A SPRIПG
OF SOULS

A SPRING
OF SOULS

William Cobb

CRANE HILL
PUBLISHERS

Birmingham, Alabama

Also by William Cobb

SOMEWHERE IN ALL THIS GREEN:
NEW AND SELECTED STORIES

HARRY REUNITED

A WALK THROUGH FIRE

THE HERMIT KING

COMING OF AGE AT THE Y

Published by Crane Hill Publishers
Printed in the United States of America

Library of Congress Cataloging-in-Publication Data

Cobb, William, 1937-
    A spring of souls : a novel / by William Cobb.
p. cm.
    ISBN 1-57587-137-8 (hc.). - ISBN 1-57587-138-6 (pbk.)
    I. Title
PS3553.0198S67   1999
813'.54-dc21   99-19145
                                                         CIP

10   9   8   7   6   5   4   3   2   1

Once again,
for Loretta.

'Tis a Spring of souls today...
Neither might the gates of death,
Nor the tomb's dark portal,
Nor the watchers, nor the seal
Hold thee as a mortal.

Easter Hymn
St. John of Demascus, 8th Century

BYRON BAILEY STANDS BY THE ROAD IN THE SUNSHINE, waiting for the church bus. Three sticks of dynamite are taped to his skin beneath his plaid shirt. An electric fuse in his pocket is attached to the dynamite by two thin wires that snake up through the hairs on his belly. Byron squints in the harsh August sunlight.

The bus comes squeaking and creaking down the narrow asphalt road. It is an old school bus painted blue, which leans to the right. On Byron's side of the road is a ditch, orange packed dirt; on the other a thick growth of dusty kudzu climbs up a telephone pole and drapes from the wires like Spanish moss. The countryside is Sunday-morning quiet, the road deserted except for the old bus.

Ordinarily the bus would not stop for Byron, a white man, but he flags it down. Hand-lettered on the side, in black paint, is MOUNT ZION HOLY TEMPLE OF JESUS. Byron sees about twenty sets of white eyes set in black faces staring down through the windows at him. It will be mostly children, picked up and carted into town for Sunday school. Byron has observed the bus for months now. He knows its every move, coming and going on its rounds on a Sunday morning.

The door is jammed permanently open and the driver observes Byron suspiciously. Byron and the driver know each other slightly. The driver, Shantua Watts, sits behind the wheel and the old bus's engine rumbles. Byron can smell the exhaust rising on the heat waves from the pavement. Byron starts to twitch and tremble as he stands there. Shantua stares at him. He nods.

"Mistuh Bailey," he says. Byron does not answer. "You lookin for a ride into town?"

"Yeah," Byron says, "somethin like that." His voice comes out high and squealing, forced, like air out of a balloon. Watts looks curiously at him. Byron still does not mount the rusted steps of the bus.

"Well," Watts finally says, "git on, then."

Byron sits on the first seat behind the driver. He does not remember getting on. The bus stutters and thumps down the road. Byron looks around. Two women sit in the seat behind him. One of them is thin, the other heavy. They wear flowered dresses and straw hats. Both fan themselves with handkerchiefs. They nod to him. Children toward the back rest their chins on the backs of seats and stare at him. Byron makes a funny face and they laugh.

"I figured you was just wantin a ride to town," Watts says, shouting over the engine, "cause I know you sho ain't going to Mount Zion."

"Oh?" Byron says, "Why you say that?"

"Well ..." Watts pauses. "Cause you goes to the Church of the New Light, don't you?"

"We're all God's children," Byron says.

"That's the God's truth," Watts says, yanking at the wheel, leaning forward to peer at the road ahead.

"Amen," says one of the women behind Byron.

"But ain't no black folks at the New Light, and ain't no white folks at Mount Zion," Watts says. He laughs like it is the funniest thing he has ever thought of.

"Well, what of it?" Byron asks sharply. Nobody answers. He looks around. Beads of sweat sprinkle his forehead and his upper lip, which continues to tremble. Byron is only twenty-four years old, and a lieutenant in the Wembly County Militia. He feels the cold explosives against his skin, the unpleasant irritation of the plastic tape. He fingers the button on the fuse. Maybe, he thinks, he should move to the middle of the bus.

"And so," one of the women says, continuing her story that had been interrupted, "I seen the girl, too. A little girl. A little white girl. Some say she a ghost. She didn't look like no ghost to me. Yesterday afternoon. I was puttin flowers on the altar for this morning, and I just knew somebody was there, and I looked out and there she was, standing there in the aisle, just looking at me. A little white girl, looked hardly no more than a baby, and I'm looking at her wondering how she got in the church and she axes me, she say, 'Have you seen my friend Pearl?' I don't know nobody named Pearl, much less some little white girl friend of hers, so I say, 'Naw, I ain't seen her. Where your mama, girl?' And you know what she say? She say, 'My Mama ain't here, my Mama moved away. She comin home though. She on the way right this minute.' I went on with the flowers and when I looked back there at her she was gone, just like she been sucked back up in the air. Don't that beat all?"

"Lots of folks done seen her. She everywhere," the other woman says.

"There ain't no such thing as a ghost," Byron says.

"What about the Holy Ghost?" one of the children, a little boy, asks as he creeps down the aisle, closer to the front. "What's your name?" he says to Byron. He wears a crisp white short-sleeved shirt, a clip-on tie and clean jeans that still smell of detergent.

"The Holy Ghost is different," Byron says, "it don't mean the same thing. Sit down fore you fall down."

The little boy sits down. Some of the other children are bunching now toward the front, looking at Byron.

"Where y'all goin?" Byron asks. "Ain't you s'posed to be sittin in the back of the bus?"

"Huh," one of the women says.

"They children," Byron says. "Children in the back, adults in the front."

"Who say?" The women stare at Byron.

"I say," Byron says. They seem to shrink back before his glare.

Byron Bailey is angry that he had been born way too late for Desert Storm, the only thing remotely resembling a war in his lifetime. When he finally reached enlistment age, he was kept out of the Marines and the Army by his flat feet and a heart murmur from a childhood bout with rheumatic fever. Then the Wembly County Militia had been organized. It was like Salvation for Byron, who saw an aimless, directionless youth come to an end. It was as though he had lived his life in darkness until then, and suddenly a bright heavenly light was leading him where he was supposed to go. Leading him right here, onto this bus on a hot Sunday morning.

Byron Bailey believes in America and the superiority of the white race. Prior to joining the Militia, his feelings had been disjointed and vague, a simple simmering hatred for all things foreign. The Militia gave him a framework for his beliefs. The white race is superior and the American white race is superior to all other white races. The New World Order is an attempt by the ungodly forces of Zionist chaos to overthrow America and all it stood for. And these forces have already succeeded in taking over the federal government. The federal government, even the U. S. military, is little more than a pawn in the hands of those who would destroy the free world by attempting to take away its guns and its religion. All the proof you need can be found at Ruby Ridge and Waco.

Byron glares at the two women, his jaw set. "I'm a Christian patriot," he blurts.

The women laugh. "I ain't studyin what you is," the thin one says. Her hat sits flat on her thin hair like the head of a nail.

"The Constitution and the Bill of Rights was meant to empower white men!" he says.

"Uh-huh," the women say together. They nod. Byron does not know whether they understand what he's saying. If they do, it's not having the effect he had intended.

"All that other stuff," he says, "all them other amendments, the income tax, giving women and colored folks the vote, stuff like that, all that is illegal. Did you know that?"

"Uh-huh," the heavier one says. "I sho did. Now tell me somethin else." She rolls her eyes back and shakes her head and looks off out the window. Her hat is like a little round straw donut on her head. Byron's insides burn with fury. His legs shake. They don't know what he has under his shirt. Opposition to all that violation of the Constitution and the common law is worthy of extreme measures. Extreme measures.

The bus rolls on toward town, the slick tires hissing on the pavement. The children look at Byron with large round eyes, curious eyes. Byron swallows. He tries to calm himself. He feels as though he is about to jump out of his skin.

"Y'all better get on back to the back, now, like I told you," Byron says, his voice thin and tight. "Fore I have to whup one of you."

"Huh," one of the women says.

The children have no intention of obeying Byron, and it infuriates him further. "Goddamit!" he says.

"Hey, this here is a church bus!" Watts yells over his shoulder.

Byron's hands shake; he grips the one in his pocket into a tight fist. In his imagination he can feel the explosives going off, the hot swift blast against his skin, the roar that will fill his ears before the quick silence comes. He shudders. A moan escapes his lips.

"What ail you?" the thin woman asks.

"None of your business, Aunt Jemima," Byron says, and the woman sniffs. Her eyes are narrowed. Then she looks at the other woman and they laugh again. They look at Byron and they laugh at him.

"Lordy, Lordy," the other woman says, clucking her tongue.

Byron seethes inside. You ain't no better than a nigger, his father would tell him all the time. All his young life. His father kept him completely off balance by being a preacher half the time and a mean drunk the other half. His father would preach in the street for days and allow no alcohol or tobacco near him. And then suddenly would come a period where his father sat in the kitchen in his sleeveless undershirt and drank beer all day and night, and told Byron over and over what a worthless shitbird he was. And his mother walked around the house naked in front of him even until he was well into his teens, and even then she didn't stop altogether. "I'm sorry, Byron," she would say, "just look the other way, sugar!"

The bus stops and an old man climbs on. He has white hair and blood-shot eyes, and the collar of his white shirt curls up around his chin, which is covered with gray stubble. He wears a black tie with bright lime-green half-moons on it.

"Mornin, Remus," the thin woman says, and the other nods. The old man passes Byron and sits. Byron smells whiskey on him.

"Bless y'all," the old man says. He looks at Byron. His eyes are watery and unsteady. The bus sways back onto the road. They are nearing town now and Byron fingers the fuse. Maybe he'll do it as they enter town. Maybe as they roll into the parking lot of the church. The old man continues to stare at him. "Who this white boy?" he asks.

Nobody answers. Some of the children still hang on the back of the seats watching Byron and the other adults. Half of them have returned to the back and play some game, swatting each other's hands and giggling. They laugh very loud.

"Y'all hush up and sit down back there," Watts yells over his shoulder. The children pay no attention to him. Byron catches Watts's eyes peering at him in the rear-view mirror. All of a sudden Byron feels as though the dynamite is taped outside his shirt, that Watts knows what he's up to. It's written all over him like shame. He feels his heart fluttering and thumping. He swallows, but his mouth is dry.

His thumb plays over the toggle switch hidden deep in his pocket. He knows Watts's eyes are shifting from the roadway to him in the mirror, back and forth. The old man licks his lips. His eyes are steady on Byron now and do not waver, even with the swaying of the bus. The old man seems ancient, his eyes coming from some other place.

"Who you lookin at?" Byron blurts.

"Nobody," the old man says. The sun beams down and glares off the narrow fields of high cotton and the naked ditches along the road between the hills. They begin to pass houses and a filling station, closed, and signs strung out along the road. WELCOME TO PIPER, POP. 3,011. A Rotary wheel: ROTARY, THRS. 7 PM, COLES BARBECUE RESTAURANT. HIDDEN VALLEY CHURCH OF CHRIST AND THE NEW LIGHT WITH SIGNS FOLLOWING. The signs are peppered with shotgun pellet and bullet holes. Orange rust bleeds down from the holes like blood.

The bus is hot, and Byron sweats freely under his clothes. He is sweating on the dynamite, on the tape. No air circulates on the bus, but the women seem cool. They sit looking out the window. Byron stands up. He stands swaying in the aisle, adjusting his body to the motion of the bus.

"You got to set down," Watts says, "no standin on the bus. Rules."

"Fuck the rules," Byron says.

"Hush your mouth," the heavy woman says. "Lordy!" They look at each other and laugh again.

Byron holds on to the metal seat frame with one hand and jams his free hand into the pocket with the fuse. He moves to the middle of the bus. The old man watches him. Byron is trembling all over. His lungs don't want to work, his breath comes in short gasps. They are in town now, passing stores, and then turning down a side street toward the black side of town and the church.

The children are singing now, loud and raucous. At first Byron can't understand what they are singing, and then it sounds to him like a jazzy version of "On Jordan's Stormy Banks." They push each other and try to drown one another out. "On Jordan's bank the Baptist's cry," they shout, "announces that the Lord is nigh!" They scream the words and giggle and shriek.

The sound of the children's voices pounds in Byron's head. The old bus thump thumps on down the street. The tires whine. Byron fingers the switch. This is it, he thinks, This is the moment. And then he sees her. The little white girl, from the old woman's story. She sits in a seat halfway back, smiling at Byron. Her hair is wispy blonde and tied with a red ribbon. Her face looks strangely like his mother's face, but he knows it is not. It is a face put into his mind by the old woman's story. The little girl is a ghost that does not exist. The little girl is a trick, a joke played on him by these people.

Byron squeezes the toggle switch. He holds his breath, waiting for the searing pain that will be intense but brief, knowing that he and the children, the old women, the old man, Watts and the bus will be, in one heroic instant, scattered to smithereens all over that part of town. But nothing happens. His head swims and he blinks several times, his sweat stinging his eyes. He squeezes the switch again.

Nothing. He licks his lips but they're like sand. The little girl stands up. She wears a white dress, like a smock. She smiles at him again and then vanishes. She is gone. Disappeared into the air. And Byron knows that no one has seen her but him. She was like a tiny baby with a woman's face. Like a paper doll. Byron's heart thuds in his chest.

Gradually he hears the sounds of the children again, their singing and screaming. He hears the street noise of the bus. The bus rocks and sways on the uneven pavement. He glances at the old man, who still watches him. The old man's eyes are fixed on him like angry snapping turtles. They frighten him, cause him to stammer. He thinks he's going to lose his balance. He thinks for a moment that he will disappear, too, into the air where the little girl has gone. But he does not.

Instead he turns toward the front of the bus. He moves slowly, like a man underwater. He is tired, exhausted. He feels nothing, not even disappointment.

"Let me out at the corner," he says to Watts, who pulls the bus over, and the brakes squeal and the transmission grinds. Byron moves stiffly down the steps. He stands on the curb. He is shaking all over. His tongue is thick and his head aches him so badly he has to squint his eyes. "Th ... Thanks for the lift," he says.

"Anytime," Watts says. And Byron watches the old bus pull away and jerk and sway on down the street toward the church. His eyes narrow and squint in the sunlight. The pain splits his skull like an axe. He sees the little white girl waving to him from the back window of the bus. She is smiling. She is laughing. She is singing with the other children. "Announces that the Lord is nigh!" she sings.

"Jesus," he says aloud.

"Anytime," Watts had said to him, "anytime."

ONE

Viewed from on high, from behind white puffy summer clouds, it is like a small town dreamed or imagined, shimmering comfortably in the sun. An emerald green valley tucked between rolling wooded nobs. A toy hamlet with one straight wide Main Street and meandering secondary streets with schools and churches and lawns and houses, many new or under construction. A child's block village with toy cars and tiny ant-like people, narrow asphalt gray roads curving away from it like arteries and veins from a heart.

Behind the high clouds hundreds of pink cherubs hover over the town and the surrounding county. They dance like plump bumblebees. They quarrel and they sing. Naked babies. Little angels. Hundreds, no thousands of them. An invisible mass of transposed flesh and wispy souls. They observe all and miss nothing. Like the blue speck that becomes a car, moving inexorably toward Piper, an old station wagon just inside the county line on one of those narrow roads.

⟲

Brenda Boykin slows suddenly and turns the old Toyota station wagon into a flat gravel parking area in front of a low concrete-block building, with a sign reading FAT MAN'S SHOP AND SNACK. The gravel pings on the undersides of the car.

"What are you stopping here for?" Jimmy asks, looking at the place with a frown.

"Something else has dropped off this car," she says. "There's a hole in the floor. I can smell fumes."

"No kidding?" he says sarcastically and makes a retching noise. He is her son. Fifteen. Potential juvenile offender. Potential youthful delinquent.

She points to a sign next to a lean-to shed on the side of the building. Mechanic on Duty, it says. Jimmy shrugs. His eyes flick over the facade of

FAT MAN'S SHOP AND SNACK. A Mountain Dew sign hangs in the window blinking green in the sunlight. And a red Pabst Blue Ribbon sign. Three gas pumps stand baking in the heavy afternoon air. Shell.

When they open the car doors the muggy late-summer air creeps over them like warm invisible fog. The air feels like hot fingers on their skin. Brenda has been living in Chicago long enough to forget how oppressive Alabama summers can be. She worries about the air conditioner in the car, which has put out very little cool air since middle Tennessee. They spent last night in a Day's Inn in Covington, Kentucky, and awakened to a crisp, cool morning. She felt good. She faced the road south eagerly, with anticipation. As she steps from the car pearl-size beads of sweat are already forming on her forehead.

Brenda is a tall woman. Her thick brown hair is only dusted with hints of gray, worn long and too youthful, she sometimes thinks, too kittenish. She doesn't care. She likes it. She brushes it out and lets it go, likes the feel of it blowing freely in the breeze. She is at least ten pounds overweight, but on her big frame it doesn't show. Her eyes are deep brown, almost black, sitting on high cheekbones, and her lips are full and without lipstick. She wears very little makeup any more; sometimes she forgets it altogether.

The store is dark and crowded and close. The only person inside is a middle-aged man with tan skin and shiny black hair. He has a large wart on his cheek under his left eye. He is not fat. He is thin and drawn. The skin hangs from his jaws like turkey's jowls. He reminds her in a weird way of her ex-husband Billy.

"Are you Fat Man?" she asks.

"Fat Man died," he says, "how can I hep you?"

"I've got a little car trouble," Brenda says. "I don't know if it's serious or not. How far is it on to Piper?"

The man blinks at her. He looks familiar to her. She thinks she knows him. "Where you coming from?" he asks.

"North," she says. "We got off I-65 near Cullman."

He snorts. "Iff'n you'd stayed on it, you'd be in Piper right now." He shakes his head as though what she has done is too stupid to deserve further comment. He has a tattoo on his forearm, a skunk in a top hat, with the words Little Stinky under it.

"We like the two-lane roads," she says. "Where's your mechanic?"

"You're lookin at him," he replies. He watches Jimmy, who slouches in front of one of the drink cases. Jimmy's jeans hang low on his narrow hips. The entire back wall of the place is lined with cooling cases, with milk and orange juice, cellophane wrapped po-boys, beer and soft drinks and bottled water. The man makes no motion toward coming out from behind the cash register.

"Well," she says, "could you take a look at my car?"

"What ails it?" His eyes are mean and singular. He can focus on only one thing at once, and he does that with an intense concentration that chokes out everything else around him.

"The exhaust fumes seem to be coming up through the floor," she says. "We may be asphyxiated." He blinks. "Or catch fire." He does not move. It's as though he has fallen asleep with his eyes open. She looks around. There are racks of cheese crackers and peanut butter crackers and rows of candy: Snickers and Baby Ruths and Goo Goo Clusters. And above the counter and on all sides of it are posted hand bills and various notices, some small, some large, some printed and some hand-written. BUGS-B-GONE PEST CONTROL. "Will keep Children in My Home, Healthy Christian Environment." Fire Wood: $45 a load. A new crisp green and gold poster advertises the upcoming football season of the Piper Christian Academy Eagles. She stares at it. A flicker of excitement passes through her. There had been no Piper Christian Academy when she had lived in Piper, and here she is coming home to become headmistress of the school.

Jimmy pulls out a large Dr. Pepper in a plastic bottle. He moves with it to where she stands and places it on the counter. Jimmy wears a wrinkled, dingy black T-shirt with a White Sox logo on the front. Good Guys Wear Black, it says on the back. The dark man still has not commented on her car trouble. She looks over his head to a large banner. THIS IS MILITIA COUNTRY, it says. LIVE FREE OR FIGHT! Under that, in script, Wembly County. The Home of The Alabama Lords of The Caucasus. WAR AND PEACE IN THE NEW MILLENNIUM. My new millennium, she thinks.

"It ain't likely you'll be 'ass-fixiated' before you get to Piper," the man behind the counter says. "They's a garage there, Coles's Pontiac and

Cadillac." He yawns. "I don't do nothin more than check oil and a occasional spark plug, to tell you the truth. That's a old sign. Left over from Fat Man." He stares at her. She does know him. He sat behind her in algebra class, at Piper High School. Jimmy picks up the drink and goes outside, letting the screen door rattle shut behind him. The man's eyes move up and down her body. They linger on her breasts. "He was a hell of a mechanic," he says. He stares at her breasts. Brenda wears no bra under her denim shirt.

"You're Larson Eubanks, aren't you?" Brenda asks.

The man's eyes are like bits of stone. He smiles and his teeth are stained. He does not answer her.

"Coles Pontiac and Cadillac, huh?" she says.

"Uh-huh."

"Yes, well, thanks," Brenda says, "how far is it to Piper?"

"Thirteen mile," he says. His hand is suddenly over hers on the counter. His fingers are pudgy and thick. He leans forward, nods toward the outside. "That Dr. Pepper there is seventy-nine cent," he whispers. His breath smells like cheese. He blinks at her. His eyes are gray and flat and dull. She slowly removes her hand, and he only gradually lets go. Brenda pulls a dollar bill from the pocket of her jeans.

"Listen, babe, how bout—"

"I'm not your babe, Larson," Brenda says. She drops the dollar on the counter.

With surprising quickness he grabs her arm. He pulls her toward him. She can hear his breathing, raspy and rapid. She hears the car door slam and she knows that Jimmy is back in the car. She can smell the man's body now, damp with stale sweat. He is a big man, and strong. She pulls against him. He grips her so hard he hurts her.

"I'll scream," she says, "Jimmy's right out there."

"Shit," he says, "I'll break that little skinny boy in two like a tooth pick."

She struggles. Brenda is a big woman, almost as tall as the man. He tries to kiss her on the lips and she turns her head and butts him in the face, and she hears him blubber.

"Goddam bitch," he says. She sees a flash of red blood from his nose or his lip. He is startled, shocked into temporary inaction. His eyes are wide and they blink. She is able to get a distance and an angle and she swiftly kicks him between the legs, square in the balls, and his mouth drops open and a cry of pain escapes him and he goes down. "Ohhhh, Ohhhh," he grunts.

"Don't ever try that again, Larson Eubanks," she says. She looks at the dollar bill on the counter. "Keep the change," she says. She struts as she walks out into the sunlight, letting the screen door slam behind her.

Outside Brenda walks over and kicks the Mechanic on Duty sign down into the dust. Jimmy watches her from the car. She is still trembling inside, jumping from the sharp edge of fear and excitement. She walks over to a rack of quart plastic bottles of motor oil by the door and turns it over. The bottles roll all over the gravel. Jimmy opens the door and stands outside, holding the Dr. Pepper. "Mom!" he says, "what ... what ..." She kicks one of the bottles of motor oil and sends it skittering.

A house trailer with a small wooden porch built at the front door sits on concrete blocks behind the store. Brenda stands looking at it, her hands now on her hips. She nods toward the store.

"Trailer trash," she says. "You drive."

Jimmy looks at her curiously. Then he nods. He goes around to the driver's side and slips in behind the wheel.

The narrow asphalt road unfolds before them. They wind through the wooded hills, thick and green. The woods seem as impenetrable as a jungle. Thousands of eyes watch from the undergrowth as the old blue car goes by. The hum of insects is like music.

They pass open fields, houses set back from the road. Brenda is struck by how many women are hanging out washing or mopping front stoops. Her mind quickly contrasts it all with the concrete sameness of Chicago. She had forgotten that women stay at home, that women are housewives. It seems strange, otherworldly, but it takes her back. Jimmy brakes and swerves slightly to go around a U.S. Postal Service jeep, white with a blinking yellow light on top, that slows at a rural mailbox. She sees a woman in a blue calico dress waving and starting down a gravel drive toward the highway.

"I've got to get out of here," she had said to her friend Marjorie, who lived in the same tired gray block of apartment buildings near Midway Airport.

"Then go," Marjorie said. They shared a ride into the city for years, to the University of Illinois-Chicago four nights a week, where both of them had finally gotten their degrees, grueling night school in harsh over-lit classrooms with weary professors. Her husband Billy, a Chicago cop, was long gone, run off with a bony girl who shook pom-poms at Bulls games. And Jimmy had been picked up for joyriding in a stolen car. Probation. He wasn't the one who stole it, but that was next.

"I'm going to take this job, sight unseen," Brenda said.

"In a freaking minute!" Marjorie said.

A man named Roger Coles. The name was vaguely familiar. He was chairman of the board of trust of a private academy in her hometown: Piper, Alabama. Her brother Lamar, who still lived in Piper, told her about the job opening. Brenda would not have given a nickel for the probability of her ever returning there in one million years.

"I remember you," Coles said on the phone, "I remember you well. Piper High School. Good Citizenship Girl." She had forgotten all about that. "Homecoming Queen," he said, almost reverently. "You probably don't remember me, but I remember you. No need for an interview at all, as far as I'm concerned."

Jimmy had not wanted to come. He had been angry, resentful. He is still a boy, not yet a man, but he will make her pay. She knows he will make her pay.

They pass through an intersection. Piper—10 Miles, a sign says. Ten miles from "home." There are more houses now, closer together. Brenda notices how even the poorest people try to fix up their homes, with hanging pots of Wandering Jew on the sagging porches, even old discarded tires painted with whitewash half buried in the yards. Cement statues of deer and birds, bottle trees. She hasn't seen bottle trees since she left Wembly County for what she had thought was the last time all those years ago. Mailboxes are decorated with blue ducks, Disney characters, cardinals. One they pass has a second mailbox high in the air, on a thin pole, marked Air Mail. She smiles and looks to see if Jimmy notices. He does and nods, a suppressed grin on his face. Then they are back passing through woods so deep and dark they might as well have been miles from any civilization at all.

She thinks of the man in the store, Larson Eubanks, the smell of him. She is sure he recognized her. She could read it in his dead eyes. She thinks of Wayne McClain. Their child, who, when Brenda was fifteen years old, the same as Jimmy is now, was aborted in the back room of a funeral home over in Mount Holley. She remembers the pain and the humiliation of it, the shame and the terror, and the dreams that have haunted her for years, dreams of the little girl that she is certain the fetus was, a little blond-haired girl even though she and Wayne were both dark-haired. She wonders where Wayne is now. She has a premonition that he is in Piper. She knows that he is in Piper. She can feel him.

There are ghosts everywhere, movements and flutters behind the thick screen of leaves. The little blond girl flits from limb to limb in the trees, watching their progress down the road. Brenda sees her long-dead mother's face in the configuration of the hills in front of them. Her mother is here, too. Brenda can hear her voice, clearly, and she says, "Like an old song, Brenda. We'll sing it together."

⟜

They have not gone more than two miles beyond the intersection when they see a roadblock up ahead. It looks like a license check, or something more. There are policemen and uniformed soldiers in camouflage fatigues. "Oh shit," she says. Jimmy does not even have a learner's permit. One of the conditions of his probation is that he cannot drive. But that was in Chicago. This is a world away. Maybe she can bluff her way through. There's nothing else to do but keep going, as the road is narrow, no place to pull over and turn around. She sees a soldier standing by the road, looking at them as they approach. He seems to be in charge. Four squad cars and two army green jeeps are parked in a row alongside the road. "Shit, shit, shit," she mutters. She is fumbling in her purse, finding her wallet with her own license.

"What do I do?" Jimmy asks.

"Just let me do the talking," she says, "and pray."

"Afternoon," the soldier says when they are stopped. He leans his elbow on the window and looks in at them. He touches the tips of his fingers to the bill of his soft cap. His name patch says "Putnam Greer, SGT." She knows then that it's not a routine license check. But Greer says, "Could I see your license?" He is very polite. He smiles at Jimmy. He peers upward from beneath the bill of the hat. He squints in the sunlight.

"Sir," Brenda says, "I'm sorry. I was teaching him to drive. The road was, well, you know, deserted. I thought ..."

"Yes mam," the man says. "It's a good road to learn on." He continues to regard her. His eyes sparkle. Fine laugh lines crinkle around his eyes, which are a pale almond color with green highlights. He is hefty and blond. After a moment of awkward silence, she hands Putnam Greer her license. He holds it close to his face. He seems to read every last word on it. Jimmy glances at his mother. Then the soldier hands the license back across Jimmy to Brenda. He touches his hat again. The other men stand in a line behind him. They stand at attention.

"Let me verify this, if you will. You are Brenda Boykin, and you will be the new headmistress at Piper Christian Academy. Am I correct?" He is oddly formal now, stiff.

Brenda is surprised that he knows that. She doesn't answer for a moment. Then she says, "Yes, that's right." She notices the soldier listening to the rumbling of her old car, smelling the exhaust. "I know it wouldn't pass inspection," she says. Not only does Jimmy not have a license, she is driving the car illegally. She had skipped last year's inspection in Illinois, knowing full well it wouldn't pass. She has been lucky, up until now. "But I'm going to have it fixed. I promise." She smiles at him.

"Inspection?" he says. He blinks. His cheeks are chubby and pink, like ripe peaches. "Don't worry, mam," he says. "We ain't got no inspection in Wembly County. We don't tell nobody what they can drive and what they can't. You can drive anything you take a notion to here."

"Oh," she says, "all right."

"Our citizens live free here. We're proud of that." He touches the bill of his hat again. "So let me be the first to welcome you back to Piper," he says. "Maybe you ought to come around and drive, though. All right? Then you just fall in behind that squad car over there. Mr. Coles wants you escorted, right on into Piper and to your new house he's got all ready for you. He says you get the full VIP treatment." He smiles.

Brenda gets out and goes around, meeting Jimmy halfway. Jimmy grins at her. She can see he is about to burst out laughing. Brenda grins back, but shakes her head no. Behind the wheel she nudges the accelerator and the car inches forward. The muffler rattles as though it's full of pebbles. The squad car pulls into the highway and she moves forward behind it. The other squad cars and the jeeps fall into line behind her. The police car puts on its lights, then its siren. The other cars follow suit. Brenda's face is a mask of surprise and shock. She cannot believe it.

"Man," Jimmy says, "Man!" He laughs almost hysterically.

She shakes her head. She grips the wheel. The lights whirl and the sirens whoop. She is embarrassed. She is flattered, in spite of herself. The procession makes its noisy and colorful way into Piper, taking Brenda home. In the dark shadows of the woods the little girl smiles. The trees and the hills vibrate with life, humming and hissing, and the voice of Brenda's long-dead mother says, again, "Like an old song, Brenda. And we'll sing it together."

⌐

Cody Klinger leaves the interstate in the late afternoon and takes the blacktopped two-lane highway to Piper. He has driven all the way from California with only one stop, in Texas. He sleeps sporadically, anyway, sometimes only needing an hour or so a night.

Cody is a young man in his mid-twenties, with pale sun-bleached hair, who is astonishingly good-looking. So handsome is he that anyone seeing him in Hollywood, where he mostly worked, would immediately assume that he was an actor, but they would be wrong. Cody Klinger is a documentary filmmaker.

WELCOME TO PIPER the sign says. Cody is having the last of his late lunch or early supper, two apples and a banana. He munches on the banana as he drives, his hand draped nonchalantly over the wheel. His old 1985 Plymouth van is not quite maroon, a kind of deep red, a color of his own mixing and application. The second seat is out and the back is packed with his video equipment and his clothes. The front seat is littered with paper bags and plastic cups from fast food joints.

Cody does not even notice the police car that pulls out behind him. When he finishes the banana he tosses the skin out the window. Immediately the blue swirling lights go on behind him and he hears the sudden blurt of the siren, just a blip, just enough to signal him to pull over. He does. "I'll be shit," he says under his breath. He has not even checked into a motel yet and already he is in trouble with the cops. He has a quarter bag of pot in the glove compartment. An eight-ball of cocaine is stashed in one of the equipment boxes in the back. Hidden way down. He tilts his mirror and watches the cop approach him.

A middle-aged man with a graying mustache, he has on a shiny badge and a metal nametag, but Cody can't read it in reverse in the mirror. He wears a white shirt and blue pants and a Smokey the Bear hat. When he comes up to the window of the van, he puts both hands on the sill and just looks at Cody. Cody can read the name tag now: Leeds Scroggins.

"I'm Leeds Scroggins, Sheriff of Wembly County," he says. "How are you, son?" His voice is deep and rumbling. It is polite but full of an irony that is not lost on Cody. It is a Southern irony that he had heard all his life, not least of all from his own father.

"I'm all right," Cody says.

"Son, you tossed some litter out of your van back there, and it's a fifty dollar fine for doin that."

"It was a banana peel," Cody says.

"Litter."

"It's bio-degradable," Cody says.

The sheriff just stares at him for a moment.

"I didn't say nothing about it being degrading," he says, "I said it was against the law."

Cody starts to laugh and then realizes that the man is not joking. "Yes sir," he says. The sheriff is looking at his hair. He shakes his head and grunts. He peers into the van, at all the clutter, at the jumble of equipment in the back.

"I notice you got California plates," he says. "What's your business here, son?"

Cody gives him the standard answer, the one they had settled on. "I'm scouting locations, for filming movies. I work for a motion picture company."

"You make picture shows?"

"Yes sir. But I'm scouting locations now. Just looking around. In case we might want to come here to make a movie."

"What kind of movie?"

"Any kind. One set in the South. You have to make them somewhere, right? I might find the perfect spot right here in Piper."

"Is that right," he says. It does not sound like a question.

"Yes sir," Cody says. "Let me give you my card." He fumbles around on the dash and finds one. He hands it to the sheriff, who holds it like he would hold a small rodent by the tail. He does not look at it. Cody is getting nervous. He can imagine himself in some dank red-neck jail cell, without even being allowed a phone call to his partner Coates back in Hollywood.

"The movies, huh?" the sheriff asks.

"Yes sir," Cody says. "It can be a boon to a local economy if a company comes in to make a movie. I can get you all sorts of information on that, if you—"

"A boon, huh?"

"Yes sir."

The sheriff seems to be chewing on a tiny ball of air. His lips move, his thick jaw sways in a circular motion. "Uh huh," he says. "Well." His hands still rest on Cody's opened window. Cody looks into the older man's eyes. He can see them shifting in color, subtly and almost imperceptibly as the man's mind works, as he considers his options. Finally, he says, "We don't take too big to strangers around here, son, because most of the time they ain't got no business here, no business atall. But," and he reaches into his back pocket and pulls out a pad, jerks a pen from his shirt pocket, "I'm just gonna give you a warning ticket. You get caught litterin the streets again, it'll cost you double, a hundred smackers, cause this warning is in the computer. You got that?"

"Yes sir. I'll remember that." The man's eyes shift quickly up to his. "Really. I mean it." The sheriff writes on the pad. "Tell me," Cody says, "is there a motel or a hotel in town?"

"Ain't but one," Scroggins says, not looking up, his face close to his writing, "The Moon Winx, out on old Highway 35. It ain't fancy," he says, tearing the ticket off and shoving it at Cody, "but it's clean."

Cody takes the ticket. He is on Highway 35. "Thank you sir. Just straight through town?"

"Straight through town," the sheriff says.

Cody nods again. "Thank you again," he says. He starts the engine. The cop stands in the street watching him. He wears his gun slung low on his hip like a cowboy. The Smokey hat is tilted at a sharp angle. Leeds Scroggins takes a toothpick out of his shirt pocket and sticks it between his lips. He chews on it. Cody waves and pulls into the street.

Leeds Scroggins stands for a long time watching the red van, its color reminding Leeds unpleasantly of hog's blood, as it moves on away from him, stopping carefully at stop signs and red lights until it is almost out of sight. Leeds rolls the toothpick around between his teeth. For years, when he had smoked three packs of Camel cigarettes a day, he had chewed on matchsticks. Since he had quit eight years ago, it has been toothpicks. At first they had poked little holes in his shirt pocket, so now he breaks the pointed ends off when he takes them out of the box in the mornings. He watches the van disappear.

Leeds isn't surprised that the boy is from the movies, because he looks like a movie star, with that tan and those teeth and those blue eyes twinkling like Leeds' wife's blue topaz ear-bobs he had given her last Mother's Day. Roger Coles will surely be interested in hearing about him. Anything that is a boon to the economy of Piper or Wembly County, Roger Coles is interested in.

Cody, together with another documentary maker named Doug Runnion, formed a production company with a man named Paul Motherwell Coates, who had named their company—for no reason at all other than the fact that they needed a name—Postwar Productions. They had done an hour-long piece on minor league baseball on the West Coast and sold it to PBS. They had done an investigative piece on the shady

practices of talent agents who preyed on unsuspecting young people with
ambitions for show business, and the film had run as a short feature in the
theater chain of a distribution company in the Midwest. That short subject
attracted the attention of HBO, which had just commissioned them to do
a full-length exposé of the militia movement growing around the U.S.
Doug Runnion is currently in Montana, interviewing and filming.

The day before Cody left California, Paul Motherwell Coates spread a
map of the state of Alabama out on his desk. Their office was on the second floor of a concrete block two-story building painted bright yellow. It
was two blocks off Hollywood Boulevard. The tip of Paul Motherwell
Coates's finger rested on a square county just to the north of the state's
largest city, Birmingham.

"Wembly County," he said. "A hotbed. They've taken over the
county. A man named Roger Coles, the probate judge of the county,
also heads up the militia. Along with Michigan and Montana, that's where
it's happening."

Cody Klinger was familiar with Alabama. He had been born and raised
in Franklin, Tennessee, just south of Nashville, and, first with his folks and
then later as a teenager, he had driven through Alabama on the way to the
Gulf Coast. His family left the South when he was a senior in high school
and moved to Rutland, Vermont, where he graduated high school and then
went on to get his bachelor's degree at Bennington College. There, he had
become an artist, majoring in film and producing a thirty-minute movie
featuring female masturbation for his undergraduate thesis.

Now he wanted to do something on the South. He felt that he knew
the South. Backwards and forwards. He had known from the start that it
would be he who would head in that direction when production began.

"I know the place well," Cody said with excitement. When he was
enthusiastic about something he tended to breathe in short quick spurts,
almost like hiccups, as though he were out of breath. "I've driven through
there on I-65. Stopped and eaten. There's a barbecue place there that
everybody drives out of their way to stop at. Best barbecue you ever put in
your mouth."

"Yes, well ..." Paul Motherwell Coats said. He was a small man, older,
fiftyish with a narrow brown mustache. A native Californian. Barbecue to

him meant stringy beef with watery sauce in cheap Tex-Mex joints. He wore a pale beige linen suit with a checkered vest. He smoked long filter-tipped cigarettes. Both Doug and Cody waved their hands in front of their faces and frowned when he lit up. But they both smoked dope and did God knows what all else. Coates was the business brain of the company. Doug and Cody were the artists. Cody slouched in his chair with his foot propped on the edge of Paul's desk.

"How long can I stay down there?" Cody asked.

"Well, no limit on it right now," Paul said. "You can take your time. The advance was substantial and since it's for television we can use tape and that'll save us a bundle right there. Get a motel room, eat three meals a day. Be normal. Nose around. Ingratiate yourself. Talk Southern. Do what you have to. We have expenses written into the contract, but the less you spend the more we'll make. I don't have to tell you that."

"Right," Cody said. Coates kept all the books. He had a way of bleeding every last penny out of whoever they were contracted to. And they needed every penny. Cody would drive across the country in his Plymouth van, with all his taping equipment in the back, along with his clothes, a cot and a sleeping bag. Postwar Productions was the very definition of the shoe-string operation.

"This is going to be a great one, Cody," Coates said. He settled back in his swivel chair and peered across the desk at Cody. The flat California sunlight, dull and muted, slanted through the dusty smeared windows. "This documentary is going to make our reputation, and then we can write our own ticket." He smiled. He fumbled in his coat pocket for his cigarettes.

"Right," Cody said again.

Cody had spent the last couple of days in Austin with an old girlfriend who was in graduate school at the University of Texas. He shot lots of tape footage of the famous bats who nested under the freeway overpass. Millions of bats. The city of Austin couldn't decide whether to get rid of them as the pests they had become or to celebrate them as a tourist attraction. "One bat can eat a pound of mosquitoes a day," his girlfriend said. She wore the same old afghan with a hole cut in it for her head that she had worn around

Bennington. It was red and green. Her hair was black and straight. She was in favor of protecting the bats.

"But they shit on people and cars," said her friend who was drinking espresso with them. Her friend was teaching two freshman English classes and working on her dissertation on Alexander Pope. They both looked at Cody to see what he thought.

"Let me get my footage of them," he said. "Then you can do with em what you want. Fuck em. Bats are bats."

Wayne "Freight Train" McClain is on his way to see Roger Coles because he wants Otis Hunnicutt on his football team for the fall season. It's going to be a hard sell, because Otis is black. Wayne, an All-American running back when he was at Auburn, is the football coach at Piper Christian Academy, an all-white school. Last year he had come within one touchdown of winning the state championship, and this year he is determined to win it all. He wants so badly to win he can taste it. The taste lingers on the back of his tongue like cold beer or good Scotch, both tastes that had gotten him fired from an assistant coaching job at the University of Georgia and reduced him to the ranks of high-school coaching. He had been on the verge of a head coaching job at a major university when the booze got so bad that Bobbye, his wife, had left him and taken their son. Then Wayne was fired. Wayne dried out and got this job—which got him his son back. Wayne for now has custody of Keith, who is seventeen. He considers this job a steppingstone on the way back up.

Wayne had grown up here, had been an All-state running back at the old Piper High School, which is now all black. Roger Coles had hired him at the Academy and given him five years to win the state championship. This is his fifth year. He can't win it without Otis. He is not going to stop until he convinces Coles to get him, even if he has to threaten to quit.

Wayne is driving his old beat up red Pontiac Firebird. He drives too fast through town. He doesn't mean to, but Wayne does everything too fast. He is hard on the boys on his team. "Good God, Coach," a parent would say, "this ain't college ball!" Wayne would just look at him or her, not deigning a reply. Lots of the boys who went out quit long before the season started, but those who stayed—his entire squad last year had numbered only twenty-four boys—were lean and hard and in such good shape they could have played a second game after the Friday night game was over. That's why his record, in his four years, was forty-nine and four. He had taken the Eagles to the play-offs his very first year, and the last two losses were in the championship games of the past two seasons. He knows he is the best high-school coach in the state of Alabama. All he needs is a chance to prove it once and for all.

Wayne switches on the radio. It is tuned to WXAY, the local 250-watt station that just a few months before had changed from a top-forty country format to all-talk. The announcer's name is Alex Gresham, and he banters and argues with and insults callers all day long. Everybody in Piper listens to the station. "The bleep bleep federal government is a conspiracy," a man's voice is saying, and Alex jumps in and interrupts him. "Watch your tongue, man. You can express your opinion without cussing. Using words like that is a sign of a poor vocabulary, and a poor vocabulary is a sign of stupidity. So go ahead, stupid!" "Well," the man says, "it is!" "Is what?" "A conspiracy!" "Wheeww," Alex says, "the joint is stunk up mightily here!" There's a click and Alex says, "The People Speak. Go ahead!" It's a woman's voice now. "Alex, I got a good recipe for a three-day coconut cake," she says. "Wow!" Alex says, "tie me to the bed-post, Mama!" "You take three cups of ..."

Wayne buzzes on down Main Street as the woman's voice drones on. He can see Coles's house at the end of the sunlit street, the huge old oak and elm trees that stand in its front yard, shading it. Splashes of white from the house show through the thick green foliage. It's the biggest house in the area, the old Piper mansion, built by the man—Mason Landow Piper—who had owned all the mines in the surrounding hills way back around the turn of the century, before he sold out to International Steel and moved his family to Florida, where he founded the city of New Smyrna Beach and became a U.S. Senator.

The woman's voice giving the recipe is shrill, and Wayne shuts the radio off. Wayne had not been able to believe his eyes earlier in the week

when he had scanned down a memo to the faculty from Coles, announc-
ing that their new headmistress was Brenda Boykin. It had taken him a
moment to place the name. Brenda Vick. It had to be. Boykin was her married name, he remembered that. He sat there holding the memo like it was
a snake about to bite him. He licked his lips. Brenda Vick.

Wayne had not seen Brenda since the summer after they had graduated together from Piper High School. They had been an item, the star of
the football team and the head cheerleader. They had gone together for all
four years of high school. They had even talked of marriage, and then
Wayne had gone off to Auburn on scholarship to play football and he
didn't want to drag the baggage of a hometown girlfriend with him. There
would be too many other possibilities. So he shafted her good. Just dropped
her. She wasn't going to college anyway, and he would be moving on to a
different level. She lived with her mother and her younger brother in a
ramshackle house-trailer on the edge of town. He remembered that she had
gotten a job in Birmingham for a while. Then that she had married a
policeman. Billy Boykin was his name, and they had moved off to Chicago
or somewhere, while Wayne was making All-American his senior year and
playing two years for the Broncos before he messed up his knee and went
into coaching.

He thinks of her now, in his cluttered car: tall, with dark hair cascad-
ing down her back, her big black bush of pubic hair and breasts like proud
grapefruits, hips wide and sturdy. Her running down the sand bar on Big
Sandy Creek, near the Warrior River, where they all used to go skinny-
dipping, plunging into the water and splashing, the drops of water flailing
like sunlit rhinestones in the air around her head. Laughing. Or lying back
beckoning to him. Spreading her legs.

He shakes his head to clear it of the images. There will be time enough
to get back with Brenda if he decides he wants to. He has to concentrate
on his mission. Otis Hunnicutt is going to be his ticket back to the big
time. Otis played last year for Piper High School. He is six foot two, two
hundred and thirty pounds. He runs the forty in 4.2. He is built like Bo
Jackson and he is the best running back to come out of central Alabama
since Bo, maybe even better than Bo. He is that good. Wayne knows the
coach over at Piper High, a science teacher who moonlights as the coach,

and he knows that every school in the South sent scouts to the games last fall or asked to see Otis's tapes. Schools like Michigan and Notre Dame are interested. This will be Otis's senior year, and Wayne wants him to transfer over to Piper Academy, where he can get the kind of coaching he needs. Wayne wants to give him a football scholarship. And then wherever he goes to play at the next level, Wayne plans to go, too. That will be part of the deal.

The only problem, and it is a major one, is that Otis is a black kid. Not really black black, but a kind of cream, or golden. Even his hair is tinged with gold. But he is a Negro, a black. No black student has ever gone to Piper Christian Academy. The school owes its very existence to the forced integration of the public schools back in the Seventies. The school struggled in its early years, until Roger Coles began to give partial scholarships, football and basketball and cheerleading scholarships to white kids who couldn't afford it otherwise. Now every white child in Piper goes to the Academy for grades one through twelve. It even has a pre-school kindergarten. Piper High and Elementary Schools are all black.

"We can tell everybody he's an Indian," Wayne says. He has rehearsed this. He is sitting in Coles's spacious office in the Coles Building, a three-story brick and glass office complex on Main Street, next to the movie theater. "A, you know, native American. We can put that down on his application."

"Are you serious?" Coles asks. Coles is tall and lean, with a prominent nose. His skin is suntanned.

"Serious as a heart attack," Wayne says, "an Indian. Why not?"

"Have you taken leave of your senses, Wayne?" Coles says. "He's a local boy." He sits behind the huge desk in his office. Coles wears khaki work shirts and pants, like a uniform. He wears the same thing every day and drives around town in his Bronco, looking over his property. He is in his late seventies, and his hair is thick and gray, plentiful and bushy. Almost white. Wayne has no idea how many millions Coles is worth. He couldn't even guess.

Wayne has rehearsed this too: "If you say he's an Indian, Mr. Coles, then he's an Indian. Everybody in Piper will believe it."

Coles settles back and looks at him across the desk. "Ridiculous," he mutters.

"He lives with that old woman he calls his grandmother, but nobody knows who his parents were. I've asked around. She ain't no more his grandmother than I am. Maybe his parents were gypsies, or something."

"Gypsies? Shit, that's worse than blacks, Wayne."

"Somethin," Wayne says, "somethin that ain't black."

"He's black and you know it, Wayne."

"Yeah. But do they know it? Will everybody know it, after you—"

"Hell, I know it. Ain't that enough?"

"Depends on how much you want that state championship, I reckon," Wayne says.

"You came close last year," Coles says.

"Close don't count cept in horseshoes and shaving," Wayne says. Coles does not respond to that. Wayne takes a different tact. "Hasn't the federal government been on your back about no minorities at the academy? Seems like—"

"We take no federal funds. None at all."

"Seems like something about violating civil rights, discrimination. That lawyer, Grist, whatever his name is—"

"Grist is full of shit," Coles says. His face colors. A.J. Grist is a black attorney in town who is a card-carrying member of the ACLU and the NAACP. Wayne can tell from the expression on Coles's face that he would like to run Grist out of town, or worse. Grist was once married to a white woman who claimed to have been a Las Vegas showgirl, and she had run off with a UPS driver, leaving A.J. to raise their daughter Karla. Karla Grist is almost white, a beautiful young seventeen-year-old woman who is a senior at Piper High. Wayne has seen her around town. Once a man saw her, he never forgot her. Wayne is certain of that. "Don't talk to me about A.J. Grist," Coles says.

"All right," Wayne says. "Back to the matter at hand. I've got to have Hunnicutt, Mr. Coles. I can't win it unless I do."

"Nonsense, Wayne," Coles says.

"He'll make em forget about Bo Jackson," Wayne says. "Think of all the good press for the Academy. For Piper. We can call him the new Jim Thorpe. We can—"

"The new who?"

"Jim Thorpe. The great Indian All-American. You know? From the Carlisle Indian School, in Pennsylvania. Hell, they made a movie about him. He's a great American hero!" Coles stares at him across the desk. His pale blue eyes are fixed on him. Wayne sees a real spark of interest there now. "Have you ever seen this boy?" Wayne asks. "Hell, he's beautiful. He's like an Egyptian prince. Or an Indian chief! He—"

"Easy, Wayne," Coles says. "Don't overdo it here."

"But—"

"Bottom line: he's a black."

"Nossir," Wayne says, "he's an Indian!"

Coles sits there contemplating. His arms lie flat on the neat desktop. The sleeves of his long-sleeved khaki shirt are rolled up two loops on his forearms. Wayne expects an answer. He braces. He knows that Coles is a decisive man, given to quick and final conclusions.

"All right," Coles says, "we'll give it a try." Wayne tries not to let his relief show. He has been holding his breath, and he tries to let it out slowly and casually. "I want that championship, Wayne." He stares at Wayne, his eyes level. "Maybe he is a goddam Indian. Who the hell knows what he is? He might as well be an Indian as anything else. What the hell."

"Good," Wayne says. He stands. He is anxious to get going.

"Wait a minute," Coles says, "how the hell do you know this boy will do it? Have you talked to him?"

"No," Wayne says, "but you just leave that to me."

"All right," Coles says. He points to the chair. "Sit back down, Wayne. One or two other things." Wayne is nervous now and jumpy. He sits. Coles leans back. His swivel chair squeaks under him. He makes a tent of his long thin fingers and contemplates it. He nods, as though he is talking silently to himself. "This is a big step, Wayne," he says. "I don't want things fucked up."

"You can depend on me," Wayne says.

"Can I?" Coles looks at him. "Stay off the booze, Wayne. I mean it. Start drinkin again and you're out on your ass. Is that clear?"

Wayne nods. He holds his tongue. Coles's tone makes him angry. He wants to tell the old man to go to hell.

"And I want you to leave Brenda Vick alone," Coles says.

"Pardon?" Wayne is not sure what he said. It comes like a thunderbolt out of a clear sky. It's as though Coles has shouted Brenda's name into his ear. At close range.

"Wh ... What do you mean?" Wayne stammers.

"Just what I say," Coles says. He leans forward. He peers at Wayne, and there is silence for almost a minute. "I order you to leave her alone," Coles says, "because I brought her back here for me, not you."

It is true. Roger Coles has been in love with Brenda Vick, nee Boykin, for twenty-five years, ever since the night he crowned her Homecoming Queen at half time of the football game, while his daughter Helen Grace who was in the same class as Brenda stood by in the court with envious tears in her eyes. Something happened to him, like a bomb exploding inside his head. It was like all the songs said, and he experienced it for the first and only time in his life. He had been struck totally dumb by her beauty, by the way the stadium lights had sparkled on her dark hair and her teeth, the fullness of her lips, her perfect young body in the black sheath of a dress with high heels that made her almost as tall as he was. He had fallen in love with her, hard. But that was back before he was King Coles, when he had barely made his first million. His wife Alberta was alive, and he had just begun his affair with his secretary, Sybil Riggs, now his Executive Assistant, an affair that had lasted all this intervening quarter of a century. And Brenda was a classmate of his own daughter's. Decency itself forbade him, he supposed. He told himself that, and felt virtuous.

When Lamar Vick, Brenda's idiot drunk of a brother, called to inquire about the job opening at the Academy, Roger knew it was providence. When he got her letter of inquiry, it was like something divinely inspired, as though he had said to God, "All right, I've got everything I ever wanted, but is there anything else that I can make mine now to give my future years the joy and pleasure that I deserve?" It was as though God had reached down and rung the phone or plopped the letter square on his desk, the letter with the return address of some godforsaken hell of a place called Summit, Illinois, but written by an angel from his past. An angel who could bring back the vitality of his middle years and stop time's flow for him. She would erase those years since that fateful night on the football field and make him forever young again. It is just too perfect, too synchronistic.

The only obstacle, perhaps, is Wayne McClain. Roger well remembers that they had been in love, had gone together for a long time. He remembers Helen Grace talking about them. Helen Grace had a crush on Wayne herself, and acted like a school girl when he moved back to town. She is married to the local State Farm agent, Putnam Greer. Putt had confided to Roger that for the first year Wayne was back Helen Grace "talked about McClain all the time. That's all she can think about!" And then it had stopped. Abruptly. Roger wondered if something had happened.

After Wayne leaves Roger tells Sybil that he is going out for a while, to ride by and check on the new McDonald's and run some errands. He has been annoyed that the construction company seems to be taking its own sweet time in finishing the McDonald's. Roger had set the grand opening to coincide with the beginning of the football season, but it doesn't look now as if they'll make it.

He likes to get into the Bronco and just cruise around town, looking at all his rental property and his projects under way. He owns a total of seventy-nine rental houses in town. Plans are on the board to build eighty more houses—for sale—and construction has already begun on half of them. He also just closed the deal buying three hundred acres of land at the future intersection of I-65 and I-459, the new northern bypass around Birmingham. He's going to build a mall there, the Twenty-First Century Mall, the biggest mall east of the Mississippi River. He is building Wembly County into what will be the most desirable place in the state for white people to live. Every white person in his right mind will want to live in Wembly County and shop at the Twenty-First Century Mall. Everything an upscale person could possibly want will be had right there: four levels of specialty shops and restaurants, movie theaters, a swimming pool and an ice rink, exercise gyms, bakeries, car dealerships, and a hotel under a sixteen-acre skylight seven hundred feet high, with Macy's and Rich's and Parisian on one end and J.C. Penney and Sears and McCrae's on the other. White people from all over Birmingham and the rest of the state will flock there likes ducks to a slough. Construction is set to begin in the fall. Roger knows that the New Millennium will be a white one, and he intends for it to reach its fullest potential right here in Wembly County.

Roger Coles has almost single-handedly turned Wembly County into a haven for like-minded, conservative people like himself. Roger is Probate Judge of Wembly County. He has run unopposed in the last three elections, and he subscribes to the philosophy of Posse Comitatus, Latin for "Power of the County." He believes, and has convinced other prominent men in the county, that all government above the county level is illegitimate. His militia is his army. Along with the other People's Militias scattered around the country, they are the only duly authorized armies in the United States. And the highest legitimate authority that exists legally is the Probate Judge. "The Supreme Court," Posse literature says, "is NOT the highest court in the land. The Probate Judge is of course the highest authority as to the interpretation of the law or as to questions concerning its enforcement."

He sits now in his Bronco watching a crew putting the yellow tile roof onto his new McDonald's. They seem to move in slow motion. But today he is not annoyed with them. Because Brenda Vick Boykin has been given a police escort into town and is ensconced in the neat little fully furnished cottage on Pineview Road that he is renting to her for the nominal sum of two hundred dollars a month. And he feels his accumulated years dropping away and disappearing into the late summer air.

THE VOICE ITSELF IS HAUNTING. IT DRIFTS OUT OVER
the valley where the village of Piper nestles in the wooded, coal mine-
dotted hills, floating on the smoky airwaves of WXAY. "Yes, that's right,"
the voice says, and it is recognizable as the voice of a black woman,
elderly, "and it ain't the first time I've seen her, either. I was comin home
from fishin. I likes to catch me a few bream for supper, they fry up real good
with corn meal and I make hushpuppies, too. I can walk to the creek from
my house. I passes down Moody Street, near where that Women's Health
Center is at—"

"It's an abortion clinic," Alex Gresham says. "Call it what it is."

"Yessir," she says, "don't make no difference to me. I calls it by what is
wrote up on the side of it. Anyhow, I'm comin along there and I see the
little girl, just standin there in the path. Right off I know this is the little
girl that everybody been talkin about, say she is a ghost or a spirit, pop up
everywhere. I know sho as I'm standin there that this is her, cause she got
fine curly golden hair like a doll baby, wearin this little white dress look like
it just been pressed."

"White or black?" Alex asks.

"She a little white girl," the woman says, "same as what everybody been
seein. Same as I seen before. But she peculiar lookin. She look for a
moment like she ain't got no body to her, then it look like her body is a
empty sack, you know, ain't got no form to it, and—"

"Oh, come on!"

"And the music goin on all around her. Like one of these flutes. I ain't
never heard no music like that. Sound like it come up out the ground. Or
like it comin out the leaves theirselves. You ain't never heard nothin like
that in your life, Mr. Radio Man. And then angels singing. Little children's
voices, comin from everywhere. Little angel's voices—"

"What were they singing?" Alex interrupts.

"I can't make it out. I can't understand the words. They don't make sense. Then the little girl, she come right up to me. It ain't like she walks, but like she floats, and I can smell her, and she smell like vanilla and rosemary. She smell like candles do when you snuff em out. She smell like the air inside it when you open up a cedar chest. The music sound like all these little children trying to drown each other out, like they all want me to hear their song but all the songs is different and don't none of em make no sense and you couldn't hear one of em by itself even if you wanted to. I'm just standin there holdin my little stringer of fish, got my pole over my shoulder, and that little girl just hangin there in the air in front of me, and them voices goin off like firecrackers on the Fourth of July! It had my head swimmin. It had me lookin for somewhere to run, I'll tell you.

"Then the light in the air changed. All around me. It was yellow, like it get sometime in August, and then it was pale green and shot through with violet. Seem like I could hear thunder, way off in the distance, it bein a clear day, not a cloud in the sky. That little girl was just lookin at me, her face all scrushed up like she wanted to say somethin but she couldn't get it out, and then she looked for a moment like a old lady, older'n me, and in the next instant she was a baby, red-faced and bout to squall. It like to killed me. It like to drove a stake through my heart ..."

TWO

The division of the Academy that Brenda most likes is the elementary school, particularly the pre-school. The little children are fresh-faced and innocent. They look at her with wide trusting eyes.

"Do away with the rows of desks, immediately," she tells the teachers in K through six. "No more of that regimentation. I want the classrooms free-form. I want you to establish 'study areas' where the children can roam at will, explore—"

"You can't keep discipline that way," Francine Holloway says. Francine Holloway is nobody knows how many years old. She was teaching at Piper Elementary when Brenda was in school. She won't tell anyone how old she is. Some of the other teachers have told Brenda that Mrs. Holloway falls asleep in her third-grade classroom and some of her students climb out the window and run away only to be found wandering up and down Main Street during school hours.

"Discipline will take care of itself," Brenda says.

"Hah!" Francine Holloway says. Her hair is thin and stringy, dull gray.

The children come running and gather around Brenda when she appears. They jump up and down. They think she is a movie star. She lets them run their fingers through her long hair. The other teachers eye Brenda from the corners of their eyes and shrug. They all want the kids to march to the lunchroom in neat, military lines, not making a sound. Brenda instructs them to let the kids walk there naturally. Visiting and talking. "A little noise never hurt anyone," she says, "a little noise is good for the soul!"

The teachers stand in groups, talking, and they fall silent when Brenda walks by. They resent her from the start. Stuart MacGruder, the former headmaster, stayed in his office all day and let the school run itself. Brenda finds a half-empty pint of Old Crow bourbon hidden in the back of one of his filing cabinets.

Alex Gresham sits behind the panel in the control room at WXAY. He is a tall young man and his hair recedes to the middle of his head so that his face seems even longer and leaner than it is, sloping to his prominent nose that hooks like a large bird's. He loves it that "Wax-ay," as he calls the station, has gone to a talk format, and he slouches in the chair with his long blue-jeaned legs crossed, his feet in scuffed and discolored sneakers. He had been ready for a change. He had grown tired of spinning CDs of country singers, all the plunking and whining, and he's beginning to get the hang of goading his callers into saying things even more outrageous than whatever they had called to say in the first place. He thinks he might have found his calling.

He can see Miss Martha Norton sitting in the glass-enclosed studio next to the control booth. She operates the bleeper. It is a large and elaborate looking taping machine that puts everything coming out of the control room on large reels of tape and delays it for six seconds before back-feeding it into the transmitters for broadcast. Miss Martha is a retired schoolteacher. She has pale blue hair and a fixed smile. When someone says something she deems unfit for the airwaves, she bleeps it out. If she misses something, Joe Callivera, the dispatcher at the highway patrol office nearby, will call immediately. Joe weighs 550 pounds and had to have his car seat special rigged so that he could get behind the wheel. He is also the local representative of the Federal Communications Commission and he monitors public broadcasts. Everytime Miss Martha has to bleep something, she laughs hysterically.

Alex has a call from a man who identifies himself as Malcolm Roland. He sounds ancient. But his voice is strong and full of conviction. "I don't need no garbage pick-up," he says. "I been livin out here near Nanafalia all my life, and now all of a sudden the county government tells me I got to pay for garbage pick-up and put one of them big old trash containers out there side the road. I ain't gonna do it."

"A law is a law," Alex says.

"Hang the goddam law," Malcolm Roland says, and Alex glances over at Miss Martha and sees her grinning broadly. "I don't have no garbage to put in it. I drive in and recycle my cans at that place in Piper. Sell em by the pickup load. Same with my plastic. And my newspaper, too, what I don't use to start my fire. Old Tommy Tutwiler eats all the scraps and gristle and bones I got left over—"

"Old Tommy who?" Alex interrupts.

"My hound dog. Tommy Tutwiler. He'll eat most anything you put in front of him. Course I'm careful what I give him. I wouldn't want him eatin nothin that would kill him. Hell no. I don't throw nothin away. I told em I didn't care to join up with the new trash route, as they called it, but they say I ain't got no choice. Join up or pay a fine or go to jail. Now what do you think of that?"

"I think you better join up or pay a fine or go to jail," Alex says. He sighs. "What are you, un-American or something? Are you some kind of bolshevik? Are you a communist?"

"Some kind a what?"

"Are you a lawbreaker?"

"I'm a law-abiding American. I fought in the Second World War. In the South Pa—"

Alex cuts him off and opens another line. "The People Speak," he says. "Go ahead."

There is a shrill whistle and then silence. Alex can hear the tail end of his conversation with Malcolm Roland coming through the speaker-phone. "Turn your radio down, please," he says. "Hello?"

"Hello? Am I on the air?"

"Yes. You are." There is another pause. Whoever it is is puzzled because they can't hear themselves coming from the radio. "You're on. Go ahead please."

"Hello? Hello?" Alex cuts the caller off and switches to the third line. All four lines are blinking.

"Alex, my man," a voice says, "how are you?"

"This is The People Speak. Go ahead. I'm fine."

"Well Alex, I represent the White Knights of the Aryan Cross. We are a brand new organization in Wembly County, and I wanted to alert you and all your listeners to our presence. You see, we feel that the niggers and the Jews are taking over this country, and we aim to stop em." Alex glances over at Miss Martha. She looks startled, as though she does not know whether to bleep or not.

"How do you know I'm not a Jew," Alex asks.

"I don't. But we'll find out if you are. Believe me. This is just our first alert. Stay tuned for more." And the phone clicks off. Alex opens line four.

"Alex, this is Newton Grable, pastor of the Hidden Valley Church of Christ of the New Light. God bless you this mornin, brother!" And Newton Grable begins his daily ramble through whatever scripture has caught his eye during his ritual Bible study. He calls every morning. Alex sits slumped in the chair only half listening as Brother Grable's voice drones on.

Then Alex's attention is arrested by what Brother Grable is saying. He is talking about a demonstration scheduled for that day at the Women's Health Center, something that Alex has not heard about. "God's men, women and children will be there, all of us surrounding that murder palace, that place that sends innocent little children to their horrible deaths, that—"

"Wait a minute," Alex says, "if you don't believe in abortion, then it's simple. Just don't get one!"

"—that persists in its sin! We will lie down on the sidewalk and block the street, anything to stop these young women from killing their unborn—"

"Too bad your mother didn't exercise that option," Alex says, and Grable falters for a moment.

"Ahhhh, yes, you would persecute me for expressing my beliefs, my belief in the Holy Scriptures, that say that life is sacred—"

"Are you a Catholic?" Alex barks into the mike.

"I most certainly am not a Catholic," Grable says. "I don't need the Pope to tell me—"

CLICK. "The People Speak," Alex says, opening another line.

⇒

Mabel Perkins watches the crowd of demonstrators from inside the clinic. Mabel is in her forties, a thin dainty woman who wears her short-cropped hair the color of an eggplant. She calls the shade "aubergine." Mabel had been Brenda Vick's best friend when they were in school. They had been inseparable until Brenda had started going out with Wayne McClain, who demanded Brenda's full attention, but the girls had remained close even then. Indeed, Mabel thinks she was the only other person who knew about Brenda's abortion, and it had been that one event more than any other that had eventually led her to open and manage the Women's Health Center. It is the only abortion clinic in Wembly County, and the two doctors who come out from Birmingham—one one week, the other the next—do so under constant threats to their lives. The Piper Women's Health Center has for years been one of the busiest abortion clinics in the Birmingham area. It has survived bombings and many attempts by Roger Coles's county government to shut it down. It does a brisk business and it always will, as long as there are pregnant women, and men who get them that way against their wishes.

Mabel has heard that Brenda is back in town. She hopes to see her soon, but she has her hands full with Brother Grable and his bunch of Operation Rescuers, who have been joined today by the local chapter of The Eagle Forum. Through the window Mabel can see Roger Coles's daughter Helen Grace, the local Eagle Forum chapter president, holding a large glass jar in which they claim is a fetus preserved in formaldehyde. But Mabel knows it is really a plastic figure someone has gotten from the UAB Medical School. Mabel had been Mabel Plunkett when they were girls, and she has never had an abortion herself. Though she has no children, she has been married four times, most recently to Red Perkins, a one-armed man who ran a poolroom downtown and who is now deceased from a bullet between the eyes, fired from a .45 by Mabel herself in what old Judge Thaddeus Stern called a classic case of self-defense.

But Mabel is a double-murderer in the eyes of her critics, because shortly before his death Red Perkins had gone down front at Grable's church and dedicated his life to Christ. And what they all did not know, or would not believe, was that very same night, Red had come home drunk and knocked out one of Mabel's two remaining real front teeth with his fist. Red Perkins was the meanest sonofabitch who ever lived, but in Brother Newton Grable's eyes, he was born again, new and innocent and without sin. His death was like the deaths of the babies in the clinic. Grable calls that murder. Mabel knows better on both counts.

Mabel is certain that her mission in the clinic was ordained by God, by God herself, because if God had to be one sex or the other then She most definitely had to be a woman. All you had to do to figure that out was look at the world and at her message that she sent through her son. Women are the only ones who understand love and can give life. Men run around scattering their seed every which way, but women are the only ones who can take it, nurture it and bring forth life from it. And they're the only ones who can decide when not to do that, too, though Roger Coles and Newton Grable think it ought to be them who decide, because they are men. Mabel, of course, knows it shouldn't be them, and for exactly the same reason.

Young Dr. Pitts is here today, and he is scared to death. "These people will kill you," he says to Mabel, peering out the window at them. His hands shake. He can barely hold his coffee cup. He wears a white smock with WHC over the breast pocket in blue script.

"Anybody killed by one of those nuts goes straight to heaven," Mabel says. Her smock is pale blue with red letters.

"Thanks, but no thanks," Dr. Pitts says nervously. He is thin and slight, with a sandy mustache. They have aborted two pregnancies this morning, two country girls, one of whom was so dull that Mabel was sure she didn't even know how she had gotten pregnant. The other was thirteen and told Mabel that the father was her own father. She was hysterical, weeping and begging that they "get the monster out of her!" Mabel is breaking the law in not notifying the girl's parents.

"Just stay out of sight," Mabel says to Dr. Pitts. Another local woman, Pixie Dixon, a prominent housewife in town, has already missed an appointment today. Mabel had known that she wouldn't show up with all these people here. A young black girl is due in a few minutes. Mabel goes to the front door and opens it.

The people surge forward toward her. "Murderer!" they yell. "Baby killer!" Helen Grace Greer is right in the front, with several other women, their faces strained and contorted with their screaming at her. Several deputies are posted on the lawn, and they smile self-consciously. It's one of the first cool autumn days, crisp and high blue. There are no clouds in the sky.

"Stay behind the barriers!" they say, "get back, now." They motion toward the demonstrators, wave them back.

Brother Newton Grable, in the middle of the street, prays through a bullhorn. "Jesus Lord take pity on these poor murderers, for they know not what they do!" he says, his voice electric and distorted and echoing loudly in the trees. His followers are on their knees in the street. Their faces are turned to the high sky, their arms upraised. "Reach down and fill their sin-ful hearts with the merciful dew of your blessing! They have murdered hun-dreds, nay thousands, of babies, and the babies' souls are not dead! They are angels and they are with God in heaven! Bless Jesus!" Brother Grable is really not that concerned with Heaven. He's more interested in the mani-festation of God's plan here on earth. Here and now.

Purcell Dewberry stands behind Mabel. Purcell works for her, and he is huge and black. His arms bulge in his white T-shirt; the afternoon sunlight gleams on his skin. A car nudges its way up the street, stops, and the young girl gets out. She is frightened. The crowd swirls around her. They hold out the jars of phony fetuses. They beg her, some of them on their knees, for her child's life. Mabel and Purcell go down the sidewalk to where the girl stands terrified, looking around, her mouth hanging open, her eyes wide with fear. The girl wears a plain purple sundress, and her skin shines yellow like melting butter in the sunshine.

Purcell puts his arm around the girl and the three of them begin to make their way back toward the clinic. Angry, reddened faces surround them, screaming at them. "You murderer!" "You will murder your own child!" Mabel can feel the young girl trembling against her. "Please, please, listen to Jesus!" Then something hits the ground at their feet. Mabel looks and knows immediately what it is. She's seen it all. Nothing surprises her anymore. It's bloody and real and dead and it looks like a human fetus, but Mabel knows it's a hog fetus. Another one lands next to the first, and the young girl tenses and cries out. She begins to shake violently and Purcell and Mabel hold her.

"Look! Look at what you do! Look at what you will have done!" Their shrieking is a litany now, a steady loud chant. The defiant faces swirl around them. The girl seems rooted to the sidewalk. They cannot budge her. "Yes! Yes!" the women scream, "she's having second thoughts! The Lord is working in her! The Lord is—"

Two sudden and explosive shots ring out. They sound like loud firecrackers and there are screams and cries all around. "Uhhhh," Mabel hears, "Uhhhhh." She looks around and Purcell is holding his arm, gazing with surprise and disbelief at the blood that oozes between his fingers. The girl stands crying with her eyes clenched shut. "Nooo," she says, "Nooo." The demonstrators, the women and Grable's people, billow all around them. They move chaotically, surging back and forth.

Mabel drags the stiff-legged girl, her eyes shut tight, toward the door, and Purcell Dewberry follows, still looking at where the blood streams out over his hand and down his arm and drips in large thick drops to the grass. It's copious blood, crimson and slick. Mabel can smell it, urgent and warm.

Inside Dr. Pitts helps them to an examining room and begins to look at Purcell's arm. They can hear the people outside, milling and shouting, crying, as though the sounds of the shots have driven them finally crazy. They can hear police sirens, whining and moaning.

"A flesh wound," Dr. Pitts says.

"It hurts like hell," Purcell says. "It burns like fire."

The doctor begins to bathe it with alcohol. Purcell winces. A deputy comes inside.

"Who did it?" Mabel asks. She looks at the deputy. He is young, hardly more than a boy. "Willie Mays Crews," his name tag says.

"Somebody in the crowd," Willie Mays Crews says. "We don't know. Could have been anybody. Most of em have scattered."

"You didn't catch him?"

"Or her," he says. "Could have been anybody. No, we didn't catch em."

"And you probably never will," Mabel says.

"Never say never," the deputy says. He looks at her with his pale flat eyes, the color of a salmon's skin. He does not blink. "Like I say," he says, "never say never."

⌐

Cody gets great footage of the demonstration and the confusion and disarray after the shooting. He happened on it by accident, drawn by the crowd as he cruised around town in his van.

He checked into the Moon Winx, a small strip motel at the edge of town. Its sign was a round green moon painted with a face with one eye winking. The desk clerk, a girl named Willodeen Makepeace, told Cody she was a cosmetology student at Bevil State Community College over in Mt. Holley. She got off at eleven and joined Cody in his room. They made love six times, and between the fifth and sixth time she said to him, "I want you to put me in this movie, now, son," and Cody, knowing that this was only the first time of many that he would hear this, had said, "Oh Lord. Well, hell yes. Of course I will." Willodeen Makepeace had breasts like ripe oranges and beautiful teeth. She was gone when Cody awakened.

⌐

Brenda knows the girl is her niece even before she has been introduced to her. She knew her brother had a girl, a little older than Jimmy. But the effect when she first sees her is jolting. It's like looking in a mirror and seeing herself blond and twenty-five years and twenty pounds ago.

Because for a brief moment Brenda thinks that this is her daughter, the little blond girl who has drifted through the back of her waking and sleeping thoughts for years. Who has floated like a wisp of smoke always there, hovering. She has not realized until now that the child she envisions is a mirror image of herself, altered, even distorted, by the light hair and the blue eyes instead of black, and when Darlene fixes her with her eyes in a casual passing in the hallway, eyes like the autumn sky, Brenda is rocked to the bottoms of her feet. She is speechless.

Darlene sees her aunt and hurries on by. The hallway is crowded, between classes. Her aunt is a woman she does not know, a woman from Chicago, another universe. "She's always been uppity," her father said about her, "always thought too much of herself to suit me." Darlene wonders what it would be like to live in Chicago. A big city. She has never been out of Alabama in her life, hardly out of Piper. She works nights and weekends at the local movie theater, the Piper Twin. She works behind the candy counter, shoveling up popcorn. Sometimes she works in the ticket booth out front. She watches a lot of movies, so she's not at all surprised or alarmed by the person who visits her in the night, who materializes out of the darkness when Darlene is all alone in her bed.

"What would you think if ... if you ..." she asked her classmate Shannon Stephens, "if you had a visit from the Virgin Mary?" Shannon is not really Darlene's friend. Darlene has no close friends.

Shannon looked at her sideways. She was chewing gum.

"What are you tellin me? That you did? Come on," she said. She shook her head.

"No, really," Darlene said.

"When was this?"

"At night. In the middle of the night. Sometimes."

"And how do you know this dream is the Virgin Mary?" Shannon asked.

"Because," Darlene said. "Because she said so."

"Jeez," Shannon said. She chewed her gum. She shook her head again. "Only Catholics really see the Virgin Mary," Shannon had said.

The Piper Twin is managed by a man named Duane Justice. He is married with three children and he won't leave Darlene alone. Duane Justice is forty-seven years old and very good-looking. He has a thick black mustache, like Tom Selleck. Sometimes, when they are in the office together toting up, Mr. Justice takes out his thing and asks Darlene to rub it. It is the only one she has ever seen. It gets hard and is long and thick and warm to her hand. She feels her breath quicken when she touches it. It's so big she cannot imagine it going inside her, but, after weeks of coaxing and begging and kissing her, when it does slide inside her it does so with ease.

"I know it's wrong," she says to her visitor in the night. "It's a sin."

"Not necessarily," Mary says. "It depends on the circumstances." Darlene can see her standing there, in the shadows. She stands in a violet haze, and her hair always looks as though it needs washing. There is a strange smell about her, like hot candle wax.

"But he's married," Darlene says.

"Maybe it is wrong," Mary says, "but it's not because he is married." Darlene can hear the faint whispering of the television set in the front of the house. It sounds like an infomercial about a revolutionary new fishing rod. "Marriage as you know it on earth is changing," Mary says. "It's an invention, by and large, of men. It's not anything like marriage in heaven."

"What is it like in heaven?" Darlene asks softly.

"It's based on love," Mary says. "That's all."

Then Mary is gone, faded back into the dark, and Darlene is alone in her bed again. She lies very still. The only sound is the distant television set in the front of the house. Her father sometimes watches television and drinks beer all night and then sleeps most of the day. He is between jobs, he says. She lies there thinking of what Mary has said. She doesn't feel guilty now. Mary has given her permission to enjoy what she is doing with Mr. Justice.

And it makes her happier than anything in her life before now. It's like a fantasy, unreal and distant. Mr. Justice drives a red Mustang convertible and wears wrap-around sunglasses. He goes to Atlanta and sometimes to Los Angeles to see all the new movies before they're released. He tells Darlene about all the stars he meets. "Yes," he says, "I shot a game of pool with Brad Pitt. He's an okay guy." Half the girls in town have a secret crush on Duane Justice, but it is Darlene that he makes love with.

"Hey, gir-friend," Shannon says to her. They meet in the new McDonald's. They sit at a small table for two next to the front window that looks out partially on the enclosed playground with its twisted multicolored tunnels and its bin of red, green and blue plastic balls. The window also looks partially out on Main Street, across the street to the red-brick

Planters and Merchants Bank with its columns in front and its broad drive-through at the side, wide enough for three lanes and a fourth lane for the ATM. "What's happenin, baby?"

"Nothin," Darlene replies. She has a small cone of soft-serve. They are giving them away during the Grand Opening, and there's a line halfway down the block. The McDonald's is crowded. Ronald McDonald has been there for several days handing out balloons, but he's gone now.

Just then Cody Klinger walks by down the sidewalk. He carries a video camera dangling at the end of one arm and has a black leather satchel slung over his other shoulder. He wears a navy blue turtleneck sweater and jeans. Both girls watch him go down the street. His gold hair bounces in the sunlight.

"All that and a bag of chips," Shannon says. "Wow!"

"Amen," Darlene says. She licks her ice cream cone.

"Fine babe," Shannon says. "He's from Hollywood, here to make a movie."

"Really?" Darlene asks. She sits up straight. She watches his back until he disappears.

"Yeah," Shannon says, "it's gonna have Sean Penn and Wynona Rider in it."

"Naww."

"Yep. That's what I hear."

Brenda has startling moments of deja vu, as though periodically she transforms back into the child she once was in this place. The town has changed so much that it's hardly recognizable. But Brenda sometimes will be abruptly stopped and arrested by a sudden scene: the afternoon sunlight on a side street, say, the way it falls across a hedge; or the quick smell of new bread when she walks by the bakery on Main Street; or the scent of honeysuckle in a vacant lot as she jogs by. Her body will grow warm, relaxed. It will seem for a moment as if she has drifted outside real time.

She feels that way when she looks at Darlene, when she sees the look in her eyes. The way her eyes dart back and forth, avoiding others' eyes.

She stops Darlene one day after school. The girl lopes when she walks, hunches her shoulders as though to make herself less tall.

"You are Darlene Vick," Brenda says. "I'm your aunt."

"I know," the girl says. She ducks her head, then she straightens up and looks Brenda in the eye. Brenda cannot read her look.

"I guess anybody could tell by looking at us, huh?" Brenda says. She smiles.

"I guess," Darlene says. She shifts from one foot to the other. She is gangly in her clothes. Brenda knows that one day soon she will be graceful, tall and slim. Now she is awkward. She looks at Brenda out of the corners of her eyes.

"Maybe we can, you know, you and I, maybe we can get to know each other," Brenda says.

"Sure," Darlene says again, "why not?"

And then she is gone, slipped away into the crowd of adolescents in the hallway. Brenda called her brother Lamar once since she's been back and he was drunk. "I'm on bad times, Brenda," he said bitterly, "bad times! But you wouldn't know nothing about that! Miss high and mighty!"

"You need to work more hours at that theater," her father says to Darlene. "Tell that pissant Justice fellow that you need more hours." Her father is drinking beer in the kitchen. He wears an old T-shirt with a hole in the back of it.

"Let her alone, Lamar," her mother says. She is shaping a pound of ground beef into a meat loaf pan, and she will pour a can of cream of celery soup over it and bake it in the oven. Her fingers are bloody from the meat.

"I ain't botherin her," her father says. "Hell, Justice don't pay her but six dollars an hour. How come she can't get more hours and bring more money home?"

"I work all the hours I can," Darlene says. "I have to study."

"Shit. When have I seen you studyin?"

"Git off her back, Lamar!" her mother says. She flicks her fingers at him and several specks of blood hit his cheek. He recoils.

"Hey! Shit!" he says, rubbing his cheek with the flat of his hand. He spits on the floor. "Bitch!"

The late afternoon sunlight slants through the dusty windows. The red formica table top is piled high with cereal boxes, boxes of soda crackers, an opened loaf of bread, a six pack of Diet Coke, a case of Miller Lite, paper plates and cups and forks. They eat off paper plates that her mother can bundle up and throw away. They eat supper at four in the afternoon.

⌐

Darlene walks after supper along Shell Creek, a stream that curls through the middle of town. She walks down the running path that goes by the abortion clinic. The cinder-covered path, built by the town fathers for jogging and walking, runs for several miles along the creek. The street in front of the abortion clinic is littered with candy wrappers and crushed paper cups, but there's no one around.

The early autumn dusk is already beginning to descend. Not many people walk on the path after dark, because this is where so many of the reports of the ghost of the little girl have come from. Several of Darlene's classmates have seen her. They say she is vicious looking with long sharp teeth and flashing red eyes. The ghost growls threateningly at them from the bushes. "I think it's Bigfoot," a girl named Lorene Wagstaff said one day in English class. "Ha, you wish!" said a boy named Ernest Bridgewater. Lorene had blushed pink and everybody had laughed.

Darlene looks up at the twisted shapes in the trees above her head, the high leaves brushed pale golden by the setting sun, and she thinks about the ghost. She smells the damp rotting of the creek bank, covered along here with brown pine needles and ferns. The ferns arch over the water as though they are thirsty. The moving water makes a low, throaty gurgle. Everything else in the woods is so still that it seems to be about to burst, as though it is holding its breath.

She walks further along the path, deeper into the woods. It's darker here, but still light, the trees and shrubs and picnic pavilions and garbage cans mounted on the trunks of trees all still retaining their shapes, but muted and softened by the twilight.

Way into the woods she comes to a clearing where the last shafts of light from the dying sun pierce the treetops and she stops for a moment. Someone had built a fire here, and the cold black remains of it are inside smoke-stained bricks arranged in an odd star-like shape. Other shapes, off-kilter geometrical figures, are scratched in the ground as though with a sharp stick. Darlene leaves the path and goes closer to the ashes. She can see what looks like charred bones there, the bones of what appears to be the carcass of a small animal. A silence as thick as fog hangs in the clearing.

Then Darlene hears someone coming, quick footsteps along the path, the sound of someone running or walking very fast, and startled she turns and sees her aunt coming down the path, jogging, breathing easily, her hands in fists pumping before her. She wears a purple headband and a dark—black or navy—sweatsuit, cotton, the kind you buy at Wal-Mart. She does not see Darlene at first, and Darlene thinks for a moment that she will run on by, but her eyes jerk to the side, toward Darlene, as though suddenly drawn there, as though Darlene has moved or shouted or made some other noise, but she hasn't.

Brenda stops. She runs in place for a moment. She has a good sweat and her skin feels cool under the sweatsuit. Her niece stands in the center of a circle drawn in the ground, a circle with an X drawn through it. Brenda had not expected to see anyone, much less her niece. She stands still for a moment. Shadows fall across Darlene's face and body. She wears jeans and a plaid shirt, green.

"Darlene," Brenda says. Then, "Hello."

"Hi," the girl says.

Brenda sees the charred black wood of the old fire. The scattered bricks. The smell of the fire-site is acrid with a hint of decay. Brenda has run by here often and has never noticed it before.

"What ... what are you doing?" Brenda asks.

"Nothing," Darlene says, "I was just walking."

Brenda pauses. "Which way?" she asks. "I'll walk with you for a while." The girl points back toward Vine Street, the direction Brenda is going.

Brenda is near the end of her jog. She always goes up Vine Street to where it crosses Pineview and then on back to her house, the last mile of her route.

"Okay," Darlene says. She comes out of the clearing to the path.

"What's all this?" Brenda asks. She squints into the glooming clearing.

"I don't know. Some crap, I guess."

"Crap?"

"I don't know. Kids, I guess."

Just then a sudden breeze comes up, rattling the dry and dying leaves in the towering trees. The breeze is warm, like a breath, like a summer wind before a thunderstorm, but there are no clouds. Both women instinctively shiver. There is a gust and some of the topmost branches bend with it. The leaves sough and sigh. They break free and come tumbling and curling downward, all around them, littering the ground and drifting against the tree trunks. The wind picks up and whistles in the branches. It makes a sound like children singing. There's a strong smell of talcum powder and roses.

"Wow," Darlene says.

Brenda feels herself tingling all over. Her hands seem light and weightless, and she holds them close before her eyes. They have become the hands of a young girl. An ink spot that had been on the back of her right hand all day—that was there a moment before—is now gone. She squints at Darlene in the dimness and she can see fine lines around her eyes and the corners of her mouth, lines she now sees on her own face in the mirror every day. Darlene tilts her head, and her eyes flame and she is smiling at Brenda, grinning, and she laughs out loud. The leaves swirl around them. They can hear what sounds like other laughter coming from up in the trees.

The blue of Darlene's eyes has the intensity of the sea now, a broiling wet deep blue, and laughter rings all around them as the leaves dance in the air. Darlene's laughter is edged with hysteria, bubbling, delighted and wicked. The earth shakes and trembles. Now the wind is cold, frigid, and both of them hug their arms. After a moment Brenda reaches out to her niece. "Why, you ... you're ..." For a moment Darlene looks like a child, a little girl that Brenda has never seen before.

Darlene backs away. She looks frightened now. Her hair shakes and streams in the gusting wind. Brenda blinks. Then the moment passes and Darlene looks like herself again, her skin smooth and untouched.

They stand there for a long time. Neither one of them moves. Whatever it is back in the shadows breathes softly now, gently, like a baby's sleeping. Her aunt turns and begins to walk. Darlene falls in beside her. She knows she looks so much like her aunt that it frightens her. Her aunt is tall. Darlene knows that she herself will be even taller than she already is, as tall as her aunt. She is still growing. She feels her bones hurting in the night as they grow. Her face is a mess. Her nose will grow for several months, then her jawbone, then her chin. They never match. She wishes all the parts would grow at the same pace, at the same time. She hates her face but Mr. Justice tells her she is beautiful, that she looks just like Helen Hunt.

They walk along in the silence for a while. Brenda looks at the young girl walking beside her. Darlene is only half formed, if that much. She walks with a stiff, hesitating gait, as though she has to pause for a fragment of a second with each step to let her brain tell her leg to move. Brenda remembers being that self-conscious about her body, but she has not thought of it for a long time.

The girl bounces ahead of Brenda and pulls a twig off a bush and chews on it. Her lips are full and ripe, without artificial color. Her eyes are now the color of cornflowers, a gentle and delicate blue. They glitter. Darlene says suddenly, "I want to live somewhere far away from here. I wouldn't mind living in Chicago."

"Huh," Brenda says, "not my part of Chicago, you wouldn't."

"You didn't like it?"

"No," Brenda says.

They stand there for a moment. The glint of fear in Darlene's eyes has gone away. She smiles. She seems about to speak again, but she doesn't. And then she begins to walk again, and Brenda falls in behind her and catches up to her and soon they are almost back to Vine Street and the flickering streetlight up ahead.

⌐

"Azaleas! That's what you need, azaleas!" Roger Coles says, looking around the yard.

"Well, that's—" Brenda begins.

"No, no. I'll have some sent over and planted. I own a nursery. No problem. Your yard will have azaleas! Every yard needs azaleas!"

"Well, thank you, sir," she says.

"Please don't call me 'sir,'" he says, "it seems condescending."

"All right."

"Call me Roger."

"All right."

"Well, go ahead. Call me Roger."

"All right, Roger!"

"That's better," he says, grinning at her.

"Well, okay," she says.

So she has finally met the famous Mr. Coles. He moves with a kind of youthful quickness around the yard. His hair is snow-white, but his movements are lithe and graceful. She wonders how old he is. She wonders if his well-pressed khakis and work boots instead of a business suit are an affectation. She vaguely remembers him, remembers the family. His daughter had been in her class, a mousy girl named Helen Grace Coles. She and Helen Grace had competed for Good Citizenship Girl. And for Valedictorian. Brenda had won both. She recalls dimly that her friend Mabel Plunkett told her that Helen Grace had cried in the girls' rest room when one or the other of the awards—maybe both—had been announced. The awards had not meant all that much to Brenda. Maybe because she had won them.

"I must take you into Birmingham for dinner at Arman's," he says. "You've never eaten at Arman's."

"No," Brenda says.

"Superb food." He looks around. "What do you need? Anything? Everything to your satisfaction?" He looks at her. His eyes are gray and sharp. His face is lean and angular, well tanned. "If something's not right, why you just say the word and it will be replaced. Money is no object."

"Mr. Coles—"

"Roger!"

"Roger. Why are you being so nice to me?" She inspects him. "I mean, why this treatment? Escorting me into town like that? And this house for two hundred bucks? What's the catch?"

"No catch. Don't be ridiculous. It's because I want you to be happy. I know you're going to be the best headmistress Piper Academy ever had, and I don't want you to leave us. I want that school to be the best around. Let's just say that whatever I do for you is an investment that will pay off handsomely in the future. I'm very confident of that." He licks his lips. Something in his gray eyes makes her uneasy. He looks at her hungrily, eagerly.

The house is a small, three-bedroom cottage with a fenced-in yard. He told her on the phone that it was furnished. So she loaded up a lot of stuff before she left Chicago and took it to the Salvation Army. She shipped a few things. Otherwise, she and Jimmy brought only what they could get into the station wagon. Which suited her fine, because she wanted this to be a total new beginning.

They walk up onto the porch and sit down on a glider. It is well oiled and silent. "Well," she says, "I appreciate everything you've done for me."

"Don't mention it again," he says. "We have a ... well, a unique situation here in Wembly County, and you can have a significant and important place in the...well, the scheme of things."

"I don't know," she says, "all this militia business I hear about, it gives me the willies."

"The what?" He frowns.

"The, well, you know. The willies. The heeby-jeebies." She smiles. He does not smile back. "I don't care for it," she says.

"That's because you don't know anything about it," he says curtly. "But let's not talk business today. I came by to welcome you to Piper. I'll do so more formally at the opening reception at the Academy. It will be your official introduction to Piper. Your 'coming out,' you might say."

"Ahhh," she says, "my long-delayed debut." She laughs.

Coles does not laugh. He stares at her. His eyes seem to flare, to widen, and then he squints at her as though he is suddenly half blind. He stands up. He is very tall, and he is so thin that he looks even taller. The boots have two-inch heels. Though they are work boots, they are shined to a high sheen. Brenda thinks that all he needs to complete his outfit is a riding crop and a pistol strapped to his hip.

"Let me tell you something, Brenda," he says. His gaze is level on hers, from high above.

"All right."

"Wayne McClain is a dangerous man," he says.

"Pardon?" She has no idea what he's talking about.

"My advice to you would be to steer a wide path around him. He is a good football coach, but his morals are, well, dubious, at best. And he has been known to partake much too heavily of the bubbly, if you follow what I mean."

"Well," she says. She wants to laugh out loud, but she doesn't. "All right," she says, "thanks for the warning."

He reaches out and touches her tenderly on the arm. He smiles then. "Good," he says. "Very good!" He pauses. "I'm sending a few things over. Some nice glasses, and a case of Jack Daniels bourbon. And a calf-skin recliner—"

"A what?"

"You know, a recliner. A chair!"

"Mr. Coles, I don't need a recliner."

"Roger!"

"Roger. I don't think—"

"But I do! I need a chair to sit in when I come to visit you."

She does not know what to say. So she finally says, "All right."

⟶

Jimmy Boykin stands in the dim confines of LEROY'S GRILL AND BILLIARDS watching two other kids shooting pool. He is drinking a Coke and eating a package of pork skins. The other boys are dressed exactly like him, T-shirts and jeans and grubby sneakers, and he thinks that he might as well be in Summit or South Chicago except for their accents. They speak to each other in a slow country drawl instead of the harsh and foreign-inflected tones he would have heard up there. They pay him no attention. They ignore him.

"Ain't no sense in a whole lot of worry," one of them says.

"You telling it right," the other says. "Moon come up," and he pauses and does a little dance step and punches the air, "and it goes down! Whooey."

"Play the winner, loser pays?" Jimmy asks.

They ignore him.

"Louise, now," the first boy, tall and skinny with his head shaved up to a flat-top across his crown, says, "she's spreadin it all over town, what I hear. A regular herpes factory. I wouldn't touch none of that with a ten-foot pole."

"Like you had that much," the other, shorter, stockier, says. He wears a red baseball cap turned around backwards.

"Man, I wouldn't touch her with my little two-inch pole!"

"Shit. You got to get a boner to get a inch and a half."

"I ain't heard you complainin when you took it in the fudge," the first says. He leans over and taps a corner pocket with his stick and pops the eight ball briskly into it. "Next," he says, and he looks at Jimmy for the first time. His eyes are hazel and vague, close together. "Say you want to pay for this next game, feller?"

"Yeah," Jimmy says, putting three quarters on the edge of the table.

Jimmy breaks. The tall boy says his name is Ernest Bridgewater. The short, heavy boy goes and pays for the game and comes back with two Mountain Dews. He introduces himself as Clarence Peevy. Jimmy and Clarence shake hands. Jimmy misses his first shot.

"You new in town?" Clarence asks. One of his eyes seems to have a cast in it. He tilts his head sharply to the side when he looks at you and speaks to you.

"Yeah," Jimmy says. "I just moved down here from Chicago. I'm going to the Academy."

"Who ain't?" Ernest Bridgewater says. He punctuates his question with a slam of the nine ball into a side pocket.

"What grade you in? You gonna play football?" Zip goes the one ball.

"Tenth. I'm thinking about it," Jimmy says. "You guys play?"

"'You guys,' you hear that? 'You guys,'" Clarence says.

"Yeah, we play," Ernest says. "I play end. Clarence there is a fullback. He got his eye knocked out last year against Belle Ellen."

"Out?" Jimmy asks.

"Clean out," Clarence says. "Stood there holding the goddam thing in my hand. Talkin about fucked over. Man."

"Skipper whacked him across the back of the head. Said 'Stop blubberin, man. It ain't nothin but an eye. And hell, you got another one! Besides, the damn thing's gone now! Ain't no use in cryin over it now!'"

"Skipper?"

"Coach McClain. The coach. Hell of a feller. Made All-American at Auburn." Blam. The three ball. "Don't take no shit, Coach don't. If you go out, be ready to sweat your balls off. He'll make you wish your ass was dead." Ernest misses a shot. He stands up straight, leaning on his cue. "But man do we play football. We are some mean motherfuckers. We beat the shit out of everybody we play, it's some great fun, man-alive!"

"Yeah. Ain't nothing like it," Clarence says.

"Is that right?" Jimmy says.

"Yeah, that's right," Clarence says. He is sitting on the next table, his legs dangling. He sucks at the Mountain Dew. "You ain't shit in this town if you don't play football at the Academy," he says.

"Yeah," Ernest said, "all the pussy is reserved for us."

Jimmy lines up a shot and misses. His cue ball banks and nicks the eight ball and scratches it into a corner pocket. Ernest stands gazing down at the table.

"Shit man," he says, "where'd you learn to shoot eight ball?"

"South Chicago," Jimmy says.

"You settin us up or what?"

Jimmy grins. He is thinking of football. He has made up his mind. He wants to be somebody in a new town. He sure wants in on the girls. If these yahoos can play football, so can he. "Yeah," he says, smiling, "I'm settin you up. What kinda town is this, anyway?"

"This is a fuckin no-count town," Ernest says.

"Ain't nothin in this town," Clarence says. "Nothin but a bunch of ghosts!"

"Ghosts?!" Jimmy says.

"Yeah," Clarence says, laughing, "ghosts. People always seeing ghosts. Fuckin ghosts all over the place."

"No shit?" Jimmy says.

"'No shit?' You hear that? You hear the way he says 'no shit?' You talk like a yankee, man. Live down here a while, and you'll get rid of that fuckin accent," Ernest drawls.

⟜

Wayne pushes open the door to the small apartment he shares with his son Keith. It's six o'clock, and Keith will soon be on his way back from Birmingham where he takes violin lessons. Keith is a musician, and he wants to go to the Juilliard School of Music in New York City. Keith is a total puzzle to Wayne; he's just about everything that Wayne is not. His head is shaved bald as a cantaloupe, and he has rings in both ears, his lower lip, his right nostril and sometimes his tongue. He wears the rings except when he goes to classes at the Academy, where they're against the established dress code. The old headmaster, Stuart McGruder, even tried to change the code for boys' hair when Keith had enrolled. Wayne raised hell at a faculty meeting when McGruder brought it up and the old man backed off. He knew better than to cross Wayne in this town. Wayne had had mixed feelings. He would have loved an excuse to make Keith let his hair grow back out. But he would be damned if he wouldn't defend his own boy when the crunch came, no matter how ridiculous Keith insisted on making himself look.

"The only reason I give in to something stupid like a dress code," Keith told Wayne, "is that I want to finish and get my degree, so that I can get out of this dumb nowhere town and go to New York and study."

"Then you understand the point," Wayne said. "That's the reason everybody conforms. So they can get what they want."

"Huh," Keith said.

"You think this is my idea of heaven? You think I want to stay in this 'dumb, nowhere' town any more than you do? I'm serving my time in hell! I don't belong in high-school coaching. I belong at the top! I'm on the way out of here, too, son!"

"Huh," Keith said.

Wayne's ex-wife Bobbye has all of a sudden, in typical Bobbye fashion, decided she wants custody of Keith again. She had custody of him for several years after their divorce, because Wayne was a drunk and out of a job. He had had to go through a rehab program and then a couple of years of after-care and then A A meetings and twelve-step programs. And he finally found this job and got sober. For the most part. By then Bobbye, a party girl herself, moved from Athens, Georgia, where they had lived, into Atlanta. She started dropping hints that it might be good for Keith to live with his father, that every growing boy needed a father figure and all that. Wayne knew she just wanted her freedom to kick up her heels. So they went through all the legal business and Keith moved in with Wayne, who was by then established as a successful coach at Piper Academy. Now Bobbye was engaged to a fellow named Meadows, who owned a chain of funeral homes all over the Southeast, and she had decided that maybe she might want Keith back.

"No way, Bobbye," Wayne told her over the phone.

"Listen, Wayne," she said, "Mr. Meadows (she still called the sonofabitch 'Mr. Meadows,' he was sure because he was a rich old bastard) and I want to send Keith to Juilliard. We'll be able to, Wayne, and you won't. You know that."

"The hell you say," he said. "I can send him. I don't need any 'Mister Meadows' sending my son to school."

"Don't be such a macho prick, Wayne," she said. "You haven't changed one bit!"

"Yeah? Well, fuck you, too, Bobbye," he said and slammed the phone down.

Keith is almost eighteen. He will graduate in May. And Wayne will take care of his future schooling himself, thank you very much. That is one reason Wayne is anxious to get back into college coaching. He makes a pretty good salary at Piper Academy, but not nearly as much as he can make in college, especially with his share of the shoe endorsement fees and the bowl bonuses and all that. They had enjoyed a mighty good life style when he had been an assistant coach at Georgia. A state championship will put him right back on that level.

He remembers their sunny little house in Athens, near the campus, when they had all been together as a family, remembers tossing a football or playing catch with Keith, who seemed, in his early years, a natural athlete ready to follow in his father's footsteps. Keith had played peewee football and Little League baseball and was very good. But then the years immediately after that were a blur. Wayne lost more than a few years of his life to the bottle. He can't remember those years very well at all. Wayne might as well have been someone else or dead, for all he recalls of those days.

When the opportunity came, he wanted his son back. But the boy who moved in with him he had not known at all. He hadn't even recognized him. The boy was sullen, not at all interested in the things Wayne had devoted his life to. His hair then was long, halfway down his back. And Wayne told him he had to cut it, so Keith shaved his head. Keith cared not one dick for football or any other sports. He began playing acoustic guitar with a local rock band called the Velcro Moonpies, who looked to Wayne to be a bunch of dope-heads. He figured Keith was into drugs himself and didn't have any idea what to do about it. He was relieved when Keith asked for violin lessons, and Wayne had called around and found an old man named Richbourgh Smiley, a retired first violinist of the Birmingham Symphony, who rarely took new students anymore but who relented when Keith auditioned for him. Mr. Smiley told Wayne that Keith was one of the most talented students he'd ever had. Which is all fine and dandy, but the lessons cost a lot of money and Keith needs a car to get back and forth, a used Honda, which seems to drink gas. It's all Wayne can do to put a little money away toward Juilliard. But he's determined that no Mr. Meadows is sending his son to college. No way.

Wayne looks at his watch. He has at least a half hour before Keith is back from Birmingham, so he goes into his son's room and flips through a stack of CDs next to his stereo. Most of them have been checked out from the Birmingham Public Library. He sneaks in here to listen when Keith is not at home. He doesn't want Keith to know he's doing it. He chooses Mendelssohn's Violin Concerto in E Minor, played by somebody named Zino Francescotti, and he puts it on, puts on the earphones and sits back to listen. It is sad music. He sits there thinking hard of Keith. The key to the mystery of his son is probably somewhere down inside this sad music. Keith. He might, at that very minute for all Wayne knows, be smoking dope with some friends on Southside. Or doing crack or some worse substance. All of his friends have tattoos and nasty body jewelry festooned all over them and look like they've escaped from some loony bin somewhere.

Then he thinks of Otis Hunnicutt. What a body. Absolutely pure and golden and unadorned. His skin the color of fresh baked bread. And what natural ability. Talent. The kind that will take the boy to the big money in the pros if he doesn't get hurt like Wayne had. Otis Hunnicutt, just earlier this afternoon running laps around the patchy, weed-clumped football field at Piper High, and Wayne leaning on the fence when he passed, watching him through four or five laps until Otis stopped. He was breathing easily, barely sweating, the sleeves ripped out of his T-shirt to reveal bulging muscles, his thick thighs under his tight shorts as slick and hard as marble.

"Hey, coach," he said.

"Otis," Wayne nodded. After a minute of silence, Wayne said, "Can I talk to you for a minute, son?"

"Yessir," Otis said. He looked suspiciously at Wayne.

"I want you to come over and play for me at the Academy."

"Say what?" The boy scratched his head. Then he laughed. His hair was curly and golden. He laughed again and looked at Wayne as though he were making a joke.

Wayne spoke quickly. "You want to go to a major university? Play in the pros? Get the big money?"

"I'm gonna do that, all of that," Otis said.

"Not if you don't get some better coaching," Wayne said. "You'll wind up going to some backwater college, get drafted in the twenty-fifth round and be a back-up. I can make you into a star. The third best running back this area has ever produced, after me and Bo." Wayne smiled.

"I'm already the best," Otis said. He smiled back at Wayne.

"All right. You may be the best. You got the potential. You come play for me, you will be, and every college in the nation will be slobbering all over you. We'll win the state championship. You'll go over a thousand yards before halfway through the season, and by the play-offs everybody, I mean everybody, will know who you are."

The boy ran in place for a moment. He squinted at Wayne. "Don't no brothers go to your school, Coach. You know that. Quit shittin me."

"I ain't shittin you, son. You're gonna be the first. On full scholarship. And maybe a little under the table for your grandmother."

"Naw," he said.

"What, your grandmother won't—?"

"It ain't that. Naw. I can't do it."

"Come on. Why not?"

"Cause these crackers'll kill me, that's why not."

"They ain't gonna bother you, cause you gonna be my boy—"

"—I ain't nobody's boy!"

"Just a figure of speech, Otis. You gonna be my tailback, you gonna be my man! My man! Wayne McClain's man! What do you say? A little over four years from now you gonna be richer than old man Coles himself!"

"Shit."

"You come over there and play for me, it ups your value to the big universities. I'll teach you all the skills, the tricks. Your stats'll be so good—against decent competition—that you'll be able to name the university you want to go to, and there'll be extra benefits in it for you, too, when you sign with somebody. I'll see to that. It can be fixed so you can carry your grandmother with you wherever you go to play. Decent housing for her, too. At the right place, in three or four years, the pros come with their hands full of big bucks. All you'll ever need for the rest of your life."

Otis's eyes were dark and brooding. His skin gleamed in the sunlight as though it were polished.

"Full scholarship," Wayne said.

The boy looked off across the field. Finally, he said, "You'll have to talk to Muh-dear."

"Your grandmother? No problem. You want to do it, then?"

The boy looked around. There were other kids running wind sprints in the far end zone. He looked back at Wayne. "All right," he said.

⟶

Wayne sits up and takes the earphones off. He shuts the equipment off. He thinks he hears Keith's car pulling into the alley where they park. Their apartment is on the second floor, over Deluxe Cleaners, a block off Main Street. It's dingy and cluttered. Some of Keith's instruments and some of the Velcro Moonpies' sound equipment gather dust in the corners. Newspapers are scattered all over the floor in the living room, the remains of last evening's pizza in its box on the coffee table before the television set.

The furniture in the apartment is secondhand, even cast-off stuff, and neither one of them cares. It's a place to light, a place to sleep. Wayne pays three hundred and fifty dollars a month for it, to Coles Realty.

"You couldn't find a furnished place like this in Birmingham for less than seven hundred," Coles said, and Wayne said,

"Yeah? Well, this ain't Birmingham."

"It's sure not," Coles replied, "thank God!"

Wayne hears Keith coming up the metal outside stairs. The boy comes into the living room, carrying his violin case and a stack of sheet music under his arm. It is bulky and he holds it awkwardly.

"Where's your backpack?" Wayne asks.

"In my car," Keith says.

"What, then? You don't have room for the music in it?"

"I don't know where my car is," the boy says. "Somebody stole it."

"What?!" Wayne says. "What? Somebody stole your car? Somebody—"

"Yes! Somebody stole it! They must have hot-wired it or something. I came out and it was gone." Keith puts his violin case in the corner, the stack of music on the cluttered coffee table.

"You came out and—" Wayne begins. He stops. He stares at Keith. "You came out of where? Where the hell were you? Southside?"

"Mr. Smiley's apartment. On Highland Avenue. I was at my lesson."

"You sure you weren't in some dive on Southside? With your goofy friends?"

"No, Dad," he says. He sighs.

"How'd you get home?"

"Jody gave me a ride." Jody was the drummer in their band.

"So. So how'd you get up with Jody?"

Keith sighs again. "I called him, Dad. I called the cops, too. I took care of it, okay?"

"What'd they say?"

"They said it would turn up. Eventually. They're looking for it. In the meantime, Jody said I could borrow his brother's car. Until I can get some more wheels, or something." Jody's brother Mark had just joined the Marines.

Wayne stares at his son. The overhead light glints on the jewelry, on the metal. It makes a white spot on the crown of Keith's head. Keith's denim shirt and his jeans look as though they're about two sizes too big for him. He stands staring dreamily off into space. He is not the least upset that someone has stolen his car. The boy inhabits another world. The world that exists mysteriously beyond that music that Wayne studiously and secretly listens to.

"That car damn sure better be clean when the cops find it," Wayne says sternly.

Keith looks at him. He sighs. He shrugs. "I just washed it last Sunday, Dad," he says. He smiles. He goes down the short hallway toward his room.

"Goddamit!" Wayne says. He stands there shaking his head.

Then he goes into his room and strips down and puts on running shorts and a fresh T-shirt. This one says ATLANTA BRAVES, WORLD CHAMPIONS, 1995. He puts on a battered pair of running shoes. He goes out and slams the door behind him. He jogs up the slight hill to Main, then turns south through town. Most of the stores are closed now. He passes LEROY'S GRILL AND BILLIARDS, which will be open till way past midnight. He can smell greasy hamburgers and onions. His stomach clenches. He begins to jog faster, picking up his pace to a run. There are no cars on the streets, no pedestrians. It's just twilight. Supper time. He can see Coles's big house through the trees up ahead. His feet pound the pavement rhythmically, steadily. By the time he reaches where the street turns sharply to the left in front of Coles's house and grounds he has broken a slight sweat, cool against his skin under his shirt and shorts. And he has forgotten about Keith and the car and the look in his eyes.

He goes by Coles's house and turns down Meador Drive. People sit out in their yards on folding chairs, and they all wave as he goes by. "Freight Train! Freight Train!" the children call out. The men nod and raise an index finger in greeting. The women all watch him eagerly. He wears skimpy running shorts that let the bottoms of his tight buns poke out, and he knows that his legs are hairy and still firm. He has a paunch now that pushes against the waistband of whatever he's wearing and his hair is sprinkled with gray but it is still thick. He hasn't lost a strand of it. He pumps his arms and nods and smiles and occasionally punches the air with his fist. "There goes the coach! Out on his run!"

He passes the little house on Pineview Road where he knows Brenda lives. He passed it daily before she got here, the small pale green cottage sitting forlorn and empty. Deserted. He had had no idea it would soon hold Brenda Vick Boykin. A light is now on inside and an old beat-up blue Toyota station wagon with an Illinois tag sits in the driveway. Bitch Bitch Bitch Bitch Bitch he says under his breath in time with his pounding soles on the asphalt. He does not even turn his head in her direction, panting evenly now, getting a second breath, his legs moving like fluid pistons, flexing the muscles of his back with his arms, almost dancing, knowing surely that she's at the window secretly watching him as he goes smoothly and evenly and powerfully by on his nightly and lonely run through the little town.

THE LITTLE GIRL SITS IN THE TOPMOST BRANCHES of a towering hickory tree. She observes Wayne McClain as he runs down the street, running as though the furies of hell are hot out after him. The dusty dry leaves, thick all around her, hint of their incipient autumn turning with barely visible streaks like thin brushstrokes of yellow and red against the deep green. She watches Wayne McClain every day on his run. She watches him with a fervor, an earnest unwavering gaze that registers his every move, his every twitch of muscle. Her eyes are faded blue, and when Wayne is out of sight they eagerly sweep the town spread out below her. From where she is perched she can see all the way over to the Academy, where four women in leotards and an old man in white shorts walk briskly around the oblong track that surrounds the football field, their arms pumping in rhythm with their strides. All of them wear pleased, self-satisfied expressions. The old man's wife, a thin woman in yellow slacks, sits on the aluminum bleachers and watches him.

The sun has set, streaking the sky with purple and orange. Great shafts of pastel yellow light still pierce through the swollen clouds. Main Street is deserted now, and the smells of grilled meat and simmering vegetables drift through the still-warm air. Over her shoulder, as she turns her head, the little girl can see the pale, almost translucent moon hanging in the deepening blue sky like a perfectly rounded smear.

THREE

Coles goes up the gracefully curved staircase to the second floor, carrying a heavy silver tray on which sits a steaming bowl of Campbell's tomato soup, a saucer of crackers, and a glass of cherry Kool-Aid. His mother drinks eight or ten glasses of it a day. She is still spunky, even though she is ninety-nine years old and confined to her room.

Coles has reached a major decision, and he always informs his mother first. He thinks of her as a Goddess, the heart and soul and conscience of Wembly County. She lies propped up, gray and wizened and wise, up there towering high over the town of Piper, over the treetops and rooftops of all the smaller houses, square in the middle of his domain. In the center of his enclave, his sanctuary.

His mother now lies in her tall, hospital-type bed and watches television all day and most of the evening, muttering under her breath and talking back to it. She watches talk shows, every one that comes on: Rikki Lake and Montel Williams and Leeza and Oprah, Geraldo and Rosie O'Donnell, Jerry Springer, every one. And tabloid news shows. She loves those. Phyllis, their maid, though she has a family and a small house across town, usually sleeps in a downstairs bedroom at the back of the house. She is a heavyset and brooding black woman who does everything for his mother, bathing her and fixing her meals and adjusting her television set and calling the cable company for her when it goes out. She cleans the house and does their laundry. Roger prepares his mother's dinner on those rare occasions when Phyllis takes a few hours off, and whenever he does she never wants anything but a bowl of soup.

He goes down the long hallway, noting all the little trinkets and doodads sitting on tables and in glass-front cabinets, little glass figurines of angels and horses, a collection of unicorns and one of milk-glass black and white Scotty dogs that first his mother and then his wife Alberta had collected over the years. He loves the house, the order of it. It's a symbol to him of just how high he has risen in life.

Roger anticipates a loose board in the floor, hearing it squeak slightly under the runner as he steps on it, hearing the tinkle of glass and metal from one of the cabinets as it moves ever so slightly with his passing. His mother's door is open and he looks in. The evening news is on, droning against the wall, but his mother is lying in the high bed gazing out the window, her arms folded across her belly. She doesn't hear him in the doorway and he stands for a moment inspecting her. She wears a lacy bed cap over her thinning gray hair and her nose is long and pointed, her toothless mouth a faint line, little round spots of rouge on each cheek. She insists that Phyllis make up her face every morning. She plans to live forever, and Roger is quite sure she will. He is certain of it.

"Mama," he says gently, and she turns toward him, smiling, and he comes into the room with her dinner. He rolls the bedside tray to the bed while she eagerly pushes the button that raises her upper body higher, smacking her lips, rolling her eyes.

"You're so good to me, son," she says. She grabs the spoon, holds it in her fist like a child.

"You better let me," he says, and she hands him the spoon and he spoons the red liquid to her thin lips. She takes a sip, nods her head.

"Crunch me up some crackers in it, son," she says, and he does. He stirs it, then spoons it to her mouth. She drinks the cherry Kool-Aid through a straw. When the bowl is half empty she says, "I'm full as a tick, son," and he pulls the tray away and sits down across from her. She glances at the news on the television. She sighs.

"NBC?" he asks.

"What does it matter?" she says. "They all tell the same lies. I was lying here this afternoon looking out that window right over there and I saw the black helicopters again. They fly over this house at least once a week. Checking up on us. They know this house. They watch us. And there has never been one iota of news about it on the liberal television news. Lies."

"I know it," he says. He has seen them himself, hovering overhead, probably filming whatever was going on below.

She had seen an item on a talk show about the mysterious numbers that were painted on the backs of various road signs. It had been on public access TV, on a show run by a man named Thomas T. P. Bloomsbury, who also owns the local radio station WXAY, an absentee owner who is an old colleague of Roger's and who lives clandestinely somewhere in Birmingham. These numbers had been put there by the federal government as secret symbols that would guide troop movements when the New World Order took over. Roger had the soldiers of his militia go along and paint over the numbers with silver paint. At least there would be no such secret symbols in Wembly County.

"Penny for your thoughts, son," his mother says, startling him. She is smiling at him. "Why are you so happy?"

"Do I look like I'm happy?"

"Yes. What is it?"

"The woman I hired, to run the Academy. She is here."

His mother looks levelly at him. Her eyes are light gray-blue. "Is this the woman we talked about?"

"Yes," he says.

She pauses, staring at him. After a minute she says, "You must try this woman out, son. You would if you were buying a racehorse, wouldn't you? And she will be queen. When you are king, she will be queen. You need her, to take Alberta's place." He nods. He smiles at her. Alberta has been dead now for almost ten years.

Her eyes narrow. "Is she a lesbian?" his mother asks.

"Of course not," he says. He laughs jovially.

"You never know," she says. "I saw it on Rikki Lake. Your best friend could be a lesbian and you wouldn't even know it."

He dismisses her concern with a wave of his hand. "Forget it, Mother," he says. "I have something else important to tell you."

"What?"

"The secession. I've decided. It will be soon."

"Oh, goody, goody," she says.

"I'm going ahead with it, and of course I wanted you to be the first to know. We will secede, first from the state of Alabama, and then from the U. S. of A. We will live in the Free State of Wembly!"

"And you'll be President. Prime Minister! King!"

"All of those," he says.

"When?" she asks.

"Soon," he says, "very soon."

She looks proudly at him. And then she frowns. "They will attack you, son," she says. "They will try to crush you."

"But they won't succeed," he says, "because Right is on our side."

Suddenly she sits up and motions to him. "Listen, do you hear them?" she asks. She puts her finger to her lips and cocks her head.

"What?" He hears nothing.

"The helicopters! They're back! The black helicopters!"

She is excited and agitated. Her face flushes. He gets up and goes to the window. He scans the dimming sky. Sure enough, there is a helicopter. He can hear it now, a high faint droning. It is crossing the early evening dusk, a mile or two away. Its running lights are on, blinking. He gets the binoculars from his mother's chifferobe and focuses on the helicopter. He can see it then as clearly as if he were standing next to it. Then he sees another. And another. They are like a swarm of wasps. They are black, with dark tinted windows. They look evil and threatening. They have no markings on them and they could be from Hell. But he knows where they come from.

He lowers the binoculars. He watches their progress across the horizon in the direction of the city.

"Do you see them, son?" she asks.

"Yes," he says, "yes mam."

He looks back at her. She now looks oddly like a much younger woman, even a young girl. Even a child. A sudden wave of love for her leaps through his body like an electric jolt.

⟃

The Rotary Club meets in the large back room of Coles's Cafe, and Roger pulls his Bronco up right in front of the plate glass window. Opening the door of the Bronco he immediately smells the pungent hickory smoke and the sweet vinegary aroma of the barbecue sauce. It hangs like incense in the early evening air. The sauce is a secret formula he created years ago, when he first opened the place, a rich thick sauce with ground jalapeno peppers and powdered mustard. He bottles it and sells it in supermarkets all over the Southeast. COLES DOWN-HOME, it's called, with a sketch of him in a tall white chef's hat on the label.

Rotary has been meeting at Coles's Cafe for forty-five years. Every Thursday night Roger gathers with the other prominent business men and professionals and civic leaders of Wembly County in the back room of the cafe to eat ribs and cole slaw and hear a speaker. Coles's Cafe ribs are famous all over the state, all over the South. It's not unusual for people to drive from as far away as Nashville or Mobile to eat the ribs. Coles and another businessman named Ted Irving and a Birmingham attorney named Geoffrey Malone are currently working out the details of franchising the cafe all over the region. There's a waiting list of investors and potential franchisees, and two locations, one in Roebuck in Birmingham and another down near Montevallo, have already been announced. Many people drive out from the city just to see the collection of antiques that Coles decorated the place with: old signs, spinning wheels, handmade buckets and baskets, old harness. Coles found a lot of the treasures up around Highlands, North Carolina, where he has a vacation home. The franchised places will carry the same decor, except the relics—authentic reproductions—will be manufactured in a factory outside Morristown, Tennessee.

Coles moves through the front room of his cafe, nodding and smiling to the ladies, clapping fellows on the back, shooting youngsters with his index finger stuck out and his thumb cocked like a gun. A hush falls around him as he moves through the room. Everybody knows him. Everybody is in awe of him. He is the most famous figure in that part of the state. People are always glad to see him. Many of these people are glad to see him because they owe their jobs, their very livelihoods, to him—both directly and indirectly. Many of them work for one of his many businesses; many who don't work for him rent their houses from him or lease the places that house their own businesses from him. "Hey, Mr. Coles, how you doin?" they say, "how you gettin along?" And some of the men call him Roger and are proud to do so. They swell up when he shakes their hands.

Most of the Rotary has already gathered. He sees Randy Capshaw, the mayor of Piper, just inside the door, talking with Brother Newton Grable, the pastor of the Hidden Valley Church of Christ of The New Light With Signs Following, who is to be their speaker for the evening. Roger makes his way around the room, shaking hands and greeting everyone.

Roger looks around. He picks a table with only one other man, an optometrist named John "Doc" Stewart. Doc is a pathetic, eager little man who tries to stand and sit very straight to disguise how short he is. He has a round, flat face and thin pale blonde hair. His feet are tiny and flat, like a midget's. Roger points his index finger at him and pulls the trigger, and Doc grins. Roger knows that Doc is pleased and flattered to share a table with him.

Grady Morris, the president of Rotary, bangs the little gavel, and chairs begin to scrape as everyone finds a place. The room is almost full, at least thirty men. Some Rotary Clubs allow women now, but not, by God, Piper's. Slabs of ribs are piled on platters in the middle of each table, with pitchers of iced tea and plates of light bread. Grady asks Brother Grable to say grace and he goes on too long, punctuating each sentence with a long drawn out "Je-he-ssuss!" Roger does not have much patience with fundamentalist preachers. They annoy him. He believes, of course, that all the people in their movement are "Identity Christians." He agrees that the new resistance is a Christian movement as opposed to the godless federal government. But people like Newton Grable aggravate him, going on like they do. When Grable is through praying everyone falls to eating and the conversation is at a minimum.

Roger and Doc don't exchange more than ten words during the meal. They both sit back and pat their bellies when they finish. Doc pulls out a package of Winston cigarettes and Roger frowns at him.

"Smoking's allowed in here, right?" Doc says. "None of that 'no-smokin' business in Wembly County, right?"

"No," Roger says, "new rule. No smoking on the premises."

"Since when?" Doc asks. "I thought—"

"Since just now, when I said it. I just passed a new law. You got a problem with that?"

"No sir," Doc says.

Roger looks at Doc. "Damn, Doc, how old are you? How long you been smoking?"

"I'm sixty-six," Doc said. "I figured it up. I been smoking fifty-one years. Three packs a day, that's sixty cigarettes a day. Four hundred and twenty a week, twenty-one thousand eight hundred and forty a year. Fifty-one years, that's one million, one hundred thirteen thousand, eight hundred and forty cigarettes, give or take a few. It ain't killed me yet."

Grady Morris is introducing Newton Grable, who fiddles around adjusting the microphone. Then he adjusts the volume controls so that his voice booms and fills the room when he starts to speak and Grady has to reach over and change the setting. The preacher wears an electric-blue suit the color of a Clorox box. It's stiff and ill-fitting. He is thin, with a long neck like a pencil and close-cropped, mouse-colored hair.

Grable says, "We are the hope of the new America." He pauses. He says, "Bless Jesus." His eyes blink rapidly. "Brothers," he says, his voice just above a whisper, rumbling ominously out of the loudspeakers, "a great need has arisen!" He pauses again. "There are 35,000 Communist Chinese troops bearing arms and wearing cleverly disguised powder-blue uniforms poised on the Mexican border, preparing to invade San Diego. Right now. The United States has turned over, or will at any minute, its Army, Navy and Air Force to the command of a Russian colonel in the United Nations. Almost every well-known American or free-world leader is, in reality, a top Communist agent. A United States Army guerrilla-warfare exercise over in Georgia—and you can drive over there and see it if you want to, Brothers! I have!—called Water Moccasin III, is in reality a United Nations operation preparing to take over our country!" He pauses again, leaning over the podium. None of this is news to Roger or to anyone else in the room. He looks around. The other men's eyes are wide with anger. "And everybody knows, Brothers, that the federal government is training these street gangs, the Bloods and the Crips, with gangs of them right over there in Birmingham," he points, "urban street gangs, to take away people's firearms!"

"No sir!" someone says in the back of the room.

"Gun control ain't but one thing," Grable shouts, pounding the lectern, "and that's people control!"

"You tell em, Brother!" "Yeah!"

Grable is really wound up now.

"Yes sir," he shouts, "We are God's chosen people, my friends, right here in this room, and don't you let anybody tell you any different. The Jews are imposters! The covenant that God made with Abraham has been fulfilled not with Jews but with White Christians! And America is, or was, the promised land. Now maybe that promised land is right here in Wembly County! This is our land, right here!" Roger couldn't have made this speech at this particular time any better himself. "Wembly County is Eden! And out of Eden was cast the seed of Cain, the evil wicked Cain, who killed his white brother and then ran off to join the nonwhites who had been created subhuman, created with the animals, all according to their own kind, on the fifth day, created below man, below white man!" He pauses. "Jews!" he says. Leaning forward he peers out over the Rotarians. "Jews. You got your nigger Jews, you got your Asiatic Jews, and you got your white Jews. They're all Jews and they're all offspring of the Devil! Turn a nigger inside out and you've got a Jew."

Grable's face is fire red. The Rotarians listen with rapt attention. Doc Stewart, sitting at the table with Roger, says under his breath, "Amen, brother." Doc Stewart had been a member of the Ku Klux Klan in Wembly County for years, before it had been replaced by the Militia. Many of the other men in the room had, too. Including Roger Coles.

"So it is important to support our private army," Grable says, "with money and manpower and most of all, with prayers. They will come after us eventually, just like they did Randy Weaver, just like they did the Branch Davidians at Waco. They will come after us. Nostradamus prophesied a long time ago that around the year 2000 'from the sky there will come a Great King of Terror!' My fellow free men, that great king is the U.S. government, with its black helicopters, and it is coming!" He pauses. "And we will be ready."

There is applause. Scattered grunts. Even some laughter. Coles sits watching the little man in his stiff suit sit back down, a broad grin on his face. Coles considers getting up right then and informing them all of his Declaration of Secession that his attorney, Goodloe Bedsole, had drawn up for him just that afternoon. But he does not. He will choose a better time. Later, when he has his Queen all tamed and in place.

Brenda talks every night now to her mother. She wakes up long before dawn, lying awake in the neat little house, and at first she had started merely thinking of her mother. She visited their graves, the narrow plot, the small headstones, her father's dull and gray, her mother's still surprisingly shiny clean and new-looking even after more than twenty years. HESTER LAMAR VICK, 1921-1962, her father's stone said. She remembers how her mother worried all her life about how and where she was going to be buried, putting her money dutifully away to pay for her burial policy. Brenda has no burial policy, no such shackle binding her to the earth.

She had stood looking at her mother's stone. SANDRA LUANNE GIBSON VICK. 1924-1973. Forty-eight years old. Only two years older than Brenda is now. Brenda blinked back tears as she imagined again her mother's lonely death, how sad it must have been to be so alone that that oily gun barrel in the mouth would seem like some kind of answer. Reading the name she said simply, "Mama."

Brenda had been the one who found her. To this day she cannot bear to remember the scene in the bedroom of the house-trailer. Brenda had come out from Birmingham because her mother wouldn't answer the phone. Everyone thought she was on a drunk. The door had been unlocked, the television playing, a half-empty bottle of vodka sitting on the kitchen counter. And her mother was on the bed, naked, the pistol, which must have been one left there by one of her men friends, still in her hand, and half her head and face blown away, and the one eye that Brenda could see staring emptily at the low ceiling, the smell of blood at once terrifying and nauseating.

And Brenda had to go back out there after the funeral, to sort through her mother's things. Sitting in that forlorn, unheated, cleaned-up and scrubbed trailer all by herself, she looked through the faded underwear with sprung elastic, the few personal belongings that her mother had possessed: a souvenir cushion from Christus Gardens in Tennessee, a miniature statue of the Life and Casualty Building in Nashville, gotten on some trip to the Grand Ole Opry with one of her men—a trip that Brenda had heard many drunken versions of—and in a closet in a back bedroom, the room that had been Brenda's, she had found her high school yearbooks and a stack of her papers that her mother had saved, compositions marked with big red A's, her DAR Good Citizenship Girl certificate, her Beta Club pen, the detritus of Brenda's young life. And piles of her mother's shoes. Curled and scuffed, but never thrown away. Hundreds of shoes. Brenda had taken everything she could gather up, the shoes and the yearbooks and the underwear, everything, out into the back yard and had burned them in a wire incinerator. It had taken her the better part of an afternoon to burn everything. And she had wept the whole time.

She opens her eyes in the quiet of the early morning darkness and the image of the gravestone pops into her mind, and she says again, "Mama," and a voice says "Yes?" She is not frightened, not even startled, not surprised at all. She knows it is her mother's voice. It's as familiar as her own voice. It's as though no time has passed at all. "Mama?" she says again.

"Yes, Brenda," her mother says, a note of impatience in her voice. "What do you want?"

Brenda tenses. She looks upward at the pattern of the ceiling tiles, only faintly visible now in the creeping light.

"Why, Mother?" she asks. "Why did you do it?"

Her mother does not answer for a long time. Then, "I think you know, Brenda," she says. "You broke my heart. You and Lamar both. When you were little you stepped on my toes. When you got older and almost grown you stepped on my heart!"

"But Mama," she says like a child, "I—"

"She's here, Brenda," her mother says, interrupting her. "The spirit of that little child that you got rid of. She'll be with you forever, just like I will."

"I can feel her presence," Brenda says. "Ever since I came back. I've dreamed of her all my life, but now I feel her. I can almost hear her. I can almost smell her."

"Of course. You can hear me can't you? We're the same, Brenda. She and I. We're the beginning and the ending. The first and the last. We complete the circle, Brenda. We keep it unbroken."

"But you're ... you're ..."

"Dead? You can say the word. We're dead, but we're here. We're always here."

"You are?"

"Of course," her mother says, "we're always here. We've been here forever. Where did you expect us to be?"

"I love you, Mama," Brenda says.

"I have only one eye now, Brenda," her mother says. "I'm hard to love, always was. I'm hideous now, an old hag. Aging doesn't stop when you die. It gets worse. Roger Coles says all the time that time stands still in Wembly County. It doesn't. Not even Roger Coles can stop time." Her voice begins to fade. "Beware of that man, Brenda," she says, "beware ..."

"I can handle him," Brenda says, "don't worry."

"I never worry," her mother says, her voice faint now, distant. "Go see your brother. He's your family. Go see Pee Wee. I never worry ..." And she is gone.

Brenda lies there in a sweat. She hears the ticking, settling of the house. She hears the rumble of the ice maker in the kitchen. She thinks of Lamar, drunk and complaining. She has not thought of him by his old nickname Pee Wee in years. She knows that Jimmy is sprawled face down on his mattress, in his room, his arms flung out, his breath adolescent sweet and steady. She closes her eyes and sleeps.

⌐

Or she does not sleep. She does not know if it's a dream or she is remembering something that actually happened. Recently. Maybe the first time she actually saw Wayne McClain again. He is standing in front of her holding a red pencil. His hair is combed the way he has always combed it, medium length, straight back, and she can see the marks left by the comb. He wears a T-shirt that says PIPER CHRISTIAN ACADEMY across the chest. His arms are still thick and muscular, but his eyes are paler, more tan than brown, like old pecans. His face is weather- and sun-beaten. Tiny ruptured veins criss-cross his cheeks. She knows immediately that he is a drinker.

"Well, Brenda Vick! I'll just be goddamed," he says. His eyes are fixed on her breasts. She is wearing a plain white blouse like a man's shirt and faded jeans. They are at the school, she thinks. She can smell chalk, new books, lemons. He stares at her breasts the way Larson Eubanks had done. Strangely, he is even less familiar to her than Larson, who had only sat behind her in algebra class. He is a stranger: the father of her first child. Not a child. A cluster of cells. No. She is and always will be the secret mother of a nameless little girl, two children and not one. She has two children. She has never told a living soul this. They will think she is crazy, hysterical.

"Well, Wayne," she says, "I didn't know I would get the opportunity so soon to tell you in person what a lowdown shit-headed son-of-a-bitch you are."

"Hey," he says, "don't hold back now!" He grins at her.

"Kiss my ass," she says.

"Not right now," he says, "I ain't in a romantic mood! Don't rush me."

"Fuck you," she says.

"We can arrange that, too—"

"Stop it, Wayne."

He wears dark blue sweat pants. They're tied with a white string, in a loose bow that drops down in front of his crotch. She sees his erection, then, poking at her, always there and ready, like an overripe plum about to burst. She sees it as clearly as twenty years ago.

"I'm the best goddamed football coach in the state of Alabama," he says. "I'll do my job better than any of these other misfits on this faculty, don't you worry. You can tell these other goons what to do, they need it, but I don't need any help, thank you very much. I'm gonna win the state championship for you, that's all."

"Rah, rah, rah," she says.

"I see you ain't lost your cheerleading touch," he says.

Brenda's eyes pop open. She lies there in the crawling gray of the dawn. It is a new day, another in a long series of new days. She met yesterday with her faculty, a remarkably colorless and dull bunch. She carefully outlined her plans for the year, and she didn't think any of them even heard her. The only teacher who had spoken to her was one who stopped her after the meeting, a little short fellow who teaches senior high English, John D. Wisham, Jr. He always uses his whole name. When he first introduced himself to Brenda it had been as John D. Wisham, Jr. He says it as though it's one word: Johndwishamjr. The reason he had detained her and followed her to her office was to assure her that he had a master of arts degree in English and not a master of education. "I want you to know that I am a scholar," he said. "I am not an educrat, God forbid!" He had given her a copy of his thesis to read. It is bound in heavy black leather with the title stamped in gold on the front. Back in her office, she placed it on her desk and glanced at the title: THE SOCIAL AND CULTURAL IMPLICATIONS—RACIAL, SEXUAL, POLITICAL—OF PAT THE BUNNY: A DECONSTRUCTION, By John D. Wisham, Jr.

She hears the television playing inside as she stands on her brother Lamar's front porch, the house like all the fifty or so others in Minetown, the house exactly like the one she had been born in and raised in. It could be the same house, for all she knows. As she stands on the sagging front porch she's swept backward in time. She is a child again, with the same smells—faint sewer and garbage stinks and cooking smells, grease and frying meat—in the same air. All the streets in Minetown look the same and always did, the same plastic toys faded in the sunlight and the rain, in the same patchy sandy crabgrass-choked front yards. Row after row of the houses, peeling and dirty white-washed exteriors and rusty screen porches. No curbs, no sidewalks. Children play in the street. She and Lamar are two of them, her mother young with her apron on and her father still alive, home from the mines, rubbing liniment into his stiff muscles in the living room.

When her father died she and her mother and her brother Lamar had taken the small insurance pay-out and bought a double-wide. They parked it on the other side of town and then Lamar quit school and left home to work in the cardboard box factory over in Belle Ellen, leaving her there with her mother who worked as a waitress at a beer joint called The Top out on the Birmingham Highway. And there had been a succession of her mother's men friends in the trailer, salesmen and businessmen from Birmingham, the longest tenured one being a man named Ronnie Phillpott, who ran a large discount furniture store on the Bessemer Superhighway and drove a long white Cadillac. He starred in his own television commercials on local stations and spent much of his time accidentally surprising Brenda in the shower or walking in on her in her room, finally forcing himself on her one night when her mother was working, slobbering and biting her between the legs and frightening her to death. That had gone on almost a year, when she was thirteen. She had been scared to tell her mother. She knew instinctively that her mother knew all about it, but Brenda was terrified to put words to it and make it real. She never had told her mother.

She raps on the screen door. A hole in the screen about eye level is stuffed with cotton. Emily opens the door and Brenda realizes that she would not have recognized her sister-in-law if she had passed her on the street. Emily is of medium height, not as tall as Brenda, with pale blonde hair cut short in a punk cut. She has on gray sweat pants and a baggy sweatshirt that reads PROPERTY OF LOS ANGELES POLICE DEPARTMENT across the front. Emily stares at her for a moment. It has been almost twenty years.

"Well," Emily says. "Well."

"Hello, Emily," Brenda says.

They both hesitate for a moment. Then they hug, still tentatively. Emily is thin and bony in Brenda's arms. Emily squeezes Brenda quickly and lightly. Her hair smells like cooking oil.

Emily steps back and opens the door wider. "Well," she says, "come on in. What can I getcha?"

"Nothing. I just stopped by. How are you?"

"Fine."

"And Lamar?"

"Fine."

"Where's Darlene?" Brenda asks.

"At work. She works at the movie theater. She ought to be home soon."

Brenda looks around the living room. It's crowded with furniture, and the television set plays in the corner. Emily has been watching Geraldo. It is cool, almost cold, in the house. Window air conditioners hum. Geraldo is interviewing a man in a chauffeur's uniform.

"He was Madonna's driver," Emily says. "You wouldn't believe it. So, how've you been, Brenda?"

"All right," Brenda says.

"Billy, he ... where is Billy?"

"Hell, I don't know. Milwaukee, I think. What do I care where the son-of-a-bitch is?" She laughs and Emily giggles.

"You sure you don't want a Coke or something? Coffee?"

"Okay," Brenda says, "coffee." Emily disappears toward the back of the house. The living room smells sweet and perfumy, like cosmetics, and Brenda can see stacks of pink boxes against the wall, in the corners and piled on table tops, everywhere. Emily is selling Mary Kay. Brenda looks around. On the dining room table, visible through an archway, are more pink boxes.

"I mean," Geraldo is asking, "what did you do, man, arrange the rear-view mirror so you could see what was going on in the back of the limo, or what?"

"Something like that," the man in the uniform answers and smirks. The audience laughs like maniacs. Geraldo has a pious, disapproving look on his face.

"Even Madonna is entitled to privacy," Geraldo says. The man shrugs and holds his hands out to the sides, palms up, the smirk still on his face. The audience laughs again.

Emily comes out of the kitchen with a cup of coffee for Brenda. Brenda sits down on a vinyl sofa with her coffee. "Thanks," she says. She sips her coffee.

Emily goes over and switches off the television set. "That Geraldo," she says, "he's a mess, ain't he?" She sits down and looks at Brenda. "So," she says, "you're, like, back, huh?"

"Yeah," Brenda says. "I'm back." Emily just looks at her. "Where's Lamar?"

"He's probly on his way home. He went over to interview for a job driving a Pepsi Cola truck. He won't get it."

"Why is that?"

"Brenda, that brother of yours is the most hard-luck man that ever come along the pike. Seems like everything is stacked against him. His back is bad and there's so much he can't do. He's got all these problems. And driving around filling up drink machines involves some lifting even though the man on the phone said he would have a helper with him. I don't know."

"Maybe he'll get the job. Is he drinking now?"

"Yeah. Drinkin and smokin some dope, too. He's got a problem."

Just then they hear his footsteps on the front porch. Lamar comes inside and stands there looking at Brenda. He has aged mightily, but he is still her little brother. Brenda stands and embraces him. At first he is awkward and tentative, but then she feels his arms growing tighter. He releases her and steps back. He wears jeans and a wrinkled white dress shirt with a frayed collar. He has lost a couple of front teeth since Brenda last saw him and it gives him a rough, snaggled appearance. He is thin and lanky, with a prominent Adam's apple, and his voice is coarse and deep, the same voice he has had since he was a small child and some people called him "Foghorn." It seemed he always had one nickname or the other.

"Hey, Pee," she says. It was her own name for him. His family nickname had been Pee Wee and she had shortened it to Pee. He looks much older than she does. Older and tireder.

"Hey, Sister," he says, and when his breath wafts over her she can smell the whiskey. He comes on into the room. "The job woulda been perfect," he says to Emily. Then he looks at them both. "I woulda had a helper to tote the cases of drinks. But they discovered those DUIs. I had my license suspended twice, Sister. Shit. They get you in the damn government computers, you can't ever get away from it."

"You'll find somethin, Lamar," Emily says.

Lamar sits down across from them. "Well, Brenda," he says, "you've done gone big time on us. You are Mr. Coles's fair-haired girl, the new headmistress of the almighty Academy!" He laughs. "I would say that you are a piece of trailer trash that's done rose up in the world, a piece of shit that's floated to the top! Don't forget I helped you get there! I heard about that job, don't forget. Don't forget your old poor relations, now."

Brenda laughs. She shrugs. "It's a job," she says.

"Darlene's on a full scholarship to that school. She's smart as a whip."

"I know."

"She said she met you," Emily says. "She said y'all went for a walk together."

"Yeah," Brenda says. The house is the exact same floor plan as the first house she remembers. The light is the same, filtered through the dusty glass of the windows. The old familiar smell of stale gas from all the hundred past winters' spot heaters still clings to the rugs and curtains. Lamar and Darlene are her only living blood kin other than Jimmy. Brenda sits there with her legs crossed at the knees, taking a deep breath.

There is a rattle at the front door and Darlene comes in. She has seen the old blue Toyota out front, so she shows no surprise. She smiles. They are all together in the same room and there's nothing to say. They all smile. Disappointment seeps up around them like a chill. Brenda stares at Darlene. In this old recalled house the girl is even more Brenda in another time than when Brenda had first seen her. Their eyes lock for a moment and then Darlene looks away.

She wears a kilt-like skirt and a light green sweater. Her face is flushed fresh from the outside air, pink-tinted and alive. Brenda feels the girl in the room, a steady vibrating buzz that registers in Brenda's feet and her legs and her hips. She hears it, too, in silence like an absent hum. There's not so much an aura about Darlene as a kind of inner sparkle, as though she is lit from within. She stares off into space, looking at something a millennium away.

It takes Brenda a long moment before she realizes it, before it hits her. My God! Brenda thinks, my God! Darlene is pregnant! She can tell it as certain as if it were her. As if it were her all over again. My God.

BYRON BAILEY, WHO IS SLIGHT OF BUILD AND SHORT, five foot six or so, gets into a fight with the much larger Phillip Moon, or Boligee Phil as he's called, in the pool room at LEROY'S GRILL AND BILLIARDS one night. Boligee Phil is six foot three, two hundred and eighty pounds, and plays right tackle for the Piper Christian Academy Eagles. He is actually twenty-six years old, but never finished high school and lied about his age in order to play football at the Academy. He presented a forged birth certificate, which had been accepted without question. Phil rarely attends classes and spends most of his time pool-sharking.

Byron is into Phil for eighty bucks and is trying to win it back in a fifth game, and Phil is taunting him. As Byron is lining up a difficult shot, a bank to put the seven-ball into the near side pocket, Phil says,

"If you really had any balls you'd kill somebody."

Byron misses the shot. He thinks for a moment that Boligee Phil knows what happened on the bus that day. Color rises up his shaved neck and settles into his prominent ears. He says nothing. There's no way that Phil can know about that. After Byron's miss, Boligee Phil runs the table. "Corner pocket," Phil mutters, tapping the worn leather lining with the tip of his stick, and he rattles the eight ball in. He stands there, leaning on his cue. Byron pulls out another twenty and puts it on the side of the table with the others.

"I tell you," Phil says, "if it was to do over, over there in the Desert Storm, I think I'd fight on the side of the A-rabs."

"The who?" Byron asks indignantly.

"You know. Saw-damn, all a them. Them nomad people."

"Against white people?" Bailey says, swelling up more.

"Hell yes."

Byron swings, catching Phil on the nose, and Phil brings the butt of his cue up sharply between Byron's legs. The pain shoots all through Byron's body, doubling him over. He swings out blindly again, his fists falling harmlessly on Phil's hard body, and Phil catches him with a roundhouse right that straightens him up and lifts him backwards and onto the next table where he feels the back of his head crash and scatter balls that had been racked and waiting. He can see little sparks of light flickering before his eyes. He can smell the sharp acrid cigarette air of the pool room, see the shaded fluorescent light dangling over his head, over the center of the table. He hears the bartender, Robertson Reboul's, voice. "Hey! Hey! What the hell's goin on back here?" There have been several other men watching them play, and he hears them laughing.

"Nothin," he hears Boligee Phil say, "now." There is more laughter.

"Well, take it outside," Reboul says. "Any more fightin, take it outside!"

Byron feels hands lifting him, dragging him toward the men's room. His legs work, but it feels as though he's walking under water. He is furious at Phil. His anger is blinding him as much as Phil's awful blow to his face. The very idea of thinking it's a joke to run white people down. That's what's wrong with people. Wrong with the world.

The men's room is damp and smells of piss and disinfectant. He jerks his arms away from whoever is helping him and flails backwards at them. They back out and leave him alone. The wash basin is stained and dirty, and he runs cold water and splashes his face, discovering blood, but not all that much. He mats his face with damp paper towels. He stands there, his breathing returning to normal. He looks at his face in the mirror. His left eye is swelling, and there's a cut on his cheek. His eye will be black.

That's all right. It will be a badge of honor. It will be purple, not black. The cold towels are soothing to his face. He stands there for a long time. Next to the bathroom mirror is written: "For the best blow job in town, call Pixie Dixon, at 689-2518." Under that is scrawled "God is Love." Byron's eyes scan around the walls in the narrow, dank and dim bathroom.

Then he focuses on his slim face in the warped mirror. He stares into his own eyes. He does not move for a long time.

And then, with a sharp pop like the report of a rifle, the mirror cracks. From the upper right-hand corner down to the lower left, the quick fissure is like a silver slash through Byron's face, and Byron does not even blink. His face is contorted and misshapen beyond recognition by the shattered, fragmented glass, and Byron leans in close to it, his hands on the edges of the sink. He squints as though perceiving himself for the first time.

FOUR

Everybody in town and throughout the area is talking about the Indian that Wayne McClain has recruited to play for the Eagles. "He would have to be an Indian," Brenda hears a woman say on WXAY, "else he couldn't play in the private school league. They have strict rules, they—"

"What do you have to do?" Alex Gresham interrupts. "Present a pedigree?"

"You can look at him and tell he's an Indian," the woman says.

"Looks are deceiving, mam," Alex says, "things are not always the way they look."

"But sometimes they are."

"I can't argue with you there, mam," Alex says.

⁓

"This is absurd, Wayne," Brenda said to him one day at the school.

"Absurd ain't the word for it," Wayne replied, and winked.

"People are going crazy with this thing. They stop me on the street, in the stores—"

"Don't worry about it," he said, "this is my department."

"It's disruptive. It's got the students all in a dither," she said.

"I said, don't worry about it," Wayne said curtly.

⁓

"All right, all right," Roger Coles had told a reporter from *The Birmingham News*, "you prove to me that he ain't an Indian, okay?"

⌐

Brenda listens to the radio driving to work. Jimmy leans his head back against the seat and pretends to be still asleep. "He's a Seminole," the woman says. "His people come up here from Florida. From down around Okeechobee. I know this to be a fact."

"Facts lie," Alex says.

"Facts don't lie," the woman says. She sounds as though she is about to cry now.

"Are you a fool, or do you just sound like one?" Alex asks, and the woman hangs up.

Alex says, "The Peo—" but he is interrupted. Another voice comes on immediately.

"America is the Zion of Bible prophecy!" It is another woman, this one with a deep and guttural voice. The voice growls, "Our government is now completely under the control of the international invisible government of world Jewry—"

"Hey," Alex breaks in, "wait a minute now. Where did you get all this stuff? Are these your own crackpot ideas, or what?"

"Our United States government, our Bill of Rights and our Christian law has been trampled under the mire and filth of the international money barons of high finance who now control the government of the United States!"

"Whew, lady, have you escaped from the loony bin?"

"I can tell you—" She is shut off.

"The People Speak. Go ahead."

"This is Malcolm Roland. I just want to bring you up to date about my garbage cans." Brenda glances over at Jimmy. His eyes are shut tight. Brenda remembers that back in the sixties WXAY played top-forty rock-and-roll at night. In the mornings and afternoons it had played easy listening, Ella Fitzgerald and Frank Sinatra. Both dead now. She turns the dial. "... partly cloudy and hot, with a high of eighty-six. Low tonight seventy-two. Chance of thundershowers tomorrow. This is country weather, WZZK, in the Magic City. In the next half hour, Reba McIntire and George Jones!" She switches the radio off.

Brenda dreamed last night about her mother. She was in the chapel of the funeral home where her mother's funeral had been held. She was in the back row, and someone was with her. The two of them went down front to view the body and they stood gazing into the coffin where her mother lay in a calm repose. She was whole, complete, no signs of her violent end. Even young. Her mother's coffin—all those years ago—had actually been closed, but now it was open and her mother lay in peaceful sleep, wearing a navy blue suit. Brenda realized that she herself was dressed in torn jeans and a wrinkled blouse, and everyone in the pews was looking at her, disapprovingly she knew. She turned to the person beside her. It was her mother. "Don't you have to be getting on back to Gordo?" her mother asked. Gordo was a town in the next county. Brenda didn't remember ever having been there. She awoke in a cold sweat. She knew there was more to the dream, but that was all she could recall.

She drives through downtown. It is a neat town now, attractive. The storefronts are painted in deep dark blues and maroons lined in gold, and the plate glass windows are stencilled in antique script. Large pots of impatiens sit on the corners. Brenda remembers the main street's being dingy when she was a child, with deserted buildings and trash in the gutters, but now it looks prosperous. There are ice cream shops and gift and pottery shops. What had once been a seed and feed store is now an antique store called Trash & Treasure. There's a large store called Piper Flooring & Design. Everywhere are signs of a building boom. "We are the newest bedroom community for the city," Coles told her. "People will continue to flock here, I can assure you, and you will head the best school system in the entire state, not just that one school but a whole system!"

"Yes, well ..." Brenda replied.

"You will! I'll see to that. Now, I don't want to hear any more about it, hear? It's signed, sealed and will be delivered!" She had not known quite how to respond.

Brenda's secretary is a woman named Virginia Martin, a hefty freckled middle-aged woman who wears her graying reddish hair in a severe bun at the back of her head. She wears pearl-rimmed glasses that hang around her neck on a silver chain, and her clothes are box-like, her skirts as wide at the waist as at the bottom. Her mouth is perpetually set in a thin, flat line, an expression that mocks the portrait of George Washington that hangs on the outer office wall. It hangs next to a well-known print of Jesus praying in the Garden of Gethsemane, a beatific look on his face. Jesus seems to be gazing up at the top of George Washington's head.

"On his form Otis Hunnicutt did not check Native American," Virginia Martin says to Brenda. "He wrote in 'multi-racial.' What does that mean?"

"What does it matter?" Brenda says. "Let it go." She has been looking at records at the school. They are a mess. Attendance records, grades. Everything is sloppy and incomplete. There are no black students at all.

"But we are required to list the race of each student. I must say we've never had this problem before." Virginia Martin sniffs the air.

"What problem? The kid is in, it's a done deal. Forget it."

"I think you should know that he told Billie Wilcox that A.J. Grist told him to write that. Told him to put 'multi-racial.' I don't think we ought to allow him to do that. I think—"

"Mrs. Martin—"

"Everybody else has to check one of the boxes. Caucasian, Negroid, Asian, Native American! Why aren't those categories good enough for him? He was supposed to check Native American!"

"Maybe he doesn't want to be a category. Maybe he considers himself multi-racial. It's not your concern, Mrs. Martin."

"It most certainly is my concern, Mrs. Boykin! I am responsible for these records!"

Brenda laughs. Virginia Martin glares at her. "All right," Brenda says, "I'll take responsibility for that one."

"But there is no 'multi-racial' box!"

"Leave it alone, Mrs. Martin! Do you hear me? Leave it alone!" Brenda speaks curtly, maybe more harshly than she had intended. The woman leans back and peers at her. She looks Brenda up and down. She sniffs. Brenda wears black slacks and a brown mock turtle. She wears her scuffed running shoes. Her dress habits have already been the subject of much gossip around the school. "You know we do have a dress code here," Mrs. Martin said to her the very first day.

"For the students? Or for the teachers?"

"For everybody," Virginia Martin said, scowling.

"Well, we'll have to look into that first thing, won't we?" Brenda said. "Everything can be changed for the better, after all, right?"

"'If it ain't broke, don't fix it,' as they say."

"With that kind of thinking, Mrs. Martin, we would never have invented the wheel, now would we?"

Virginia Martin sniffed.

⊷

"Hey, girlfriend," Ernest Bridgwater says to Darlene Vick. They are on campus right after school. It's a clear, sunny afternoon, the sky as light blue as water-thinned ink. Crowds of students mill about, laughing, bicep punching. They are grouped in crowds of boys and crowds of girls. Some couples. Darlene is strolling by a bunch of boys who are ready to go to football practice.

"I'm not your girlfriend," Darlene says. She ducks her head, pulls in her chin. Her light ashen bangs hang over half her face. She wears a plaid kilt but her legs have grown so long that it's almost a mini. Her legs are smooth and shapely. They look soft.

"You're a girl, ain't you? What are you, my enemy?"

"No."

"Well, then you're my friend. My friend girl. My girl friend."

"Chill out, Ernest," Clarence Peevy says. "Can't you see you make her want to hurl?" Darlene hurries on away.

Lolly Phillips walks by. Lolly is a petite girl, curvy and quick with a laugh. She's a cheerleader.

"Suck my mouth!" another boy says to Lolly. It's Boligee Phil.

"Oooo, weeee, shaky puddin," Clarence Peevy says.

"Fuck you," Lolly Phillips says. She keeps walking briskly.

Jimmy is on the fringe of the group of football players and he watches them taunting his cousin and the other girls, but says nothing. He's two grades behind Darlene and younger than most of the other boys. Darlene is not very friendly to him. His mother seems to think they should be friends or something, just because they're cousins. "She's shy, Jimmy," his mother said. But Jimmy has no time or patience with her.

He follows the gang of boys to the gym and stands outside the coach's office. He can hear the team laughing and shouting in the dressing room as they dress for practice. Ernest had showed him the new dressing rooms and the weight room, modern and gleaming in the bright lights. Jimmy looks up as the coach comes out of his office. Jimmy has never seen an all-American in person before, not this close up anyway. He had seen Michael Jordan once, coming out of an Italian restaurant downtown. And his dad had once taken him to Comiskey and he had gotten to shake Robin Ventura's hand before the game. Wayne McClain is shockingly old compared to those two. His eyes are watery and almost bloodshot. His cheeks seemed chapped and raw and his hair is long and oily, sprinkled with gray like Jimmy's mother's hair only more so. He wears a T-shirt with PCA FOOTBALL on the front over tight gray running shorts, and he has a little belly like a honeydew mellon.

"Yeah?" he says when he sees Jimmy standing there.

"I ..." Jimmy hesitates. "I want to go out," he says.

The coach looks him up and down. He shrugs. "What grade you in?"

"Tenth," Jimmy replies.

"Why haven't you come out before now? The first game's a week away."

"I just transferred in."

"Yeah? Where from?"

"Chicago."

The coach's eyes go thin. He seems to squint at Jimmy for a moment, nodding. "Chicago," he says. "Are you Mrs. Boykin's son?"

"Yes sir," Jimmy says. The coach looks him over almost like a piece of livestock. His lips are pursed. It's queer the way the coach looks at his body. It makes Jimmy uneasy. He wonders if the coach is a faggot.

"You ever played before?" the coach asks.

"No sir. Just some baseball. Playground basketball."

"All right. We'll put you on the weights. But hell, you're big enough to play some now. I might have a uniform to fit you." He grins. "As of now you're a wide-out. We'll check your speed, but I could tell you down to the nanosecond what it'll be, just by looking at you. I'll write it down and we'll see how I do, okay? And you'll go one hundred seventy-six and a few ounces. Five eleven, right?"

"Yes sir."

"All right. You'll have to go see old Dr. Mason, get a physical. Wait a minute," he says, and he goes back into his office and rummages around on his desk, finds a memo pad and scribbles on it then rips the memo off. He comes back out and hands it to Jimmy, along with a larger form. "Give that to Dr. Mason, he'll charge it to the school. The other one is a release form and permission slip that you'll have to get your parents to sign. In your case, just your mother."

"Yes sir," he says.

"Go on over to Dr. Mason's office now. You can't practice until you have your physical. Don't worry about it. Unless you've got a heart murmur or a hernia or something you'll pass okay. He'll stick his finger up under your balls and tell you to cough. You cough, and that's it." He continues to stare at Jimmy. He has a questioning, strange look in his eyes. Almost as though he's trying to figure out if he knows Jimmy from somewhere, had known him somehow in the past. "Practice is right after school, three-thirty. Tomorrow. And every day thereafter, except game day of course, until the season is over. You know J. D. Hill?"

"No sir."

"Well, J. D.'s the trainer. He'll have a practice uniform for you, show you how to wear the pads. The other guys will help. Don't let em talk you into puttin your jock on your nose."

"Okay," Jimmy says. "I know what a jock strap is."

"Good," the coach says. "That's a start." He turns and goes down the hallway toward the dressing room. Jimmy stands there holding the memo and the permission form, watching him walk away.

⟜

Wayne stands out on the practice field squinting in the declining sun. A breeze has kicked up and he can feel it on the thin layer of sweat against his skin. The team is running wind sprints now, and he watches Otis. The boy is truly something. He had seen him in the dressing room in only his jock, pulling on his pads, and his body is hard and rock-like, shining golden like sunlit marble in the white glare of the overhead lights. He towers over some of the other boys, whose bodies are pale and in some cases still too flabby and soft. Summer baby-fat. Most of the boys avoid Otis, sneaking looks at him. They're glad to have him but frightened of him, too. Only Boligee Phil jokes with him, and Ernest Bridgewater. And Jimmy Boykin, who has the locker right next to his. He is like another species to most of them, even a creature from some other world. Otis ignores them, moving as though in some cyst that isolates him and encloses him, shutting out the noise of their horseplay.

Otis's first days of school at the Academy had been chaotic. Everybody wanted to see him. People stared at him when he walked down the hallway but nobody wanted to sit next to him in class. The students yelled at him, called him Geronimo. Most of them had known him all their lives, and only recently had they learned he was not a Negro at all but an Indian and they were confused. Classes were hard to teach for a few days. Then things seemed to settle down. He was in the senior class. Wayne told Johnny Wisham, that fag English teacher, that Otis had to remain eligible. "You're his advisor, and I mean it," Wayne said, glaring at Wisham, "if he misses a game because of grades, I'll kick your ass. I want him to graduate and qualify for a Division I college. I want him to score at least twenty-five on his ACT. You got it?"

"I'll do what I can, Skipper," Wisham said. He clapped Wayne on the back.

"How does it feel to be an Indian?" Wayne asked Otis.

"Coach," Otis said, "I'd be a fuckin Chinaman to get out of this town and take my Muh-dear with me." He began to chant. "Uh, uh, uh, uh! Tonto, Tonto."

This afternoon Otis scrimmaged with the team for the first time. Wayne gave him a playbook less than a week ago and Otis already knew all the plays. Running from tailback Otis would explode at the line like a mortar shell. Only Philip Moon was able to stop him before five or six yards, Philip and one other boy, a sophomore named Claude Autry Bowers, nicknamed Ironhead, whose neck was as thick as Wayne's thigh and who was six five and weighed in at a trim two hundred and sixty. A couple of times

Ironhead stopped Otis in his tracks, and Wayne made them keep running the play over and over again, the two young, strong bodies like two compact cars in a head-on collision. "Let's play cowboy and Indian," Wayne said. "Come on. Show me what you're made out of!" The last time they had run the play, Otis knocked Ironhead flat of his back and stepped in his chest on the way to the goal.

Their first game is against Belle Ellen Academy, a week from tonight. Wayne looks up in the stands. There are at least a hundred men sitting in the aluminum bleachers watching practice, most of them retirees. They have come to see the Indian. One of them is probably a scout from Belle Ellen. The men sit in clumps of threes and fours, leaning back, shading their eyes with their hands and fanning themselves with their hats. They would call out to Wayne when he'd come near. "Hey Wayne, buddy, that Indian can run like a scalded jackrabbit," one of the men calls out to him. "Hey, Freight Train, he don't need no horse!" yells another.

Otis is quiet and brooding. He seems narrowly focused on exactly what he is doing, shutting out everything else around him. His movements are restrained and controlled. There's no wasted effort with Otis. None at all. Wayne could not have asked for a better athlete. He had put him through a drill earlier in the afternoon to show him how to hold his arms and hands for a hand-off, how to receive the ball so as not to fumble. Otis had not been taught even those basic things. He took hand-off after hand-off, with rows of hands and arms slapping at the ball. After twenty minutes or so he looked as though he'd been doing it the right way all his life. Not even Ironhead's massive hand could dislodge the ball. And Wayne knows that unlike some of his boys Otis will not lapse, will not forget it all by practice tomorrow afternoon.

Most of the boys have finished their wind sprints now, and Wayne can see the Boykin boy standing over by the water cooler. Wayne had known who he was immediately because he looked just like his mother in the eyes and nose. There's something through the eyes that all those Vicks have; their eyes are either too far apart or too close together, Wayne can't decide quite which. He has caught himself watching the boy a lot. Jimmy is athletic, but raw and undisciplined. Unfocused.

Wayne calls the boys back to the middle of the field. Some of them still breathe heavily. They group around him, leaning on one knee, holding their helmets. They smell like fresh sweat and grass and mud. They look up at him as though he is their supreme hero, even their savior. A joke around town is that Wayne can walk on water. Some of the boys are so young and skinny that their shoulder pads dwarf their heads. Wayne looks around at them, meeting their eyes. His eyes come to rest on Jimmy Boykin's. The boy looks back at him with a kind of cocky, knowing look. He probably knows all about Wayne and his mother. She has probably told him. Wayne thinks suddenly of the child the two of them had aborted, probably a boy. He had thought at the time that it was a boy. He has not thought about that in years.

Boykin smiles. Wayne does not know why he's smiling. He thinks for a moment that the kid is reading his mind. He thinks then of Keith and wonders what his and Brenda's boy would have grown up to be like. He thinks he would have been more like Otis, only white, of course. He would not have been a musician. He would be something like Jimmy but he would have a body like Otis's. Wayne is thinking then of Brenda's body, strong and lean and smooth; he is standing there in front of these boys, including her own son, thinking of her naked and open, beckoning to him. Remembering vividly the way she used to look. He shakes his head and frowns.

"Men," he says, "one week from tonight! We can quit blockin and tacklin one another and kick some new ass! We're gonna rub those Belle Ellen boys' noses in the dirt, and then we're gonna stomp on em, we're gonna squash em till they bleed! We're gonna kick the livin shit out of em!"

"All riiiight!" says Boligee Phil. The other boys murmur and shout. Some of them punch the air with their fists. Ernest Bridgewater and Clarence Peevy kneel on both sides of Jimmy. They both nudge him with their elbows and grin.

"We're gonna do it fair and square, and we're gonna do it for Jesus," Wayne says. The boys assume serious expressions on their faces. They all look down at the grass. He requires that they all belong to the Fellowship of Christian Athletes. He finds that lots of prayers, before games and at half time, have a settling effect on them. "Now we're gonna scrimmage again, we're gonna scrimmage till dark! We're gonna have these plays down so good you can run em in your sleep! We're gonna get tough. Anybody pushes you, push back! Before the whistle blows, find somebody and put em on the ground! I want to see your man's ass covered with mud, all right?! Come next Friday night, I don't want to be able to even read the numbers on the backs of those Belle Ellen Panthers' jerseys! I want you to stick somebody! I want you to get mean! All right, now, let's go!"

The boys jump to their feet. "Do it! Do it!" they yell. They pound each other on the back. They head-butt. They run in place and scream like animals. Wayne can feel their energy. Their young juices swell almost to bursting inside them. Their eyes glint. They look feverish, maniacal.

They run some pass plays. Wayne puts Jimmy Boykin in at flanker to run a simple slant. Johnny Mack Reeves is the quarterback. "All right, you got it?" Wayne says to Boykin, after walking through the play. "Yes sir." "Okay," Wayne says, "we might as well see what you're made out of, too. We might as well see what they're makin Chicago boys out of these days." Some of the boys laugh. Boykin looks nervous.

Johnny Mack calls the signals, drops back two steps and fires the ball over the line. Boykin catches it neatly on the tips of his fingers, pulls it in, and is hit with a vicious tackle by Chris Warnock, a defensive back, who drives his shoulder pads into Boykin's side and midsection. The breath goes out of him and the ball flies into the air, and Boykin goes down heavily in the grass. He lies there gasping.

Jimmy feels as though his chest is locked and paralyzed, as though his lungs will never work again, and his whole body aches like a boil. He rolls over and looks up, into the low sun, and the coach is standing over him. He's looking down at him. Tears jump to Jimmy's eyes. He heaves for breath that does not come.

"Get up," the coach says, "get your ass up and get back in there!"

Jimmy cannot move. He lies there. The air inches into his lungs, enough to let him know he will live.

"Whatsa matter, Chicago boy," the coach says, "you takin you a nap?"

"N ... no sir," he stutters, his voice a terse, tight whisper.

"Can't you take it, Chicago boy?"

Jimmy struggles to his feet. His arms hang at his side, weighted down with fatigue. He had thought that, after the earlier scrimmage, after running down under punts and laps and wind sprints, he would not be able to move again. He staggers back to his flanker position.

"All right," the coach says, "same play. And this time hold onto the fuckin ball, Boykin!"

Jimmy is dizzy. His head swims. He hears the signals from Reeves, hollow and distant, echoing as though from down in a well, and he sprints into the pattern. The ball zips toward him and he tenses, anticipating the hit, and the ball sails by him and he relaxes for a split second before he is blindsided again, not expecting it after the ball is gone. Warnock drives into him and over him and presses him into the damp ground. Jimmy is blinded by fury and he shoves his hand inside Warnock's face mask, his fingernails raking across the other boy's cheek, and Jimmy hears him curse and cry out. Jimmy is licking his own lips that burn and are numbing and he knows there's blood there too because it is thick and warm and salty and Warnock pounds his sharp fist into Jimmy's belly and then his neck. The two boys roll around on the ground.

"Git off him, you asshole," a voice says, and Jimmy feels hands grappling him, and another voice, Bridgewater's he thinks, says "Leave him alone! Goddamit!" and a body falls over his and Warnock's, and then another, and he hears grunts and moans and cries of anger. "Asshole! Sonofabitch!" They all swing out blindly, hitting whatever they can hit, whoever.

Wayne watches them for a moment. Half the team is punching one another out. The others, mostly the younger boys, stand around looking on with frightened, curious looks. Otis looks on with a smile. There's a slight, crooked smile on Wayne's face, too. He lets them go for a few seconds longer. He does not want one of them getting hurt. He wants them fired up, but he doesn't have that many boys to risk a real injury. He's glad Otis is not in the middle of it. He looks over at the boy. Otis rolls his eyes and shakes his head. "Oh, man," he says.

"ALL RIGHT!" Wayne bellows. "CUT IT OUT!" He blows his whistle, several long, shrill shrieks. "STOP THIS SHIT YOU BUNCH OF GOLDBRICKS!"

They struggle apart. Several wild parting punches are thrown. Wayne can see puffy eyes, split lips. There is blood all down the front of Boykin's mud-smeared practice jersey. "All right," Wayne says, in a calmer voice, "here's a valuable lesson for you. If there's a fight," and he looks around, meeting their eyes one by one, speaking in a slow, explicit cadence, "when there's a fight, keep your fuckin helmets on!" He laughs. "When you get home, admire yourselves in the mirror. Look at your blood and whack off. And then forget it. Now," he says, "line up and run that goddam play again!"

A.J. Grist guides his dark blue Buick Century to a stop at the curb on the street overlooking the football stadium. He sits there looking down at the tiny figures scampering about on the clipped felt-like grass. His motor rumbles quietly and comfortably, and the air conditioner whispers.

A.J. is a small man and he wears a dark gray vested suit with a blue-and-red-striped tie. His close-cropped hair, which he has to drive all the way into Birmingham to get cut, is salt and pepper, and the narrow mustache under his nose mirrors that. He is an intensely black man, so black that sometimes white people and some black people too do a double take when they first see him. He is not just brown or dark brown. He is flat out coal black. Sometimes, looking in the mirror, he widens his eyes to large, minstrel-like circles, and the contrast between the whites of his eyes and the blackness of his face startles even him, makes him laugh out loud.

He squints down at the field, picking out Otis Hunnicutt. This Indian business is the most absurd thing Roger Coles has come up with yet. A.J. had advised Otis to go along with it. "Hell, they all of a sudden got a brother enrolled at their lily white school," he said.

"Yeah," Otis said, smiling, "but I'm an Indian."

"You ain't no more an Indian than I am. Or than Karla is." He had plans for his daughter. "Doesn't she look like an Indian to you, though? Ain't she an Indian, too?" He laughed. They were sitting in his office, in a little red brick house on the edge of downtown. The house was beautifully restored for Grist's law offices, and there was a black sign outside with ornate gold script: A.J. Grist, Attorney at Law. His plan is to send his daughter to Piper Christian Academy. He plans to claim that she was an Indian child that he and his wife had adopted in Nevada. He has already drawn up false legal papers to that effect. The truth of the matter, though, is that both Karla and Otis are multi-racial, more black than white, and once he got them both in the Academy he would proceed from there. He is certain he can use it against Roger Coles, even if he just embarrasses him.

He knows that he is a great mystery to the town of Piper. They can't figure out why he stays here. He had been married to a white woman, who ran off with the UPS driver when their daughter was little more than a baby. And Karla: he has raised her himself. She is beautiful like her mother, statuesque. As poised as a Paris model. Highly intelligent.

He sits there gazing down at Otis Hunnicutt, his smooth fluid motions, the power of him evident even at this distance. Jesse Owens, A.J. Grist is thinking, yes, Jesse Owens. In the time of the New Nazis. Jesse Owens. He smiles. His teeth are astoundingly white.

There is a parade, a Fall Harvest Parade. "We love a parade," Sally Witherspoon, who teaches French, says to Brenda in the teachers' lounge, with a knowing smile. Sally Witherspoon would have called her own smile a glowing smile. She is in her mid-fifties, blond, stately and stylishly pretty.

"This town is parade crazy," John D. Wisham, Jr., says. "It gives all these machos a chance to strut around in their military uniforms and get the fire trucks out and blow the whistles and sirens. You never heard such noise in your life."

"Everybody loves a parade," Sally says, cutting her eyes at Wisham. "Everybody normal, anyway!"

Brenda had not even known that Jimmy had gone out for football until he had come home with the bloody lip and the scabbed eye.

"What is this?" she stammered, "what the hell is this?"

"I had the physical. Coach told me I could. I—"

"Coach? Wayne McClain? I don't want you under the influence of Wayne McClain, Jimmy!"

"Why?" He stuck his bruised, sullen lip out.

"Because he's a shithead, that's why!"

"But you have to play football in this town. You have to—"

"You don't have to do anything!"

"All the guys say—"

"I don't care what the guys say. Maybe you could be in the band. Look at you. Look at your—"

"Only faggots are in the band," he said sullenly.

"Dammit," she said. She looked at him across the table in their kitchen. The windows were dark. They were eating pork chops and peas she had cooked when she got home. There was blood caked on his chin. His right eye was swelling. "What the hell else have you gone and done that you haven't told me about?"

He just looked at her, brooding. She looked away.

And Piper Christian Academy has turned out to be a circus. The faculty manages to violate every single principle Brenda studied in her education courses. And some of the textbooks are a joke. The biology text dismisses evolution as a ridiculous, unproven theory. In its place is something called "Creation Science." Roger Coles and the local board of the Academy have purchased old social science and history books published twenty years ago and long since rejected by the public schools as hopelessly out of date. "We have to use these books. Everything now is just revisionist history," Virginia Martin told her, "and none of it's true." And the high school reading list is limited to books suitable for very young children. The seniors are required to read *National Velvet*.

"We cannot have books with cursing in them," John D. Wisham, Jr., told her. "The parents would have a conniption. This is a Christian school, after all."

"Christians don't cuss?" Brenda asked.

"They don't admit it if they do," he said, "not these, anyway."

"All this is not good, not good at all," she said to Roger Coles. "I—"

"That's why I brought you in as headmistress," he said. He smiled warmly. "Brenda, Brenda. There's plenty of time for that. Let's not talk about work!"

They were sitting at a table in Arman's, an expensive Italian restaurant in Birmingham. He reached across the table and put his hand over hers. "Do you need anything?"

"Yes," she said, "I need all new textbooks. I need—"

"I mean you personally!" He waved his hand in the air, dismissing her concerns. "Anything. A new car? Let me buy you a new car. How about music? Would you like a new CD player?"

"No," she said. "Are you crazy?"

"Yes," he said, "crazy about you! What kind of CDs do you like?"

He tried to talk her into riding in the parade with him. He was planning to ride in the back of a new Cadillac. She insisted that she would not do it. He told her about a man in town who was shooting videotape of various locations for a movie company. "They want to make a movie here," he said, "it'll be good for the economy. He'll be shooting the parade!" Back at her house he had kissed her roughly, plunging his tongue into her mouth. She had forgotten how long it had been since she'd had a man. He was tall and lean, and his cologne smelled strange, like an old trunk, dusty and mysterious. His tongue was thick and warm. He had fumbled at her breasts like an adolescent boy.

There are over fifty fire trucks in the parade, from all over the area, and they blow their sirens and little children cry and try to run away. Thoughtful mothers have brought cotton balls to stuff into their little ears. The noise is deafening. It's unbelievable. The trucks stop at the main intersection of town and raise their snorkels into the air. Firemen climb the ladders and throw handfuls of hard candy down on the eager upturned faces of the crowds below.

Brenda, true to her word, watches the parade from the sidewalk. She sees Coles go by in the open car, waving to the crowd that lines the main street. She watches the Wembly County Militia, marching in step, in camouflage fatigues and white helmets, following two tanks that grind down the street. The football team walks by, wearing their bright green jerseys. Without their pads, the jerseys hang on them like collapsed pup tents.

Wayne walks with them. Brenda sees Jimmy, ambling casually along, his hands in the back pockets of his jeans. All the boys pretend they don't notice the crowd. Jimmy walks right behind Wayne and Otis Hunnicut. The Eagles have won their first three games, and Jimmy has gotten to play in the last two, because they have beaten their opponents by the scores of: 63-10, 78-0, and 69-6. Otis has gained over three hundred yards in each game and has already scored seventeen touchdowns. He is phenomenal.

Brenda sits in the stands at the games, seething with resentment at Wayne McClain. She thinks that he has stolen her son. She plans to do something about it, but she doesn't know what. The games are frenzied, carnival-like affairs. The stands are packed, and the cheerleaders turn cartwheels down the sidelines every time the Eagles score. The band plays constantly. Wayne paces the sidelines with a pair of earphones on, looking self-important.

At the parade Brenda presses her fingertips into her ears to protect herself against the sirens. It's Saturday morning and she will walk back home. She wears her sweats, after her jog. She is brought up short by the sight of a young blond man with a large video camera on his shoulder. Her eyes fasten on him like glue and she's reluctant to turn them away. His faded jeans hang low on his hips and cup his tight buttocks. His buns look as hard as iron. When he turns she sees that on the front of his sweatshirt is the image of Mickey Mouse. His blond hair is long, curly and gleaming clean in the morning sunlight, pulled back into a short pony tail. He is astonishingly handsome. Their eyes meet. His eyes are a light green, almost colorless, distant, focused on her and through her at the same time. When he looks at her she feels a jolt almost to her heels. He looks to be in his twenties, not that much older than Jimmy. She starts to walk on.

"Hello," he says. He has seen her before, around town. He has heard talk about her in Leroy's and he knows who she is. She wears no makeup and her eyes are clear and sharp, a deep dark brown like coffee. She is as tall as he is, maybe even taller. Her body looks solid and substantial. He senses more than sees her breasts under the black sweatshirt. She pauses. She looks at him again.

"Hello," she says. Their eyes seem to lock together for a moment. She nods, and a slight smile flickers at her full lips. Then she disappears into the crowd. He winces as another siren goes off.

Cody parks his van and is walking down the sidewalk with his video camera over his shoulder when he sees her jogging up the driveway of her small white house. He walks quickly and gets to her house just as she's going up to the front door. The house has pale green asbestos tiles, a screen porch on the front, and forest green awnings on the windows.

"Hello, again," he calls out, and she stops and turns and looks at him. She regards him calmly, without alarm or surprise.

"Hello, again," she says. It is a narrow yard, and they're not fifty feet apart. The high-noon light glints in her dark eyes. He thinks he sees interest there. He wonders what part in the movie she will want to play. He hopes she's not interested in that. He hopes she has never seen a movie in her life.

He moves halfway up her front walk. "That was some parade, wasn't it?" he asks.

She seems to hesitate. Her eyes perch on her sculptured cheekbones. She wears her hair long, youthful, and he can see from this closeness that she's pushing fifty. The skin of her face looks as smooth and supple as fine-grained leather that has been used well. Her body seems heavy like a seasoned melon is heavy. He knows that she's the principal of the local private school. "A widow, I think," one of the men drinking beer at Leroy's had told him. "I hear she likes women," another had said. Cody thinks she looks as though she would smell good, not like perfume, but woman-good.

"Yes," she says. "Loud." She smiles.

Brenda wonders how old he actually is. He stands there with his camera and a black leather bag slung over his other shoulder. She looks at his Mickey Mouse sweatshirt. He might be as old as thirty. His features are delicate, almost feminine, and the curly blond shoulder-length hair contributes to that effect. He is facing her but she remembers how his butt had looked earlier at the parade, hard and tight like two clenched fists.

"I'm Cody Klinger," he says. He shifts his load and steps closer to her and sticks out his hand. She grips it. His hand is soft, his skin cool. His eyes are changeable. They are now the color and shape of Greek olives. He is so good-looking it makes her teeth hurt. She wants to bite him. "I'm in town—"

"—scouting locations for a movie," she finishes for him.

They both laugh.

Her whole face laughs. Her eyes squint first and then her mouth follows. She would photograph beautifully in natural light.

"Well," she says, "it was nice to meet you, Mr. Klinger."

"Wait a minute, I—"

"Yes?"

"I'd like to interview you, if I could," he says.

"Interview me?"

"Yes, really, I ..." he says. "Really. I'd like to talk to you," he says again. "Actually, I'm not in town scouting locations at all." He moves closer to her. He can feel their nearness, and he can tell she feels it, too.

"You're not?" she asks. Her eyebrows arch over her forehead.

"Not altogether. Actually, my company is doing a documentary on militias. I'm here to shoot all the footage I can get. And I need to talk to some local people." He peers at her, his greenish eyes narrowed. "I'd rather you not say anything to anybody about what I'm really doing here," he says.

"Okay," she says. She watches his tongue as it licks his lips. She can see bits of stubble left on his chin from his careless shaving. Like Billy Boykin. He probably leaves streaks of lather in the sink. Little tiny bits of beard like dust specks. He is probably impatient with having to waste the time shaving every day. He's so close to her she can smell him. Sweat. A sweetness of skin. "I promise," she says, "I won't tell a soul."

"Then you'll talk to me?" he asks.

"Of course," she says, "when would you like to get together?"

BRENDA AWAKENS AND GOES GROGGILY INTO THE KITCHEN to put on coffee. She stands there yawning and scratching. She looks out into her back yard and thinks she is still dreaming. Her entire back yard is filled with flowering azalea bushes. It is startling. White and pink and red blooms burst like a fire out of control in the early morning sun. She shakes her head to clear it.

She goes down the short hall to the front of the house. Her front yard is full of the azaleas as well, the bright blooms looking false and cartoonish against the changing orange and brown leaves of the trees and the dullness of the autumn grass. When she had gone to bed her entire yard had been neatly clipped grass. It's now a jungle of flowering bushes.

She rips open a note tacked to the front door. "I told you you needed azaleas," the note reads. "I can even make azaleas bloom in October! Especially for you! They bloom at my command! Love, Roger." She stands there with sleep mussed hair, in an old extra-large T-shirt of Jimmy's with SHUT UP AND PITCH printed across the front, holding the note at arm's length to read it without her glasses. She squints at it in the early morning light.

She slowly waggles her head back and forth. She runs her fingers though her hair. As she stands there a breeze comes up, swaying the heavy clusters of blossoms, and she imagines she sees something moving in the explosions of color, something like a small person, or a child. She blinks. And then the sensation is gone, and there are only tiny green leaves and hues of red and tints of pink, like paint splatters, dancing in the earliest wind of the day.

FIVE

Wayne McClain walks into LEROY'S GRILL AND BILLIARDS and goes straight to the bar and orders a Budweiser before he even thinks about it. He has not planned it, and there's absolutely no logical reason for his doing it but the fact that he's doing it. The cold beer runs down his throat in a slaking stream of pure, refined pleasure. He can feel it jumping into his veins and lifting up the back of his brain. Its taste is as comfortable and familiar as one of his thumbs. Even as the beer bubbles in the pit of his stomach he is thinking, Well, it's back to the Elks Hall for the old Skipper. The Elks Hall, on the second floor over the NAPA Auto Parts Store, is where the Piper chapter of Alcoholics Anonymous meets.

Wayne's Eagles have just won their ninth game of the season against no losses, 66 to 0 against Shelby Academy, a team from south of the city. Wayne had stayed late in his office and watched the films of the game all the way through two times, making notes as he went. Otis had scored seven touchdowns. Scouts were there to see him from as far away as Southern Cal and Northwestern and Penn State. Wayne is feeling great.

It's late, long after midnight, and the only other man at the bar is Bo Stern, a mechanic at Coles Pontiac and Cadillac. Bo is drinking boilermakers, shots of Early Times bourbon followed by Dixie Beer in long-necked bottles. Robertson Reboul, the bartender at Leroy's, is half asleep behind the bar. Wayne wakes him up, yelling "Bud!"

"Goddam, Wayne, lemme buy you a beer," Bo says. "That team a yours is hell on wheels!"

"Ain't they?" Wayne says.

"Unbeatable. State champs for sure," Bo says, shoving a couple of dollars across to Robertson, who blinks sleepily. A neon Miller Lite sign bubbles red and golden behind the bar. Wayne can hear the crack of billiard balls in the back room. It's nearly two in the morning and a game is still going on. Friday night. After a game. Wayne remembers the way it was at

Auburn after a game. King of Fraternity Row! Free booze, all you could drink. And women. Corn-fed and blue-eyed, cinched waists and bursting out of their clothes like their bodies were stuffed with a swelling sweetness rising like biscuit dough. But that was a long time ago. That was another life.

"I've got another engagement, Wayne, but thanks anyway," was what Brenda Boykin said to him when he asked her if she'd like to go out with him after the game. He tried to do it very casually. He felt like a tongue-tied schoolboy. He figured her "engagement" was with Roger Coles or she made it up just to put him down. Well, to hell with you, too, sister.

He downs the beer almost in one chug-a-lug.

"Goddam, you musta been thirsty," Bo says. "Robertson, set this here gentleman up again." He reaches in his pocket and pulls out a thick roll of bills he tosses on the bar in front of them. "Keep em coming. He's only the greatest football coach that ever lived, that's all."

"Don't I know that?" Reboul says.

Both men sit quietly watching Reboul get Wayne's beer. The man moves slowly and deliberately, like a mechanical toy winding down. "You're tired and sleepy, Reboul. Why don't you take a nap and just let us help ourselves?" Bo asks. They all laugh.

"Shit," Reboul says. He is bald with yellowish blond temples and thick glasses with aluminum rims. He blinks behind the glasses like a sleepy owl. "Homecoming comin up, eh Wayne? Big parade and all," he says when he sets the beer in front of Wayne.

"Parades, parades," Bo says.

"We got more parades around here than the Pope's got beads," Reboul says.

"Next week," Stern says. "Homecoming."

"Yeah," Wayne says. "Gimme another Bud." He seems to be absorbing it, soaking it in like those thick paper towels advertised on television.

"Hey, those flowers you brought me looked nice in my office," Brenda said to him after school, squinting at him in the afternoon sunlight, almost closing one eye. He had brought her a handful of fall wildflowers, on impulse. And her saying that had emboldened him, led him on. She looked so good. She had on jeans stuffed into short blood-red boots. She had taken to wearing jeans to school, causing an earthquake in the teachers' lounge and in the PTO. "How can we expect the students to obey a dress code when we don't?" Sally Witherspoon asked haughtily in teachers' meeting.

"Dress codes are archaic," Brenda said. "They are an anachronism."

"Not here in Piper," Sally Witherspoon snorted.

"At my school they are," Brenda said. "I'm taking steps to get rid of the thing."

"Since when is this your school?" Billie Wilcox, who taught junior high math, asked. "I haven't noticed the board changing the rules in that regard."

"It's my school since I became headmaster," Brenda said. Wayne was watching all this with silent amusement from the back of the room. Brenda stood before the whole group with her hands on her hips wearing a blouse that looked like a man's white shirt, with a button-down collar. Her breasts threatened to pop the buttons in front.

"Headmistress!" Billie Wilcox corrected her. She was a short woman with close-cropped strawberry red hair.

"Headmaster!" Brenda said, and the air in the room dissolved into a heavy strained silence, and Wayne could see the stiff backs of all the teachers.

So Wayne asked her out later. And she had an "engagement."

Just then Cajun Rhodes and his brother Bumpy come into the bar. They are farmers from out in the north of the county. Everybody knows that for years they've been making whiskey up in the hills, in the hollows back among the old closed-down and sealed-off mines. They are headed for the poolroom when they spot Wayne and stop.

"You whupped them yippies asses good," Cajun says. "All riiiiight." Wayne figures he means "yuppies." Shelby County, home of Shelby Academy, is upscale, suburban.

"Whupped em good," Bumpy says, giggling.

"Hey, Wayne, they's a rumor goin round that that new principal up at the Academy is a Lebanese," Cajun says.

"A what?" Wayne asks. "She's American as you are. She came from right here in Piper."

"Don't make any difference. They tell me a woman can become a Lebanese over night, just like that."

"You dumb shit," Bo Stern says, "you mean a lesbon." He grins at Wayne. "Sumbitch means a lesbon."

"Who you callin a sumbitch, grease monkey," Cajun says. He grins and claps Stern on the back. He cups his genitals. "All that good-lookin bitch needs is a dose a this," he says.

"Country pecker," Bumpy says. "Whooeee."

They're getting on Wayne's nerves. He wonders why he ever came here in the first place. His head buzzes with the beer. He hadn't had a drink of anything in over a year. He had been standing in front of his apartment with his car keys in his hand. Looking up at the stars, he felt the warmth from the still-hot engine of his car, which was so dirty someone, probably a student, had written "Wash me pleeze" in the thick dust across the trunk. And then he'd found himself walking up the hill toward the main street and heading to Leroy's like he was on automatic pilot. And he is all of a sudden drunk, and now people are saying that Brenda has gone queer. She ought not to stand up in front of everybody and call herself a headmaster, he thinks. He finishes his beer and slides off the stool.

"You be good now, Wayne, you hear?" Reboul says as Wayne floats toward the door.

Outside the early morning air is dry and cool. It has become autumn all of a sudden, sneaking in like all the seasons in this part of the world, and Wayne stands there for a long time, thinking about Brenda Vick Boykin. He is relatively certain that she has not gone queer. But she had said an "engagement." Why hadn't she said a "date"? He feels a deep, gnawing anger, and the beer only intensifies it. He has lately realized that he has been angry as hell at Brenda for years, ever since the day he dumped her before he went off to Auburn.

He goes back inside and buys two cold six-packs to go.

Brenda stands naked in the middle of the floor. Coles looks at her, licking his lips. He is still fully clothed. She wears a faded royal blue sash over her right shoulder and down over her left breast that reads "HOMECOMING QUEEN, PHS, 1968," in dulled gold letters.

"Where did you get this?" she asks. The silky sash tickles her nipple. She laughs and shakes her head in amazement. "Is this ..."

"No, no," he says. He licks his lips. "No. I had it made at the costume shop down at the Alabama Shakespeare Festival. I've given them lots of money. They were glad to do it. Looks authentic, doesn't it?"

She laughs again. "Authentic, and a little ridiculous," she says.

"Oh, come on. It's fun."

"I don't know," she says. She wonders if he is lying. She wonders if the sash is the real thing and he has kept it all these years. The thought makes her feel cold, makes her skin shiver. She moves to take it off.

"Wait. No. Don't take it off," he says.

"Roger, I—"

"No, I said. Now listen to me. Keep it on." His face is a thick dark mask, and then suddenly he smiles. He smiles warmly at her. He can change from cold to warm in an eye-blink. "Wait till you see this," he says, chuckling. He hands her a brightly wrapped package he has brought.

She feels silly unwrapping it, standing there completely naked except for the sash. He watches her every move. She feels on display. It is not unpleasant, but strange. It's Roger who makes it strange. He continues to smile but his eyes are searing and hard, almost penetrating her with their stare.

Inside the package is a tiara, a queen's crown like the one she must have worn that night all those years ago. She pulls it out. The rhinestones glitter in the muted light of the bedroom. "Well, I'll be," she says. She puts it on her head for a moment and then holds it out and looks at it. She looks at Roger. "The costume shop again? Or is this the real thing?"

"Well, it's not the one you wore, if that's what you mean. I'd give anything if I had that one. Didn't you keep it?"

"Me? I don't know. I suppose I did. I suppose I burned it."

"Burned it? Why would you do such a thing?"

"I burned a lot of things from those years." She turns the crown around. The rhinestones seem to glow from inside. The metal has a rich sheen. She holds it closer to her eyes. She wishes she had on her glasses. "You had this one made?" she asks curiously.

"Yes. At a shop in Palm Beach."

"Palm Beach?"

"Yes. They're real. The diamonds. And it's real silver."

"Don't shit me, Roger," she says. The crown suddenly feels heavy in her hands.

"No. Really. They are real diamonds. I had it made especially for you."

"Oh, come on. You didn't either. This thing must be worth ... well, how the hell would I know?"

"Three quarters of a million," he says. He beams at her.

"What?" she says. She drops it to the rug, as though something has yanked it from her hand. He stoops down and picks it up. It is slightly bent. He straightens it out. "Look, I'm sorry," she says. "Don't hand it to me again. I'll drop it again. I'll throw it out the window, okay?"

"What's the matter? Put it on."

"No."

"Put it on! I had it made for you, goddamit!"

"I don't want to, Roger. This is too much. Fun is one thing, but—"

"Listen to me! It's my money, and I paid for it! Put it on!"

He looks on the verge of a white anger that frightens her. His jaw is clenched, his eyes burning and feverish.

"Oh, all right," she says. She puts it on. He hands her a couple of bobby pins from her dresser and she pins it in place on her hair.

"Now," he says. His hand grips her upper arm so hard that it pains her. He moves her to in front of the full mirror on the back of her closet door. He knows the layout of her house better than she does. His house. She looks at herself in the mirror. The sash slashes her body at a sharp angle and the exposed nipple is erect. His eyes move slowly up and down her body, fastening on her coal black pubic hairs—too much hair she had always thought, ever since she was a girl, too thick and the patch so much bigger than the other girls her age. It poked out of her bathing suits around the legs and she had to shave to wear a bikini, but she had learned early on that men loved it that way—his eyes pausing lingeringly there until they move up to the crown that reflects tiny points of light that twinkle in the gold glow of the bedside lamp.

His hand loosens on her arm and he caresses it. His breathing quickens, and his hand slides slowly down her back and cups one buttock, gently rubbing, then he slides his flattened hand between her buttocks. Her knees tingle and grow liquid, and she watches him in the mirror, his eyes manic and bright now as he stares at the tiara. Her skin is warming, sensitive. His mouth hangs open. She can see his erection bulging against his khaki pants.

"Loosen up," he whispers. "Risk a little. Let's go for the sky."

"All right," she says quickly.

They breathe together in a quick unison as she leads him to her bed.

＊

Lemuel Bluett trips over the first row of azalea bushes in the dark and mutters "Shit" under his breath. He has observed at Brenda Boykin's house several times already, and the last time there were no bushes right here in this spot. He peers around. The whole yard seems covered with the shrubs. And they are blooming. He has to pause at the sight. He rubs his arms in his light blue windbreaker against the chill of the night air. Azaleas don't usually bloom in early November, he doesn't think. He doesn't really know. Plants don't interest him. His wife plants stuff in the yard all the time and wants to talk about it, but it doesn't interest him.

He moves stealthily through the yard, expertly avoiding the new bushes. The moon is thin, low in the sky, and it gives just enough light to see. The stars are like sparks sprinkled on a canopy. They always make Lemuel think of the ceiling of the Fox Theater in Atlanta, where his daddy had taken him to see the Original Ted Mack Amateur Hour when he was a child. Call For Phillip Morris! He had liked the little midget in the red suit best of all. There's a dim glow in the principal's bedroom, like a nightlight, except that Lemuel knows that it isn't a night-light, unless it is new.

The night-light is in the bathroom. This is probably one of those little reading lamps that sit on her bedside tables.

Lemuel is thirty-six years old, and he has been doing this—prowling around looking in people's windows—for over twenty years. He has been caught he doesn't know how many times. He has been shot at and beaten up. He has had counseling and his wife has left him twice and taken the children with her, but she always forgives him and comes back. He has served a couple of stretches in the county jail. The last time, for six months, he had to report to the jail at night and sleep there and they would let him out in the mornings to go to his job. He works as a lumber grader for Godwin's Timber Company, a firm that makes railroad ties and creosote fence posts and other treated wood products. You can smell the chemicals from the plant, located a mile outside Piper, hanging in the air when you go anywhere in that direction. And Lemuel's skin smells like creosote, too. He can't wash the smell off.

He eases up to the window. The shade is drawn, but there's a good inch down the sides. Lemuel feels his groin tingling, just anticipating. He knows because of the light that she probably isn't asleep. On the other occasions he has watched her undress and change into her nightgown, which is an old T-shirt. Her breasts are large and melon-like, with big dark nipples the size of silver dollars. Her bush is black and thick. She is a big woman, and there is lots of her to see. He leans his head to the side and squints through the crack.

Bingo! Jackpot! She is astride somebody, and they are going at it like jackrabbits. Her heavy breasts are jiggling and bouncing up and down and the man has his hands on them pulling at them and rubbing them. All she has on is something shiny and glittery on her head and some kind of blue cloth sash over her shoulder. It flaps with her movements. Lemuel stares at her round full buttocks, moving back and forth. He grabs his own gonads, now hot and hard. He can barely see the man, and he changes his position slightly, closing one eye to get a better view. The man has white hair. Gray hair. He turns his face toward the window. Lemuel can't believe his eyes. It's Roger Coles, banging the new principal! Roger Coles is so old that Lemuel is surprised he can still get it up. He has seen lots of things in his years of peeping—people jacking-off in all manner of ways and men nuzzling one another's naked crotches and women doing themselves off with candles and hairbrush handles, and all kinds of other things, too—and Lemuel had thought he wouldn't see anything else that would surprise him, but this one does.

The two of them get so frantic that Lemuel can hear the bed squeaking through the wall. He lets his own member out to taste the cool air and he can feel himself getting ready. He can tell that Brenda Boykin and Mr. Coles are getting there, too. Lemuel's mouth forms words but no sound comes forth. He is careful not to move his feet, not to rustle anything, not to touch the house. "Oh, oh, oh, oh," he hears her saying, her voice faint through the glass. "Yes, yes, yes," he hears Mr. Coles say.

Lemuel's knees go weak and he grunts audibly. He spills his seed on the ground. That is what always goes through his mind at these moments: I spill my seed on the ground. Like Onan. It gives Lemuel a sense of belonging, even of tradition, to remember his kinship with the Biblical figure who had gone before.

⟿

"We would be undefeated even without Otis," Ernest Bridgewater says, having to shout over the noise from up front. They are sitting around a table in the back room at The Owl Cafe, a large restaurant and dance hall on the outskirts of town. The jukebox is thumping in the dance hall, rattling the walls, and they hear the stomping of feet. Old people in ten-gallon hats and cowboy boots are up there doing country line dancing. They can hear them laughing like hyenas, drunk as skunks.

"He's a great ballplayer," Jimmy Boykin says. He is the youngest one here. He is drinking beer.

"He's cute," Lolly Phillips says. She has a pug nose. Her breasts are like softballs. "He's one hot nugget."

"Hush your mouth, girl," Clarence Peevy says. One of his eyes, his glass one, is darker than the other. Clarence scored two touchdowns earlier, both in the fourth quarter. He is feeling pretty good about himself.

"I could do him if I wanted to," Colleen Purdy says. She's in the National Honor Society. She holds her long-necked Pabst Blue Ribbon like a teacup. She smokes Eve Cigarettes. Her face is pasty white, her hair dyed coal black. "How about you, Darlene? You want to do him?"

Darlene ducks her head. "No," she says.

"Why? Because he's an Indian?"

"Because I'm a Christian," Darlene says.

"If you're a Christian," Ernest says, "then why are you sitting around in here drinking beer?"

"Jesus drank wine," Darlene says.

"That's right," Colleen says. She slides her chair closer to Darlene.

"Unfermented," Jane Ann Dewberry says. "It was unfermented grape juice." Jane Ann is tall and thin with an overbite. She and Lolly are cheerleaders.

"The Bible says wine," Darlene says.

"My father says unfermented grape juice," Jane Ann says. She laughs and toasts them with her Miller Light.

"I wouldn't mind doing him," Lolly says.

"Who? Jesus, or Otis?" Colleen asks.

"Otis!" Lolly says. "He's carrying a major package. What do you think, Jane Ann?"

"I wouldn't know," Jane Ann says.

"I mean, he's rockin on his own private planet," Lolly says.

Ernest has bought the beer for them all, because he has a phony ID, a fake Virginia driver's license that lists his name as James Knox Polk. John Shannon Shanahan, the fat man who owns The Owl, likes to at least go through the motions. Jimmy's six-pack of Red Dog is under the table and he's on his fourth. These people drink as much as anybody he had known in Chicago. They do grass, and something called Special K that he has never heard of. "And we make our own stuff, joy juice, peace milk," Colleen Purdy told him. "You'll have to join us one night for one of our, uh, parties." Jimmy thinks he knows what the pale, pasty face and the sooty hair means; Colleen is into some dark stuff. He is checking out Lolly Phillips. She's the one he has picked out. Her eyes are pale blue and she frowns slightly when she sips her beer. Her lips are as plump as ripe cherries.

The music pounds through the walls. All they can talk about is Otis. Jimmy likes Otis, but he feels sorry for him. He has never known an Indian before, never even seen one. He's not even sure that Otis is an Indian. He overheard his mother on the phone to Mr. Coles. "He's not an Indian, Roger," she said, "you know that very well, but I don't give a shit at this point what he is." There had been a long pause, then his mother had said, "I'll use the word 'shit' whenever I want to, Roger," and she had hung up. Otis seems lonely, isolated. Their lockers are right next to each other, and they are the two new guys on the team.

Earlier, after the game they sat on the benches in front of their lockers and watched the others, naked and pink, pushing and shoving and shouting. Bragging and boasting. Steam boiling out of the shower room. "We're number one!" they chanted. "We're gonna be State Champs! State Champs!" "We're gonna whup some ass!" "Who's number one?" Boligee Phil yelled, standing naked in the middle of the room, his body wet and hairy and his dork hanging down like a hose pipe. "Who the fuck's number one?!" "We are! We are!"

Otis had not joined in the celebration. "These crackers are some crazy motherfuckers," he said.

Jimmy wonders if Lolly goes to these parties Colleen told him about. Colleen is now sitting practically in his cousin's lap. Colleen looks at Darlene and licks her black, shiny lips. She looks like she uses soot for lipstick. Lolly is sipping her beer and frowning. Jimmy can't wait to try this Special K, this peace milk. The music is so loud and drumming through the thin wall that it's giving him a headache.

⌐

Colleen Purdy is the leader of their coven. She is known among them as Miz Luce. She has an upside-down cross carved into her upper arm. This is the Cross of Satanic Justice. She has a Cross of Nero branded into her back. Neither her father nor her mother has ever seen it, and if they did they would think it was a peace sign from the sixties. But to Colleen and the others the upside-down cross in the circle signifies that the arms of the cross have been broken in defeat of Christianity, in Satanic victory.

In the darkest of the morning before dawn, they gather in the woods along Shell Creek, the shallow stream that ambles aimlessly through the town of Piper. The air is cool and crisp, full of the night's last mist. Keith McClain is there, and Karla Grist. There are just four of them tonight. The fourth is Lolly, who now wears baggy black pants and a T-shirt turned inside-out, and red high-stop tennis shoes. Colleen is dressed exactly the same, and Karla wears black slacks and a black turtleneck. Keith is in loose baggy denim, his day's clothes, and he displays all his body jewelry: rings in his nostrils, lips and tongue, his pierced navel and nipples and eyelids. His bald head gleams in the light from their campfire. The flames glitter on his jewelry.

They have captured Miss Holly Polliday's old dog Grover from his pen. He knows them—they've borrowed him before—and he has come with them willingly, high squeaking whines of pleasure escaping his throat when they pet him. The old dog stays locked in the pen all the time, pacing back and forth and around and around so that he has worn a path in the shape of a figure-eight several inches deep into the ground. He is glad to be let out. He's excited at the attention. He sits on his haunches and eagerly watches their every move, the yellow flames reflecting in his eyes.

Colleen has peace milk in a Mason jar. It's a thick liquid distilled from wild Morning Glory seeds, Hawaiian Rose seeds and Jimson Weed. Colleen puts it on Ritz crackers; the others kneel and she puts the crackers on their tongues like communion wafers. It's a solemn ceremony. They sip from the jar one by one. It's a powerful hallucinogen, and it's not long before they begin to see the shapes and forms in the trees, the geometric patterns that become ghosts, ghosts of small naked babies with blank faces, flitting from limb to limb like cupids. At first they're just pale shadows and then they're outlined in blazing bright colors, pulsing with light, blinding in their intensity.

Keith hears music as though it rumbles up from the bowels of the earth. He hears violins tuned to some otherworldly scale, a harmonious caco- phony that fills his head and bounces with the babies in the trees. The pink of their skin is luminous. In Keith's eyes they are all little girls, but to the three girls they are boys, with stiff outsized members like satyr's organs. And the organs spurt a red liquid, like blood.

Colleen hits old Grover expertly in the back of the head with a hammer, and the dog emits a startled half-bark, then goes down heavily to the ground. Colleen hits him again several times in the top of the head, the hammer dull and thudding as though in packed dirt, and while the cherubs frolic overhead they can all see the life fade gradually from the old dog's wide, surprised eyes. He smells rancid, like damp dirty rags. His body is heavy when they turn him over, and Colleen plunges a butcher knife into his skin just inside the legs.

The knife is razor sharp and the blood spurts warm and sticky over all their hands as they rub them on his belly. They chant sounds, not words but moans and soft cries, and Colleen begins to strip the skin from the dog's body with the knife. She slashes. She looks upward as the stars grow round and large and soft like moons that hover just over the treetops.

She chants: "Not to go on all fours! That is the law! Not to claw bark or trees, that is the law. Are we not woman? Not to snarl or roar. Not to show our fangs! We are woman! And woman is God! We are Gods!"

The little girl is there, in the sky. She watches them, her arms outstretched, and they see her. Her white robe is smeared with the old dog's blood, bright and shining with a metallic sheen. She is not a child now but is their age. They see her budding painful breasts, seeping a pale yellow liquid against the robe. Her hair is stiff, unruly, and her eyes are angry and deep and staring inward and outward at them at the same time, watching them as they smear the blood on their arms and faces and pull the old dog's carcass over the leaping flames of the fire. The smell of seared meat and black billowing smoke spreads throughout the clearing and drifts upward to the girl, who hangs suspended in the sky, heavy rusted nails through her hands, the skin of her face raw and chapped and stinging in the night air.

They are exhausted now, their nostrils clogged with the smells of blood and smoke. The three of them sink to the ground around Colleen, who stands holding the blood-smeared knife and hammer. Colleen smiles. The music rages; it is something that has lost all semblance of form or order.

Everything around them bolts and shudders like an earthquake. The forms above them are a giant kaleidoscope, changing shapes with each pulse and heartbeat, and over it all hovers the girl, her gaze as steady as a statue's.

"Oh Great Goddess," Colleen chants, holding her tools, "I have found her. I have found us a virgin. A Christian virgin."

There is not an ounce of excess flesh on Cody's body. Brenda can see the pale outline of his Speedo over his narrow buttocks, and his penis curves from its little nest of golden hair and sways back and forth when he walks.

He stands unselfconsciously before her.

"You should come to California with me when I get done with this," he says.

"I can't," she says. "I came here to ... I don't know." She thought maybe she would find her old self wherever it was that she had left it. "I want to do some good, make a difference," she says.

He stares at her. "That kind of talk went out with the hippies and the people in the sixties. This place is dangerous. The people are going postal."

"Going what?"

He shrugs. "You know."

She does. She has already realized what he means. "About to explode. The people are crazy," she says.

He shrugs again and his penis wiggles. "Whatever," he says.

"She's a movie star," one of the children in the pre-school says. "She's starring in the movie that that man is making."

"Naw," Melanie Shephard says. "She was a prostitute in Chicago. My mother said so."

"We're all in the movie. The movie is about us."

"Naw."

"We're all making up the movie as we go along. My brother said so!"

"If she's a movie star, why ain't she already been in a movie?"

"She has. It just hasn't come to Piper yet."

"You fulla bull."

"My brother said he saw it in Birmingham!"

"He's fulla bull!"

She is so very different from the rest of their drab teachers. She walks in light. Her dark hair is full and thick with clean sparkles. She never talks down to them and they have been quick to pick up on that. She is old but there is something young about her. She is big and tall but she kneels down on one knee to look them in the eye. She laughs with them. She understands when they say something funny. She does not erase them with a blank adult stare.

⌐

It is late in the third quarter of the last game of the season, the Homecoming Game against Heiberger Academy, and Piper is leading 49 to 0. All the energy available in Piper, in most of Wembly County, is concentrated right here under the powerful lights that illuminate the bright green grass of the field, the white lines as sharp and distinct as needles. Both bands play incessantly, a steady stream of marches and fight songs and jazzy versions of popular radio ballads.

The game is still difficult for Brenda to follow. She cringes every time number 80 is involved in a collision. She is edgy and anxious. She has never liked football, even when she was a cheerleader. Back then her back was always to the field and their cheers were practiced little rhyming dances and such. They cheered when the crowd cheered, and Brenda had never really known, nor cared, what they were cheering about.

She is sitting with Lamar and Emily on one side of her and on the other side a couple whose daughter is a B-team cheerleader who struts up and down the aisles in her little short skirt selling programs. The couple's names are Paula and Lemuel Bluett. Lemuel Bluett tells her proudly that he is the son of Calvin Bluett, adjutant general of the Wembly County Militia and a member of the board of trust for the Academy. Lemuel Bluett looks at Brenda in a strange, lingering way that soon annoys her. He seems to be waiting for her to say something, staring at her inquisitively with his eyebrows cocked, an odd, wan smile on his lips. "My son plays pee-wee football," he says. "You must like azaleas. I drove by the other day and saw your azaleas?" It is phrased as a question.

"Yes," she says, "I do." She knows his son. The boy's name is Calvin Bluett the Second, and he is a chubby bully who picks fights with much younger and smaller boys.

"I've always liked them, too," the man says.

The outcome of the game was no longer in doubt at half time, when the Eagles led 28 to 0 and the homecoming queen, Jane Ann Dewberry, was crowned. Jane Ann said on the loudspeakers that she owed it all to the Lord Jesus. Brenda wondered how that made all the other girls feel who had not won. I finished last because that's where the Lord Jesus wanted me. The band played "Let Me Call You Sweetheart."

Lemuel Bluett seems to be sitting very close to her, and she moves away from him. "Did you go to the homecoming parade this afternoon?" he asks, and she keeps her eyes on the field, concentrating, trying to ignore the man. "It was a good parade." She does not answer him.

The parade that afternoon had been another elaborate affair, with twenty-one—Brenda had counted them—fire trucks, all blowing their sirens and whistles again and flashing their red lights. And there were police cars as well. And Shriners from Birmingham dressed as clowns, some in little open toy cars labeled with the title of whoever was inside. There was the Director of Units, the Assistant Director of Units, and the Associate Director of Units. The Hidden Valley Church of Christ of the New Light had a float with an angel on it, and when it passed close Brenda recognized the angel as Marthetta Green, in the tenth grade. She was chewing gum. And of course the local Militia, their troop carriers and their tank, and men marching in formation with rifles. It was a show of military might, like those parades in Russia she used to see on television.

Wayne had come by in an open car. He waved to the crowd. Even from the curb Brenda could see that his eyes were bloodshot. He seemed shaky earlier in the week. He had a bud-vase with a single red rose, a balloon with a yellow smiling face attached to it by a long string, sent to her office. "You're the Greatest" was printed on the balloon. The card had read

"Happy Homecoming Week! Freight Train." His players straggled along behind him, walking casually, refusing to keep straight lines. They slouched, hands in pockets, as though they were completely unimpressed with the goings-on. Jimmy waved to her. He was walking beside Otis Hunnicutt. Otis's eyes were straight ahead, looking neither right nor left. He seemed to be walking in time to the band, which had already passed but whose peppy music could still be heard.

Brenda caught sight of Cody, his camera on his shoulder, taping the parade. Her eyes fastened on him like glue and she had been reluctant to turn them away. His blond hair was curly and shining in the afternoon sunlight, and he wore heavy boots. He was lost in the trance of what he was doing, unaware of anything else. He had been to her house a couple of times now. He was like a kid, not that much older than Jimmy, not much more mature. He sat naked in the calfskin recliner Coles had sent over and that had amused Brenda.

She was with Coles at the parade, and he had noticed her looking at Cody. "From Hollywood, California," he said. "He's the one who's in town scouting locations for his movie company. They are looking for a typical small Southern town to make a movie in, and he's right impressed with Piper."

"Really?" she asked. Coles was still watching her; she had been devouring Cody with her eyes. She flushed. She looked away at the parade, but in a few seconds her eyes jerked back to the boy as though his body were a magnet, her eyes acting on their own accord as though she had no control over them at all. "He's very good-looking," she said.

"That's what they tell me," Coles said. Indeed Sybil had come back into his office after Cody Klinger had left, fanning herself in an exaggerated manner with a newspaper.

"Jesus H. Christ," she had said, "I'm running all down the insides of my legs and my headlights are on high beam!"

"Act like a grown woman, Sybil," he had snapped.

Mabel had seen him around town, too. "My God," she said to Brenda, "God sent him to us. Have you ever seen anything as good-lookin as that?"

"He's a child," Brenda said.

"You know what they used to say about us girls, back in junior high school," Mabel said.

"What?"

"Old enough to bleed, old enough to butcher!"

"That's right. That's absolutely right," Brenda said. They were drinking coffee in Mabel's office at her women's health center. Brenda had been dropping in on Mabel, renewing their old friendship, for a couple of months. Her office is a large spacious room with a picture window that looked out on woods and the creek. She had told Mabel about her and Coles.

"He's so rich he doesn't know how much he's worth," Mabel said. "And powerful. He runs this county, lock stock and almost barrel, because he doesn't run me or my clinic. But he'd like to run me, all right, run me right out of the county!"

"He runs that school, that's for sure," Brenda said.

"Right. And it's now about the only school in the whole county that matters. It's the school, and he's got you runnin it for him. Why you?"

"Why me?" Brenda echoed. "He says he loves me. Says he's been in love with me for twenty years, ever since he crowned me Homecoming Queen. He's a little crazy. I don't know. He frightens me, but he's sweet. You know?"

"Yeah. He's a charmer. Butter wouldn't melt in his mouth."

"He says he wants to marry me," Brenda said. "I wouldn't marry him if he was the last man on earth. In fact, I wouldn't marry the last man on earth, period."

"You wouldn't have to fight me over him," Mabel said.

⌐

The game is almost over. Brenda can see Wayne pacing the sidelines.

"How do you like it in Piper, Mrs. Boykin?" Lemuel Bluett says to her.

Brenda still does not look at him. "Fine," she says through tight lips. She dislikes the man intensely, and she doesn't know why.

She watches Wayne down along the sidelines. The Eagles are still moving the ball down the field. They have the ball on Heiberger's twenty-five yard line, first and ten. Wayne is talking with one of his players, who then sprints onto the field with a play, she knows, because Lamar has told her that's the way they do it. The teams line up. The people in the stands are almost as noisy as ever, and Brenda watches as the quarterback, Number 2, a kid named Johnny Mack Reeves, fades back to pass. He throws the pass over the middle, toward Number 80, Jimmy, who leaps for it. High in the air. He soars, a ballet-like motion, reaching for the ball, and one of their boys tackles him, rams his legs from behind, and Jimmy turns a complete flip in the air and comes down heavily on the back of his neck. It takes Brenda agonizing seconds to realize that he has hit very hard. To realize that she is not watching a movie or something far removed, that it's Jimmy and he lies on the ground, not moving, as still as a statue. All the players stop running. An ominous hush settles over the crowd. The other players, both teams, stand looking at Jimmy on the ground. Brenda can not take her eyes off Jimmy's limp, still body; she can not move. She sees Wayne running onto the field, several players now motioning frantically for him.

Suddenly and inexplicably it is as though she is the only person there. Surrounded by complete silence, she sees the play again in her mind's eye: Jimmy leaping and hanging in the air as graceful as any dancer. It is as though the play is in slow motion, and she can clearly see the back of his helmet hit the ground, his shoulders twist with the momentum of his own body, and she imagines she can hear the dull snap, the horrible wet sound of bones breaking, and she knows, in that instant, without doubt, that her son is dead.

"He probly just got the breath knocked out of him," she hears Lamar say, his voice distant and hollow and shaky and filled with doubt.

⌐

In retrospect she would remember the next few hours in vivid and brief snatches of time and images. She is on the field, not knowing how she got there. She is under the glaring lights, conscious of the strong clean scent of clipped grass, of its sponginess beneath her feet. She stands beside Wayne, the two of them watching paramedics work over Jimmy. They are careful not to move him, and the ambulance is coming onto the field.

"He'll be all right," she will remember Wayne saying. "These things are usually just temporary jolts. They just don't want to take any chances." Her mind is acute, her vision clear. There are no tears in her eyes. She watches the paramedics place the inflatable cast around Jimmy's neck; they have not removed his uniform, not even his helmet. She sees them place him carefully on the stretcher and push the stretcher into the ambulance. She is aware that they are looking questioningly at her then. She does not know why. "You go with him in the ambulance," Wayne says. "I'll be on after the game." He is standing very close to her, and she thinks she can smell alcohol on his breath.

She moves automatically, her arms and legs numb and without feeling. She realizes that it's becoming hard for her to breathe, and she inhales the night air deeply. She climbs into the back of the ambulance. Her back is against the side, against the row of small windows. There is little room. The paramedic across from her is young. He looks no older than Jimmy. His face is contorted with worry and concern.

"Mama," Jimmy says, his voice muted and soft. She holds his hand. It is lax, without strength.

She hears the siren begin and sees the red lights flashing around them as they leave the stadium. She is only dimly aware of the lights reflected from the storefronts as they race through town. She does not know how long they've been on the interstate when she realizes where they are, and soon she sees the tall buildings and the lights of the city. In the dusky interior she sees the young paramedic smile at her and nod.

"Mama," she hears Jimmy say. She can smell the sweat from his body, the dirt and grass on his uniform. His arms and legs are strapped to the stretcher with bright yellow straps. "I can't move, Mama," he says. She can barely hear him over the sound of the ambulance, the siren. She looks at the young man across from her.

"Swelling," he says. "The area will swell, press the nerves. Maybe that's all." He looks away, then back at her. "We're almost to the hospital." She cannot breathe.

They are in traffic now, among tall buildings.

⇌

Keith McClain and Karla Grist are parked in Jody's brother's car at an overlook near the Warrior River. Keith has told Karla in hushed tones about Jimmy Boykin's injury. It frightens them both. They comfort each other. Then they kiss passionately. Keith has Karla's bra up around her shoulders and is nuzzling her breasts. His tongue flicks over her nipples and makes her feel warm all over, like she has been dipped in a hot fresh bath. She feels his fingers inside her panties and realizes that her jeans are already unzipped and down around her ankles. Keith is moving fast. She feels her panties come off. She pushes his head downward and he kisses her belly and then stops. His naked head is motionless. She looks at the smooth skin of it. She caresses it softly. She thinks it's very sexy. She pushes his head downward again.

He resists and looks up at her. The radio is playing softly (The Eagles's "Desperado") and she can see his face and his eyes in the dim light from the dash. "You want me to do that?" he asks with mock innocence. Then he laughs, and she shoves at his head.

"Yeah," she says. "Get with it, honky."

"I read somewhere that black people didn't like that," he says. She can see him grinning in the dimness.

"Do I look black to you?" she asks, roughly guiding his head and his face and finally his mouth to where she wants it to be. "I'm an Indian, white man," she says.

⇌

Brenda sits in the crowded waiting room of the Trauma Unit. It is Friday night in the city, and she has seen several stabbing and gunshot wounds come in. She sits remembering another visit to a hospital emergency room, this one in Chicago, when once Billy, drunk, had beaten her so badly she had lost several teeth and had part of her right ear ripped from her head. That night is still as fresh in her memory as yesterday, as vivid as the scars hidden by her hair. She had forgotten how much worse it could be, had forgotten what it was like to have her child in danger, his life threatened. She shifts in the hard plastic chair. The air smells of harsh floor cleanser and stale cigarette smoke. A television set plays high on the wall, some golf match. The announcer drones on. Nobody is watching.

She sits among dozing family members, assorted night people. Three nurses eat their lunches in a corner. Two uniformed policemen sit near her, talking quietly, one of them writing from time to time in a pocket note-book. She feels dry and empty inside. She is tired and yet curiously ener-getic, as though she is two people at once. She keeps looking at the double doors through which they had carried Jimmy. It is now past midnight and she has long since finished answering all the questions at the window, wel-coming the diversion of the paperwork, the endless details. She had been surprised that she had her insurance card with her. She has her purse, but she does not remember grabbing it up and bringing it along. Coles has called twice, sending her word that he's on the way.

She is looking at the doors when she sees a young doctor come through. He is short, with straw colored hair. He wears surgical greens. She sees him looking around and she knows instinctively that he is looking for her, and their eyes meet. He nods and approaches her. He sits down next to her in another plastic chair.

"I'm Doctor Nance," he says, "Mrs. Boykin." He shakes her hand, oddly formal. The skin of his hand is cool and smooth. He seems very young.

"Yes," she says, "how is he? Is he ..."

"I must tell you that it does not look good," he says, and she feels as though she has been kicked in the heart. "Not good at all. Injuries of this type are always serious. However, we won't know the full extent of the damage until the swelling goes down." He looks calmly at her. "He cannot move anything below his chest region, Mrs. Boykin. He has no use of his arms and he has no feeling at all in his legs. At least now. Of course, any paralysis might well be temporary, and even serious paralysis is reversible in some cases."

"How long before we know?" she asks. She whispers it.

"Two or three days," he says.

She sighs and sits back. She feels suspended in time, as though all this is not actually happening.

"What we have here," he says in a professorial tone, as though he were in a lecture hall, "is a probable fracture to the third or fourth cervical vertebra, or possibly both. But, as I say, we cannot really know until we determine the degree of inflammation. When the swelling is down we'll do some X-rays. We'll do a CT Scan or an MRI scan of the neck. Of course surgery is always a possibility, to decompress whatever pressure we might find is being exerted on the spinal cord. But right now he's stable. He may develop pulmonary problems, which is sometimes the case with a rupture of the third or fourth vertebra. I must be honest with you. I must tell you that most patients with this fracture die within a year." She gasps and looks sharply at him. He blinks and almost jumps.

"I'll tell you this, Mrs. Boykin," he says quickly, "because I believe that complete honesty is the best course in these matters. Fractures of the third cervical vertebra are almost always fatal. Your son's life is not in immediate danger. But you must prepare yourself for the fact that he may never walk again, even if he survives the year." She is stunned speechless by what he is saying. He looks closely at her. "On the other hand," he says, "there are breakthroughs in the treatment of spinal cord injuries every day. We are treating him with a new drug, methylprednisolone, which is miraculous in preventing further damage in the next thirty-six to forty-eight hours. We—"

"When can I see him?" she interrupts.

The doctor persists. "We will also treat him with a ganglioside known as GM-1, which will help prevent further damage to the white matter in the cord and will stimulate nerve repair." He makes Jimmy sound like an illustration in a textbook.

"When can I see him?"

"Right away. He will be transferred up into intensive care within the hour. I think you should wait and see him up there. It won't be long. He'll be woozy, but he is stable for now. Oh, yes, he'll have a catheter, to prevent urinary tract infection. Other than that, all we'll really do within the next twenty-four hours is keep him completely immobile. He'll be fed intravenously. Hopefully, he can rest. Try to reassure him."

"About what?" she asks.

"About all that I have said," he says.

"You've sat here and told me my son is going to die or be paralyzed for the rest of his life, and you want me to reassure him?" Her voice is shrill and tight. "Reassure him about what, Doctor, about what?!"

"Please keep your voice down," the doctor says.

Her eyes suddenly flood to overflowing, and she feels as though someone has kicked her in the small of her back. "Fuck you, doctor," Brenda says.

⟶

Wayne sips on a beer. He is sitting in the living room watching an old movie on television, *Niagara,* with Joseph Cotton and Marilyn Monroe. He had fully intended to go into town to the hospital, to be with Brenda, but he had not. Every time he thinks of the boy's injury he shudders. He knows it's bad. He has been around football long enough to know a bad one when he sees it.

And he likes Jimmy Boykin. The boy is wiry and tough. He is the boy that he and Brenda would have had, no doubt about that. He had dreamed Jimmy actually was their child together. In his dream the boy leaped full-grown from between Brenda's legs, wearing a football helmet and a jock strap, and he looked right at Wayne and smiled and said, "Dad." The dream had been so real that it awakened him, and he had been startled to find himself tangled in the wrinkled sheets in his darkened bedroom, all alone. He had lain there listening to that single word echo all around him. Dad. Then, when he was wide awake, staring around in the darkness, someone whispered it to him, from the corner. "Dad." He sat up. Nobody was there. Only empty shadows.

He hears Keith's key in the lock. The boy comes into the living room. He just stands there looking at the beer in Wayne's hand. Even from across the room Wayne can smell perfume on the boy. At least he's been with a girl. Or Wayne hopes it's a girl. He wouldn't put it past some of those creeps in Keith's band to wear perfume. A long silence passes between them. Finally, Wayne says, "What?"

"You know," says the boy.

"It's just for a little while," Wayne says. "I'm gonna handle it this time."

"Shit," Keith says.

"Listen, wise-ass," Wayne says, "this stuff ain't half as bad for you as all that LSD and Angel Dust and shit that you put in your head, so don't 'you know' me, okay?"

"I don't do drugs," Keith says.

"Yeah, yeah, yeah," Wayne says. He can see the lamplight glinting on all the gold and silver in Keith's ears and nose and lower lip. The crown of his head is shiny like a polished melon. He is incredibly thin and he wears little steel-rimmed glasses shaped like eggs. "Shit, anybody that looks like you do takes drugs. Don't shit me."

"What does the way I look have to do with it?"

"Everything. Don't bug me. Go on to bed."

"It's your liver, and your life," Keith says, shrugging.

"You're goddam right," Wayne says.

"Dad," the boy says, and Wayne looks sharply at him. The boy's bald shiny head reminds Wayne of when he had been a baby, when Wayne and Bobbye had played with him on the floor, on a bright red-and-green hooked rug in the house in Athens. Wayne wonders for a moment what became of that rug. Bobbye probably sold it at a yard sale when she moved to Atlanta. He sips his beer.

"What?" he says.

"It ... it scares me when you do that," the boy says.

"Do what?"

"You know ... drink."

"You think you don't scare me? You think you don't scare me every time I fuckin look at you?"

"All right," Keith says. "I should have known you didn't care."

"I care, all right! Goddamit, Keith," he says. He realizes he is drunk. "I'd give just about anything if you ... if you ..."

"If I what? Was a jock like you?"

"No. If you'd just stop ... stop building up these walls between us. Building these barriers between us."

"Me?" Keith asks incredulously. "Me build barriers? Jesus!"

"Well, you do! You're whole life style, the way you look, everything, the things you do, are an affront to me and everything I hold decent!" He knows he is slurring his words.

"Good God!" Keith says. "There's no talking to you, is there?" There are tears glistening in Keith's eyes.

"Where have you been tonight?" Wayne blurts. "What have you been doing?"

"Where have I been?" Keith repeats. The tears are running down his cheeks now. Wayne does not know what to say or do. "Where have I been? I have been swimming with the divine sisterhood," he says.

Wayne blinks. He holds the beer can out to the side. He looks sternly at Keith. "What? What did you say? Sisterhood?" Wayne peers at his son. "Sisterhood? I guess you're goin faggoty on me now, too, huh? Is that it?"

"No, Dad," Keith says. "That's not it."

Wayne sits staring at his son's back as he goes down the short hallway to his room. In a minute Wayne hears music coming from back there, loud harsh unpleasant rock music. It sounds like a series of traffic accidents. Wayne sits there. Somewhere along the line all the fun has gone out of drinking. Bobbye will be on his ass the next time she calls, because she can always tell, even long distance, if he's drinking. Wayne envies the hell out of Bo Stern and the Rhodes brothers, who are probably sitting around Leroy's right now having fun. Everybody else can drink and have fun. Being a fucking rummy is not fair, and it's no fun at all.

He had fully intended to just have a few beers last Friday night, just one short week ago, but he had found himself so shaky the next morning he could not wait to slake that fear of trembling that nagged at him. And the only thing that would do it was another cold one, and he had very conveniently put two in the refrigerator for just that purpose. By Monday morning he had him a couple of pints of vodka tucked away, one in his desk at school and one in the glove compartment of his car. He was not worried. He could coach better drunk than all the other coaches in the state could coach cold stone sober.

"THE LORD NEVER MEANT FOR THERE TO BE NO MIXING of the races," the voice says, and Alex Gresham knows that the voice belongs to a black woman. He is never wrong about something like that. He has become an expert on voices. If it had been some white person pretending to be black, he would have known it in a minute.

"You don't believe in integration?" he asks.

"Depend on who being integrated with who," she says.

"Are you an African-American?" Alex asks. He senses he has a live one here.

"I ain't no African, no sir," she says, "I come from right here in Wembly County."

"I mean your race."

"My name Tanisha Burns, and I a hoo-doo. I put the voo-doo hex on folks. You mess with me I put a little powder of ground-up bone of mink's dick in your coffee, and ever time I blink my left eye you'll fall down in a fit." Alex looks over at Mrs. Martha Norton. She completely misses the reference to a mink's dick and it will go out over the air. Mrs. Norton just smiles benignly back at him.

"Yes, well," Alex says, "get on with what you want to say, Tanisha Burns. We have other callers, you know."

"Don't you now?" she says. Through a big plate glass window Alex sees the office phone begin to blink and he knows it's Joe Callivera calling about the mink's dick. "These white folks round here crazy," Tanisha Burns, if that is her name, says. "They callin up talking bout Otis Hunnicutt really bein a black man after all and not a Indian, well, hell"—Mrs. Norton is now pushing her button—"actin like black folks want to mix up with white folks, mingle and mix up the races, get together between the sheets, if you know what I means. Ain't no white man can match up with a black man in that department, no sir. Little white mens just as well forget it.

They got lil ol bitty whamburgers, they is." Mrs. Norton looks extremely confused. "They pale like a frog's belly, they is. Skin got freckles on it, look like it done got mildewed. What would a black woman want with juice like that, mess her up? No sir. White mens can kiss my nappy—"

CLICK. "The People Speak. Go ahead."

"Alex, this is Malcolm Roland. I've finally got a court date ..."

CLICK. "The People Speak. Go ahead, please."

"How bout them Eagles?!" the voice, a man's, shouts, and Alex says, "Is that a question or a statement?"

"Hey, how bout them Eagles?"

"Are you bragging or complaining?"

"I love them Eagles, man. They gonna whup up on them Bulldogs, man. They gonna go through the play-offs like a banshee!" Miss Martha Norton's finger is poised over her button. It is an excited male voice and she knows that any minute now he will get carried away as they always do. She wonders momentarily what a "banshee" is, then lets it pass. She thinks she has heard her husband Carl use that word, and he never uses profanity. She looks through the thick glass at Alex. He is smiling. Apparently "banshee" is all right. "That Otis Hunnicutt is somethin else, man! I don't care what he is, Indian or Chinaman or A-rab, for all I care! And Freight Train McClain! Man Alive! Has there ever been a coach that ever lived as good as he is?!"

"Why do you keep asking me?" Alex says. "You sound like a nut."

"I am, man. I'm a football nut. I'm a Eagles nut! And I'm proud of it, too!"

"Well, good for you," Alex says. CLICK. "The People Speak."

"Alex, I want to talk to you about this here sex course they plannin to teach up here at the Academy." It's a woman's voice. Mrs. Norton gets ready. The word "sex" is a red flag. "I think the last thing in the world these young people need is some adult tellin em it's all right to have sex. Sex is ugly! Sex is what's wrong with America today! Sex is—"

"Hold on! Hold on," Alex interrupts. "You sound like a walking hang-up."

"This country was founded by Puritans. They kept the functions of the body behind closed doors and in the dark. They knew, and I agree with em, that the ugliest thing in the world is the naked human body! 'And they clothed themselves,' it says in the Bible when Adam and Eve committed the sin of fornication—"

"Wait now," Alex says, but she doesn't.

"They lay down with each other. Sex, that was the original sin in the Garden of Eden, fornication. And today everywhere you look there's sex, sex, sex. Pay attention! Sex is what the devil uses to break down society, to tear down family values! You can't turn on the television without you see some people in bed together, goin at it like a pair of hound dogs, and I wouldn't take my family to no picture show, I can tell you that, with all the bad language and sex in it." Mrs. Norton thinks the woman's heart is in the right place, but she is so passionate that she, too, might slip up and say something she will regret. She is already bordering on it, with the remark about the hound dogs. So Mrs. Norton stays on ready. "I'm just tellin you like it is, Alex. Sex is somethin a man and a woman ought to do to make a baby. That's what the good Lord intended it for. And all these people out there are trying to make it fun! Like it's some form of entertainment or something! And now they gonna teach a course in it to little young'uns with galloping hormones! It's the devil. That woman they got up there at the Academy is the devil's disciple! That's what I think. I call em like I see em, Alex! I've got her number. She's one of these women's libbers. She is a agent of the devil. She is a witch!"

"Her son is in the hospital," Alex says.

"Serves her right."

SIX

Cody picks out the young man because he is wearing army fatigues. They look new and pressed and his boots are shined. His clothes are not from an army-navy store. That is confirmed when the boy tells Cody his name: Byron Bailey, the same name stenciled over the pocket on his fatigue blouse. BYRON BAILEY, PVT. His hair pulled back in a ponytail, Cody wears jeans and a light seersucker jacket with very wide lapels. He had discovered a thrift store on the outskirts of Piper and had bought the jacket there for ninety-five cents.

"Yeah, I'm Wembly County Militia," the boy tells him. He is drinking a strawberry milkshake and eating fries at the new McDonald's. They're still giving away free soft-serve yogurt for their Grand Opening, and the line stretches down the block.

"Could I talk to you? Just for a few minutes?" Cody asks. He puts a small tape recorder on the table between them. He can get some voice-over. Then, if it goes well, some footage later.

"What's that?" Bailey asks, nodding toward the tape recorder.

"I'd like to interview you," Cody says.

"About what?"

"About your experiences in the Militia. Anything you want to talk about."

"You from the paper?"

"*Time* magazine," Cody says.

"The liberal media, huh?" Bailey says, and Cody thinks Uh-oh. But he can tell the boy is flattered. He can tell he is eager to talk.

"I do balanced stories," Cody says, "not like some of these jerks. I'm from the South, originally."

"That right?" Bailey cocks his eyebrow. He looks Cody over. Cody sees his eyes drift over his hair.

"I live in California now," Cody says. "Hollywood."

"Hollywood?"

"Around," Cody says, "you know."

"Yeah." The boy is looking at him sideways. "If you from the South, what do you think about that nigger that sneaked on the football team?"

"I think it's a shame," Cody says. He leans closer. "I hate niggers."

"Yeah?" Bailey says. "You the guy that interviewed Buster?"

Damn, Cody thinks. Why the hell did I say that about *Time* magazine? "Yeah," he says, trying to remember how he had identified himself to Buster. Buster Shirley, his name was. An older man, a supply sergeant out at the Militia compound. He was a television repairman. He had told Cody, "I woulda been career military if it hadn't of been for lettin the queers in. Can you imagine bein in a foxhole with a guy and findin out he's a fairy?" Cody knows he should have stuck to the one story about who he was and what he was doing—the movie scouting—but he can't resist making up things as he goes along. It makes the whole project a lot more interesting.

"Well, I can't tell you a whole lot," Byron Bailey says, "because a lot of what I do is classified top secret."

"I wouldn't want you to reveal any secrets," Cody says.

"I can tell you this," Byron says. The tape recorder is whirring away silently. "Something big is going to happen soon. We're just looking for a cause. And some people think that nigger that claimed to be a Indian might just be it!"

"A cause?"

"Yeah. Something, you know, big."

"Big in what sense?"

"A cause, you know!" Bailey looks impatient. "You have to find a symbol, man. A symbol! You know, like the Federal Building out in Okie City. Something—"

"Wait a minute—"

Bailey holds up his hand, palm out. "Now I didn't have anything to do with that, now. You wait a minute. Don't be tellin me no 'wait a minute.'" He pauses. He seems very angry all of a sudden. "That wasn't the Militia!" He leans close. He whispers to Cody through tightly clenched lips. "You know how I know?" His eyes are feverish.

"No."

"Because," he whispers, "it was bungled. It was the work of amateurs. Those children wasn't supposed to die."

"How do you know that?" Cody asks.

"Never mind how I know," Byron Bailey says. He pops a french fry into his mouth and chews. "Because it's common sense, that's all."

Cody sits staring at the boy across the table from him. He is small and slight. He has clean blond hair and blue eyes. He is what Cody has always thought of as "apple-cheeked." He also looks like a storm trooper. Maybe the time has come to level with him, to let someone, other than Brenda of course, know what he is really doing there. He doesn't want to jump the gun. He could be run out of town before sunset. He leans across the table. "Listen," he says, "how bout if I let you in on a secret, too?"

"Huh?" the boy says. His eyes are open and curious now.

"Let's let this be just between me and you for the time being, okay?"

"My word of honor," Byron says. Cody thinks he is going to salute, but he doesn't.

"Actually," Cody says, "I'm making a documentary on the militia movement in this country. I want to show how patriotic you all are, what makes you tick. I want to show how you're going to save the country, how—"

"Hold on. You are?"

"Yeah."

"What's this, docu-what? What?"

"You know. A nonfiction movie. For HBO."

"HBO? Really?"

"Really."

"Well, I'll be fucked," Byron Bailey says. He glances down at the tape recorder. Then he shrugs. He seems excited.

"But this is just between us, now, for now, okay?" Cody says. "Because we don't want to make the other fellows jealous. That would ruin it. And I'd have to change everything all around, re-write the script and everythi—"

"Wait. Change everything? What are you talking about?"

"You know, I've picked you out. I want to make you one of the center-pieces. One of the stars of the movie."

"Git outta here."

"No. Why does that surprise you? Why not?"

Bailey seems to ponder this for a few moments. He takes another fry and chews slowly and then sips his milkshake.

"You are going to save this country," Cody says, "and I am going to be there to record it. Like that guy who made that picture of the Marines putting up the flag at Iwo Jima. Like the cameramen who were there when the Allies liberated Paris. I'm going to record it for history. For all future mankind."

"Go on," Byron Bailey says, grinning, his face flushed. He nods. After a few long silent seconds he speaks. "Hell," he says, sitting almost at attention, "You are, ain't you?"

~

Wayne sits in the AA meeting in the Elks Hall upstairs over the NAPA Auto Parts store. It's hot and stuffy in the crowded room, the air so heavy with cigarette smoke that Wayne can hardly breathe. One thing about drunks: most every one of them smokes like a stove-pipe and they seem to feel that if they have to give up one vice then by God they aren't going to give up another. Wayne's gut hurts and he shivers with anger. He is angry at them for smoking and he is angry at Roger Coles for what he has done. Wayne's whole season has gone into the pits before his eyes. His chance at a state championship, his new job as a college coach, sending Keith to Juilliard in New York City, every damn thing.

"My name is Tim, and I'm a grateful recovering alcoholic," a fellow says. He sits slouched against a wall in a red ROLL TIDE sweatshirt. They all use only their first names, of course, but Wayne knows everybody in the room. He has known Tim Brabner all his life. He is a pipe fitter and lives over near Calcis.

"Hi, Tim," everybody says in unison.

"I ain't had a slip in eight months," Tim says. There's some scattered applause, maybe from those who haven't made it as far as eight months yet. Most of the people in the room have been sober for years and they aren't impressed. Tim seems to be on a nine-month cycle anyway. About every nine months he falls off the wagon and goes on a toot. "I started drinking when I was eleven years old," Tim says. Wayne squirms in his chair. He is next. He has heard Tim's story about a hundred times, and he knows Tim will drag it out as long as he can. Wayne is looking forward to speaking. To letting his frustration out. They all will have figured out that he has started drinking again because people have discovered that his prize running back is a black after all, and Roger Coles has had the boy expelled from school right here as the play-offs for the state championship are about to begin. A lot of people in this room think they know all the answers. Wayne can't wait to tell them otherwise.

⌐

"But you knew it all along," Wayne said to Coles, "you cheated on his application! You—"

"But nobody knows that, Wayne," Coles said. "Hell, he looks like an Indian. He had us both fooled!"

"Goddamit, I need him," Wayne said.

"Don't raise your voice to me, son," Coles said.

"All right, goddamit, then I quit!"

Coles blinked at him from across his desk. They were in Coles's office. Coles leaned back in his swivel chair. "You better think about that, Wayne," he said, "you just better give that a bit more thought!" Coles eyes were as hard as concrete.

⌐

"I was a violent child," Tim says. "My mama told me I used to head-butt her and bite her on the leg all the time. My daddy used to tell me I was the stupidest thing that ever come down the pike, and he used to whup me when I'd mess up my mama. I bit her so bad on the inside of her thigh that she had to have stitches and she'd bleed like a stuck pig, and I blacked both her eyes a number of times. Nobody could control me. My daddy, who was a big man, would wrap me up in a blanket and set on me, sometimes for two or three hours, me yanking and wiggling and carrying on. I can just barely remember all that. When I started taking a few drinks it would settle me down. It was like medicine. I would break out all over with the hives, look like I'd been stung by a swarm of wasps, and take a few drinks and the hives would go away. You talkin about fucked up, I was. By the time I was eighteen years old I stayed drunk all the time. Got fourteen DUIs by the time I was twenty. I'd leave the house and couldn't even remember where I was going nor how to get back home. And I come to AA. I been sober before for as long as a year. I'm grateful for that. By God." Tim takes a drag off his Marlboro. He looks around the room defiantly, as though challenging anyone to suggest that he isn't grateful.

Then everyone looks at Wayne. "My name's Wayne, and I'm an alcoholic," he says.

A chorus of voices: "Hi, Wayne."

"I fell off," Wayne says. "I fell the fuckin off!" He looks around the room. They all stare at him. There are people in their twenties and middleaged and old people, men and women, and none of them show any reaction, much less surprise. "I don't know," he says, more calmly, "it was just one of those things. I was drinking even before I knew I was going to."

There are appreciative chuckles around the room. It has happened to every one of them before, just like that. "I mean, I had no reason to drink," he says. "I don't need a reason to drink. I know you think—"

"If we ain't got a reason, we'll make one up," Joy Hilpert interrupts. She is a fat woman with a double chin. Big as she is, she is still light on her feet. She is known as the best dancer in Wembly County. She has blond bangs cut in a straight line across her broad face. "It's either a celebration or a wake, Wayne," she says. "We all know about the colored boy."

"It ain't that," Wayne says.

"That's right," someone else says. "Some big disappointment comes along. Take one sip and you're a goner."

"One's too many and one hundred ain't enough," Joy says, nodding her head.

"Goddamit, I don't need an excuse to drink," Wayne says. "I got plenty if I need em. But I don't. If I want to take a drink, I'll by God take a goddamned drink!"

"You need to go to more meetings," a man named Morgan Coleman says.

"I ain't got time to go to meetings," Wayne says, and everybody laughs. Some of them go to a meeting a day, all over the Birmingham area. Sometimes two a day. If you call AA in the city you can find a meeting somewhere most any time of the day or night. "I guess I mean I don't want to go to meetings."

"Who's your sponsor?" someone asks.

"I don't have a sponsor," Wayne says. "I don't need a sponsor."

"There you go. You do, too, you need a sponsor."

"I don't want a fuckin sponsor," Wayne says. All of them smile knowingly at him.

"Uh-huh," Joy Hilpert says. "Of course you don't. A sponsor wouldn't bullshit you. A sponsor would tell you what a dumb fuck you are."

"Maybe so. I'm just telling you how it is, that's all," Wayne says.

"We know how it is," an old man near the back of the room says. "Don't talk the talk unless you can walk the walk!"

"Listen," Wayne says, "I've been sober for years before. I—"

"Dry," the old man says, "not sober. You'll never be sober till you die without any alcohol in your blood. None of us will."

Wayne is getting more depressed. It isn't working at all the way he had wanted it to. He wants again to tell them about what had happened to him in the rehab hospital, but he can never find the words for it. He has never told anybody, because he knows they will laugh at him. Wayne had seen Jesus, really seen him, one day in group therapy. He had actually seen Jesus in the flesh. He knows instinctively that they will not understand it, because everybody, even these drunks, think they know where Jesus hangs out. And they don't. He's not the same Jesus all these church freaks talk about, the same one they pretend to pray to at the Academy.

It had been during family week, the last week he was there, and Bobbye was there. They were in a recovery room with five or six other couples or families, and one boy—a kid spaced out completely on crack, a kid off the streets—and his father—a tired, depleted old man in overalls—had been standing in the middle of the room, crying and hugging each other for the first time in ten years and something had just washed over Wayne, something warm and soft to his skin. And he had felt it clearly because it was as though every one of them in the room—the boy and his father, Wayne, all of them—were as naked and vulnerable as the day they were born and Wayne had been crying, too, knowing that somehow he had finally surrendered. And he had looked up over the kid and his dad's head and there He was, Jesus, just hovering there, looking down at Wayne and smiling, and Wayne was not surprised at all because he had known for a long time—even if he hadn't known that he had known it—that if he ever saw Jesus it would be somewhere like that and not in some church. And Jesus had said to him: "Wayne, this right here is what it's really all about, man. Not all that prayin and singin hymns and stuff." And then he had added, "Don't worry. Just go and use your talent!"

And Wayne is not worried. Damned if he is worried. Not worried, but haunted maybe. Haunted by Brenda Boykin's face. Her face now and her face the way it had looked that hot muggy August afternoon all those years ago, her big liquid eyes collecting their hurt and sadness like a cistern collects water. Standing in the dusty yard in front of that double-wide. She had left the door open and her mother yelled to her from inside to close it because she was letting all the cool air out. Her mother a waitress at a honky-tonk called the Top out on the Old Birmingham Highway, drunk again, probably. "They're white trash, Wayne," his father had said. "You don't want to tie yourself down to people like that. There'll be a million girls at Auburn. Listen to me."

His father had been wrong about most every thing he had ever told him. Big-bellied and blow-hard, Kenneth McClain, a puffer of big, stinking cigars. And his mother Ruth, quiet and dark and thin, rarely speaking above a whisper, his father answering questions for her, speaking for her, speaking for Wayne, too. His parents had moved to Montgomery when he had been at Auburn and they were there at all his games. His father is dead now. His mother is still living, at the Masonic Home in Montgomery. She doesn't know who anybody is. Not even Wayne. She can stay there until she dies because his father had been a lifelong first-degree Mason. His father had died in prison: he had finally been caught enticing—with the promise of candy—a little girl into the back room of his service station and molesting her there among the stacks of tires and the close smells of grease and motor oil. His father. Wayne would never forget his first baseball glove. It had wide stitching around the inside of the pocket. His father bought it and brought it home to him, and all the other boys taunted Wayne, laughed at him. "You've got a softball glove," they yelled at him, "you've got a girl's glove!" His father bought it because it was the cheapest one. And Wayne hung in a kind of equilibrium, a balance between a guilty hating of his father and a need to defend him because he was his father.

Wayne stands up. His face is flame red. "You fuckers don't know shit!" he says.

They all stare at him. He feels himself start to tremble from the inside out. He thinks of Keith's nostril and his lip with the rings in them. "I can't do anything, Wayne," Brenda said to him when he went to see her about what Coles was doing. "The man runs everything around here, including this school. What the hell am I gonna do about it?" She seems sapped of energy these days. Jimmy's injury has taken a lot out of her.

"You're the boss," he said, "where is your backbone?!"

"The only reason you're concerned about Otis, Wayne, is because you need him to play football!" she shouted at him.

It made Wayne so furious that he was blinded by it. Now he thinks of that moment. He thinks of Coles. He looks around at all his fellow drunks.

"I just want you fuckers to know that I quit," he says. "I fuckin quit. I'm not gonna coach another day."

"Awwww, Wayne," Tim Brabner says.

"Listen to me! I quit. To hell with em! To hell with everything!" Wayne glares at them all. "I need a drink!" he says, and he plows toward the door and then goes through and slams it shut behind him.

⌐

Barbara Gleason is the night clerk at the 7-Eleven out on Highway 35. She is a tiny woman who can barely see over the counter. Some in town say that her parents were midgets who worked in the circus, but Barbara doesn't talk about it. She lives alone in an efficiency apartment in an old house near the Shell Creek Covered Bridge, which is listed in the National

Registry of Historic Places, and she sings in the choir at the Church of the New Light With Signs Following. She had to have a special choir robe made, and her head comes up to just above the waists of the other choir members, all women.

It is just after two AM on a Wednesday morning when Barbara looks up from her book—she is reading *The Celestine Prophecy*—and sees the young man and the girl come into the store. She recognizes the young man immediately from pictures of him in the Wembly County Weekly Republican. He is the football player Otis Hunnicutt, the Indian they are now saying is a Negro. He is a handsome boy, light skinned with curly, soft-looking hair, and to Barbara's amazement he looks neither like a Negro nor an Indian. He looks more like someone from the Middle East, from Iran or one of those countries over there, Saudi Arabia or somewhere.

The girl is white and blond, about thirteen or fourteen, pretty. Barbara has never seen her before. She thinks she has seen every teenager in Piper at one time or another, coming in to buy Dr. Peppers or Skoal or Snickers or cold cases of Old Milwaukee she keeps especially for them in the back room. But she has never seen this one before. Both of them seem nervous and Barbara thinks that she would be nervous, too, a white girl running around with a colored boy in the middle of the night in Wembly County. And then almost immediately she knows why they are so nervous. They are going to rob her.

Barbara has been clerking at the 7-Eleven for thirty-four years, and she has never been robbed. There is very little armed robbery in Wembly County, and she has never worried about it. The man who owns the place, Roger Coles, insists she keep a loaded .357 Magnum pistol behind the counter, but Barbara has never fired it. She doesn't really know whether it's loaded. She would not even know how to hold it.

"What can I get for you?" she asks the two youngsters. She's actually a little excited that she's going to be robbed.

The boy pulls a small silver-plated pistol from his pocket. He points it at Barbara. "You can get us all the money in the cash register," he says.

"Oh, I couldn't do that," Barbara says. "It doesn't belong to me. It wouldn't be right." She looks at them. They just stare at her. "It doesn't belong to you, either."

"It does now," the girl says.

Barbara thinks now that she looks familiar, but she can't place her. When Barbara looks closely at her she sees she's older than she first thought. And then the girl suddenly looks younger. There is an ageless quality about her. She's as beautiful as an angel.

"Y'all ought not to be doin this," Barbara Gleason says.

"Why not?" the girl asks.

"Cause y'all are nice chillen," Barbara says, "I can tell. Y'all ain't crooks."

"Yes we are," the girl says, "and if you don't open that cash register you'll find out the hard way."

"Hah," Barbara says, and the boy tightens his grip on the pistol and holds it out toward her. She sees it shaking. The boy wears a tight white T-shirt and jeans, though the night is chilly. The girl has on a nice white dress, though it is scuffed and dirty, wrinkled and stained. Barbara thinks the faint stains look like bloodstains. Barbara stares at the muzzle of the pistol. It is tiny and black, like an eyeball. "It's computerized," she says.

"What?" the boy asks, puzzled.

"The cash register."

"OPEN IT!" the boy says, shoving the pistol in her face.

"We don't keep but twenty dollars in change on the premises at all times," Barbara says.

"Bullshit," the boy says.

Barbara knows that every single bit of this is being taped by the security camera. It will be jerky and black and white and shown on the evening news. Barbara plays it out in her mind. She sees the gun buck in the boy's hand, sees herself grab her chest and go down behind the counter, sees the boy and the girl grab money from the open cash drawer and scramble for the door. It all unfolds in a washed-out, ghostly light on her television set at home, like an old silent movie. Except that she's wrong in the details: Barbara suddenly and unaccountably grabs the loaded pistol from its nesting shelf beneath the counter and comes up firing. She gets off two shots point blank at the boy's chest from three feet away, just as he fires at her, so that the resulting loud quick roar sounds like this: ba-ba-boom! The bullet catches her just under her right eye and exits her head behind her left ear. She registers a flash, a sudden smell of smoke, and a yank as though someone behind her is fiercely jerking her head back. And then she goes black.

~

They get seven hundred and fifty-four dollars. They cut on foot across a pasture behind the 7-Eleven and through some woods. The girl tells him that she knows of a cave along Shell Creek where they can hide for a while. She has food there, and bottled water. "Then you can steal you a car," she says. "Don't worry."

"I've stepped in the shit now," he says. "Ohhh, Jesus."

"Yeah," the girl says, "but I'll take care of you." The woods are dark and shadows fall across her face and hair. Her name, she has told Otis, is Willie Clyde Pitts. "Call me Clyde," she said. She had appeared at the door of the sagging Minetown house Otis shared with his grandmother. She seemed to know everything about him. "You got a rotten deal," she said.

"You don't go to the Academy?" he asked, but it was more a statement of fact.

"No," she said.

"You live in Piper? How come I ain't ever seen you before?"

"Maybe because you ain't ever looked," she said.

All the big universities had seemed to lose interest when Otis was expelled from school. The recruiter from Notre Dame, a fellow named Barnie O'Dwyer, said to him, "We can't recruit you if you don't finish school! And we can't help you do it. We'd get caught for sure. So get back in school."

He had gone to see the Skipper. "I'm tryin, Otis! Believe me, I'm tryin!" Coach McClain said. His eyes looked tired. His hair was limp and unwashed. The little red veins in his cheeks looked like a drawing of capillaries in Otis's biology book. Coach had shaved, but not very well, and there was a tiny cut on his chin and a dried blood smear.

Mrs. Boykin, the principal, seemed distant and preoccupied. "I hate this, Otis," she said. "But ... but ..."

"But what?"

"I don't know if I have the strength to fight the man. He makes the rules. I ..." and she stopped, her eyes drifting off to her office window and out into the parking lot. "I haven't been sleeping well," she said. "I'm sorry."

"I can't stay in no cave for very long," Otis says, "I got to get my Muh-dear and get out of this town!" Then he moans. "I killed that woman!" He is crying.

"You sent her to a better place," Clyde says. "She had to live her whole life as a dwarf."

"You're crazy as a loon," he says.

"It's okay. Believe me."

They sprint across a field and back into more woods. After a while the girl asks,

"Do you know Mabel Perkins?"

"No, I don't know no Mabel Perkins." They hurry through the woods and stiff winter briers grab at their clothes.

"The woman who runs the abortion clinic?"

Otis stops, and the girls stops beside him in the darkness. Otis stands still and silent for a long moment. "Why?"

"Because I want you to go and kill her. Shoot her."

Otis can feel the pistol pressing against his hip, in the pocket of his tight jeans. The woods are black with night and thick, early morning quiet. "Don't fuck with me, Clyde," he says.

"I'm not," she says, "come on!"

⟜

Brenda stands outside in the cool night. The stars are vast over her, like a huge upside-down cup that covers the village and closes it off from the rest of the world.

She wears her sweat suit, but she is not running. She never runs at night. The house is too quiet, too empty, so she comes outside to cry with her mother.

"He's your grandson," Brenda says, "I know how you must feel."

"Yes," her mother says. "And Darlene is my granddaughter. We go on, don't we, we continue on in one way or another."

"Jimmy's dying. They don't give him much hope at all. I want to die myself."

"Don't," her mother says, "it's overrated."

"I've never been this low," Brenda says. "He's all I've got in this world. How can you ever recover from losing a child?"

"Don't bury him yet," her mother says.

The stars are like light airy sprinkles overhead, but a thick heavy weight pushes Brenda down toward the ground. Her legs ache from the constant pressure of it.

Brenda says, "You want something as simple as just the chance to be yourself and live your life, and everything in the world gets stacked up against you."

"You're feeling sorry for yourself."

"You're right," Brenda says, "I am."

⟶

The Pike County Militia is having a daylong training camp at their facility, a large farm that belongs to Roger Coles in the northern part of the county. There are seven hundred and seventy-six members of the Militia, and they wear crisp fatigues and carry US Army issue .45s as sidearms. They have recently acquired a third tank, adding to their vehicle pool that already had six armored personnel carriers, fourteen jeeps, two heavy trucks and a black limousine equipped with the latest in computerized communications equipment. They own two helicopters and two small Cessnas which use an airstrip Coles built on the farm.

The men have been conducting maneuvers and firing-range activities all morning, with AK-47s and rocket launchers. It's now afternoon and they have just heard a lecture on land mines delivered by a man named Austin Potts from the Michigan Militia. Potts wears five stars on his fatigue hat. From the way he looks and the way he carries himself, some of the

younger men thought he was Oliver North when he first appeared. They
are gathered now at a large hunting lodge that has been converted to
their headquarters. Presiding over it all is Calvin Bluett, the general in
command. He wears only two stars. Bluett owns a fleet of oil tank trucks
serving all of Wembly County and most of the northern suburbs of the city.
Roger Coles is commander-in-chief. There's never any doubt as to who is
really in charge, even though Coles rarely attends training sessions such as
this one.

Their chaplain, Newton Grable, is leading them in prayer. "Dear Lord
Jesus," he chants, "help us to lift the heel of the oppressor's boot from free
Americans everywhere. Help us to tame the ATF and the FBI and all the
other three-lettered devil's disciples, the federal government which would
try to take away our God-given liberties! As our Lord said in the Gospel of
John, 'and just as Moses lifted up the serpent in the wilderness, so must the
Son of Man be lifted up, that whoever believes in Him may have eternal
life!' Lift us, Lord! And teach us to lift! Amen!"

He sits down and Calvin Bluett stands up. Calvin paces back and forth
in the front of the room. His camouflaged dress fatigues are starched and fit
his chunky body as though they have been tailor-made. He carries a riding
crop, which he uses as a pointer and for emphasis. "Today," he says, "we are
going to learn about the Freikorpsmen." He stumbles over the German
word. He writes it on the portable chalkboard. The class of young
militiamen begin to take notes earnestly. "The Freikorpsmen," Bluett goes
on, pacing, "were proud and powerful German officers who refused to sur-
render after World War One. The war was never over for them. They later
became the core of Hitler's Storm Troopers. To us, like to them, there is
always a war. The war is never over for us, either! Because there is always
them out there threatening to take away our liberty!" He points out the
window with the riding crop, at the rolling sunlit hills of the farm. The
thick green of the pastures is dotted with yellow and brown autumn wildflowers. The windows are open, and lazy wasps bump against the screens.
"We are the modern American equivalent of the FREIKORPSMEN!"
Bluett shouts. The soldiers write down every word he says.

⟶

Roger Coles smiles to himself as he gets the box of Fruit Loops from the kitchen cabinet. He is pleased he has been able to solve the problem of Otis Hunnicutt so easily. He acted as soon as word got out. He's disappointed that the Eagles probably won't win the state championship, but he doubts that that rummy McClain will really quit. But he wouldn't mind having him out of the way. Roger is troubled by the way Brenda has resisted him, wanting to defy him about Otis.

"My God, Roger, he's a child, a boy," she says.

"He misrepresented himself," he says. "He has to go."

"What difference does it make? No, I can't do it."

"Do it or you will be relieved for insubordination," he says calmly. "And who would pay your son's medical bills if your insurance were abruptly cancelled? I tell you this, Brenda, for your own good. Do as I say. Because I have your best interests at heart. After all, I love you."

Brenda looks very tired. "Enough, Roger, please," she says.

He brings her gifts every day. New dishes. A case of Jack Daniels.

"We need to plan the wedding," he says.

"No, Roger," she says. "I'm not marrying you!"

"It should be a big state occasion, I think. I wish I could marry us myself! But I suppose that idiot Grable will do. I—"

"Roger! Listen to me!"

He looks at her. He smiles. He nods. "Or a small simple wedding, whatever you prefer," he says.

Roger's mother had seen the Fruit Loops advertised on television and insisted Phyllis get her some. He shakes a small portion into a bowl and goes to the refrigerator to get some milk. He has let Phyllis spend the night at home across town with her own family, and he's alone in the sun-drenched kitchen. He can hear his own footsteps echoing in the large house. He always feels good in the mornings, always wakes up with energy, looking forward to the day ahead. He still sleeps soundly. Awakes refreshed. He gets out an opened pound of bacon and sets it on the counter to soften while he is upstairs. Every morning Phyllis fixes him two pieces of bacon and two fried eggs, over medium, exactly the way he likes them, exactly the way his mother always made them for him and his father. He taught Phyllis himself what an over-medium egg is.

He thinks of his father, so long dead that his memory is as vague as a fleeting dream that stuns you with its vividness even though you can't quite remember it. Roger can barely recall the rambling old wood frame house where he had been born, on the family farm in West Alabama, almost in Mississippi. So close to Mississippi, his father used to say, that he could spit out the window and it would land in the Magnolia State. It had been his mother's idea to move to Birmingham after his father died. "You'll not be a farmer, Roger," she said. "Farm if you want to be dirt poor all your life," she had gone on, "go to the city if you want to find your fortune." His mother always pushed the men in her life. It hadn't worked for his father, but it worked for Roger. He and his mother had crossed the Tombigbee and Warrior rivers going east and had come to what everybody was calling the Magic City. The opposite direction from where everybody else was going. People in America always went west, toward water, toward the mighty Mississippi, toward the Colorado and the Pacific. The Coles had come east and now everything Roger touches turns to gold. King Midas Coles, they ought to say. And he owes it all to his mother. If you want to know a man, Coles feels, then get to know his mother first.

With the bowl of cereal and milk on a silver tray, along with a glass of cold orange juice and a small pot of coffee and the delicate off-white bone china cup and saucer—with the matching sugar bowl and cream pitcher—that his mother favors, he mounts the stairs. He hears the grandfather clock in the front hall chiming seven. The house is extremely quiet this morning with Phyllis gone and he realizes he doesn't hear his mother's television. That is strange, since she always watches the Today show. She looks forward to the day when Willard Scott will announce her name for reaching one hundred years of age. She has already written him, sending her picture and alerting him to the exact day. The stairs creak under his weight, and he goes down the dim cool hallway with its waxy, Lemon-Pledge smell. His mother's door is open, the sun spilling into the dark hall in clearly defined rays, and he can see tiny dust motes floating in the shafts of yellow morning light. He pushes into the room, the tray before him like an offering.

He knows something is wrong as soon as he sees her. He stops stock-still, frozen in mid-stride. He feels a sudden coldness, an emptiness that descends upon him so quickly that he is almost overwhelmed by it.

She lies on her side, her face toward him, her eyes open and lifeless and unseeing. Her mouth is open and her thin dry lips are formed into an astounded O. She is so rigid and immobile that immediately he knows that it is not really her, that someone has substituted some poorly made effigy for his mother, his mother of over seventy-five years. Her body is mostly out from under the sheet, as though she had kicked the cover down to the foot of the bed sometime in the night. Her nightgown, too large for her, lies crumpled and bunched atop her fragile body. Her expression is one of mute astonishment, of almost total surprise that this sudden discomfort has stolen upon her in such an unforeseen manner. He stands looking expectantly at her, but she does not move. Her expression does not change.

"Mama," he says, "stop this." She is playing possum. She is playing a trick on him, the way she used to when he was a child. There's no way, after all this time, that God would do this to him. He is Roger Coles. He is King Coles.

He sets the tray on a bedside table and stands looking down at his mother. She can not die. Life is unthinkable without his mother. He thinks of Alberta, of the funeral home with its sickening odor of flowers and air freshener. He remembers the slash in the red earth, covered up by the fake grass, the vault and the dull gray coffin, the surface like tarnished coins, and he can not bear to think of his mother going through that. She will not have to. Ever.

⇀

Alvis Earl Butterworth, the mortician, sits in Coles's living room sipping on a cup of coffee. "I don't know why this couldn't have waited until some more convenient time," he says. It's eight o'clock in the morning. He and Coles have known each other for years. He sits in one of the pair of antique green velvet chairs—one a man's chair with one arm, the other the lady's with two—that Alberta had bought in Highlands, North Carolina.

Coles called Butterworth and asked him to come over, told him he and his mother wanted to discuss plans for her eventual funeral. When Alvis hesitated—"I've got two bodies laid out, Roger," he said—Coles said, "And plans for my funeral, too, Alvis. These are going to be two big, expensive, important events."

"All right," Alvis said. He wears a dark suit and his eyes are sunken and wan, with yellowed bags under them. He wears a permanent expression of mourning. Coles does not know whether it's because he had been born a Butterworth—who had been morticians in Wembly County since before the Civil War—or because he had trained himself so well, or whether his face was locked the way parents tell children their eyes will lock if they cross them. Coles has often wondered just how it would affect a man to embalm dead bodies for a living and go to one and sometimes two funerals every day, seven days a week.

"I don't know what you're in such a hurry for," Coles says. "In your business your customers ought to be pretty patient. Where the hell are they going, anyway? Those two you've got laid out, for example, they—"

"It ain't them, Roger. It's their families. You wouldn't believe the stories I could tell."

"I guess so," Roger says. He does not know how to proceed. He sips his own coffee. Alvis is sitting in the lady's chair, in front of the cold, spotlessly clean fireplace. Phyllis has polished the brass andirons to a dull sheen.

"Well, shall we go up and talk to her, or what?" Alvis asks, glancing at his wristwatch.

"No, we better not," Coles says. And Alvis tilts his head and peers curiously at him. But he says nothing. They sit there in silence, the only sound the ticking of clocks. Alberta had put clocks all over the place. Roger knows that the cuckoo in the sitting room is about to go off. He has fantasies of sitting with his shotgun across his lap and blasting the cuckoo when it sticks its head out, especially to signal the half-hour, when the thing abruptly will pop out and give one sharp quick squeak that never fails to startle him. Maybe he doesn't sit in the sitting room enough to get used to it. He sits there holding his cup and saucer. Alvis Earl is still inspecting him.

"She can't talk, Alvis," he says.

"Oh? Why is that?"

"Because she's passed ... passed ..." He stops.

"Passed away?" Alvis asks. He doesn't seem shocked or surprised. He gives no indication that Coles has chosen a strange way to tell him, if indeed that's the case.

"Don't say that," Coles says. "My mother will not 'pass away!' She is passed to, well, another state. That's all."

"She's gone on a trip?" Alvis asks suspiciously.

"No, no, no, you idiot! Another state of being!"

"Oh." Alvis's flat, solicitous expression does not change. He could be about to say "Your house is on fire" or "Merry Christmas" or "Go fuck an elephant" for all his facial demeanor gives away. His lips slightly pucker. After a minute, he says,

"Everybody passes away sometime or another, Roger."

"I will not allow her to be passed away. I won't," Coles says.

"Sometimes there's not much we can do about it, Roger."

Roger puts his cup and saucer on a small round marble-top table and stands up. He paces to the windows across the front of the house. He looks out through the white columns, across the broad, dull-green lawn strewn with dead leaves. He stands that way for a long time, his hands clasped behind his back. Finally, he says,

"I want you to embalm her, Alvis. Right here. I want her up there in her bed. I want—"

"I can't do that here, Roger, I—"

"I'm not asking you. I'm telling you. Can't you bring your equipment over here? Set up in the sun room or something?"

"You want me to make a house call? I've heard it all now," Alvis says.

"Yes, why not?"

"Because I can't. I've got my equipment over there, my ... my chemicals." He sets his cup and saucer on the carpet next to his chair. "You mean you want her back over here to lie in state. All right. But I'll have to take her over to the home first." He looks around. "Right in here would be nice," he says, "you and Helen Grace will need to come over and pick out a casket—"

"No, I don't want a casket," Roger says. "Listen to me! Pay attention."

Alvis Earl just looks at Roger. He has known Roger Coles a long time. He is not surprised at anything he might come up with. But this one takes the cake. It's very clear to Alvis that Roger does not want to admit his mother is dead—if, indeed, she is—which is a reaction he has seen millions of times. It is equally clear that Roger, unlike all those others, intends to do something about it, that he even thinks he can. "What are you gettin at, Roger?" he asks.

"I want her in her bed. Propped up. Watching television. I want you to ... do what you have to do, fix her so she's, you know, so she won't ..." He looks in terrible pain. He is only making it worse on himself.

"Roger," Alvis says, "let me go up and take a look at her. Are you sure she's dead?"

"Don't use that word, goddamit!" Roger says.

"What are you asking me to do, Roger?" Alvis asks.

"How long ... I mean ... how long ..."

Roger stands framed by the big picture window. "No more'n a week, Roger," Alvis says. "Using the standard, you know, procedures. But I can't do that. There are laws—"

"I'm the law here," Roger says, "and I want her up there in that bed propped up just as long as you can make her last. And I want that to be a long, long time. Do you understand me? You are good. You know what you're doing. What about those Egyptians? How did they do it? Surely you can, too. I'll pay you quadruple. And I order you to do it, Alvis Earl. That's that."

Alvis feels very frustrated. "You don't understand, Roger," he says, his voice a whine, "when you see em in a casket, laid out, it's already started. Sometimes their arms will move up a foot overnight, you can't hardly push em down to get the lid closed, they're like concrete, and the smell—"

"Goddamit," Roger interrupts, "don't tell me all that crap! Just do it! You said using the standard procedures. Well, use superior standard procedures. Consult somebody, but don't tell a soul why you're doing it, you hear? Do some research. I want her preserved, Alvis. I want her right up there in that room propped up in that bed!"

⁓

It makes absolutely no sense at all to Phyllis that Mr. Coles forbids her to go into the old lady's room any more. "I will see to her wishes from now on," he tells her, "or Helen Grace will. She's on a new diet, and she doesn't need much. Dr. Mason says so. And we won't need you here at night any more, so you just come in and wash up the dishes and do the laundry and cleaning and dusting and such all over the rest of the house except for her room. I'll do that. Do you understand?"

"Yes sir," she says.

"Under no circumstances are you to go in her room. And if you can't live with that, then I'm going to have to let you go." She just stands there in the kitchen. He pays her very well, more money than she could have made anywhere else in town. And she does not want to lose her job.

"Yes sir," she says again. And so she stays downstairs. She can hear the old lady's television playing away, turned up louder than usual. Phyllis can hear it faintly even when she runs the vacuum cleaner. She marks the passage of the morning with the shows. Leeza and then Sally Jesse Raphael. Then it's the local news. Mrs. Coles rarely watches the local late-morning newscast because it comes on at the same time as Rikki Lake. The old lady loves Rikki Lake. "Isn't she cute?" she would say to Phyllis if she happened to be in the room. "Isn't she adorable?" Phyllis would mumble inaudibly. She thought Rikki Lake looked like a fat white slob. She acted like she was running for the beauty queen or something. She acted like she was tickled to death at all these fools that went on her show.

Rikki Lake not being on makes Phyllis wonder what's wrong with Mrs. Coles. Mr. Coles ought to have known that forbidding her to go up there would just make her curious as a cat, and surely he knew she would go up there anyway. That's what she's thinking as she goes up the steps. She is carrying her dust mop and her dust rag. The stairs creak with her weight as she labors up. They get steeper every year. She has been working for the Coles since way before Miss Alberta had her first operation, and all that time the old lady has been confined to that corner bedroom in the back. "Phyllis," she would call out, "Phyyyyylis!" "Yessum," Phyllis always said. "I'm comin. I'll be there when I get there."

White folks—the old lady in particular—are some crazy people. Once she asked Phyllis, "Phyllis, do you think you descended from apes?"

"Nome," Phyllis said.

"Well, you are right. There has been very little evolution where you people are concerned."

"Yessum," Phyllis said. And you stink like dog shit, too.

On another occasion she said, "Phyllis, can you read?"

"All I care to," Phyllis replied.

"Can you read the Bible?"

"I can read anything I take a notion to read," Phyllis said.

"Well, here," the old lady said, holding out her Bible. "Read me something from it."

Phyllis took the Bible and opened it at random and said, "Jesus wept!" Then she tucked the Bible under her arm and started out the door.

"Phyllis! Bring me my Bible back here this instant."

"Nome," she said, "I got some more readin to do."

"Phyllis! Phyyyyyyllis!" she could hear the old lady calling as she went on down the stairs. Mrs. Coles is a mean old thing. She once called Phyllis a nigger to her face. Phyllis said, "I wish you wouldn't call me that, Miz Coles." And the old lady looked genuinely puzzled. She said to her, and Phyllis could tell she was sincere, "I don't see why you would object to that, Phyllis. That's what you are."

Phyllis approaches her door. It's almost closed, just cracked, and a thin bolt of sunlight slants into the hallway. The television is louder now, blaring, and Phyllis can tell by the voice that it's the skinny baldheaded man giving the weather. He always acts like the weather is funny. He ought to get together inside the television with Rikki Lake. Phyllis chuckles to herself. They would make some kind of weird looking white babies, they would. She laughs out loud.

Then she steps through the door.

The old woman is propped up in the bed facing the television. Her arms are outstretched as though for some all-encompassing embrace. Her eyes are wide open, little round bright circles of rouge dot her cheeks, and her head is tilted at an odd angle. The first thing that comes to Phyllis's mind are the mannequins in Newberry's window in downtown

Birmingham, the way their heads lean forward in an unnatural way and lock there, so that they appear to be looking at some spot about six inches off the ground about ten feet in front of them. Mrs. Coles is as motionless as a statue. The baldheaded man continues to give the weather. He says that tomorrow will be sunny, with a high of 61. There's a strange smell in the room that reminds Phyllis of turpentine.

"What ails you, Miz Coles?" she asks. Of course the old lady does not answer. She is frozen, inert, her glazed eyes open and staring blankly at the television. Phyllis stands looking at her. "Sweet Jesus Above," she says aloud. "This old lady finally dead."

"I SENT OFF THESE SOIL SAMPLES?" THE VOICE SAYS, a question, and Alex says, impatiently,

"Yes, yes, go on, please."

"You know, took em up in various places around my yard and sent em over to Auburn to have em tested. You have to do it in the winter time, you know."

"What is your point?" Alex asks sharply.

"My point is, the soil around here is heavy with lime. Now, I already knew that. All you have to do is look at your element in your hot water heater, you know? Everybody around here has to replace those dang things ever six months, because they get all caked up with lime rock, and it'll clog up your coffee maker, too, if you don't run vinegar through it now and again. White vinegar, not cider vinegar, because—"

"Yes, yes, your soil! What about it?"

"Well, here's what about it. You have to do things to it if you want it to grow things right. You can't just put the seeds in the ground and then expect it to—"

"That's absolutely right," Alex says. "For best results you have to use wild deer and boar manure gathered during a full moon, and when you spread it over the ground you hold your breath and turn around three times and then say 'Abba Abba Do Do.'" Mrs. Norton glares at him. She doesn't like the "Do Do," but she isn't about to bleep Alex himself.

There is a long silence on the other end of the line. Then, "Ahhh, Alex, I believe you're puttin me on."

"How'd you guess?" CLICK. "The People Speak."

An image, curious and singular, begins to form in the dead of night on the windows of a building that sits between Coles Pontiac and Cadillac and the Piper Twin Theater. The building—built by Roger Coles to serve as his headquarters and as rental property in 1959—is a fifties-modern narrow three-story office structure. It houses, in addition to Coles's Holdings on the top floor, a CPA named Alexandra Robertson, the offices of a construction company called AppleTree Construction, and at street level a hair salon called Way AHead and a small coin operated laundry. On the front of the building, in the center between unbroken outer walls of yellow brick, are nine large floor-to-ceiling panes of plate glass, three on each floor level. It is there that the image forms, faint at first and pale in the streetlights on the deserted street, empty except for Lemuel Bluett who makes his way quickly down the sidewalk in a black windbreaker which he holds tight around his throat against the damp, misty air. He doesn't notice the image, so intent is he on his own next destination, which is the home of Frank Natali, the manager of the NAPA store. Frank has two teenage daughters, Amy and Valeri.

The image on the glass begins with several gracefully curved streaks of color that slowly emerge: blue, yellow, pink and green. It is like a rainbow with a sharply defined curve, outlined in a blue that gradually changes to purple. Up close the design of the image is at first unclear. But from across the street, even as it begins to solidify itself in the glass, it's obvious that the likeness is to a woman, a woman standing, wearing a hood, and the face is a mysterious flesh-colored, cloud-like smear, soft and fuzzy, and the colored lines show a draping stole on the body, a gown, multi-hued but predominantly the same blue and purple. It finally becomes a perfect image, symmetrical and harmonious, like the finest stained glass. It is an astonishing likeness of the Virgin Mary. When Cindy Stockman, the hairdresser who runs Way AHead—the last person in the building for the night—had locked up, the panes had been clear and glistening clean from a recent removal of the water-based green and gold paint that shouted in large letters GO EAGLES! and WE'RE NUMBER ONE! By morning, when the first orange rays of the sun play across the glass, the effigy is firmly in place, the head tilted gently forward toward the street, the faint hint of hands clasped softly across the breast.

SEVEΠ

"Come here," Roger Coles says, "come here now." He unbuttons his shirt. It's always at Brenda's house, never his. This is the time he has set aside for her, a brief stop on his tour of all he owns in the town.

"Women can never be equals to men," Roger has heard Grable say, "in the church, in a marriage, in government, anywhere. It is scriptural. They are unclean, vessels for childbearing. They exist for that." And for the pleasure of men, Coles thinks. He has some problems with what Grable says, but he is not sure precisely what they are. Brenda's body fascinates him, draws him on some animal level. She has a strong smell, but it is rich and fecund. Coles responds to it with an impulsive erection, as quick and tight as a sixteen-year-old's. He has no need for Viagra. No sir. But it is as though Brenda controls his arousal, dictates it. He loves her but she makes him feel helpless. He has never felt that way around a woman before.

"Do you douche?" he asks her, and she looks at him as though he is insane. Her eyes flash with anger.

"Never," she finally says, "get out of my house!"

"I was just jok—"

"Out! Now!"

"No!" he says, "not a chance."

He grabs her. Holds her tight. She is strong, but he is stronger. She curses at him, spits at him. He holds her until she calms down. He kisses her cheek. He is willing to play the game. "I'm sorry," he mutters.

She is not very interested in sex these days, since her boy is in the hospital. She is distant and preoccupied. He forces himself through her shell, because he knows what's good for her. She doesn't need to be dwelling on all that.

Roger tells her when and in what position. "You came," he says, "it was good for you."

"Give it a rest, Roger," she says. He can't figure her out. He is not sure how good it is for her. Sybil always moans and gasps. She thanks him afterwards. These days Brenda acts as though the whole thing is unimportant to her. She is already thinking of something else. He penetrates her body but not her person.

He will try again. "Come here," he says.

⌁

With Wayne it is sustained, longing looks, like a deserted puppy dog's. He wants to erase the years, too. He wants to pretend their history together never happened. Sometimes around Wayne, Brenda has to fight the impulse to cry. He brings too much old baggage, wearing it like a sweater.

She needs emotional involvement. She has it only to a tiny extent with Coles; he is like a picture in another town's newspaper. She is lonely for someone to share her grief over Jimmy but there is no one there.

Wayne would be another flawed child in her life. She does not even consider letting him past the door. She covertly inspects his body, solid and hard inside the thin layer of encroaching middle age. It is better than Cody's in some ways because it is worn and used like an old pair of leather gloves. It would be comfortable and warm. Cody is hot with young juices. Insistent and demanding, like youth. Like her own son. She shudders. With fear and pleasure. She puts her arms around Cody and holds him but he is not there. He has already gone away. His body smells like Ivory soap and garlic.

"Go with me," he says.

"You're here. You're not going anywhere."

"I'm always going somewhere," he says. "We'll take Jimmy with us."

"He can't leave the hospital," she says. "Hush. Just lie still." He struggles, wriggling out of the bed. He is restless and jumpy. He is beautiful, finely sculpted. He pulls on his black bikini briefs.

She wants to be enchanted. She needs an escape. She wants another person who does not have to be told anything. The house seems empty, too quiet. She finds it restful and boring. Soft and nagging, like a mattress with one loose spring.

"I want us to set a date," Roger says.

"Roger, I—"

"There will be a big, a huge, development. Soon. A political thing, but very big. I want you by my side when it happens."

"Look, I don't know—"

"All right. Soon. Look at a calendar. We'll make it a weekend celebration. Hell, a week-long celebration. A state occasion."

"You're not listening to me, Roger."

"No," he says, "I'm not."

◠

Brenda eats supper with Mabel at the Women's Health Center. Mabel has a small apartment in the rear of the two-story Victorian that houses the clinic and she rarely leaves it.

"What I need is a wife," Brenda says, "not another husband. I guess I need to tell that to Roger Coles." She takes another bite of the salad with grilled chicken that Mabel has prepared. She sips her wine. It is icy cold and mellow. The wine is from a green-glass half-gallon jug that sits on the table. "Hmmmmm," she says, smiling. The two of them have almost killed the whole jug.

"Amen," Mabel says. She laughs. "Maybe I ought to kill him for you. I don't think they'd let me get away with killin another one, though!" Her laughter is harsh, like breaking glass.

The two women eat then in silence. The high walls of the old house rise into dimness. Upstairs, in one of the rooms, is a young girl named Kawanna Jackson and her little baby boy Raymond. She has run away from her husband, who does not know where she is. "He'll find out, though," Mabel said. "They always do."

"Roger Coles wants to pay for specialists for Jimmy," Brenda says. "Money is no object, he says. The doctors say it's hopeless, but Roger says we'll find the best doctors in the world. Spare no expenses."

"Wow," Mabel says, "you must give good head."

They laugh again. "I'm going to let him pay it. It makes me feel like a whore."

"Yeah," Mabel says.

"He acts like he owns me," Brenda says.

"He acts like he owns the world, and everything in it," Mabel says.

Brenda pats her mouth with her napkin and puts it down. She frowns. "Dr. Nance doesn't seem to know what to do next. He seems surprised that Jimmy's still alive. He ... he doesn't seem sure of anything."

"Doctors are never sure of anything."

"You can say that again."

"These doctors who come out here, God bless em, some of em are just babies. Some of em don't know doot. And scared of their shadow." Mabel smiles. "I'm grateful for em, though. What the hell would I do without em?" Mabel is a small woman. She is almost fifty but she is still girlishly pretty and her body is trim. She calls herself a freelance social worker, because she has no degree. The clinic is actually owned by a medical group in the city, the only way it can be licensed.

It is a foggy night, warm for December but still chilly. The fog rubs and scrolls against the tall windows. The old house settles and creaks.

"Don't you get scared here by yourself, with all those crazies out there?" Brenda asks. She shivers.

"Sure," Mabel says. "But then I'm hardly ever by myself." She rolls her eyes toward the ceiling. "I've got Kawanna."

"Shit," Brenda says. "And her husband. Suppose he comes after her? What do you do then?"

"I try to reason with him. I call the cops. I dial 911. Whatever."

Brenda stares at Mabel across the table. "Why do you do this, Mabel?"

Mabel shrugs. She looks away, at the dark black windows. "I don't know," she says. She looks back at Brenda. "Because I want to," she says. She stares at Brenda. "Because of you."

"Me?"

"And that pregnancy. All those years ago. It was ... awful. It was too sad."

Brenda swallows. A mist of tears stings her eyes. She does not speak for a long time. "Jimmy may die," she finally says, "my son. And I've got this other child, and she is real, not in this world inhabited by me and you and

Roger Coles and Wayne McClain, but in a narrow private world, in here."
And she touches her chest, over her heart. "She's my secret child, Mabel.
And she's like those children that you read those terrible stories about,
children chained to beds in attics or starved in closets, and I'm the only
one who knows she exists. I know her. I know the shape of her nose and
the color of her hair and her eyes. And I failed her miserably."

"No," Mabel says, "you didn't fail her." She reaches across the table and
puts her hand on Brenda's. The touch of her hand is hot and concentrated, like the sun through a magnifying glass. The two women stare at
one another.

After a long silent moment Mabel says, "Maybe you do need a wife."

Mabel comes around the table and stands behind Brenda. She puts her
arms around her. She kisses the top of Brenda's head, her hair. Brenda does
not move.

"Maybe," Mabel says. She steps back.

Brenda holds her hand. She squeezes it.

"Maybe," Brenda says. She smiles.

"Love you, girl," Mabel says.

"I know," Brenda says. "I love you too, sister."

In the dim cave in the woods Willie Clyde looks at Otis across the
sputtering fire and says,

"Now. Go kill her. Mabel Plunkett. She'll take you in. Tell her you
need help. Then you can shoot her, too."

"Why?"

"Because."

"Why would she even let me in the door? She don't know me."

"Because she is an angel, and you are an angel, too. Or halfway there,
anyway," Willie Clyde says. "Now. Tonight. Take the pistol," she says.

Otis trembles in the dampness. "Why do I want to shoot her if she's an
angel?" he asks. His voice shakes. It is hoarse. His head burns with fever.
He can barely see Willie Clyde, her blond hair and her eyes. She does not
answer him. He puts the pistol in the pocket of his jacket.

Lemuel Bluett is standing on a flagstone patio before wide glass sliding doors. The drapes on the doors are open and the room within is well lit. This is the home of Frank Natali and his daughters. Amy and Valeri are fifteen and sixteen, and they often walk around the house in their bras and panties and sometimes even less. The younger daughter, Amy, is on the B Team cheerleading squad with Lemuel's daughter Krista. Lemuel knows that Frank Natali goes to bed around eight every night because he has to get up at four to open the NAPA store at five-thirty. Lemuel has often looked in on him in the dark early mornings, when he sits in his kitchen and drinks coffee out of a blue mug with WAR EAGLE printed on it in orange letters. Frank watches "The Country Boy Eddie Show" on a little television set sitting on the kitchen counter while he drinks his coffee. Then he spends thirty minutes on the toilet reading *Field and Stream* magazine. He is a widower.

Tonight Lemuel has hit the jackpot. Amy and Valeri are having a sleepover and the two girls staying with them are helping them decorate the Christmas tree. Lemuel knows the girls: Jane Ann Dewberry and Lolly Phillips. Lemuel had earlier perched on the porch of an old playhouse in the back yard, a place that afforded a perfect view of the older girl's room, where all four girls had changed into their nighties. They had giggled and examined each other's breasts and made each other pose in front of a full length mirror on the back of a closet door, rolling their panties down into G-strings and bumping and grinding and carrying on. It was a veritable feast. Now they are in the den and Valeri Natali is on a stepladder, and every time she leans into the tree to put an ornament near the top, Lemuel can see her plump bottom poking out like two smooth pink honeydews.

All the girls but one wear skimpy little nighties with their bubble breasts and nipples plainly visible. Lolly Phillips wears a floor length flannel nightshirt, red and blue plaid, an L. L. Bean, Lemuel knows, because he has one exactly like it. It's cold on the patio, but Lemuel is hot under his clothes. He does not mind the cold. It is a damp, misty night. Rain and storms foil Lemuel, but not cold and mist. Cold and mist he can handle.

The girls frolic around the Christmas tree like nymphs in a pagan ritual. Lemuel then gradually becomes aware that the girls know he's there. At first it's a suspicion, a spark, and then a little flickering flame, and then he is sure. The way they keep posing and "accidentally" hiking their nighties, revealing their fur: two blacks and a strawberry blond. Except for Lolly. She doesn't join in. But the others seem to be having a great time displaying themselves for him, and he is momentarily thrown by the realization that they know he's there. He is disappointed. The thrill goes out of it when he becomes sure someone is aware of him. He does not want them to know he is there. There are clearly-established rules of the game, and they have broken one.

He notices that Lolly keeps glancing at the sliding glass doors, and all of a sudden Lemuel is bathed in harsh white light, and the girls are jumping up and down and squealing. "Daddy! Daddy!" "Mr. Natali! Mr. Natali!" Lemuel is rooted to the spot, startled. For a few moments he can not move. Then he sprints across the back yard, being careful to avoid the lawn chairs stacked there and the concrete birdbath he knows is right in the center of the yard. He scales the high wooden fence, and just as he gets to the top he hears the sliding glass doors shriek open and Frank Natali yell.

"You bastard! You bastard!" Frank screams, and as Lemuel drops to the ground on the other side two shotgun blasts, one right after the other, rock the quiet winter night, and birdshot rips into the fence and into the dry leaves still clinging to the redbud tree just over Lemuel's head. Lemuel begins to sprint down the alley. "Lemuel Bluett, you dirty bastard!" he hears Frank Natali yelling from his back yard, the girls still squealing, all their voices growing fainter as Lemuel reaches the street and dashes headlong toward his house.

⌐

Darlene waits until she hears her parents go into their room and close the door. There is only one bathroom in the house and they have been drinking beer in the living room and laughing at Jay Leno. Earlier Darlene thought she smelled pot, which they also do together some nights. She hears her parents bumping the wall in the short hallway as they stagger to their room. They are giggling.

She had locked her door and gotten out the test and read all the instructions in the little pamphlet. Clear, Pink and Easy Early Pregnancy Test. A little cigar like cylinder with two tiny windows in it, and a tab she is supposed to pee on. She waits until everything is quiet in her parents' room. The night is still. Out the window a halo of thick fog surrounds the street lamp on the corner. Everything is damp and her feet are cold. Even her red chenille bedspread feels moist to the touch.

"You don't have to take any test," Mary says, "because I can assure you you are with child."

"I just need to be sure," Darlene says, "I need to know for myself."

Darlene had recently recalled, suddenly one night like thunder on a clear day, that one of her earliest memories was of an imaginary play friend she had had. Her parents thought it was very funny. The little imaginary girl's name was Mary. But she had not meant that Mary. Or had she?

"How could you be more sure of anything than if I tell you?" Mary asks.

"Well, tell me this, then. Were you that Mary? When I was little?"

"I'm always Mary," she says.

"And you talk in riddles."

"You annoy me, Darlene," she says.

"I'm sorry. I didn't mean to." But she had meant to. Sometimes she gets tired of Mary hanging around, appearing at moments when Darlene would rather she not.

"Aren't you cold, with just that thin shawl on?" Darlene asks.

"I'm always cold. And I'm always hot. I'm always whatever."

"There you go."

Darlene listens at the door. Everything is still. The house is quiet. She goes out into the hallway and there is no light showing under her parents' door. She goes into the bathroom. Everything in the bathroom is a startling bright pink: the shower curtain, the bathmat, the toilet seat cover. The walls are painted a reddish pink that does not quite match the bath set. Darlene looks at the test cylinder in her hand. Clear, Pink and Easy. The little lines in the windows are supposed to show up pink if she is pregnant. She feels smothered by pink. She sits on the toilet and holds the cylinder under her. She relaxes. She sits for a long time before the stream begins, and she worries that she may not be doing it right.

She soaks the tab. When she finishes, she's tempted to look at the little windows in the harsh pink glare of the bathroom, but she hurries back to her room and closes and locks the door. She has to wait five minutes. She looks at her watch. Only a minute has passed and she thinks she cannot possibly wait another four. She paces the floor, looking at her watch every thirty seconds. Finally, the five minutes are up. She looks at the control window. A bright pink line. She looks at the other little window next to it. A bright pink line.

"I told you so, didn't I?" Mary says.

Just then there are two muffled booms, like cherry bombs, across town, and Darlene looks at the window and then back at Mary, or back to where Mary had been standing just seconds before. She is gone.

⌐

Brenda and Mabel stand side by side at the sink and wash the few dishes from their supper. They are both still high and mellowed out. Their faces are flushed and relaxed.

"I let everything get to me," Brenda says, "that school is a zoo. I should never have taken that job."

"No," Mabel says, "you're the best thing that's ever happened to it."

"Shit," Brenda says. "You wouldn't believe it. The other day one of the little second graders—bless his heart, he was just saying it out loud, repeating what his parents had said probably—asked me if it was true that I'd been a prostitute in Chicago!"

"No!"

Brenda laughs. "Can you believe it? And the fact that I want to put that Sex Ed course in, you would think it was the most revolutionary thing ever thought of, you—"

"I heard about it. At the Piggly Wiggly."

" 'AIDS,' I said to Roger, 'haven't these people ever heard of AIDS?' And you know what he said? He said, 'There is no AIDS in Wembly

County. Because we don't have that kind of people here.' That's what he said. Do you believe it?"

"Yep," Mabel says.

"And Jimmy. If I hadn't come back here, he wouldn't be in the situation he's in. I might be gone now if it wasn't for what happened to him. Lord, I tried my best to talk him out of going out for football, but no! I think Wayne talked him into it. I think he did it just to get back at me."

"How is Wayne, by the way?" Mabel asks, and Brenda cuts her eyes at her.

"Whattaya mean?"

"Nothing. Just how is he?"

"I wouldn't know. I don't see him much, except at faculty meetings. He asked me out once, but of course I said no."

"Why 'of course?' Because of Coles?" Mabel's arms are plunged up to her elbows in hot, sudsy water. She hands Brenda a plate and Brenda dries.

"'Of course' because I would never want to get involved with him again, 'of course,' that's why 'of course.'"

"What about that kid? Cody something or other? What is his name?"

"Oh, come on," Brenda says.

"What?"

"He's young enough to be my son." Brenda laughs.

"So?"

Brenda dries the dishes without answering. She thinks of Jimmy, of the ruthless bright lights of the hospital, of the peculiar wire and mesh contraption they have put around his head and neck. She tries to shift her thoughts back to Cody, to his lean hard body, his shiny hair. She does not sleep much and she thinks of him in the night. She thinks of him sometimes when she is making love with Roger. When she was younger she would have felt guilty about that.

"Anyway," she says, shaking her head, "I want to run away. I'm going to run away."

"When?" Mabel asks.

"I don't know. When Jimmy is better. I have no idea. But I'm going to. Again. My life's going to be one long flight!"

Roger Coles is insane. Harboring that letch for her all those years. But she is impressed with that in spite of herself. And he is rich. He is the only rich man she has ever had a relationship with. He wants to marry her. She wants to and then she doesn't want to. "You're too old to be this coy," he told her, and it made her angry. "You're too old, period!" she said back, and he had stormed out of her house. She does not love him. She suspects that love does not matter to him at all. He has even told her that it doesn't.

"I don't care," he said, "I just want you. I want you to be mine. Maybe that'll be enough."

"I don't know if I ever want to 'be anybody's' again," she said.

"Be mine, like a goddamed valentine!" he shouted at her.

His temper is volatile. He never doubts that he is the center of the world. Of the universe. She has never known anyone like him in her life. He likes rough sex, and sometimes she worries that she'll be hurt or that he'll have a heart attack or something. He frightens her, but there's something completely thrilling about him, something erotic about his money and his power. She thinks her life would have been better if she had been as demanding of other people as Roger is.

Both women hear a noise, a thumping, at the same time. They stand very still. They glance at each other. They hear it again. It's coming from the back porch, which Mabel uses mostly for storage. It is a wide back porch, with rusty screens and unpainted latticework, piled high with old magazines and filing cabinets and crates of medical equipment either new and unpacked or old and discarded but not yet junked. The steps are rotting and sagging and need repair, and the back yard slopes off down toward the woods and the creek.

"What's that?" Brenda whispers.

"I don't know," Mabel says. "Listen." She tilts her head. There is nothing now. Only a distant knocking of pipes somewhere in the house. Brenda puts her hand over Mabel's; it is warm and wet, slick from the soap. It is thin and bony, as small as a child's. "Shhhhh," Mabel says. There is a scraping, a footstep, as though someone has walked into something in the dark of the porch.

"Kawanna's husband," Brenda whispers.

"Maybe," Mabel says.

"Call the police."

"Hah!"

"What?!"

"Last resort. Shhhhhh."

⟜

Otis has the pistol in his hand. He can see nothing in the dense blackness of the porch. Yellow light spills out of what must be a kitchen window, into the back yard, across a winter-withered hydrangea bush. "Just go right up to the front door," Willie Clyde told him, "Just tell her you need protection. Tell her the Klan is after you. That you need her to hide you. She'll do it, and feed you, and then you just kill her. That's all there is to it. And then we can go. We can leave here forever."

"I ain't leavin without Muh-dear," he said again.

"Her, too. Now go and do it."

But he can't. He cannot bring himself to walk up to the front door of the Women's Health Center. He stood across the street for a long time looking at the building, the old house. There were no lights in the front windows, but a single bulb burned beside the front door and another over the sign. The lights had misty yellow circles around them. He looked at the lights, the sign, fidgeting from one foot to the other. Then he went down toward the woods along the creek and circled back, up through the back yard to the back porch. Only one room, the kitchen, is lighted on the first floor, and one room upstairs.

Otis takes the pistol from his pocket when he realizes his footsteps are loud on the old porch floor, and when he does tears flood his eyes as he remembers the little woman in the 7-Eleven. "I didn't mean to do that," he said countless times to Willie Clyde, crying, unable to get the picture out of his mind, of her head pitching backward and her tiny body, like a large doll's, jerking upward and backward to follow her head, blood already spurting from where her eye had been. "I didn't go to do it."

"Of course you didn't," Willie Clyde said, "God knows you didn't."

"God knows," he said, crying, "God knows...and then you want me to ..."

He crouches down. He holds himself still. He thinks he hears someone talking softly in the kitchen. A woman. Two voices, two women. They are not more than five feet from him, through the wall. He thinks he can smell them: soap, something pink and sweet. Something clean. He can smell himself, his sour body, the dank muddy smell of the cave. "The Manger was a cave," Willie Clyde said to him, "did you know that? It was. It wasn't some clean barn with sun-dried straw. It was a dark wet cave, stinking with cow and goat and donkey shit on the sloppy muddy ground and noisy with the animals, and it was cold. And there was no way for Mary and Joseph to get any rest at all or to get the baby clean, and they cut the cord with a piece of sharp stone. Did you know that? And they fed the afterbirth to the animals, they—"

"Stop!" he said, and Willie Clyde just looked at him in the dimness of their fire. The choking dry smoke of the burning twigs rose and mingled around her head with the smoke from her joint. Her hair was matted and dirty. Her eyes glowing like the coals. She passed the stick to Otis.

The muscles in Otis's legs begin to tremble. He cannot make himself move. The porch around him is just vague black shapes in total dark. He has the sensation of blindness. He cannot see the shapes but he can feel them pressing in on him. He feels the damp cold in his bones.

He wants to whimper out loud, but he doesn't. He knows he has let himself be exploited by Wayne McClain and Mr. Coles. And now by Willie Clyde. He knows that he has betrayed something or someone, but he does not know who or what. He wishes he had never allowed himself to be pulled into that white world where he does not know the rules. He cannot quite believe Willie Clyde; sometimes she is there and sometimes she isn't. She seems to have an unlimited supply of reefer. She likes to do it with him in the cave. There's something so strange about her that sometimes he is not sure she is a girl at all.

⟜

Mabel goes into her office and comes back with a pistol. It is huge, a .45 that dwarfs her hands. She holds it between both her hands, her finger on the trigger, the barrel pointed at the floor. Brenda knows it's a .45 because it's like Billy's police-issue pistol he carried. He used to get it out and wave it around sometimes when he was drinking in their apartment.

"Is that thing loaded?" Brenda asks, still whispering.

"Yeah," Mabel says.

"Maybe you better call the cops, Mabel. Really."

"Shit. They just want to shut me down." The gun is heavy and weighs her arms down. She looks as though she might drop it on the floor. "They're all in league with your boyfriend."

"Shhhh, what's that?" Brenda says, and they listen. They hear screaming and squealing somewhere in the neighborhood. It sounds like young girls. Then they hear a man's voice, shouting angrily, followed by two loud booms, shotgun blasts, and they both jump and stare at each other. Then there is silence. "What the hell is this?" Brenda says.

They hear stirring from upstairs.

"Whass goin on?" a voice calls down the staircase. The voice trembles with fear.

"Nothin, Kawanna, just stay put," Mabel says.

"Is that Rasheed?" The question echoes in the front part of the house.

"Who?" Brenda asks.

"Her husband." She touches Brenda on the arm. "Go back to bed, Kawanna," she calls out.

"Somebody's on the porch," Brenda says tightly, "I just heard him again. Look, I'm callin 911."

"All right," Mabel says. She grips the pistol, points it toward the back door. The barrel is unsteady.

"Don't you have a security system in this house?"

"Hell no," Mabel says, "just this one." She waves the pistol.

Brenda laughs nervously. "Shit," she says.

The back door rattles. Someone is gripping the knob. The door is locked. "Ohhhhh, Jesus," they hear, "Ohhhhhh, Jesus," and both women turn and Kawanna stands in the doorway, the kitchen light on her like a spotlight. She is thin and gaunt, and her dark eyes are wide in her narrow face. She wears jeans and a pale blue T-shirt. She holds the baby against her chest. She is young, a little girl herself. "Don't let him in," she pleads, "please!" She is shaking, an uncontrollable tremor that wakes the baby and he begins to cry. "Please!"

Brenda goes by her to the phone in the office. She dials 911.

"This is 261 Pettus—" she begins.

"I know the address. I'm looking at it on the screen. What is the nature of the emergency?" The voice is female, clipped and efficient sounding.

"Someone is breaking in. We need the police. Hurry."

"This is the abortion clinic, isn't it? Is this a medical emergency?"

"No," Brenda says, "but it will be if you don't tell them to hurry."

"Is this the abortion clinic?"

"Yes, goddamit."

"Please don't use profanity," the voice says. It is peculiarly disembodied, like a machine. There is no emotion in it at all. "Please hang up and keep the line open."

"Hurry," Brenda says.

"That's all we do, mam," the voice says, "we hurry."

The girl is shaking and crying. Tears stream down her cheeks. The baby is squalling, too, and his pamper is rancid and sour. "Go back upstairs, Kawanna," Mabel says. "Close your door. You'll be all right. The police are coming." The girl runs. She is barefoot, and her feet slap on the linoleum liner on the stairs. The baby boy cries louder as he is jostled up the staircase.

⌐

Otis tries the door and it's locked. He twists the knob several times. He hears a baby crying inside the house. He wonders if he has gotten the wrong house when he circled back. He does not know why he's trying to break in the back way. He instinctively knows that if he goes to the front they will turn him away. Willie Clyde assured him they would let him in, but Otis has no idea why they would, or even if they would. It is a woman who lives here. She does abortions. "She is an angel. She performs anti-miracles," Willie Clyde had said, her eyes feverish over the fire. "Abortions. She deserves to die," she said. "Can you imagine what the world would be like if Jesus's mother had gotten an abortion? She wasn't married, you know. It must have been one hell of an inconvenience!"

Otis is breathing heavily. This whole abortion business is dazzling and confusing to him; he thinks it's because somewhere in the dim past of his childhood he had somehow aborted his own parents. He had never known them, either one of them. "Don't matter what anybody tells you," his grandmother had said to him when he was a child, "your mama was not a whore." He had never forgotten that moment. His grandmother, an old woman who now spends all her time sitting in front of the television set. He does not know if she is really his grandmother, but she has raised him since before he could remember. "You don't know who you are," Wayne McClain had said to him, "so you might as well be an Indian! Ha! You sure as hell look like one."

He had stared at his face in the mirror. His hair is not black and straight but dark golden yellow and kinky. "High Yellow!" the other children had called him when he was small. His cheekbones are high and his face is long and narrow. His eyes look sleepy, drooping and dark green. His eyes sag. They make him look calm even when his insides are surging. Maybe you could say his skin is red. Redman. It is a cream red. It is smooth, without the blemishes of some of his classmates. It looks oily but it is dry and soft to the touch. Willie Clyde runs her lips over his skin, barely touching it, as light as down. She licks it and moans. She licks him and sucks him and weaves her naked white haunches back and forth in the close acrid air of the cave.

They hear Kawanna moaning and crying out upstairs. It is almost like singing. It is a chant, a ritualistic warning away of whatever is threatening her. She is terrified of the man. Of Rasheed. "I would shoot through the door but Rasheed is only nineteen years old," Mabel says. "God, I wish she would shut up. She's driving me crazy! Where are those cops, huh? Taking their own sweet time because it's me calling, that's where." She waves the pistol. "Get away from here, Rasheed!" she calls out. "Do you hear me? Get out of here or you'll be in bad trouble!"

The doorknob rattles.

"Shoot the sonofabitch!" Brenda says.

They hear Kawanna and the baby. It is an unearthly shrieking. It throbs inside their heads. The doorknob rattles again and Mabel pulls the trigger. The gun goes off with such a roar that it startles both women. It kicks Mabel backward and the gun jumps in both her hands like it's alive. The bullet splinters the molding over the door. In the flash from the muzzle—in a fraction of a second—Brenda sees a face through the dusty smudged glass pane in the door. It's a familiar face, one that she has seen before. But the image is so fleeting that she cannot place it. And she cannot move, smelling suddenly the gunpowder and the heat of the explosion. As quickly as the face had appeared it is gone.

There is one prolonged cry from upstairs and then a silence so deep that Brenda and Mabel do not even notice it in the dying reverberations of the gunshot, and they stand there with their eyes fixed on the door, splinters of stained wood dangling from the molding. The silence is as thick as the fog that smothers the house. The gunshot still echoes in their ears. Their ears ring and whistle and then the sensation and the smell of the gunshot fade. They stand very still, looking at the door. There is an emptiness beyond it now that both women feel.

"He's gone," Mabel says.

"Yes," Brenda whispers.

They stand there for a long moment in the deep quiet. Then they look at each other, questioningly, their eyes flicking upward at exactly the same moment to the high ceiling. The stillness is tense. Unnatural and frightening.

They take the steps two at a time. Mabel still carries the pistol, dragging it at arm's length. They go down the hallway. Light spills out from one room. They stop in the doorway, crowding, shoulder to shoulder.

They see the bright red blood on the bed. They see the stained and clotted razor dangling from Kawanna's hand. The baby boy Raymond lies on his back, his head twisted at an awkward lifeless angle, his throat slashed and blood gushing rhythmically with the pumping of his fading tiny heart. They see Tawanna's eyes, hollow and empty of everything now, staring back at them from some ancient lost and mysterious region of the hopeless and the damned.

THE CALL COMES TO CODY KLINGER IN THE EARLY
afternoon of a blustery winter day. Cody is propped up on both pillows in
his room at the Moon Winx, watching an old movie on American Movie
Classics. *Wild River*, with Montgomery Clift, Lee Remick and Jo Van Fleet.
He thinks Montgomery Clift was one of the greatest actors ever. Cody has
been close enough to filming actual movies—art movies—to know what is
spontaneous and real and what is faked. He watches Clift in a scene with
Van Fleet, who is playing an eighty-five-year-old woman (the movie emcee
said she was only thirty-seven at the time). There is no comparison
between them. Van Fleet is all surface, like her makeup. Cody remembers
reading that some actors loved working with Clift, and others hated it.
Nobody ever knew what he was going to do. Not even him.

The phone rings. "Hello?" Cody says.

"Is this Mr. Klinger? Cody Klinger?" Cody recognizes Byron Bailey's
voice.

"Sure is," Cody says. "What's happenin, Bailey?"

There is a pause. "How'd you know it was me?"

Cody thinks. "Your voice is distinctive," he says. "What's on your
mind?"

"Well," Bailey says. Then, "You're not taping this, are you?"

"Naw, man," Cody says. "I don't tape anything without telling you first.
You got my word on that. Scout's honor."

"Okay. Well. Listen."

A long pause. "Yeah?"

"I've figured out somethin. You remember that clerk at the 7-Eleven
that was robbed and shot?"

"Yeah?" Cody says. He sits up straight. He grabs the remote and mutes
the TV. Dim winter sunlight filters through the closed drapes in narrow
beams. The walls are so thin Cody can hear the wind howling, hear it

rattling the gutters on the roof. "Well?" he says, when all he can hear is breathing on the other end.

"Yeah. I know who did it. It was that nigger Hunnicutt, that they tried to pass off on us as a Indian. That Wayne McClain said was a Indian. But it was really Roger Coles that tried to pull that off. It was his idea. I've figured it out. Roger Coles betrayed the white race, and now a white woman is dead, and that boy did it." Another pause.

"How do you know he did it?" Cody senses that maybe something significant is about to happen.

"What is goin on, Cody?" Paul Motherwell Coates said to him on the phone. "Have you decided to move back down there permanently? Or what? Grits got you hooked again?"

"I think I've got some good shit, Paul," Cody said.

"Well, let's hope so," Coates said. "Doug's back from Montana, and all he's got is crap. We've been editing some of it. These people are boring, Cody."

"Never mind how I know," Byron Bailey says. "I know. But won't nobody take me serious. I went to Scroggins. He said it was a professional job, out of Birmingham. Said they somehow made the security cameras not work, had to be pros. But I know better. There's just too much that don't add up, Klinger. There was blood all over the place, blood from somebody else. She shot whoever shot her, that's obvious even to dumbass Scroggins. Her gun was fully loaded and she managed to squeeze off two shots before she died—they found the shells—but they never found the slugs! The slugs must have left inside of whoever shot her!"

"That's what I read in the paper," Cody says.

"It don't add up. There was a bloody trail to the door, and then it just stopped, like the murderer had just ascended into the thin air right then and there!"

"So how does that make it Otis Hunnicutt?"

"There's somethin funny goin on. And I aim to find out what it is. In the meantime, I know that boy is still right here in Wembly County. I seen him, Klinger. I seen him myself."

"Where?"

"Say what?"

"Where? Where did you see him?"

"Never mind. But when I seen him he was runnin. Why does a nigger boy run down the street in the middle of the night? Huh? Tell me that?"

Cody almost laughs. It sounds like an old Southern riddle. He almost answers Because he stole a watermelon? "All right," Cody says. "All right. You tell me how a fellow runs down the street with two bullets in him. Running down the street could seem to me to be proof that he didn't do it!"

"Maybe it was his accomplice that got shot," Bailey whispers mysteriously. "Maybe Otis carried him off. The boy's strong. He's a athalete."

"Why are you calling me with all this?"

"Because I'm the star of your goddamed movie. Unless you've gone and changed your mind on me."

"All right," Cody says. "So. What's up now?"

"Don't fuck with me, Klinger," Bailey says.

"Hey! I just mean what's gonna happen? Now."

"I don't know. I'm just keepin you posted. I'm considerin all sorts of plans of action. And I'll tell you this. One of em concerns Mr. Roger Coles, the so-called commander in chief of our militia that you're so interested in. The script for your movie ain't been wrote yet, Klinger," Bailey says.

"Okay. Noted," Cody says.

"And the other thing is this black Indian boy. He's here. And I'll find him. I don't give a shit what Scroggins says. Scroggins ain't gonna do nothing anyhow. If he did pull him in it would be O. J. all over again." Bailey whispers this next. "I hope you can see the similarities here, Klinger. A black football player and a dead white woman. Figure it out, man."

Bailey hangs up. Cody holds the receiver for a moment in his palm. He bounces it there for a moment and then he hangs it up. He lies back on the pillows. He wonders if he hasn't made a mistake, that Byron Bailey is nothing but a harmless nut who likes to hear himself talk. He lies there trying to piece it all together. He knows there's a story here someplace and he has been hoping that Bailey will play a big part in it. Now he's not so sure.

He thinks of Coles. Cody had seen him down on Main Street when he had gone to shoot color stills of the figure of the Virgin Mary in the window of that downtown building. Articles about it had already appeared in the local papers and AP had picked it up. A full-color picture ran in *The Birmingham News* next to a picture of a teenaged boy named Michael Patton posing with his two-and-a-half-ton ball of foil he had collected since he was a baby from gum and candy wrappers. CAN YOU BELIEVE IT? reads the headline over both pictures.

So many people gathered to see the image in the window that every day now they clogged Main Street, blocking traffic. Coles was there with a man named Justice, who ran the movie theater next door, and they had already roped off the sidewalk and put some old church pews there. Both of the men had been excited.

"Why the ropes?" Cody asked. "You charging admission?"

"Oh no, of course not," Coles said. He peered down at Cody suspiciously. "It's so that people can view the miracle in peace. We call them meditation benches. We are certain that people will come from all over the world to Piper to see it." Cody could see dollar signs in both men's eyes. Hollywood invades Piper, Alabama, he thought. They let Cody get up close to examine it. It was in the glass, all right, not painted on.

"Why don't you make your motion picture about this?" Coles asked.

"Yeah," Justice said, looking on eagerly.

"Good, wholesome, religious family entertainment," Coles said.

"Just the thing that's poison at the box office," Cody said, walking off.

⟜

The sound is still off on the television set, and Montgomery Clift and Lee Remick are being pushed around by a bunch of men. It's a night scene, and it looks like an old silent movie. Cody has seen the movie before, and he knows the men are nightriders. Bigots. Southern Bigots. The sheriff shows up and they all split, leaving Clift and Remick sprawled in the mud. The camera pans down on them. They stir and sit up, both of them covered with slime. Cody hits the mute button and the sound comes on just in time for him to hear Clift say to Remick: "Okay. Okay. Will you marry me?"

EIGHT

It's a mild, brilliantly sunny December day, and Keith McClain and Karla Grist walk in the woods near the old commissary by the closed-down and sealed International Steel mines number 3 and 4. Keith had pulled Jody's brother's car off the curvy road and parked near the decaying building, its rotting timbers giving it the look of a prehistoric dinosaur decomposing in the sunlight. The area is quiet and deserted, the stillness interrupted only by squirrels barking high in the hardwood, in the oaks and hickories and sweetgums, their leaves sparse now and withered and brown against the lofty blue sky. Keith and Karla walk hand in hand, the sunlight reflecting off the rings in Keith's lower lip, nose and eyebrow. Today he also wears two studs in his right eyelid. He wears jeans and a faded and wrinkled denim jacket, and Karla wears black slacks and a black sweater.

"I mean, it's not like I need him, or anything like that. But he's my dad, you know? And when he drinks like he does, he's gone. Gone bye bye. He's all the family I've got. Except for my mom. Hah!"

"I know what you mean," Karla says. "Shit. I don't even know where my mama is. And my daddy. He doesn't drink, but he ain't there half the time, either. He's rockin on his own private planet, man."

"What is it with them?" Keith asks.

"They're all crazy," Karla says.

The sunlight dapples the woods. The path runs down along a shallow creek. They sit down on a fallen log, watching dragonflies darting about and brushing the surface of the water. They sit close together on the log, their thighs touching, her arm around his waist. His little oblong glasses glitter.

"My daddy is so crazy he wants me to go to that honky school of yours," Karla says.

"Why would he want that?"

"Because he's crazy. He said he was going to run for Probate Judge against that Mr. Coles."

"Naw," Keith says.

They sit watching the dragonflies.

"I'm not happy any more unless I'm making music," Keith says. "Maybe I was happy when I was five years old. But not any more, unless I'm making music."

"You're happy at the night ceremonies, ain't you?"

"Naw," he says, "are you?"

"Naw."

He is too thin, and she can feel his ribcage through his shirt. He looks undernourished, even sick, with his lack of hair, with the body jewelry. He is a sight. Karla thinks that next to him she is plain. She thinks that her pale blue eyes make her look washed out and bleached, like some kind of mutant. Her hair is as black as midnight and as thick, like ebony wires. Her hair is the hair of an African princess, her father tells her. But not the rest of her.

"I don't know if I even worry any more about being happy," she says. "I don't even think about it much." He seems lost in thought, watching the dragonflies. She stands up. "Come on," she says, "let's walk."

The path along the creek is well worn with use. They walk deeper into the woods. The trees close together over their heads, making a canopy and shutting out some of the light. They pass through splotches of light and warmth again and can feel the damp ground chill.

They come to a larger clearing. The creek bank is smooth and level. The creek narrows and flows faster, and they can hear it gurgling as it darts between the rocks. "This is paradise," Karla says. "This is beautiful." She looks at him then, her eyes sparkling with mischief. "How bout this?" And she yanks her sweater over her head. She undoes her bra and lets her small breasts swing free. She can feel the cool air grabbing them, caressing them like water. Her tiny black nipples are erect and tingling. She begins to dance. "You hear the music?" she says. "Huh?"

"You're crazy, too," he says. "Nuts."

She slips out of her loafers and pulls her slacks down and steps out of them. She wears only green bikini panties. She leaps around like a ballet dancer. "Come on," she says, "take your clothes off." She rolls her panties down her legs and stands there naked. "Come on. I dare you."

"You're nuts," he says, taking his jacket off. In a minute he is naked, too. His skin is pallid white. He has two tattoos. One, a rosebud, over his left nipple. The other, a mushroom cap, on his right buttock. "My dad's never seen that one," he told her, when she had first seen them. "He flipped when he saw this one," indicating the rosebud. She dances around but he just stands there. His penis hangs down from his thin body in a vulnerable, exposed way. Boys look awkward naked, like things are in the wrong place or something. It always surprises her to see that thing dangling there, looking like an afterthought.

"Come on, dance," she says. "All you got to do is listen and you'll hear the music." They begin to move together, awkward at first. They giggle. They twirl. He begins to do the twist and she can see he's getting excited. Being together, naked in the woods, just the two of them. It's better than the night group, with their friends. Wild. It really is as though they hear the same music. After a while they are in perfect sync, moving in the dappled clearing. The slanting sun seems to focus on their naked young bodies. Then, "BACK IT ON DOWN HERE, BUMPY," they hear, in the distance, yet clear and magnified in the stillness. They stop. Their faces register surprise and shock. They run to their clothes and hastily dress, panting, not uttering a sound.

And then they realize that for some time they've both been smelling a sweet and heady and intoxicating cooking smell, like molasses and cornbread, faint and thin in the winter air, a smell that could have been part dying wildflowers and part the slow fermenting of decaying leaves. Dressed, they go to the edge of the woods. They steal along the creek, close together, breathing together in unison.

At the far end of a deep gully, they can see the still, a large copper tank in a shed, a licking fire and pale gray smoke rising toward the sky. They can smell it stronger now, thick and cloying, and they can smell the fire. They recognize Cajun Rhodes, standing near the still. A double-barreled shotgun leans against a sapling next to him. He wears overalls with a red bandanna tied around his curly hair, which pokes out around the edges. His brother is backing their pickup down two narrow ruts, the back end loaded with sacks of sugar. The truck moves fast. "WHOA!" Cajun yells, holding up his hands. "Whoa, goddamit!" The truck rocks to a stop. Bumpy gets out.

Bumpy goes over to Cajun and they talk. Keith and Karla crouch quiet and still. They both hold their breath. Bumpy keeps pointing toward them. Then both men turn and look in their direction, look right at where they're hidden. There is no way they can see them, but they are looking right at them. Cajun picks up his shotgun.

Keith and Karla ease backwards and then race through the clearing and back up the path toward the commissary. It's a long way. They had not realized they'd gone so far into the woods. They run side by side, and they don't say a word until they're in the car and Keith has them back on the curving road to town.

"Do you think they saw us?" Karla asks, breathlessly, her voice tight and sexual.

"I don't know," Keith says, hunched over the wheel of the borrowed car. "I don't know, but I think they did." He licks his lips. "I think they did," he hisses, his breath quick and electric.

⟜

Roger Coles drives almost into the city before he turns off onto a service road that leads into a K-Mart strip mall in the town of Fultondale. He wants to get far enough out of Wembly County so that his chances of seeing anyone he knows are more remote. He knows the large DrugsAPlenty store next to the K-Mart will have what he wants. He feels self-conscious walking into the store, as though anyone seeing him will know what his mission is.

The store seems deserted. Christmas music plays from hidden speakers in the ceiling, a jazzy version of "Joy to the World." The store seems as large as a football field, and Roger has no idea how to find what he is looking for. The first counter holds Christmas decorations, every kind you could imagine. He browses down the aisle. Red and green lights and electric candles, tinsel and all kinds of ornaments: a whole selection of them shaped like Garfield. Manger scenes, made out of everything from metal to cardboard, stuffed bears with Santa hats on. All of it is on sale for half off because it's so close to Christmas. He doesn't want to ask for help, and besides, he doesn't see a clerk. It's just as well. Any clerk is bound to be a woman.

"Could I help you sir?" a voice says, and it's a woman. No, a young girl. Blond hair with a bright orange tint, wearing a red smock with DrugsAPlenty written in blue script across the breast, and her name: Shauna. He stares at her orange hair.

"No, that's okay. I'm just looking," he says. She starts to turn away. "Hair products," he blurts.

"Aisle Seven," she says. And she disappears.

He is on aisle one. So he retraces his steps to the front of the store. When he gets to about aisle four he sees a blind man standing there with a blue felt hat on, and dark glasses. He has on a shiny black suit and a white shirt buttoned up with no tie. On greasy looking string, a hand-lettered cardboard sign hangs around his neck: HELP YOUR BLIND BROTHER. The man holds a stack of small leaflets in his hand. Roger tries to ease quietly around him, but the man hears him, or senses his presence. Roger has heard of that, that blind people can hear better than normal people.

"Bless you, sir," the man says, holding out one of the little leaflets. Roger wonders how he knows he is a man. He peers at him, trying to get a look at his eyes behind the glasses. He can tell they are open, but they are focused at some spot near the ceiling. The man is either blind or faking it pretty good. The man is young, probably in his early thirties. Roger takes the tract: "FACTS ABOUT BLINDNESS. This person was born blind. Please buy this educational pamphlet for 50 cents, or all you care to give. This man is your brother."

"Whatever you can spare, sir," the blind man says. Roger reaches into the pocket of his khakis, searching for change. His eyes scan down the narrow page. "He was born blind so that God's works might be revealed in him. John 9." Roger finds that just the kind of inverted logic people are always finding in the Bible, the kind that would appeal to somebody like Newton Grable. How could an imperfect man reveal God's works? The blind man is nothing compared to the beautiful and holy image of the Virgin Mary that has appeared on the side of one of his buildings, and yet Newton Grable had the temerity to chastise Roger for putting up the old church benches.

"We must not have false idols before us," Grable said.

"False?" Coles said. "False? Where the hell did it come from, then?"

"It may have come from God to test us," Grable said. "Or on the other hand, it may be a sign of the Rapture to come. Jesus is coming in 2000. To take us all to heaven. But we must not worship this image."

"Wembly County is heaven," Coles said.

"Heaven on earth."

Coles's face was pink. "You'll worship the image if I tell you to," he told the stubborn man. "Is that clear?"

"This is big," Duane Justice had told Coles privately. "This is really big."

"Millions of people will come to see this," Coles had agreed. "It'll get Piper in every newspaper in the world." He was already considering building more houses. "We have to get ready for the crowds."

"Don't worry, you can depend on me," Justice had said, "I'm in show business. I know about crowds."

Roger looks at the blind man. He clucks his tongue. Roger would have called the blind man one of God's mistakes. He finds six quarters and drops them into the man's outstretched palm. "Bless you, sir," the man says.

"Yeah, well, don't spend it all in one place," Roger says. The man does not reply and Roger hurries on by. Something about beggars always rubs him the wrong way. He wants to tell them to get a job.

He finds the correct aisle and is astonished at the number and variety of hair products on display, most of them for women. He goes down the aisle, looking carefully. The whole aisle smells sweet, like a birthday cake. Shampoos and cream rinses in pastel bottles, mousses and gels and hundreds of cans and plastic bottles of hair spray, combs and brushes of every imaginable size and shape, curlers and hair dryers, shower caps and scalp massagers. Finally he comes to hair colorings, still for women; and at the very end of the aisle is a small section for men. The row of boxes at eye-level are even labeled "Just for Men." He looks at the colors. They range from "Black" to "Light Ash Blonde." He realizes he has no idea really what color his hair had once been, only that it was a sort of dark brown. He gets out his driver's license and inspects it: Eyes Br, Hair Gr is all it says. Of course. His hair has been gray for forty years.

He stands there looking at the boxes. He knows better than to get black. He has seen men with soot black hair that looks like it has been darkened with stove polish.

"Find what you were lookin for?" the girl asks. Roger jumps. She has sneaked up on him again.

"Yeah," he says. "Listen, do you know anything about this stuff?"

"What about it?" she asks. She seems suspicious. For a fleeting moment Roger has the impression that she's been watching him to see if he would try to steal something.

"Can I, for instance, get a kind of graying effect? You know, not altogether brown. You know? Leave just a little of the gray. Maybe a sprinkle or two here and there?"

"I wouldn't know," she says.

"Well, Shauna, what do they pay you for?" Roger asks. "Considering that orange hair of yours, I figured you were the resident expert."

"Read the label," she says, then adds, "sir."

Just shampoo in, the label says, youthful hair color in just five minutes.

"Is this stuff permanent?" he asks.

"Beg your pardon?"

"Permanent! Is it in for good once you—"

"Yes sir," she says. "I mean, it'll fade. With time. You'll have to do it again, I mean."

He stands holding the box. Well, he thinks, just buying it doesn't do the deed. "All right," he says. He picks out a box. "Medium Rust Brown" it says. "I'll take this one."

On Christmas day Wayne is drunk. He awoke still high from the night before and had started on vodka and orange juice. Keith is not in the apartment and Wayne has no idea where he is. Everything's a blur. Wayne does not plan to go back to the Academy after the holidays. But that's all he is clear on.

He drives down Main Street in his dirt-streaked car. Empty beer cans and bottles roll around and clink under the seat every time he turns a corner. A big crowd of people has gathered in front of what they're calling "The Miracle on Main Street." People have come out from Birmingham because it's Christmas Day and it's bright and sunny. LEROY'S GRILL AND BILLIARDS is the only business open downtown, except for the theater. Robertson Reboul told Wayne that his business in the bar has tripled since the Virgin appeared. Every time you turn around there's another television crew or newspaper reporter to take pictures of the miracle.

Wayne cannot find a parking space so he drives back to the apartment, parks his car and walks back uptown. People mill around. They stand reverently in groups or hold little children up to see. Wayne stands across the street and stares at the image in the glass. He has seen it a hundred times by now and still is stunned by it. The image shimmers in the sun. A woman stands next to Wayne; she wears a blue cloth coat and has red hair and dark lipstick. "It's a chosen space," she says to Wayne. She holds a candle. She will add it to the hundreds of others gathering on the sidewalk. "It really touches your heart," the woman says.

Wayne feels cold inside. He feels his heart constrict. His stomach is empty and sour but the vodka has soothed it. He blinks and narrows his eyes in the harsh daylight. Even though it's chilly, the sight of the picture in the windows warms him. How can nine panes of plate glass come together so perfectly? God must have done it. That is the only explanation. One of the articles in the paper said that scientists from the University of Alabama in Birmingham had examined it and were baffled by it. They said it probably came from a chemical reaction between rain and metallic elements within the window's coating. They could not explain the flawless symmetry. Wayne thinks the image may have been put there just for him. The colors are as pure and clear as the sunlight. He knows it has some connection to the Jesus he saw in rehab. It speaks to him alone in the midst of all these strangers. He wishes they'd go back to wherever they came from.

The graceful lines quiver and ripple in the glare and Wayne thinks for a moment the figure is moving, reaching out to him. He has the odd sense that the figure is of his own mother. He does not even know he has staggered backward until the woman with the red hair says, "Are you all right, fella?" She looks at him and wrinkles her nose. Her eyes flicker over his unwashed hair and dingy blue sweat suit. Wayne wants to tell her to go fuck herself but he doesn't. He goes down the sidewalk to Leroy's and pushes through the door.

After the sun, inside is pitch dark, momentarily blinding Wayne. He gropes his way through the crowded cafe. All the tables in the front are full. The Rhodes boys are at the bar, drinking boilermakers, and Wayne climbs onto an empty stool next to them and orders one. He throws back the bourbon and feels the comforting burn. He sips the long-necked beer and it mingles with the vestiges of the whiskey in his throat: cold and hot. The Blue-Gray game is playing on the television over the bar.

"You know somethin, Wayne," Bumpy says to him after awhile, "there's white chocolate and there's dark chocolate."

"Yeah?"

"Like pussy. It's all sweet. And I hear chocolate nookie is the sweetest. But some of it is white chocolate and some of it is dark chocolate."

"You're drunk, Bumpy," Wayne says.

"Shit yeah, I'm drunk. Who ain't? It's Christmas, ain't it?"

Just then Cajun comes back from the men's room.

"Why don't y'all ever clean that place up, Reboul?" he says.

"We do," the bartender says. "We can't keep up with the pissers. And if we made the whole wall a urinal, some dick-heads would still piss on the floor."

"Like me," Cajun says, climbing back onto his stool. "Me, I'm used to pissin on the ground. My aim ain't all that good."

"Don't complain, then," Reboul says.

"I ain't complainin," Cajun says. He picks up his full shot glass and tosses it back and wipes his mouth with the back of his hand. "I was just askin a question."

"We was just talkin about chocolate nookie," Bumpy says.

"Oh, yeah," Cajun says. He looks like he hasn't shaved in a week. Wayne wonders when he last shaved himself. This morning? Wayne can smell both of them. They smell like stale dirty skin and wood smoke. "You know, Wayne," Cajun says, "I've always heard that if you want to fuck, git you a white girl, but if you want to git fucked, git you a nigger. Is that right?"

"I wouldn't know," Wayne says.

"Well, maybe you ought to find out," Bumpy says.

"Maybe I will," Wayne says. "What the hell is the score?" They all look at the screen.

"Who cares?" Cajun says.

Wayne is unsteady walking home. The street is still crowded with people. They maintain a reverent silence except for a man with a gray beard strumming a guitar and singing "Amazing Grace." The man wears horn-rim glasses and a red and green caftan. Those Rhodes boys are about as trashy and mean as they come. Full of nigger talk. It makes Wayne think of Otis. He feels responsible for him, and nobody knows where he is. Wayne hurts for the boy. He had gone to the house trying to find him. The old lady was sitting in the living room watching Oprah. The house was too warm, overheated. A red formica-covered table in the kitchen held Otis's school books, propped up as though he had fled in the middle of studying.

"Don't nobody know where he at," the old woman said. "He a good boy, though."

"Yeah," Wayne said, "he is. You tell him to call me. Coach McClain. You got it?"

"I gots it all right," she said, rocking, not looking at him but at the screen.

"It ain't my fault," Wayne said. "What'd he do? Just leave?"

"He went with that white girl."

"White girl? What white girl?"

"I ain't knowed her name. Little thing. Ain't no bigger than a minute. Pretty little white girl. I reckon Otis knowed her."

Wayne feels sick every time he thinks of the boy. Everything had gone so terribly wrong. But then he hadn't promised Otis any more than he'd promised himself. He knows how angry Otis is, because he is himself. He's angry at Coles. He's angry at Brenda Boykin. He's worried about Jimmy Boykin. He's worried about Keith. The boy comes and goes at odd hours. Sometimes since he has been drinking again Wayne awakens in the morning knowing full well that Keith has not been home at all. He can tell by the stillness, the feel of the apartment.

Just as he can tell that his son is home when he opens the door. He can't see or hear anybody, but he knows. It's as though Keith's presence has altered the chemical composition of the air. Wayne stands there feeling nauseated. He takes a deep breath and the nausea passes. Maybe he needs some food. They can drive into town.

They have put up no Christmas decorations at all. For Christmas he had given Keith five hundred dollars to put toward a car. "The insurance—" Bobbye had said on the phone and Wayne had interrupted her. "That old car wasn't worth the deductible," he said, "we didn't have anything but liability on it." "Well," she said, "I'm sure Mr. Meadows—" and Wayne hung up. He hadn't even wrapped the money up and given it to the boy; he had just transferred it into his account. Bobbye had sent a pile of gaily wrapped presents for Keith. Mostly clothes Wayne knows he will never wear. A portable CD player from Mr. Meadows.

Wayne goes down the short hallway. Keith's door is closed; no music seeps through the walls. Wayne pushes open the door. "Hey, it's Christmas, let's—" He stops with his mouth hanging open in mid-sentence. There's a scrambling of naked arms and legs on the bed, and Wayne sees small jiggling creamy breasts and two sets of slim buttocks, one set skinny and pallid white with a tattoo of a mushroom, and Wayne stares at the breasts thinking Well, thank God it's a girl! Then he recognizes the girl and he blinks several times. He knows now what Cajun and Bumpy were going on about at the bar and in his confusion he can't decide whether to be more shocked or proud of the boy. Or fearful, because Bumpy and Cajun obviously knew about this long before Wayne did. "What the ..." is all he can mumble.

"Dad!" he hears Keith say and the girl is pulling the sheet up over them, and Wayne says,

"Scuse me," and he backs out and closes the door.

He goes into the kitchen and opens a beer. His pulse is racing, and he feels hot. He feels embarrassed. He goes into the living room and switches on the TV, to a basketball game, the Knicks and the Heat. He sits there staring at the screen without watching it.

The girl comes through, looking sheepish. She is so beautiful it makes Wayne's breath catch in his throat. He has seen her around town many times, and now he has seen her as naked as a jaybird in his son's bed. She stops and looks at him. She shrugs. When he looks back at her, for a moment he sees only her eyes. Her eyes are icy blue. Like mother-of-pearl or the first Sweet William blossoms in the spring. Her shoulders are slightly rounded with what Wayne takes to be her own embarrassment, but her eyes glint silver with defiance. "Merry Christmas," she says. The front door closes behind her. Keith comes into the living room, his shirttail hanging out. The rings are out of his nose and lip. So you take those out when you do the dirty deed, Wayne thinks.

"I don't want to talk about it, Dad," Keith says.

"You've got a mushroom on your ass," Wayne says.

"Yeah."

"Is it a psychedelic mushroom, or what? Don't shit me. I wasn't born yesterday."

Keith laughs wearily. "It's a tattoo, Dad!" he says.

"How long has this been going on, son?"

"I said I don't want to talk about it."

"Well," Wayne says, "It might interest you to know that those Rhodes boys from up here in the hills seem to know all about it!"

"They do?" Keith says. A grin leaps to his lips, a kind of strained smile.

"You find that funny? Goddamit, son, they're badasses. You don't want to ... to ..."

"To what?"

"Do something foolish. Something that would get those old boys riled up."

"It's not their business. Besides, just looking at me riles them up. They hate me. Everybody like them hates me, and they want to beat me up just for being me. Just for lookin the way I do."

"I got no answer for that, son," Wayne says. He takes a long drink of the beer.

"I know you don't," Keith says.

"Listen," Wayne says, "anybody kicks your ass, they got me to deal with. Cajun and Bumpy included!"

"Big man!"

"But you're playin with fire around here with that colored girl—"

"Don't call her that. Her name is Karla."

"With Karla," Wayne says. He sits looking at his son. "I'm not prejudiced, son. Why Otis is just like a son to me."

"I know! And Jimmy Boykin, too. Why aren't you down at the hospital? I thought surely you'd be down at the hospital, here it is Christmas, with your real son!"

"Keith!" Wayne says. The boy's words sting him. It is true that he has been going down there. Keeping a vigil at Jimmy's bedside. He knows what happened was his fault. As much as what happened with Otis was his fault. He has been going down there talking with the physical therapists. One, an oriental girl named Apple Wu, has shown him all the weights and machines. He told her he wants to be Jimmy's coach when his therapy starts. Apple Wu has long straight brown hair parted in the middle and wears a tight white cotton uniform and gym shoes. She just looked at Wayne, shaking her head. "It'll be a long, long time," she said. On a couple of occasions Wayne almost ran into Brenda, and he slipped out a side door. He did not know why he didn't want her to know he had been down there.

He didn't even know that Keith had noticed he wasn't home, that he had gone down to the hospital. "How'd you..."

"I know, that's all," Keith says. Keith's eyes are looking right inside Wayne's head. They read clearly Wayne's fantasies about Jimmy being his son instead of Keith, of Jimmy somehow being his and Brenda's child, the one she had foolishly aborted all those years ago. It hadn't been his idea, he'd decided. It had been her idea. And that had been the beginning of the end for them. Wayne wants to turn his eyes away from his son's gaze, so guilty does he feel. But he stares back at Keith. He is surprised to realize that he holds an empty can already. He needs another beer.

"Well," he sighs, shrugging, standing up, almost losing his balance, "at least it was a girl you were with."

Keith's eyes do not waver. He does not blink. "Wouldn't you like to know what all I've fucked and that has fucked me?" he says.

Wayne stands there for a moment. He can't think of anything to say in response to that. He decides he no longer cares, because he needs a drink. He stands there a second longer and then turns and goes into the kitchen to get his beer. He hears Keith going down the hall and slamming his door, and in another moment he hears music. It is a Beethoven Piano Sonata that he has already secretly listened to. A beautiful piece, soft and sad, as lovely and sorrowful in its way as the delicate rendering of the Virgin that stands watchful and perilous over the heart of Piper.

Wayne drives into the city. He pushes the accelerator to the floor, and the old Pontiac shakes and shimmies at eighty. He sips a Pabst Blue Ribbon as he drives, listening to Alex Gresham and "The People Speak." Everybody is talking about the miracle. "You can go down there at midnight and she moves and speaks," someone says. "Bull frocky," Alex says. Wayne is still upset at Keith and Karla Grist. He wants to go pound something. He doesn't know how a man is supposed to act anymore. It seems to him that when he was younger it was a lot simpler to be a man.

Maybe he should let Keith go and live with Bobbye and her Mr. Meadows. No, he can't do that. He'll probably have to let them pay for this expensive school in New York next year. Goddamit. The thought makes him grip the steering wheel so tightly that his knuckles turn white. He clenches his jaw until it hurts. The traffic on the expressway is heavy for Christmas afternoon but he hardly notices it. He is going eighty but cars still pass him on both the left and the right. Some teenagers in a gray Lexus cut him off. He mutters at the windshield. The Lexus must be going over a hundred as it widens the gap between them. "Rotate on it," Wayne mutters.

He keeps the car on a steady eighty in the middle lane. He becomes aware of a car next to him, going the same speed in the right lane, and he glances over and somehow the Lexus has gotten behind him and pulled back up even. A boy with long black hair and pimples is driving. He grins at Wayne. He shakes his head up and down like a maniac, sticking out his tongue, making obscene faces. Then he shoots Wayne a bird, his hand flat against the glass of the window. Wayne rolls down the window, feeling the sudden chill of the air. He tosses the half-full beer can over the car, carefully leading the Lexus like throwing to a wide receiver. The can smashes against the driver's side window, foam spewing, and the Lexus slows and Wayne watches in the rearview mirror and sees it swerve a little. He laughs, thinking of the driver's shocked expression when the can hit right in front of his face.

In a few minutes the big gray car is back up even with him, this time on the left. In the passenger seat, a blond girl, pretty, her eyes wide with anger, is yelling something at Wayne. Other kids jump up and down in the back seat. Wayne slows to sixty and the Lexus does too. The girl shoots him birds with both hands. Wayne speeds up and the Lexus stays right with him. He mouths "Fuck you," to the girl. He grins at her. He winks. The Lexus speeds up and cuts him off again, and Wayne jerks the wheel and mutters "Goddamit!" A mile or so down the interstate he spots the car in the emergency lane of the interstate. Arms wave at him as he goes by. He is almost into the city, almost to Malfunction Junction, a vast pile of spaghetti where all the interstates in Birmingham come together.

Then the big Lexus is next to him on the left again. The girl yells something to him, her face red and frenetic. Wayne motions to her to roll her window down, but she doesn't. A boy in the back window yells at him, too. Wayne grins at them. He fishes on the floorboard and finds an empty beer bottle. The traffic is heavier now that they're near the junction. Wayne holds the bottle up and waggles it at the teenagers, who keep yelling soundlessly against the glass and the wind. "Here you go, you little rich bitch, have one on me," Wayne says, smiling, and with a quick sideways toss he flings the bottle by the neck. It spins across the five feet or so between the cars and he sees the window shatter in front of the girl's startled face.

The Lexus slows, and Wayne hears horns blaring behind him. He stays in the middle lane, barrelling through the huge intersection, the tall buildings of downtown zipping by, the cold wind roaring in his ears. He sees the Lexus in the right lane behind him, way in the distance, other cars swerving around it, and just as he gets south of the junction he sees the car, tiny now in his rearview mirror, stopping again in the service lane. He smiles. He hums a nameless tune. He feels better.

Wayne finds a spot in one of the parking decks in the medical center. Instead of taking the sky walkway he goes back down to the street. The traffic is fairly heavy on Twentieth Street and University Avenue. He needs a drink, but he fears nothing's open. Surely there's something open on Southside. He walks a couple of blocks east, the cold wind whipping between the buildings and cutting into his skin. He has put on a jacket over his sweat suit, but the wind is still vicious.

He sees that the Twenty-Second Street Jazz Cafe is open. It used to be one of his favorite hangouts, back when he did things like go into the city to drink and listen to music. They occasionally have belly dancing upstairs, the genuine thing, and Wayne loved the hefty women with meat on their bones who danced. They were different from the skinny kids who table-danced at places like Sammy's Go Go. They were older and bigger. He likes big women. Like Brenda. He pushes through the doorway and almost stumbles going down the steps into the main bar. There's no band, and only a couple of people at the bar. They all look up at him when he comes in.

A boy with a long curly ponytail is tending bar. "What can I getcha?" he says, swiping at the bar with a towel. The boy is thin with a narrow prominent nose and the cuffs of his brown sweater are frayed and unravelling.

"Gimme a Jack Daniels on the rocks," Wayne says. Maybe he'll order a beer next. Maybe he'll have another bourbon. He wonders if Brenda is at the hospital. Brenda would be a great belly dancer. He can remember the way she looked naked as if it was yesterday. He winces as though in pain when he thinks of her naked. Of the way she had been completely open and submissive for him. The look in her eyes. Soft and eager. He wanted to see that look in her eyes again, instead of that hard resisting shell. Cold, all that girlishness shriveled. Dried up. All her "new woman" bullshit. He can tell that doesn't make her happy. He knows it doesn't.

He has another drink. He feels as calm and steady as he has felt in a long time. Back out on the street it is already dusk and all the lights are on, the neon tubing like a child's random sketching on the buildings. One of the downtown buildings in the near distance has its windows lighted in a Christmas tree pattern, tinted green with a yellow star on top. There's lots of traffic on Twentieth Street now, everybody heading for the restaurants and drinking joints on Southside. He hears the grinding of gears and the high wail of sirens around the medical center.

He crosses Twentieth Street with the light and hurries down the sidewalk toward the front entrance of University Hospital. He can see a few cars on Eighth Avenue, their exhausts visible in the dimming air and clouds of steam rising from the manholes. The headlights shimmer golden and seem to reflect each other in the not-yet dark. His stomach feels chilled, empty. He doesn't know how long it has been since he has eaten anything substantial.

The big glass doors open with a sucking sound. He automatically pushes floor eleven. A black nurse on the elevator with him holds a wire tray of tubes of blood. She looks sleepy and tired and she does not speak to him. Her uniform is wrinkled in the back and hiked up to reveal the backs of her thick knees. He imagines that he can smell the blood. She gets off on the ninth floor.

On floor eleven, Brenda spots him before he sees her. When he sees her standing at the nurse's station she is already looking at him, an inquisitive look in her eyes, and he stops and crams his fists into the pockets of his jacket. It's a lined green and gold silk jacket with Eagles Football in script on the breast, still zipped against the outside cold. Brenda wears brown corduroy slacks and a green turtleneck sweater. The sight of her stops him in his tracks. Her eyes are like lasers that trip some alarm inside his head and make him crazy. His first impulse is to turn and run.

"What are you doing here?" she asks.

"I ..."

"That's all right. Jimmy told me," she says. Her eyes seem to soften. She comes toward him. He can feel her body displacing the space between them. It's as physical as if she were actually bumping against him. The harsh white glare of the hospital corridor blinds him momentarily and he blinks, getting her better into focus. He thinks sometimes she has not aged at all, that she has always had the fine lines around her eyes and the almost invisible gray streaks in her hair. When he looks at her the years seem to vanish and it jolts him, stuns him speechless.

"They're bathing him now," she says. Her eyes look him up and down. They register nothing he can see. "Why don't we ..." She stops. "You want some coffee or something?"

"A walk," he says, "in the fresh air."

"You're on," she says. "Let me get my coat."

They walk west on Eighth Avenue, away from the hospital. It is dark now, but the street is well lighted.

"It's as though it's always been like this," she says. "Jimmy's always been in that hospital room, with that contraption on his head. All the other Christmases, everything, all that was just some dream I woke up from. I can't imagine it ever being any different now. You know?"

"Yeah," he says.

They walk with their shoulders hunched, their hands jammed into the pockets of their coats. Her coat is a new lined navy blue London Fog. He wonders if Coles had given it to her. A Christmas present maybe. He hadn't thought to get her anything. He thinks that if he had tried to give her anything it would have made her mad.

"I'm sorry about it," he says.

"Of course you are," she says, "I know you are." She is looking at him sideways. The wind ruffles her hair, scattering it about her face. "I don't blame you, Wayne. I want to, but I don't." He does not reply and they keep walking. "At first I did, but now I don't. I guess it's just stupid to blame you, to take it out on you." Sometimes he thinks he has forgotten most every important thing that ever happened to him, but the memory of how she felt in his arms is so vivid that it's virtually happening to him now, all over again, and his mouth goes pasty.

They cross the broad street and go into a park. The park has evergreens and shrubs and is full of shadows, and in the middle is a statue of a man in a business suit, holding one hand out before him. They sit on a bench under the statue. Wayne has the sensation that the statue is moving behind them, gesturing, grimacing, mocking them, and he turns and looks up and the statue's face is immobile, the arm outstretched and still. The statue is bronze, washed golden by the street lamps. He feels the statue's indifference. It does not even hear the traffic grinding by on Eighth Avenue, the constant distant wail of ambulance sirens.

"It's getting colder," Brenda says. She shudders, pulls her coat tighter around her.

"Yeah," he says.

He pulls her to him. Roughly. He feels her resistance. He thinks the resistance is only tentative. He kisses her on the lips. Her lips are full and astonishingly soft. Her mouth is warm and partly open. He forgets where he is, forgets the cold and the hard stone bench. His arms cling to her and she feels as sturdy and stable as a pillar of concrete. He thinks that some current is pulling him away from her and he holds on and grinds his mouth against hers. He feels her trying to pull away and he holds on tighter, desperately.

She manages to turn her face slightly and she says, "Wayne!" and he is kissing her again, his tongue thick and hot. His arms fasten around her like a vise. She struggles against his strength. He is big, overpowering. She can taste whiskey in his mouth, stale and sharp. His eyes are unfocussed; they look through her and beyond to some other place, someplace distant and confusing. The look in his eyes frightens her. She resists him with all her might.

She had wanted to tell him about Otis, about Otis's face flashing in that one brief instant at the doorway, because she has not told anyone else, not even Mabel, and in the night that one instant image juxtaposes in her dreams with a picture of Jimmy's face and then merges with it and becomes one and she wakes up sweating and wide awake and fully aware that there is some presence in the room with her that she can feel as palpably as her T-shirt, as real as the bedclothes and the night air. She pushes against Wayne with her forearms. She can smell his hair oil and the moldy masculine sweat-stink of his body. His raspy breathing rattles in her ears.

She finally pulls away from him. "Wait...Brenda..." he says. She stands up and backs away, her arms clasped across her chest.

"No, Wayne," she says. He can see her eyes glinting like black marbles. He stands up, too. She does not move now. She does not move further away from him. He takes a tentative step. He moves closer. He reaches out and touches her shoulders with both his hands. He leans forward and kisses her on the cheek. Her skin is smooth and cool. Her head is rigid and still.

They stand that way for a long time. A car goes by, its horn blaring. Then there's quiet again. The tall buildings of midtown tower over them. Then she speaks, softly, "Maybe back then was real love, Wayne. Maybe God gives you only one chance at real love and we flubbed it. And we have to live with it for the rest of our lives."

"No," he says, "I don't believe that."

A lone ambulance wails in the distance. A Southside church's carillon comes on, ringing faintly on the cold air, chiming lonely and chilled: Angels we have heard on high, singing sweetly through the night... The notes are like ice crystals floating through the darkness. Then Brenda and Wayne hear stirrings behind them, movement. They only gradually begin to realize they're not alone in the park. Both their eyes, now fully accustomed to the dark, discern that some of the shadows, lumpy and vague, have eyes, eyes that stare levelly at them. Brenda gasps and moves closer to Wayne.

It is a homeless camp. There seem to be hundreds of people, in clumps and groups, filling the corners and the shadows of the park. All the eyes seem aimed right at Brenda and Wayne. The eyes are flat and tired, ancient eyes and children's eyes, the young ones round and hollow and begging in utter bewilderment. An old man in a tattered overcoat has moved to the bench where they were a few moments ago. He grins a toothless grin at them. He wears a frayed red toboggan, pulled down over his ears. A black plastic sheet strung between two shrubs right next to the bench shelters a

man and a woman and a little girl. They are dirty and lean, their eyes vac-
uous and hungry. They wear layers of mismatched and patched clothing.
None of the three has an outer coat. The little girl shivers. Her silver hair
is clotted and stringy.

"Kiss her again," the old man on the bench says. They hear his
chuckle, dry and mirthless. They do not move. The old man holds out his
hand. "A few pennies for some wine," he says. "It's Christmas."

A horn blares on the street. The light changes at the end of the block
and tires make frying sounds on the pavement. A truck's gears grind. The
constancy of the sirens mingles with the chimes of the carillon—and the
mountains in reply, echoing their glad delight—to make a new hymn, and
Brenda squeezes Wayne's hand until it pains him. The couple under the
plastic are no older than they are. The man has a grotesquely twisted upper
lip so that his face is cruelly misshapen and the woman's eyes are dull and
lifeless. Without any energy at all. The little girl stares with her mouth
open, breathing through her mouth, her nostrils crusty and clogged.

Brenda's closeness and the alcohol that has built up through the day
cause Wayne's brain to spin and throb and the eyes to whirl around him.
He can smell Brenda's skin. In his mind, he can taste her, raw and salty, like
an oyster. In his distorted imagination, she goes with him eagerly, fumbling
at his belt, away from the people and the eyes. They are in his car in the
parking garage, in the back seat, and she heaves her body against him,
naked and open and firm and soft, and he feels his strength returning in his
arms and his legs, the wet warmth of her mouth giving him new soul and
being. It's everything he needs, everything that saves him. It is more than
anything real could ever be.

She is gone, vanished. He thinks he hears her footsteps on the pavement, fading away, but he's not sure. Bitter tears of self-pity and disappointment burn the backs of his eyes. He takes a deep breath. For a
moment he forgets where he is. It's as though he has awakened from a deep
sleep and can't remember how he got here. For a brief instant he's not even
certain that Brenda has been here at all, but he can still smell her. A soapy,
spicy smell, like nutmeg or thyme. A smell warm and moist in the harsh
mechanical air of the city. And then even the smell is gone. He looks

around. All the lonely eyes watch him. The man and woman and the child beneath the plastic sheet look at him. They do not stare. They merely look, as though there is nothing else to look at.

Wayne feels tired, drained. He stands there. He tries to remember where he parked his car. The shrubs and the small trees in the park shake in a sudden gust, and the shadows dance about. He looks at the old man on the bench. The old man grins his empty grin at him. Wayne stands stunned into disbelief, because the old man has become Wayne's father. Wayne's stomach churns and his heart jerks around frantically. He closes his eyes and then opens them again, rapidly, and his father is still there, sitting on the bench. His green work pants are wrinkled and grease-spotted, and his rumpled white shirt is stained with old rusty blood. Wayne narrows his eyes, peering at his father in the dimness. His father's right hand is missing, cut off halfway up the forearm. It is the hand that he fondled the little girl with in the grease-stained shop. It is chopped off, gone. His father holds the ragged stump up, displaying it for Wayne. He grins hideously and his eyes are wide and harsh and fixed steadily on Wayne's own eyes, his gaze as piercing as a bullet to Wayne's heart.

IT IS STILL A LITTLE EARLY FOR LEMUEL BLUETT TO BE OUT and about, but he is headed over to the duplex rented by Tray "Mully Grubber" DeWitt. Tray, or Mully Grubber as everybody calls him, had graduated from Piper Academy three or four years ago and works at Godwin Timber Company, not with Lemuel but in the creosote plant. Lemuel heard him bragging one day at break about all the women he had over to his apartment all the time, so he checked it out. Mully Grubber is a tall, lanky dark-haired boy who likes to float his false front teeth on his tongue and startle people. The way he lost his teeth is one of the legends of Piper: Mully had been a linebacker on the Eagles, and one of the play-off games his senior year had come down to an extra point attempt by the other team with one second left on the clock. Mully had blocked it. The only problem was that his helmet had been knocked off as he plunged through the line, and Mully had soared through the air and blocked the kick with his face, more specifically with his mouth. While all the boys jumped up and down and clapped him on the back and hugged him and the cheerleaders ran out on the field, squealing, Mully was searching in the grass for his teeth.

Mully Grubber bragged so much that Lemuel had to see for himself, and it turned out that Mully had not been bragging at all. If you can do it, it ain't bragging, as the saying goes. Lemuel watched him with a variety of women. One of them, Lemuel had been startled to see, was Pixie Dixon, the town banker's wife, who is old enough to be Mully's mother and then some. Pixie Dixon likes to walk around the apartment naked and do it doggy style. She is a big cheese in the Baptist Church and vice president of the Eagle Forum. Lemuel is surprised, but after all he's seen, not shocked at her behavior. He did say to himself the first time he saw her in the apartment with Mully Grubber, "I ought to write a book."

And there were numerous other women and girls in the apartment with Mully from time to time, among them Lolly Phillips and Trudy

Wilcox, the daughter of a math teacher up at the Academy. And Mully lets his friends use his apartment. So Lemuel looks in periodically, usually early in the evening, to see what's going on. He will put it in his book, if he writes it, that people who are inclined to do the horizontal dance late at night, when they go to bed, usually do it in the dark. If they do it early, they like to leave the lights on. Sometimes they turn on every light in the room.

Lemuel is disappointed to see just boys in Mully's living room, all sitting drinking beer and watching television. Claude Autrey Bowers and Johnny Mack Reeves are there. Mully is slouched in his recliner. They are watching a basketball game, and all the way through the wall Lemuel can hear Dick Vitale's voice: "Better get a T.O., Baby! Better get a T.O.!!" Lemuel thinks that Dick Vitale is an idiot. Any grown man who gets that excited over nothing has a couple of screws loose somewhere. Lemuel eases along the wall toward the back and peers into the bedroom. Empty. Then he sees the light on in the bathroom. The window is small and high, but Lemuel has watched many a woman in there, and men as well. He has lost count of the times he has seen Mully Grubber beating his meat in there. There's a trellis he can stand on, pulling himself up with one hand so that his face is level with the window, and he peeps in.

A boy is sitting on the toilet, reading a limp copy of *Sports Illustrated*. Lemuel sees that it's Clarence Peevy. Lemuel watches him. He can still hear Vitale's voice, distant now and high and squeaky. As he watches his spine tingles and his breath quickens. The boy on the toilet has no idea he is there. The boy thinks he is totally alone. Lemuel watches him lick his fingers and turn the page. The boy's jeans and his boxer shorts are bunched around his feet. He sits forward, his elbows on his knees. His brow furrows and his lips move as he reads. He reminds Lemuel of that statue "The Thinker."

Time seems to stand still, and the moment is exquisite for Lemuel. This is, in many ways, even more a violation than seeing someone completely naked or someone involved in the act of making love. There is an unshared intimacy here that thrills Lemuel. He has claimed a moment that the inno-cent boy mistakenly thinks is his and his only.

Clarence Peevy puts the magazine aside and begins to clean himself. Lemuel watches anxiously this most private of private acts. His breath comes in little pants. He realizes that he is so close to the glass that he's fogging the pane. He pulls his head back. His eyes fix on the boy as he stands and pushes the handle and Lemuel hears the gurgling flush. The boy pulls his boxers and his jeans up at the same time. He zips and then buckles. Then Lemuel thinks the boy looks right at him, right into his eyes. But he is in total darkness, like in a theater. There's no way the boy can see him out here, quietly observing and sharing in his life. Then the boy leaves the bathroom, shutting out the light as he goes.

Clarence Peevy has no idea why he suddenly becomes aware that someone is watching him take a crap. But he does. He had long since finished but he is reading an article about Greg Maddox, an old article since the magazine is about a hundred years old. The last pages of the article are wrinkled where the magazine has been wet. It looks as though it might have fallen into the tub sometime in the past. The *Sports Illustrated* smells like soap.

A strange, eerie feeling just creeps over Clarence. Right out of the blue. He knows someone is looking in the window at him, and he sneaks a look up there, over the pages of the magazine, and he sees a face. A pale, ghostlike face, with eyes fixed on him, and he knows immediately who it is: Lemuel Bluett. He thinks he would have recognized him through the misty glass even if he hadn't known like everybody else in town that this is what Lemuel does. But Clarence Peevy hadn't known until now that Lemuel watched people take craps! He must be a major pervert. The son-of-a-bitch.

Clarence doesn't want to let Lemuel know he has seen him. He wipes and then stands up, giving the guy a good look at his dork. Clarence figures he really will get off on that. He is a major queer, all right. Clarence can't figure it. He knows Bluett's daughter Krista. She is a cute sexy little thing, with a tight little ass, a B-team cheerleader. As normal as they come. Clarence wonders if she knows her daddy goes around watching people take craps.

He looks casually back at the window and the face is gone. But he senses it is still there, like the dark of the moon. He switches off the light and goes down the hallway to the living room.

"Everything come out all right?" Mully asks.

"Yeah," Clarence says, "cept for Lemuel Bluett, watching me take a shit."

"What?" Claude Autrey asks. "What the hell you talkin about?"

"Lemuel Bluett," Clarence says, "he was peekin in the window at me."

"You're crazy, man," Johnny Mack says.

But Mully is already up. He retrieves an aluminum baseball bat from behind the door. "Come on," he says. "Let's go out the front, me and Clarence'll go around to the right and you and Claude Autrey go around to the—"

"Shit, man," Johnny Mack says, "the sumbitch is lyin through his teeth. Ain't anybody gonna watch somebody take a shit, man!"

"I tell you—"

"Move, assholes!" Mully says. "We got him now!"

Lemuel drops to the ground, barely more than a foot. He eases back toward the front of the house. His mind is wandering. He is projecting ahead to where he will go next. He expected to draw a blank with Mully's place tonight, but it turned out well. Not what he had anticipated, but all right. He can hear Vitale's voice clearly again. "He's a diaper dandy, baby, but he's P.T.!! He's P.T., baby!" Lemuel will be glad when basketball season is over and they put Dick Vitale back into whatever cage they keep him in during the rest of the year. He looks into the living room and it's empty. The significance of this hits him at once. Empty.

Simultaneously he hears them coming from both directions and he only half-heartedly stumbles toward the row of parked cars in the back because they're upon him immediately, grabbing him roughly. "Goddamit," he hears Mully say, "goddamit! I knew it, you bastard."

The older man looks frightened, like a pitiful animal caught in a trap. He is a disgusting pervert, frightening all the women in town for years. And if the police won't do something about it, then Tray Mully Grubber DeWitt will, by God! Claude Autrey and Clarence have the man by his shirt, pulling him up straight.

"Please," Lemuel Bluett says, "please don't—"

Mully swings the aluminum bat with both hands and catches the pervert in the temple and he goes down like a sack of potatoes, slumping to the damp ground.

"This'll learn you, goddamit," Mully says, hitting him again, and the bat makes a dull thunk as though it has hit a ripe melon.

NINE

Alex can hardly keep up with the calls. The flashing of the six buttons on the phone bank energizes him, gives him a rush. They make a kind of silent music, with a rhythm all their own. Everybody in town has something to say about the killing. The boys who killed Lemuel Bluett have been hauled in, booked and then released, which is applauded by most callers. "A clear-cut act of self-defense," Sheriff Scroggins called it. "A man has a right to protect his house," a caller says. Alex asks, "You don't think it was terribly brutal?" and the man says "Alex, oh Alex! I can hear your bleeding heart bleeding all the way through the radio!" And they want to talk about Lemuel Bluett. Now that he is dead. Many of the calls are from people—mostly women—who want to relate their own experiences with Bluett. "I seen him right outside there, weren't no more'n fifteen inches from my nose, just a'lookin at me like some old lazy cow, he was." "Why, twenty-five times in the last year at least!" A man: "By God I took him on. I said to him, listen here you bleep bleep bleep, I'm gonna whup your bleep you come round here again, and he was scared of me, too. He knew I meant business. He knew Jeffrey Hicks don't take no bleep (Crap! Mrs. Norton has bleeped out crap!) off nobody! I'm—" CLICK. Sometimes Alex goes from speaker to speaker zip-zip-zip like a montage. Like channel surfing on the television. "What makes a man" "like a little rustlin sound in the bushes, you know right outside my" "can't understand why somebody would want to look at my wife, since bleep bleep bleep bleep bleep" "the Lord says it's a abomination—"

"What is?" Alex cuts in.

"Bein a prevert," the voice says.

"The Bible talks about peeping Toms?" Alex asks.

"Yeah. You know in that parable about Lady Godiva?"

The calls go on constantly. Mr. Thomas T. P. Bloomsbury himself, accompanied by Mr. Roger Coles, comes by the station to compliment

Alex on the job he is doing. Mr. Thomas T. P. Bloomsbury is a little old man who wears a three-piece brown suit. His hair is cut in a buzz and his ears stick out. He looks like a dressed-up small child next to the tall Mr. Coles in his khaki uniform. Both men pat Alex on the back. "You are the conscience and the soul of this town, of this county, my boy," Mr. Bloomsbury says. "Keep creating controversy everywhere you can! Your finger is on the pulse of this nation. The little people look to you. You are the high priest of their culture, such as it is. Never, never say die."

Roger Coles looks at himself in the mirror. He has to swipe the steam away with his hand, making a hole in the collected moisture, and he almost recoils when he sees himself. He looks like a different person. His hair is much darker than he had thought it would be, darker than the example on the box. He looks so different he's startled. But he has to admit that he looks younger. He has taken off twenty years at least.

He ties a towel around his waist and goes out of the bathroom and down the hall. He goes into his mother's room. The television plays against the wall. It is the local morning show. It is weeks now and she has not moved. Her skin looks shiny and pasty, like film on pudding, and her eyes are dry and dusty. But she remains poised, her arms outstretched. "I ain't guaranteeing that pose, now," Butterworth had said. "In fact, I ain't guaranteeing nothing." Coles has Renuzit room deodorizers sitting discreetly on every flat surface. The room smells like vanilla and peaches. His mother loves peaches.

"Well, what do you think?" he asks. After a minute he says, "I like it, too," and he turns to the mirror over her dressing table and picks up one of her pearl-handled combs and combs his hair, humming.

"She'll marry you now, surely," his mother says, behind him.

"Yes," he says, running the comb through his damp hair.

"You look more her age now. She'll come around. Or if she doesn't you just take her! Like Henry the Eighth!" She chuckles. "If she balks again, you just take her, son!"

Coles can see his mother in the mirror behind him. She is chuckling again. The sunlight from the window sprinkles her bed with tiny specks of diamond dust. Roger thinks of Brenda and he thinks of the beautiful image of Mary that continues to shine from the windows on his downtown building. Somebody—teenagers, he thinks, and Scroggins suspects the same— threw battery acid on part of the image. He had been infuriated, because the apparition had lost some of its artistic precision for a few days, but over one night the scar had mysteriously healed itself and now it was back like it had originally been and the crowds were larger, and the stupid scientists from universities all over the Southeast and one guy from as far away as MIT were even more confused and befuddled. Coles doesn't know where it came from or why it's there. He doesn't care. He takes it as a sign that God approves of everything he's doing, his county and his Militia and everything else. And he knows a gold mine when he sees it.

"It gives me the creeps," Brenda said.

"Why?" he blurted incredulously, wrinkling his brow, looking closely at her.

"I don't know," she said. "It's not the right place. Something's screwy about it."

"I guess you know," his mother says to him now, "that I posed for that picture down there. That woman in that glass is me."

Coles smiles, looking at his own image in the glass. He shakes his head, grinning back at himself. His hair is dark rich brown, the color of youth. The stillness of the house surrounds him like a soft down comforter.

⌐

"What's happened to Jessie Owens?" A.J. Grist asks his daughter, and she looks sideways at him, irritated.

"I don't know any Jessie Owens," she says.

"Don't get lippy with me," he says.

"I don't know him, that's all."

"The boy on the football team."

"Otis! I don't know," she says. Her father sits across the table from her. He still wears his suit, his neat tie tight around his neck. He has just walked in from his office. He looks as neat and unruffled as he had looked when he had left the house this morning.

"Because wherever he is," her father says, "he's not going to that school anymore. So I want you to go. I want you to enroll, with school started back. You're not a Negro, you're multiracial, but they don't know that. They—"

"I don't want to go to that school!"

"Do you realize how many times you've said 'I don't' since we started this conversation?"

"No," she says.

"Sometimes we have to do things we don't want to do. I don't want to run for Probate Judge, either, but somebody has to run against that demagogue. Somebody—"

"Why does it have to be you? Why don't we move away from this place? This place is shit."

"Don't talk like that."

"Well, it is!"

"I have my practice here. This is our home."

"You got to be kiddin." She sits shredding a paper napkin with her fingers. It's supper time and they will eat TV dinners from the freezer. Or they'll go and get barbecue take-out. Or a Subway or a sandwich from the new McDonald's. She has been waiting for the bomb to drop: for Keith's father to tell her father about walking in on them and then whatever her father will say. She senses that he's suspicious that she's doing somebody; they don't talk about it, but she is sure that her father will like it even less that it's a white guy. Even though her mother was white. She wants to stand up and scream. She hates all this about skin color. She wishes everybody in the world was blind and you could only go by feel.

"They've already started the new semester," A.J. Grist says.

She sighs wearily. "You can go with me," Keith had said. "New York is a big city. We can get lost there." Maybe she will. Anyplace would be better than here.

"I told you," she says. "Listen up. I'm not goin to that freakin school!"

"Among our people," he says, "young people don't talk to their parents like that."

"Our people?! What are you talkin about? You just said I wasn't a Negro. You—"

"You know what I mean, Karla. We'll talk about it later."

"No we won't, either," she says, and her eyes look just like her mother's, as sharp as tacks, and just as mean and wounding.

Colleen Purdy is reading from a black paperback. Some of the others have copies, too. *The Satanic Rituals: A Companion to the Satanic Bible,* by Anton Szandor LaVey. All the books have been stolen from various Books-A-Million stores around Birmingham. It is against the coven's rules to buy one. Colleen wears a hooded black robe.

"Before the mighty and ineffable Prince of Darkness, and in the presence of all the dread demons of the Pit, and this assembled company, I acknowledge and confess my past error. Renouncing all past allegiances, I proclaim that Satan-Lucifer rules the earth, and I ratify and renew my promise to recognize and honor Him in all things, without reservation, desiring in return His manifold assistance in the successful completion of my endeavors and the fulfillment of my desires. I call upon you, my brother and sisters, to bear witness and to do likewise."

Keith McClain is here, and Karla Grist and Lolly Phillips and Jayne Ann Dewberry. They all begin to read a response to what Colleen has read. And Darlene Vick is here, too. Darlene sits in an old aluminum folding chair with sagging webbing. They have bound her wrists to the arms of the chair with soft silk ropes. Her eyes are wide at the goings-on.

"It's a little club," Colleen told her. "A sort of sorority plus one. One guy. And we have a little initiation. It may sound weird but it's just fun. You know?"

They are in a clearing deep in the woods, along Shell Creek. A bonfire crackles with red sparks shooting upward to where the bare branches of the trees loom in a wide circle overhead, and black candles burn on a raised place on the ground. There is a small wooden table to the side with a chalice. An inverted cross hangs from a mulberry bush behind the raised ground. Darlene is uneasy with it all. "It's based on Le Messe Noir," Colleen told her, "but it's all in fun! It's way cool." Darlene did not know what she was talking about, but had not let on. She was so pleased to be asked to join. Now she is not so sure.

Lolly Phillips is the only other person with a black robe on, and she walks up onto the raised earth. Darlene is astounded when Lolly drops the robe and stands there completely naked. Then she lies down, her legs toward the group. She spreads her legs wide. Her pubis is plainly visible in the firelight. Colleen takes the chalice and places it between her legs. She puts a burning black candle next to it, and a small silver saucer with what looks like a slice of dark bread. The others look on with rapt eyes. Darlene looks around at them. She tries to shrink in the chair. "You are a virgin, aren't you?" Colleen had asked her after school, when they were walking down the sidewalk in the sunshine, and Darlene had not known what to say. "Because you need to be a virgin to join."

"Yes, of course," Darlene had said, thinking of the child growing within her. Duane Justice's child. She squirms in the chair, pulling at the ropes. She wonders where Mary is now. She is sure she is somewhere close by, watching. She looks around at the bulging shadows, the faintly visible tree trunks rising like pylons into the darkness. The first time she had seen the image of Mary in the glass she stood in awe, her entire being awash with the intense heat that radiated from it. She had trembled. Her mouth was open but she was unable to make a sound. The image was locked there in the fragile stillness of time: Darlene had known that any minute, any second, the image would disappear forever, would dissolve into vapor, and the anxiety of that knowledge had caused a deep flush to grow in her face.

"What's the matter?" Mr. Justice had said, inspecting her closely. She didn't answer. "It's really something, isn't it?" he asked.

She could not answer. She could not form words. She had no idea whether she was losing her mind completely or if this was maturity and sanity. She could feel the child stirring in her insides. The image of the Virgin seemed to pulse like a strobe light inside her head. Mary was incongruous here, trapped in the glass. On the street with people staring at Her and cars going by. Darlene got a penetrating, throbbing headache just looking at Her.

In Mr. Justice's office she watched him writing something in a ledger. He was so good-looking that whenever she was around him all she wanted to do was touch him. In her dreams she felt his heavy hard body over hers. She felt his finger tickling at the top of her vagina and his tongue all over her body. He had taught her to take him in her mouth and she had loved it, an eager learner, and after the first time she had avoided Mary's eyes until Mary had said, "Darlene, Darlene, don't you know I was watching? There are no secrets from me."

Mr. Justice was everything Darlene's inept father was not. Mr. Justice wore a white shirt and a paisley tie, and her father owned only one tie, a bright blue polyester clip-on that he wore to the occasional funerals they attended. Mr. Justice had a thick, trim mustache and smelled like Brut cologne. Her father smelled like beer and sour milk. Even the way Mr. Justice held the ballpoint pen was graceful and masculine. He was sophisticated and worldly. She wanted to be his completely.

"Mr. Justice," she said, "sometimes the Virgin Mary talks to me."

"Say what?" he said without looking up. He continued writing, chewing on his lip.

"Sometimes Mary talks to me."

He looked up. "A joke?" he said. He chuckled. "That Mary?" he asked, jabbing the pen toward the front of the theater and the street. "It's like a photograph, Darlene, like when you take a photograph. One of those guys from UAB explained it to me. Like the glass is a negative, or a piece of film or some such, I don't know, but it's the same principle, he said, kind of like a flashbulb goin off or some such, only it's the sunlight and all kinds of chemicals in the glass. This guy thought that maybe there was some woman standing there looking in the window when some lightning flashed. It's nothing."

"No," Darlene said.

"He was a scientist, Darlene," he said, glancing back at the ledger, "some kind of biochemical some such. He knew what he was talkin about."

"No," she said again.

"What the hell do you mean, 'no.' It's one of those natural phenome-noms. When they made *The Greatest Story Ever Told* they had to get some of these scientists to figure out what Noah's flood really was, you know? And *The Ten Commandments*? What really happened when Moses parted the Red Sea? They had to figure all that out, Darlene. Don't be naive."

"Yes sir," she whispered.

He continued writing. She could hear the gentle scratching of the pen on the paper. After a few minutes he looked up suddenly. He wrinkled his forehead. He stared at her for a long time. He licked his lips.

"Say that again?" he said.

"What?"

"What you just told me."

"I said Mary talks to me. She appears to me and talks to me. She tells me things."

"What things?"

"Things."

"Uh-huh." He sat behind the desk, still staring at her. There were framed pictures on the wall behind him. One, of Brad Pitt, was inscribed "For Duane, party man, Brad." All the rest were not signed. There was one of Mr. Justice and Brooke Shields standing outside the Beverly Hills Hotel. "We're really, uh, just friends, Darlene," he had told her, and she could tell from the way he said it that he wanted her to think otherwise. It didn't make her jealous. It thrilled her. He may have had glamorous movie stars, but he was here now, with her. "Uh-huh," he said again, peering at her with interest, "and when did this, uh, conversation take place? And where?"

"Mostly in my room," she said, "at night. But ..."

"But what?"

"She's everywhere. She's like, you know, God."

He just looked at her. He was chewing his lip, tapping the pen on the ledger. "Has she ever, uh, talked to you here? In the theater?"

"Oh," Darlene said, "sure."

His eyes lit up. His face broke into a wide grin. "Well," he said. "I mean ... well done, Darlene." He nodded vigorously. "Do you know what this means?"

"Well," she said. "What what means?"

"This is a shrine, Darlene!" he said, his arms sweeping around, taking in his office and the lobby and she supposed the theater itself. "This is a shrine. A Holy place."

She was pleased to have made him so happy. She smiled too. "Yessir," she said.

⇋

Colleen takes the chalice from between Lolly's outstretched legs and holds it high over her head. She comes and stands right in front of Darlene. Darlene feels self-conscious and frightened. She pulls against the ropes but her wrists are tightly bound to the chair.

"Come, oh mighty Lord of Darkness," Colleen says, "and look favorably on this sacrifice we have prepared in thy name." Colleen's robe is made of thick black wool, rough, with specks of dirt and sticks and trash from the woods clinging to it. She offers the chalice to Darlene's lips. The chalice—which was stolen from Grace Episcopal Church in Fultondale— is gleaming silver, heavy, with IHS engraved on the side in fancy script. It contains a cloudy liquid, pale green in color. Darlene shakes her head no, her lips tightly closed. Colleen glares at her.

Colleen goes to where the others kneel on the ground. She passes from one to the other and they all take long draughts of whatever is in the chalice. Colleen then stands before Darlene and drinks herself. She offers it to Darlene again. She frowns.

"What is it?" Darlene whispers.

Colleen continues to frown, so Darlene allows the chalice to be placed against her lips. She sips. It is bitter, yet sweet. Oily and smooth. She lets the thick cold liquid rest on her tongue and then she swallows. Colleen gives her more. The potion tastes vaguely salty, like turnips. It has an odd smell that is familiar but that she can't identify. It seems to relax her. Her arms and legs tingle.

Colleen picks up the paten with the bread. She takes the bread and rubs it over Lolly's breasts, which look spongy and pert even lying on her back, and then Colleen rubs the bread over Lolly's private parts. She carefully inserts part of it into her vagina. Darlene can't believe what they're doing. Whatever was in the chalice has made her lightheaded and she wants to laugh, to giggle, but she doesn't. The impulse passes quickly and she licks her lips and narrows her eyes and looks on eagerly. Each corner of the piece of bread is pushed inside Lolly, and then it's broken up and the pieces are poked there as well, and Darlene knows what's coming next. She watches Colleen put the pieces on the outstretched tongues of the others, and when Colleen stops in front of her, her eyes glittering with the firelight and the candles, sparkling with excitement, Darlene sticks out her tongue, takes the bread, chews it, swallows it down. A shiver runs all the way through her and her breath catches in her throat, and her arms and legs and now her belly burn with pleasure. "Hic est calix voluptatis carnis," Colleen whispers, and she makes the sign of the upside-down cross over Darlene's face.

Though it's a cool night Darlene feels hot. She is sweating. Colleen gives her more of the liquid in the chalice. Darlene watches, riveted, as Keith rises and goes to the altar and takes off his clothes. His erect penis stands out like a white stubby flagpole, and he goes forward and quickly plunges it into Lolly. His narrow buttocks begin to work rhythmically, and all the others are breathing heavily. From somewhere Colleen takes out a long pink dildo—"Phallus!" cries Colleen, and Jayne Ann and Karla echo her, "Phallus!"—and Colleen covers it with KY Jelly from a silver tube and she inserts it into Keith's anus and slowly pushes it all the way in. Keith cries out, whether from pain or pleasure Darlene does not know, but she knows that saliva is flowing so freely in her own mouth that it drips from the corners, and shadowy images dance behind her eyes.

Hands untie her wrists and lift her from the chair. Her legs are so weak she can hardly stand and yet she is so keenly aware of what is going on that everything is overlarge, giant like they're all on a huge outdoor movie screen. And she feels the cold air against her skin as her clothes come off and she helps them pull herself toward the altar where Lolly has moved aside and they put her in Lolly's place. She is trying to tell them, "No, no," trying to say, "No, I'm not a virgin, I lied, I'm not," when she sees Keith hovering over her, sees his swollen penis being guided between her legs by many eager hands and she spreads her legs wide to accept him and suck him all the way in.

At just that moment, twenty miles away in a room on the eleventh floor of University Hospital, Jimmy Boykin has a wet dream. As he jerks awake it takes him a moment to realize that he has felt the sensation sharply and explicitly and he can even feel the cooling sticky of the hospital gown against his lower belly. His head and neck are locked so firmly in place he cannot move, and though he concentrates and tries with all that is in him to move his legs or his hands he cannot do it. It's as though there's some breakdown in transmission between his brain and his extremities. Some block that he cannot get through.

The room is darkened, lit only by the illuminated gauges on the machine that beeps incessantly beside him. But he can see the ceiling. He can see the blank screen of the television set mounted high on the wall. He closes his eyes and tries to remember his dream. He thinks it was of Lolly Phillips, of him and Lolly Phillips, but it seemed to be taking place back in Chicago, in a car behind a service station on a deserted street, and Lolly seemed to be older, a mature woman almost his mother's age, and then she would be a very young girl barely more than a child, and there was something threatening them, making them hurry. He did not know what.

Tears squeeze from his tightly closed eyelids and slide unchecked down the sides of his face. He can feel their tickle. He can feel the cold sticky down there. The nurses will find it. It's the first time he has felt anything below his neck. He tries again to remember what had happened to him. He cannot remember the game, or much of the day of the game. All he remembers, oddly, is talking to a boy named Ernest "Jingle" Bales at lunchtime. Jingle was a slight boy with thick glasses. Lolly had walked by and they had been talking about her. "Wow," Jimmy had said, "how do you get close to that?" Jingle had said to him, "What you ought to do is just go up to her and say 'Why don't we do it in the road?'" That is the last thing he remembers. Before waking up here in the hospital locked as stiffly immobile as if he'd been a statue of himself. He thinks he knows now what a statue feels like. The impulse to move that feels quick and clear and then drops away into some vast and dark and empty pit. Why don't we do it in the road?

"I missed my downfield block. It was all my fault," he hears Otis say. Otis is right here in the room with him. Jimmy opens his eyes. Otis stands there leaning over the bed.

"You're growing a beard," Jimmy says.

"Naw, I just ain't shaved in a while. I been living in a cave."

"You're shittin me, man."

"No. But, hey, listen, how're you doin?"

"Okay. You didn't miss any downfield block. Get serious."

"I did. The guy that tackled you was my man. I didn't get out there fast enough. And he whacked you good, man."

"That's what they say. I don't even remember it."

"You don't remember it?"

"Naw."

Otis's long narrow face looms above him. His eyes are like lumps of dulled gold.

"It doesn't matter," Otis says, "we lost the play-offs. Coach quit. It's shit, man."

"I know. He told me."

"He told you?"

"Yeah. He comes by here sometimes. He talks to me, rambling, like he doesn't think I can even hear him. He carries on. I think he's drunk. I can smell it. He talks about my Mom. He's got this thing for my Mom."

"No shit?"

"Yeah. They used to go around together in high school. You know?"

"Hard to believe."

"Why?"

"I don't know, man. Listen. I got somebody here I want you to meet. This is Willie Clyde."

The girl leans over the bed. She is so pale white next to Otis that she almost glows. She is milk to Otis's caramel. Her hair is blond and silky. Her skin looks so soft that Jimmy wants to reach up and touch it, but of course he can't. Jimmy is stunned. Her lips are like ripe cranberries. Her eyes are coal black. He thinks she is the most beautiful girl he has ever seen. She is like some vision out of one of his tossing dreams. He thinks for a moment that she was the girl in his wet dream and it was not Lolly at all, but he knows that's ridiculous because he has just now seen her. Or maybe he has seen her before. Yes, he has, he knows he has. Somewhere. Somewhere in that measureless, enormous void that is his recent memory. Yes. He has seen her before.

"Hi, Jimmy," she says. And her voice is as familiar as the sound of his own breathing. He cannot take his eyes from her face. From her eyes. "We're going to get you out of here," she says.

"Yeah, man," Otis says.

"What...what do you mean?" His eyes sting from looking up at them, and he blinks them several times.

"We don't know exactly. We're working on it," Willie Clyde says.

"But—"

She puts her finger against his lips and presses. She smiles. It is as though a light has come on in the room. He can feel the heat of her touch on his mouth. His whole body seems to relax and go slack. He realizes that he can feel his muscles easing all over his body, all up and down his arms and his legs. He can't imagine being away from the smells and sounds of the hospital, being free of them ever again. He has never had any existence but this. It is what he is, what he has become.

But her touch sets him on fire.

"We'll have you out of here in no time," she says. He stares up at her. He cannot utter a sound. He gapes at her face, astonished. She looks so much like him it's as though he's looking into a mirror. It's as though he is looking into his own face, his own eyes.

❧

It is not Mary but Lemuel Bluett who watches over the children in the woods. He has climbed a sycamore tree at the edge of the clearing with a dexterity that surprises him, with a strength he has never had before. He has watched the kids before with their satanic carryings on. He has seen some things that would blister your eyes. He watched them take a red hot iron from the fire and brand one girl's inner thigh with the image of a light-ning bolt while she screamed and the rest of them held her. He saw them put garbage bags over their heads to inhale something he figured was freon. One night he watched the coach's son and the girl Colleen Purdy both get fucked by a big black dog. A few weeks later he saw them kill the same dog and burn his body on a bonfire. He never knows what he might see when he happens upon them.

Tonight he is surprised to see old Lamar Vick's daughter with them. Lamar would have a conniption fit if he knew it. Yep, I ought to write a book, Lemuel thinks again, but he knows, of course, that he will never write it now. He can't. That one blow from Mully Grubber's softball bat has immortalized him and finally fixed him forever in his own self-appointed role as conscience of the town. He can roam as freely as he wishes, invisible, for eternity. He can't help but smile.

ALEX GROWS INCREASINGLY IMPATIENT WITH THE CALLERS. He begins to feel trapped, imprisoned by the clear glass walls of the studio. It's as though he has been sitting in the control booth all his life, listening to the voices. The voices become a chorus from one of the circles of hell. They blend and weave in a mind-bursting disharmony and they keep coming with a shrill regularity. Many are familiar but many are new, and it is those new ones that can still surprise and delight Alex, but they have also started to frighten him too. He had not known there were so many people out there listening to him and the sheer volume of them overwhelms him. Sometimes just the rhythmic flashing of the button to denote a new caller makes him tense up and he does not understand why. He begins to suspect that sooner or later he will get "the" call. The one important call that all the others have been building toward. He has no idea at all what that call might be, or even if there is such a thing, or where the idea that there will be one might have come from. He doesn't know if he will know such a call when it comes. Something just begins to nudge his mind, ever so slightly, so that every time the buttons flash something tucked away back inside his brain wonders: maybe this is it?

"Alex, this is Malcolm Roland, and—"

"Stop calling me, Mr. Roland! Nobody cares about your stupid garbage and your stupid dog!" CLICK. "The People Speak?"

"Alex, Lemuel Bluett is not dead!"

"Oh, get real." CLICK.

"I seen her again, Mr. Radio Man! The same little white girl ghost. This make the fourth time since I—" CLICK.

The voices burble and gurgle and drift out over the airwaves. They billow like invisible smoke in the wind. They float out over the rooftops and through the trees, some now springing with the tiniest of new buds. The thick blending of voices hovers like haze over the valley. To the west of the village, the future northern bypass, which will someday intersect with Interstate 65, is still just a curving swath of cut trees, stumps, cleared undergrowth and wooden stakes with orange tags. Nearby, yellow earth-movers crawl about the naked red hillsides like giant ladybugs, flattening the hilltops and filling in the valleys to form the broad flat foundation for the Twenty-First Century Mall.

"It ain't too early to be thinkin about plantin your garden, Alex," a voice says.

"Are you the guy with the soil samples?"

"Hey! You remembered!"

"How could I forget? You must be the most boring person since eighth-grade algebra class."

"Awww, Alex, you're puttin me on!"

"No," Alex says, "actually I'm not."

"You want to make your garden grow, Alex. Get your hands in God's good earth. See the fruits of your labors, see—"

"What can I get from a garden that I can't get from the Piggly Wiggly, easier and probably cheaper?"

"You can get your hands dirty, Alex! Make your garden grow! I can't tell you how great it is! I can't—" CLICK.

"The People Speak. Go ahead."

"Alex," the voice says, soft and muted, "this is Barbara Gleason."

"Who?" Alex asks, but he knows who Barbara Gleason is—or was—because the papers had been full of it and he had fielded thousands of calls about her, the little tiny midget woman killed in the 7-Eleven robbery.

"Barbara Gleason," she says, and Alex squints at the caller ID. "Out of Area," it says.

"Well, Barbara," Alex says, "I suppose you are calling from beyond the grave."

"Yes. I'm calling from death's other kingdom."

"Pardon?"

"Never mind. Yes I am, Alex. I'm calling with a message for you and your listeners."

"You are? Well, let's hear it, then." Alex sits up, staring at the speaker. His sneakered feet hit the floor with a thump. He winks at Mrs. Norton.

Her face looks drained and pale. Her hand hovers over the controls of her machine. Maybe this is the call, Alex thinks. Mrs. Norton certainly seems to think so. Alex can hear only a fluttering breathy sound on the phone. Then a crackling static. "Ms Gleason?" he says. He hears a swirling, howling wind. "Barbara?"

There is no reply. Then the line goes dead, and after a few seconds comes a steady dial tone. Alex and Mrs. Norton sit there listening to it as it flows through the phone line and then through Mrs. Norton's machine and into the transmitter and up the tall tower out back and out over the air, inviting everyone who hears it to dial now.

†ЕП

The Piper Twin Theater makes a perfect shrine. It is located right next door to the Miracle on Main Street. Duane Justice puts this on the marquee out front: THIS IS THE SPOT WHERE THE VIRGIN MARY SPEAKS TO A YOUNG GIRL. Bus loads of people from as far away as Cincinnati have already come to see the image in the glass, and Roger Coles has wasted no time in getting the word out further. He has placed an ad in the back pages of the *New Yorker:* "Retire to Wembly County, Alabama, where God has put his stamp!" He has put half-page spreads in the real estate sections of *The Birmingham News*, the *Nashville Tennessean*, the *Atlanta Journal-Constitution*, the *New Orleans Times Picayune* and the *Memphis Commercial-Appeal*, all with full-color photographs of some of the half-million dollar homes he is building in the rolling wooded hills around Piper. "Buy your own little piece of Heaven," the ads say. Sybil Riggs and her crew can hardly handle all the new business and Coles Realty has hired three new people just to answer the phones.

"I want to build three or four new schools," Coles says to Brenda. "I want you to be superintendent of all of them. I'll pay you triple what you're making now. Quadruple."

"I thought you wanted me to marry you," Brenda says.

"Of course. But you can do that, too. You'll have your own money. Your own career. You'll have everything! Isn't that what women want these days?"

Brenda thinks of the way Cody Klinger looks when he walks around in her little house naked. His lean body is hairless and smooth, as hard and slick as warm marble. He is insatiable. "Whoa, son," she is always saying to him, "whoa! I'm an old woman." "Shit," he says, grabbing her again.

Coles is not a good lover. He is impatient and demanding. He is self-focused. (His new hair color doesn't help. Brenda laughed when she first saw it. "What's the matter?" he asked, irritated, and she said, "Nothing, oh nothing.") "What did you expect?" Mabel says to her. "Forget Coles," she says, grinning. "Tell me about Cody Klinger again." Mabel pants like a puppy.

Cody is literally like a child with a new toy. He is twenty-six, he tells Brenda. She thinks he may be lying, adding a couple of years. "Hell, what does it matter, he's legal," Mabel says.

"Yes," Brenda says, "lethal!"

⟿

The phone rings constantly at Lamar and Emily Vick's house. It's the Associated Press, or the *New York Times*, or NBC News, or the *Star* or the *National Enquirer*. At first her parents had been disbelieving. "Why didn't you tell us?!?" they said. "Are you sure you're not making this up?"

Darlene is not sure, as a matter of fact. She has not seen Mary—except the image in the glass downtown—since she told Mr. Justice about her. Darlene thinks she might have dreamed her. She paints her fingernails black and stains her lips dark purple with some stuff Colleen Purdy gave her. And her father says, "What the fuck is all this shit? Have you gone completely crazy?" Her father now realizes what good fortune it is that she was the one Mary chose to speak to—or that she was the one everybody believed Mary had chosen—and he wants her to wear a neat dress and put her hair up in a bun. He has sold Darlene's life story to the *National Enquirer* for $50,000, and Darlene's mother is writing it. All Darlene can think about is that she's pregnant and soon will have to do something about it: one thing or the other. She thinks that her father will kill her if he finds out. She knows he will.

And Mr. Justice has not touched her since she told him about talking with Mary, except to put his hand protectively on her shoulder or her back. "Do you think She would appear here on the stage, in front of people?" he asks her.

"I don't know," she says. She wants to cry. She does not feel unhappy but she has a strong impulse to cry.

"Maybe She would appear to you behind the curtain, and then you could come out and tell everybody what She said."

"Maybe so," she says.

Mr. Justice's dark eyes are sharp and penetrating. She can tell he wants to believe her. She can sense his need to believe her. But she knows it finally really doesn't matter to him whether he believes her, as long as other people do. She wonders what he would say if she told him she is pregnant with his child. He was always real careful, using a rubber every time. One of them must have broken. Every time she looks at him she thinks she feels the child stir. But it's not really a child. Not yet. It's just a cluster of cells. She shudders when she thinks that, like when a rabbit runs across your grave.

"Why the dark eye makeup, Darlene?" Mr. Justice asks, staring at her.

"Well, you know," she says. She shrugs. She tries to smile.

"I don't think it goes with your blond hair," he says. "Maybe you should go without makeup. For a while."

"Okay," she says. She shrugs again. Whatever he says. Everybody is all of a sudden concerned with the way she looks.

And she is suddenly very popular at school. After school that afternoon Jayne Ann Dewberry offered her a ride home, and as Darlene and Jayne Ann were walking to the car they heard a short, quick whistle. It was Ernest Bridgewater.

Ernest had put his thumb and forefinger together in front of his lips and puffed. His lips made dry sucking sounds. "Huh?" he said. "You girls in the mood?"

"I don't know," Jayne Ann said.

"You Darlene?" He was looking at her curiously. She couldn't remember Ernest Bridgewater ever even speaking to her before. Several other boys came up behind him. They were football players, popular guys. "I got some good stuff. Come on, we'll ride out to the river. Come on, Jayne Ann."

"No, I'm mad at you," Jayne Ann said. "You just want to use my car."

"What you mad at me for?" Ernest said with exaggerated shock.

"I'm mad at you, dude, you know why. Come on, Darlene." But Ernest grabbed Darlene's arm. Jayne Ann stared at him. "This dunce hurled in my car Friday night, Darlene," she said. "Major suckage, man. And I went over

to his house Saturday morning to get him to help me clean it out and he
was gone."

"I had to shoot pool," Ernest said.

"Yeah," Jayne Ann said.

"Whatever."

"Come on, be-otch," Jayne Ann said, pulling on Darlene's other arm.
The two of them tugged at her. She had never been fought over by friends
before. She pulled her arm free from Ernest's grip.

"Some other time, dude," she said.

Mr. Justice looks at her across the desk with his large brown liquid eyes
and he says to her:

"You are precious to me, Darlene. I hope you know that."

And that is all it takes to make her start crying, to make the tears flow
like from a suddenly wide open tap.

⌐

The Piper Chapter of the Eagle Forum meets in the educational building of the Church of Christ of the New Light With Signs Following. Helen
Grace Coles Greer is the president, and she presides. Virginia Martin is
here, along with Anna Belle Grable, the preacher's wife. Hudora Seesay,
one of the most prominent women in Piper and one of the founders of the
local chapter, is here, along with forty or so other women. Hudora Seesay
is in her seventies, of medium height and bone thin, and her hair is coal
black, her face covered with myriad wrinkles like a roadmap. She speaks:

"This sex course is the last straw. This is social engineering. The only
thing these children need to know about sex is to refrain from it until marriage. Our school is a Christian school. They can learn all they need to
know about sex from the Bible."

"Amen," Anna Belle Grable says.

"The textbook the woman is making them use is a disgrace. Thank you,
Virginia, for bringing us copies of it. It is totally unacceptable. It discusses
'safe sex,' whatever that is. It has pornographic illustrations that amount to
a how-to manual on perverted forms of fornication! Can we actually stand
by and allow our children to be exposed to such filth?!"

"No! No!" the women chorus.

Virginia Martin is proud to be publicly thanked. She wears a benign smile. Her corduroy skirt is high-waisted, fitting just under her ample breastline—one continuous bulge across her chest—pushing against her starched print blouse. She has a yellow pencil stuck into her reddish hair over her right ear.

"The woman is a disgrace," Virginia Martin says. "She doesn't fit the image of the new Piper. She should be run out of town on a rail!"

"She is a whore, or worse," one of the woman toward the back says. "Witchcraft! I hear witchcraft!"

Helen Grace Coles Greer wants the woman gone and out of town more than she has ever wanted anything in her life, except maybe the Good Citizenship Girl Award all those years ago. And the Homecoming Queen crown, which Helen Grace had campaigned strenuously for, begging for votes, humiliating herself. And now Brenda Vick wants Helen Grace's father. And along with him Helen Grace's inheritance. "We'll be lucky if there's a few pennies left," Putt had said.

"We are at war with her," Hudora Seesay says. The women consider the Eagle Forum the women's auxilliary of their local Militia, which is of course all men. They like to employ military language. They all swell with pride at Mrs. Seesay's mention of the word "war."

⟝

At that very moment, across town, A.J. Grist is sitting in Roger Coles's office. What he has just said is the equivalent of dropping a bomb on Roger's head. Roger sputters for a moment. Then:

"Probate Judge?" Roger asks incredulously.

"Yes," the neat little black man says. He sits in one of Roger's visitors' chairs. He fingers the crisp crease of his suit pants, charcoal gray and conservative. He nods his graying head, which Roger would have called "wooly." "Your term is up next year, and I think I might just run for that office. I think I'd be a good Probate Judge. After all, I do have a law degree."

"Well, now, A.J.," Roger says. He is angry. His face feels hot. He pauses. The very idea of this man suggesting that he's less than qualified because he doesn't have a law degree. But he tries to hold his rage in check. He speaks through clenched teeth. "See, I've been Probate Judge for twenty years. Nobody's ever run against me. That's because everybody is more than satisfied with the way I run things."

"Maybe so. We shall see," Grist says.

"Now see here, you—" And Roger stops. He peers at the little man, squinting his eyes. Then he snorts. "You wouldn't stand the chance of a fart in a whirlwind," he says.

"Mr. Coles, be that as it may, I want to run."

Coles stares at him. His mouth turns white at the corners and his face colors more deeply. "Why?" he asks. Coles is shouting now. "Why in hell would you want to do a damn fool thing like that?"

"I want to give something back to the community," Grist says. Coles examines him curiously. The man has lost his mind. He sits there looking back at Coles, his eyes level, showing no guile at all that Coles can see. He seems sincere. His little mustache is neatly trimmed and his eyes are bloodshot and sleepy. "And another thing," he says. "I am going to enroll my daughter Karla at Piper Academy. I want your permission for her to enter late. She will—"

"Wait a minute. Your daughter?"

"Yes. You see, she is a Native American. You would call her an Indian. My wife and I adopted her from a reservation in Montana. She is actually the daughter of a chief, a direct descendent of Sitting Bull. She—"

"Hold on, goddamit," Coles says. "What kind of crazy shit story is this?!"

"There is no reason to be vulgar, Mr. Coles."

"There is every reason in the world to be vulgar, Mr. Grist," Coles says.

—

Byron Bailey sits in his little Honda Civic and watches Roger Coles's black Bronco go down the street. His eyes narrow as he sees the older man, his hair darker now, sitting erect behind the wheel. Byron fingers a shiny clean 30.06-lever action rifle that leans against the seat beside him. He can smell the pungent gun oil he had applied slowly and lovingly to the rifle last night, rubbing the barrel for a long time with a soft cloth while he watched TV. Also on the passenger seat is a .45 automatic pistol, fully loaded, and on the floorboard behind the front seats are three live hand grenades that Byron has sneaked out of the Militia compound.

When Coles goes by Byron starts the Honda and eases into the street behind him. He keeps a half block's distance between them. Then he moves up closer, so close he can read Coles's vanity plate: COLES 1, it says. Coles was quoted in the local paper recently telling people that the time would soon come when they wouldn't have to buy car tags any more or even have drivers' licenses. Byron knows all about that. It is the Posse Comitatus. It is the freedom from big government that he is fighting for. It is part of what Roger Coles has betrayed.

The two cars roll down Main Street, past the crowd of people looking at the Miracle. They stand around on both sides of the street, crane their necks and gawk. Byron does not know what to make of the miracle. He is secretly scared of it. He had gone in the dark of a rainy night and flung battery acid on the glass, scaring and disfiguring the image, and then the picture in two days had healed itself. He thought surely that it was some crank scheme of Coles's, some way of further cementing Coles in his role as a dictator. Byron thought it blasphemous. He wanted to reveal it for what it was, a fraud, and it had gone and healed itself! He does not look at it when he goes by. Just being this close to it makes the back of his tongue go dry.

He follows Coles through town. He does not take his eyes off the back of the Bronco. His jaw moves rhythmically as he chews on a fresh wad of Juicy Fruit. He intends to follow Coles everywhere he goes for at least three days, carefully noting his comings and goings in a spiral bound notebook. He will do this several times before he is satisfied. He is planning this one carefully. He does not want the same thing to happen with this that happened on the church bus that day. Just remembering that day makes Byron shiver with shame.

⌐

Cody is with Mindy Miller, a TV reporter from NBC Five in New Orleans. It is late afternoon in Leroy's and they are drinking together. It is crowded and noisy. Cody wears an old faded fishing vest he bought at the thrift store. Twenty-nine cents. Mindy had come in with her cameraman and immediately spotted Cody's equipment on the little round table in front of him. Cody had known they were curious. It had not taken them long. They both had come over to his table with their drinks. Mindy was drinking something in a tall, frosted glass with a quarter of a lime and a cherry. They wanted to know if he was network.

"Freelance," he said, and Mindy's eyes twinkled with interest. She is young, little and dark and pretty. She has her hair streaked with gray. What do they call that? Cody can't remember, but whoever had done it for Mindy Miller had put in too much gray. It makes her look weird. Like a little girl in her mama's wig. Frosted! That's what they call it.

Her cameraman's name is Karl Ramsey. He is tall and thin and wears a huge silver belt buckle on his black jeans. He is drinking an Icehouse in the bottle.

"What's coming down?" Mindy asks him.

Your britches, Cody thinks. She wears an opened blue windbreaker with NBC FIVE and a big number 5 embroidered over the left breast in red. Inside the windbreaker Cody can see that her breasts, under a white T-shirt, are like a couple of juicy wine-sap apples. Cody imagines gripping them like he is about to throw a curve ball. She looks at him over the rim of her glass. Cody has seen hundreds of girls exactly like her on the news, standing in front of a burning building with her hair blowing in the wind or interviewing some weeping old lady whose house trailer has just been blown to smithereens by a tornado. Looking satisfied when she finally coaxes the old lady into saying, once again, that it had "sounded just like a freight train comin through!"

"We came up this morning. Is it real?" she asks. Her eyes seem locked on his.

"It's real," he says, "as real as anything ever gets." She can't take her eyes off him. She keeps looking at his hair, his hand gripping his beer bottle, his eyes. Then back to his hair. Karl Ramsey has a ponytail, too, but his is straight and black, more like a thin pig's tail. Karl's hair is thinning on top in the front. He says nothing, just sits drinking his beer.

"Yeah. We interviewed some people," Mindy says. "Same old shit."

"Can I buy you another, you know, like, whatever it is you're having?" Cody asks.

"Sure," she says. "Tom Collins." And Cody snaps his fingers over his head at Robertson Reboul.

Cody and Mindy spend the night in his room at the Moon Winx. They smoke a lot of dope and Mindy Miller is athletic. "I was a gymnast in college," she says, "at Tulane. Hold on to the side of the table there and I'll show you." She knows positions that Cody had not encountered even in California.

The Militia gathers on the compound in the north of the county. Some of the men pass a bottle of Old Forester around. Some drink beer from cases of Pabst Blue Ribbon provided by Roger Coles and Coors sent by Calvin Bluett. Calvin called the distributor and found out that Roger was sending nonpremium beer. So he sent Coors. They are decked out in their camouflage fatigues. They have been marching on the dusty parade ground. "Right Oblique, Haaarch!" Byron Bailey called out, to little avail. His platoon is ragged. They step all over one another and laugh. He has the Rhodes brothers and Lamar Vick, and Putnam Greer and Donald Dixon, the banker. They don't take the drilling seriously. If he needs anything to convince him that his new lonely plan of action is the right thing to do, this kind of behavior would be it. He knows now more than ever that his destiny is to take things into his own hands once again.

Big grills—fifty-gallon drums sawed in half and set on welded metal legs—are fired up, and venison is roasting, the smoke and smell of barbecuing meat drifting on the early spring breezes all over the compound.

Cases of Down Home Barbecue Sauce are available, with Roger Coles's picture on the label, and the cooks are basting the meat with it. A large hand-lettered sign, tacked to a pine tree, hovers over all the activity. NO NIGGERS AND JEWS ALLOWED, it says.

Calvin Bluett arrives with other men. Several car loads of other men. Everyone knows they come from militias in other parts of the country. Calvin wears his officers' dress uniform. The other men wear fatigues or overalls or hunting clothes. Some wear ten-gallon hats and down vests. They are the Freemen from Montana and are sweating in the unexpected Southern heat.

The leaders all gather in the hunting lodge where the other men bring them cold beers and plates of barbecued venison. The plates are piled high with cole slaw the women's auxiliary sent, along with chocolate cakes and coconut cream pies for dessert. There's an air of excitement, of anticipation. Everyone knows that something big is going to happen, but they don't know what. There is much horseplay, much harsh cursing. The men pride themselves on the quality of their cursing.

Word comes that a helicopter is hovering over the woods in the upper compound. A black helicopter. Anti-aircraft weapons are brought out and set up. The men hold their automatic rifles at ready. Byron makes his awkward platoon form. "Preseeent Haaarms!" Byron barks, and Dusty Rhodes hands him his rifle and giggles. All the men laugh. They point their rifles at the sky, jabbing them toward the high puffy clouds. "A goddam dove shoot!" Donald Dixon says.

They hear the helicopter, rumbling and thumping in the distance. They shade their eyes and strain to see. Then more copters come in a roar, all solid black with no insignias, no markings, and they dart about in the sky like dragonflies. There must be a hundred of them, filling the northern sky. The men stand flat-footed, staring at them. Then someone starts shooting. From all around the compound come the sharp cracks and pops of automatic weapon fire, followed by the concentrated boom of one of the anti-aircraft weapons.

The helicopters dance about, dodging the shells and the bullets, and the men on the ground can feel the hefty thump, thump of the multiple blades in their bellies and the ground underneath their feet shakes, trembles, quakes. The guns set up a steady clamor and Byron thinks By God it is like a dove shoot! and smoke from the muzzles drifts around and converges with the smoke from the barbecue grills and the sharp scent of burned powder mixes with the rich smell of the barbecued meat. The noise is deafening, the whumping of the helicopter blades now drowning out even the anti-aircraft guns and the rocket launcher which has been rolled out, but none of the helicopters are hit.

They are so thick in the air that it would seem impossible not to hit one, but there are no flames and no smoke. They hover so close that the men on the ground can see the cockpits but the glass is tinted almost as black as the bodies of the crafts so they cannot see inside. The powerful down-drafts from the blades whip up twigs and leaves and dust from the ground and spin miniature whirlwinds all about so that the loose fatigues on the men flatten against their bodies, and their caps and helmets blow off and out and up, and they try to protect their eyes from all the flying debris.

Then as quickly as they had come, the helicopters are gone. The sound of the engines and the whirling blades dies away in the distance and the last of the solid black copters disappears behind the light green and newly leaved treetops to the south. The men stare after them. Their clothing is disheveled, their hair in disarray. They heft their rifles. They strut and curse.

Byron Bailey stands on the edge of the parade ground, his narrow face cocked to the side, his trim boy's body poised. He does not move for a long time, looking after the hoard of black helicopters, the expression on his face one of complete and total calm and repose.

"I'm pregnant," Darlene says to Brenda. Brenda feels her stomach lurch like on an express elevator, and she reaches out around her for something solid to steady herself with. It is not that she's surprised. It's just that simultaneously she hears herself saying the exact same words to Wayne McClain twenty-five years ago, and he had looked back at her then and said, "What? What?"

"What?" she says now to Darlene, "who..." She shakes her head. She had known it that day. As certain as she'd ever known anything. "Never mind. It's none of my business. I'm just ..."

"Shocked? Ashamed?"

"No. No, not that." Brenda thinks of Lamar. Of what he would say. "No, of course not," she says. She examines her niece. Darlene is changing before her eyes. She wears black fingernail polish. Her face is pasty white like Colleen Purdy's. Brenda has seen the two girls together, whispering in the hall.

"How long?" Brenda asks.

"Two months, maybe," Darlene says, "I don't know."

They stand in the parking lot next to Brenda's car. The sun is bright and the day is warm. Brenda squints her eyes against the brightness and continues to stare at Darlene. It was months ago that Brenda had known the girl was pregnant. It doesn't add up. The girl looks away, then back at her. She looks down at the pavement.

"What are you going to do about it?" Brenda asks softly. "Does your mother know?"

"No!"

"Well, I mean ... Well, what's the deal? Is this some guy you're dating, or what?"

"Not exactly, no," Darlene says.

"You do ... know ...?"

"Oh, yes, absolutely. It could, like, only be one person. You know?"

"Does he know?"

"No!"

"So I'm it, huh?"

"Yeah."

"Well," Brenda says. "How does all this gibe with the Virgin Mary and all that? I mean—"

"Oh, She knows. She knew before I did."

"Is that right?" Brenda has no idea what is going on with the girl. She is not sure of much these days. Brenda had been sitting on one of the meditation benches one day when Wayne had come by and stood for a long time looking at the image of the Virgin in the glass. He had not seen her.

He looked tired, washed out. He had already turned in his resignation at the Academy and cleaned out his desk. She watched him go on down the street and disappear inside Leroy's Grill and Billiards. And after a while she had seen Darlene stop and sit on another bench down the way, and she had watched the girl stare at the image, trance-like and still. Darlene had then reached her hand out to the image, a slow and longing gesture that seemed almost dreamlike in its intensity.

Brenda has changed her mind about the image. She has taken to going by the shrine daily, just to spend some time there. There's something calm and peaceful about it, even with the people. The crowds continue to be large. Tour busses line Main Street every day. She had asked Darlene one day about the visitations. "Weird," was all her niece had said, shrugging. The marquee on the Piper Twin reads: COMING SOON! THE VIRGIN MARY!

"It's that ghost of that little girl, all of this," Mabel said. "They're all tied up together somehow. Connected."

"I know," Brenda said. And her mother's spirit, too, that she still talks with almost nightly. "Brenda," her mother said one midnight, "you know I always thought Wayne was a nice-looking boy." "Oh, Mother," Brenda said aloud, "shut the hell up!"

"So," Brenda says to Darlene now, "so what does She...does Mary, have to say about it?" Her voice quivers when she asks the question.

"I haven't spoken to Her lately," Darlene says. "She just told me I was pregnant before I even took the test. And She was right."

You've been pregnant for a long time, Brenda thinks. "Have you seen a doctor?"

"No."

Brenda sees tears standing in Darlene's eyes, sparkling in the sunlight. The girl licks her lips. They look chapped underneath the dark, plum-crimson lipstick. Her lips look bruised and overripe. Like grapes waiting to be crushed.

"Then come to the women's health center, see one of the doctors there."

"I'm not ... I don't want ..."

"It's all right. They do more than abortions, Darlene. It's a health center. It's where you should go."

"All right," the girl says.

"But you'll have to decide," Brenda says, "no matter what, you'll make a choice. One way or the other."

"Yes mam," the girl says.

Darlene turns away. Brenda imagines that something is inside her now, kicking in the womb the way Jimmy had when he kicked so hard she could see the covers move. She thinks of Jimmy's fat baby legs kicking. She thinks of his legs grown long and strong and now locked still and motionless. As she watches Darlene walk away she begins to cry. The tears blind her eyes, shimmering silver-white in the sunlight. She stands very still as she cries. She stands there, by herself, for a long time. She is crying for herself. And she cries for Darlene and Jimmy and her mother. And for all the dead and the unborn.

⌒

"The girl is not pregnant," Dr. Pitts says to Mabel. He is still pulling off his latex gloves. "She is hysterical. Maybe this is some more—" He stops and looks sideways at Mabel. "Maybe you should go in and talk to her."

Mabel goes into the examination room and finds Darlene still on the table. The girl sits on the edge, her legs dangling. She has on a green disposable paper gown. The fluorescent lights are blinding, and everything in the room is white but the gown. There are narrow tear paths down each of her cheeks.

"I've missed three periods. I know I'm pregnant," she says. Her voice quavers.

"Sometimes—" Mabel begins.

"I've felt it there. I know I have. I've felt it move. And ..."

"And maybe you know from other sources," Mabel finishes for her.

"Yes."

It is raining outside, a spring thunderstorm, and both women can hear the rain whispering on the roof and burbling in the gutters of the old house.

"Women know," Mabel says. "We know things like that."

"Yes."

There is a sustained and muffled roll of thunder. The storm is moving away, the center of it distant now. The room smells of alcohol and disinfectant. Darlene looks at the older woman, her aunt's friend. Mabel Perkins is small and dainty, with fine lines around her eyes. She has nicotine stains on two of her fingers. Her fingernails are bright crimson and long and pointed. She wears a light blue smock buttoned down the front.

"Dr. Pitts," she says, "says the tests—and his exam—all indicate that you aren't pregnant. He thinks maybe ..."

"What?"

"A young girl. Going through trauma. A hysterical pregnancy, sometimes—"

"Crap," Darlene says. "I'm not going through any trauma. I've never been more serene in my life."

"You are becoming famous. All this. You know? The interviews, everything."

There is a soft, discreet knock on the door. Dr. Pitts sticks his head in. He sees them and comes on into the small room. He wears a stethoscope around his neck, like a child playing doctor. He is a small man, boyish. He looks no older than Darlene. "You look like you're feeling better, Darlene," he says. Under his smock he wears faded jeans.

"She is," Mabel says.

Dr. Pitts smiles. He shakes his head, looking from one to the other. "Not only is this young woman not pregnant," he says, "but from the physical exam, I would have bet my medical degree that she is a virgin." He smiles at Darlene as though she is a child he has caught at mischief. "I find no evidence that she has ever engaged in penetrative sexual intercourse. None at all. But I suppose she is the best authority on that, right?"

"Right," Mabel says. She looks at Darlene, her eyebrows raised on her forehead.

"What?" Darlene says, after a minute.

"I said," Dr. Pitts says, smiling smugly, "that your hymen is intact, Darlene. Your, uh, maidenhead, as it used to be so quaintly called."

"But—"

He holds up both hands, palm out. "Just a simple medical opinion, that's all," he says sarcastically. He shakes his head. He looks from one of them to the other and then goes back out.

The two women don't say anything for a long moment. Then,

"But—" Darlene begins.

"Shhhhh," Mabel says, putting her nicotine-stained index finger against Darlene's lips. "What the hell does he know, anyway?" she says.

⇌

Outside, the rain has stopped. Everything is clean and wet, the sidewalk, the grass, the fresh leaves on the shrubs and trees. Everything glows pale green after the long winter. It's chilly after the storm and the air is sharp and clear. Darlene stands on the front stoop of the clinic. She feels the child burning inside her. She knows it is there. Sometimes it's like a tiny pin prick; sometimes like an expanding fist. She looks around, up and down the street. The only person around is a girl across the street, at the edge of the woods, who stands there looking at Darlene. There's something strangely familiar about her, but Darlene does not know her.

The girl stands very still, but she seems to list to the side. She looks dirty and hungry. Her clothes are wrinkled and stained. Darlene wonders for a moment if she is homeless. But she had heard Mr. Roger Coles, in a speech at the Academy, say, "We are proud that we have no homeless in Wembly County!" The girl is blond and pale. Darlene realizes suddenly that she is the ghost that everybody has been seeing, that people have talked about over the radio. She looks almost transparent. But all those people have seen a child, and this girl is as old as Darlene or older. She seems to age even as Darlene is looking at her.

The sound of a truck coming down the street causes the image of the girl to fade even more, and Darlene takes two or three steps toward her. The girl sees this and raises one hand in a kind of gesture, a brief awkward wave that seems part greeting and part farewell as she withers and diminishes and disappears into the woods like smoke blown by a sudden breeze.

The pickup truck screeches to a stop in the street and Darlene looks up and into the face of her father. His face is contorted with anger. His eyes bulge in his head. He is drunk and looks as mad as she has ever seen him, and she is terrified. She has been caught. She knows from the look in his eyes that he knows exactly where she has been and why.

"Darlene," her father says, "git in this truck."

"No," she says. "I don't want to." It is not her father's truck. He is riding with someone else, a shadowy white face behind the wheel. The truck idles, rumbling. She can smell its exhaust, hot and oily. The pickup is rusty red.

Her father glares at her. "Did you hear what I said? Git in this truck! Now!" She does not move. It's as though the soles of her shoes are glued to the pavement. Her father shoves the door open. He steps down. "Are you gonna git in, or am I gonna have to put you in?" he snarls. He looks like a rabid dog. His eyes glint. He has not shaved.

Darlene moves like a robot toward the truck. She feels tears begin to gush behind her eyes.

"You git your ass in here," he says, and he handles her roughly, his fingers cutting into her arms. She can tell that he is trying to impress his friend. The seat is high, rough, patched with electrician's tape. The knob on the gear-shift lever has a color picture of a naked woman, sitting with her legs spread. "Goddamit," her father mutters, "this ruins everything!" She feels the truck thrust forward. The cab smells of motor oil and stale beer and raw whiskey. She is aware of the driver, next to her, but she does not know who he is. One of her father's friends. She is embarrassed. She cannot squeeze the tears back and they flow down her cheeks. "Goddamit, Darlene, you think I don't know why you would be in that place?" her father says. "There ain't but one reason a girl goes to that place, and you think I don't know it?"

"I'm not pregnant," she says, "the doctor says—"

"Well, now, that don't matter, since it looks like you thought you was, and that don't mean but one thing!"

When he gets her home and Emily sees the look in his eyes, she begins to scream almost immediately. "No, Lamar! No! No! No!"

"Shut up, woman," he yells back. The neighbors come out onto their porches or go to their windows and look out. Some little children making a mud dam in a ditch down the street stop what they're doing and listen.

It's not the first time they've heard such noises coming from one house or another along these streets, or even from the Vick house. They are all secretly glad that it's not coming from their own house this time.

Lamar slaps Darlene with his open palm and a red splash of blood appears immediately on her lower lip. Emily sees it and begins to wail and cry louder. Darlene is blinded by her tears. She can taste the hot blood in her mouth. Her father jerks her roughly back and forth by the arm. His fingers are like knives in her flesh. He slaps her again and her head snaps back in the other direction. "Goddamit," he says, "we had a chance! To git out of this dump! And here you go ruinin it, acting like a slut!" and he hits her again, this time with his fist, and Darlene feels a splitting pain in her nose and her eyes. The force of his blow whirls her around and sends her headlong against the dining room table with all its pink boxes of Mary Kay scattering and crashing to the floor. The corner of the table cuts into her stomach with the power of an axe blow, and she feels sharp hot pain shoot all over her body, all up and down her arms and legs and in her head. Everything is dark. She cannot see.

She hears her mother screaming. "Lamarrrr! Lamarrrr!" Her mother's voice sounds distant, as though it is coming from the next block. The next town. Darlene tries to walk and staggers into the wall. Then she knows where she is, in the hallway, and she struggles toward her room. Her legs will not work and she has to force them. They feel as though they're on fire.

Inside her room she slams and locks the door. Her head throbs with pain. Her body is numb. She cannot see out of her right eye, and she swallows the blood in her mouth. It is warm and salty. She looks down and there's bright fresh blood dripping from beneath her skirt, onto the floor, almost a stream now, puddling there. She thinks she's going to pass out. Darlene looks around, hoping Mary is there, but she can feel the emptiness of the room on her skin. She feels deserted, abandoned. She cannot believe what Dr. Pitts had said. She had hated his hands on her body.

She looks down at the widening puddle of blood. She knows what is happening but she is helpless to stop it. A searing pain forces downward inside her, weighing her down, pulling her toward the floor. She feels as though her body is being split in two. She loses consciousness on her feet for a few seconds, then she staggers toward the bed. She falls to her knees.

She rests her face against the cool smooth cloth of her bedspread. She forgets for a moment where she is and what is happening to her.

She hears her mother screaming. "Call an ambulance!" her mother screams, "call an ambulance!"

Darlene turns around and rests her back against the bed. She is so totally exhausted that she cannot even raise her arms. The room is dim and her right eye still stings like ten thousand needles and the rest of her face feels deadened, anesthetized. She squints her left eye, peering into the gloom of her room, and she sees her then, the girl, the same girl who had waved to her earlier in front of the clinic. She sits naked in the pool of blood, looking calmly at Darlene, her body streaked with Darlene's blood, her hair matted with it, and Darlene begins to scream. She screams even as her father begins battering at the lock of her door with a hatchet, even as her mother continues to yell, "Call an ambulance!"

Darlene trembles all over, shrinking back against the bed. The girl's skin is pink and glistening, like a newborn's. Her eyes are filmed over, pale gray. She raises her arm and hand as though completing the gesture that had been interrupted earlier on the street, and Darlene closes her only good eye and screams as loud as she can. She heaves her chest with the effort. And the girl sits calmly in the puddle of thick blood, her now-unseen gesture continuing unabated, her bloodstained hand waving back and forth, back and forth in that gentle motion that signs both greeting and farewell.

⌐

And thirty miles away, on the eleventh floor of University Hospital, a nurse named Heather Franks goes into Jimmy Boykin's room and begins to putter with the machine next to the bed. Heather is overweight, and she is tired at the end of her shift. It's two or three minutes at least before she even notices that the bed is empty, that Jimmy is gone, that he has simply disappeared.

THE TOWN OF PIPER DECORATES FOR EASTER IN A BIG WAY.
Shrubs in yards are bedecked with brightly colored plastic eggs hanging on
strings from freshly budding branches. Pastel bunnies in gingham dresses
and miniature OshKosh B'Gosh overalls dangle in trees. HE IS RISEN,
INVITE HIM IN reads the new portable marquee in front of the Church
of Christ of the New Light With Signs Following, long before Easter, long
even before Holy Week.

All the shop windows downtown are decorated and painted for the
occasion. The crowds continue to come, in chartered busses and automo-
biles and yellow school busses, making their pilgrimages to Piper. The marquee on the Piper Twin Theater still reads COMING SOON! The trees are
half-leaved now, the breezes warm and smelling of rain. Yellow daffodils are
everywhere, raising their coquettish heads along the sidewalks and the
byways, and the dogwood and redbud are in full bloom in the hills around
the town.

Inside the Coles mansion, Helen Grace Coles Greer makes her way
slowly up the carpeted staircase. Her father is not at home; his executive
assistant, Sybil Riggs, has told her he is in Birmingham and will not return
until late. The air inside the quiet old house is cool, the furnace now shut
off for the spring. Helen Grace has not seen her grandmother in months.
Her father—in his ridiculous new hair—has forbidden her to see her.

"She is busy," Coles had said, "she is writing her memoirs. She does not
want to be disturbed. Under any circumstances."

"Writing her what?"

"Her memoirs! What is so odd about that?"

"I never knew Damuddy to write anything in her life, that's all."

"Well, there's a first time for everything," her father had said.

She feels hurt and incensed about his hair. It's that woman. He's making a total fool out of himself over that woman. Helen Grace is sure Brenda

Vick Boykin is a witch. There have been rumors of witchcraft in the area—people have found all sorts of signs in the woods—and Helen Grace is certain that Brenda Vick Boykin brought it from Chicago. That would certainly be an explanation for her father's crazy behavior. And Wayne McClain had seemed to have his life back in order until she came home to Piper. And now he has gone straight to hell in a handbasket!

Helen Grace cannot believe the woman's vulgarity. "I don't see how you could possibly be attracted to her," she said to her father, sitting across the table from him in his large kitchen. Her eyes strayed to his darkened hair, the strangely artificial color. She could not keep from staring at it. "The woman is coarse!" she said. The hair does make him look younger, if only because it seems something impulsive and absurd and unexplainable, something that one of her twin sons, Matt or Mark, who are twelve, would do. Something adolescent. But she does not want her father to look younger, necessarily. She wants him to look like a father. A grandfather. And to act like one. "It is just beyond me," she said, "I just don't see what she—" and he said, interrupting her,

"That's because you're not a man."

She had seen her husband Putt—his name is Putnam, but everyone calls him Putt—sniffing around the woman, acting like a helpless hound dog around a bitch in heat. She told herself that if Putt ever touched Brenda, she would get back at him by having an affair herself, with Wayne McClain. It would serve Putt right and it would surely save Wayne McClain's life. She was certain of that. He needed a woman who would straighten him out.

"You're right," she said, "I'm not a man and I'm thankful for it!"

"It's not your concern," he said.

"Not my concern?!? The woman is obviously a gold digger, Daddy, she's after your money. Everybody in Wembly County knows that. And she's a ... a ..."

"A what?" His eyes were like fiery coals. She was afraid to say it. She swallowed. "A what, goddamit?"

"People say she's a whore," Helen Grace blurted. "So there! They say she sleeps with everybody who comes along. Wayne McClain and that young man from Hollywood. The one making a movie, you know—"

"That's ridiculous," Coles thundered. But his eyes were searching and hurt and she immediately felt sorry for him. She could see her father's eyes turn inward with suspicion. "It's not your concern," he yelled. "There's plenty of my money to go around, so don't worry about it!"

"Daddy, Daddy," she said, starting to cry, "I'm the only one who would tell you! I'm the only one who loves you—"

"Don't be ridiculous!" he said.

"—the only one who loves you like that. I'm your daughter!" She began to wail.

"You're just worried about your inheritance. You and Putt. Well, let me tell you, let me—"

"No, Daddy!"

"There's plenty of me to go around! Always has been, always will be! You got that?"

"Yes sir, Daddy," she said, sniffling.

⌐

She reaches the top of the stairs, the upstairs hallway. There are no lights on but afternoon sunlight filters through a curtained window at the end of the hall. Helen Grace can see her grandmother's doorway, the door propped slightly open. She can hear her Damuddy's television. She pauses a moment and cocks her head to listen. It sounds like Mayor Ed Koch and "The People's Court." She looks at the row of curio cabinets that line the hallway walls, her grandmother's and her mother's collections of glass animals.

She moves stealthily down the hall. She realizes she is listening for a typewriter, but other than the television there is silence. Maybe her father has bought Damuddy a computer, a word processor. More than likely she's writing in longhand, with a pen, on a lapboard. Of course. Damuddy will have a lot of stories to tell. She will tell stories of the early days, when she was practically a pioneer woman, and she will tell stories of her only grand-child, Helen Grace, and her great grandchildren.

There is a peculiar smell in the hallway, like turpentine, and under-neath that a heavy barnyard odor. Helen Grace glances at Damuddy's bathroom door, which is closed. She is certain that Phyllis takes advantage of Damuddy and her father, because her grandmother is so old and her father is a man. Phyllis only half cleans and then doesn't do a good job of even that, and her father would never notice. Helen Grace wonders if a mouse or a squirrel has died in the walls or in the attic. It would be just like Phyllis not to even bother to look for it.

Helen Grace stands outside her mother's bedroom door. The smells are stronger here, and the television louder. "I cannot find for you," she hears Judge Koch say, "because you have lied to this court." "But—" "Let me finish, please!" His voice rises. "By your own admission—"

But Helen Grace has ceased to listen to it, because she knows something is wrong. She suddenly remembers Damuddy telling her how she would never watch "The People's Court" again after they replaced Judge Wapner with Mayor Ed Koch. She had been very angry about it. "Never, never, never again!" her grandmother had said, her little gray curls shaking. Her grandmother had been in love with Judge Wapner and had talked about him all the time. "I detest Ed Koch!" she had said, shuddering. "Someone should just shoot the man!"

Helen Grace reaches out, pushes open the door and steps inside. She almost chokes on the smells. The room is full of sunlight, the television playing away. Helen Grace stares at the wall. She is afraid to look at the bed. And when she does she is so horrified by what she sees that she cannot move, cannot react. Damuddy, or what is left of her, sits propped up in the bed, her back against a pile of pillows. One arm is outstretched toward the television, the skin on the arm discolored spotty and black, like an overripe banana. The skin on the side of her face closest to Helen Grace seems to have slid downward, revealing the yellowed skull underneath, the bony eye socket with the wide open and staring and shrunken eye fixed so steadily and penetratingly on Helen Grace that she recoils backward.

Part of her grandmother's lips are gone and her dentures sit in her mouth at an odd angle, an appallingly hideous grin, and the nightgown and the sheet covering her lower body are stained a greenish maroon. Her grandmother's thin, wispy gray hair has fallen from her scalp in fleshy clumps that rest on her thin shoulder and on the bedclothes around her, and Helen Grace gags on the smell, the fumes in the room. She cannot breathe. She jerks quickly backward and bumps the door with her head. She is so stunned that she can scarcely comprehend what she is seeing, and the one eye locks on her and paralyzes her, freezing her, bidding her closer and inviting her in, and she screams.

ELEVEN

Wayne has not had anything to drink for five days. His reason for stopping was as unaccountable and mysterious as whatever had made him start again in the first place. He had awakened on a Monday morning and had lain there knowing this would be the day. He would quit drinking. And it has now been five days. Five days in which he has desperately searched for something to do, something to keep him busy, something to keep his hands from reaching for a drink or a cold beer.

He spent a couple of those days methodically going through his fishing tackle boxes, sorting out the popping bugs he likes to use with a fly rod to catch bluegills. He rearranges them countless times in their little bins. He checks his leaders and treats his lines. He treats all of them several times. He has not been fishing in he doesn't know when. At least since way back before Keith had started his lessons with Richbourgh Smiley. They had once fished together a lot. It was one of the few things he and his son had ever done together. Maybe they can do it again, Wayne is thinking. Wayne needs to go fishing. He knows that much.

Wayne knows that he'll probably fall off the wagon again. Eventually. But he knows better than to worry about that. He is stopped. For now it is real. And that is all that matters. Something can be real without being real. Wayne wishes everybody in the world knew that as well as he did. He sits watching a plump housefly dart about the room. It sits for a while on the kitchen table, then lifts off and flies to the blinds over the kitchen sink, where it perches. It stays, apparently content.

⌣

"Maybe I've finally really hit rock bottom," he says to the AA group.

"Most of us wouldn't know rock bottom if it jumped up and bit us on the ass," Morgan Coleman says. "You need to go to meetins, son. That's the only way."

"No, Wayne's right," Joy Hilbert says. "All of us have to find our own rock bottoms. No two rock bottoms are alike."

"Bullshit," says Tim Brabner.

"Your rock bottom is wide, baby," Lucy Lette says to Joy. Lucy is back in the group after a long absence and is angry about it.

"Sit on it," Joy says to her.

"I'm at a meeting," Wayne says to old man Coleman. Acrid gray smoke drifts through the air of the Elks Hall. Wayne almost gags. Not even the air in Leroy's smells this bad.

"I'm talkin about two meetins a day, seven days a week," Coleman says.

"I know you are," Wayne says. "And I've told you, I don't have time for that!"

"Shit, man, you ain't got nothing but time."

"You people got time," Wayne says. "Me, I'm going fishing."

"Get you a sponsor," Joy says.

"No. I'm going fishing."

⟜

Wayne buys two new fly lines, hollow ones guaranteed to float, but he treats them anyway. He goes through his collection of lures again. He handles the delicate little pieces of painted cork, the tiny yellow and green and red bugs with their feathered skirts or rubber legs. His hands and his fingers don't shake. They're steady. He still feels fluttery inside, but his hands are steady.

The tackle boxes smell damp when he opens them. They smell of the outdoors and of the water.

"Fishing?" Keith says, and his voice sounds like his mother's.

"You used to like it. The weather's beautiful. Come on."

"Fishing? Really?" Just like his mother.

Bobbye had said to Wayne on the phone: "You're a worthless son of a bitch, Wayne."

"I know it."

"You'll never stop drinking."

"Maybe not."

"I'm getting custody back. You can't stop me. I'm cutting you off, asshole."

"You're a real princess, Bobbye, you know that?"

"Yeah. Tell me about it. Listen. His letter of acceptance came. Here to the house. I opened it. He's in, and I called him and told him—"

"He told me, Bobbye!"

"—and Mr. Meadows and I want him here. As soon as school is out. We'll take him to New York, scout out somewhere for him to stay, all that, buy him some clothes—"

"Hah!"

"As soon as school is out, Wayne. Listen. Don't fuck with me, son."

"Don't worry, baby, that's the last thing on my mind."

Wayne could hear her laughing. "Goodbye, Wayne," she said, hanging up.

⁓

"All I want is my music," the boy said to him. "That's all I care about."

"And you got it," Wayne said. "You have evermore got it, boy."

He sits now in his son's messy room, when Keith is not at home, listening to his music on the headphones. He leans back on his son's narrow single bed, the sheets wrinkled and smelling of his son's body. He is listening to Mozart, a soaring symphony. He does not know which one and does not bother to look. He imagines Keith, playing in some symphony in New York or London or somewhere, dressed in a tuxedo, concentrating, holding his mouth the way he does when he plays—a stiff, childish pursing of the lips—and Wayne gets tears in his eyes. He feels the music in his chest and he blinks back the tears because he does not want to feel sorry for himself. He is afraid Keith will come in and find him sitting here blubbering like a baby. He wants a drink, and he closes his eyes tight and concentrates on the music.

"I want to fly," Keith says to him. "I want to be able to just fly away from here."

"Tell me about it," Wayne says. "You don't think I do, too?"

Keith stares at him. They're eating pizza from a box, watching "Wheel of Fortune."

"You're not drinking," Keith says.

"I quit," Wayne says, his mouth full of pizza.

"Yeah, sure," Keith says.

"I quit, okay? So what?" He swallows. "You'll be flying. Soon. First to Atlanta and then all the way to New York. Send your old man a postcard."

Keith squints at him. He seems about to say something. He seems to be thinking. Hard. Then he says, "Okay. Sure."

⌒

It is April already, and warm, almost hot. On this day there's not a cloud in the sky. Wayne asks Keith if he will walk uptown with him to look at the image in the glass.

"For what?" the boy says.

"To look at it," Wayne says.

"I've already seen it."

"Well," Wayne says, "then you can just by God see it again!"

They walk together up the hill to Main Street. The boy wears sloppy loose-fitting jeans and a wrinkled shirt. Wayne wears a gray sweat suit. He will run out of money soon and he doesn't know what he'll do. He has no job prospects. "Something'll come along," Reboul had said to him, "it always does, Wayne. Yep. Something always comes along."

"Hey, coach!" people say. "How you doin, coach?" Wayne is proud that so many people greet him. He is not a disgrace, which is what Coles had called him. No matter what Coles says, he is not a disgrace. Drinking doesn't make you a disgrace, no matter what anybody says. He had learned at least that in treatment. The crowds of people from all over everywhere are still coming, packing Main Street. Khaki-clad Militiamen stand about, a row of them near the meditation benches as though they're guarding them. They carry automatic rifles. Some of them stand under the marquee of the Piper Twin Theater, smoking cigarettes and talking.

There is a holiday atmosphere every day now on Main Street.

The marquee on the theater reads: COMING SOON! SHE SPEAKS TO ONE OF US!

"You know that girl? Darlene Vick?" Wayne asks.

"Yeah," Keith says.

"She's in the hospital, I heard."

"Yeah. Her dad beat her up."

"No shit?"

"Yeah."

"She's Brenda Boykin's niece."

"Yeah," Keith says.

They find a place and sit on one of the meditation benches. The sun is high, bright. They have to squint at the image of the Virgin, at the sun's silver reflection on the glass. Keith seems impatient, fidgety. Coles and Justice have set up a souvenir stand in front of the theater, where they sell candles and full-color post cards of the image and key rings and plastic icons of the Virgin Mary. People crowd around. Next to the souvenir stand, a trailer sells ice cream and popsicles, and children push and bunch up in front of it. Down the way another trailer dispenses barbecue; COLES'S DOWN HOME, the huge sign says, with the familiar drawing of Coles in a white chef's hat, the same one from the label on the sauce. The air smells of barbecue and popcorn.

"Well," Wayne says.

"Well what?" Keith asks.

"Well, I don't know," Wayne says. He stares at the pavement between his scuffed running shoes. He needs to start running again. He needs to sweat all that down-deep alcohol out. He looks at his son. Keith is looking back at him questioningly. "Things just seem so ... so out of balance, son," Wayne says.

"Yeah," Keith says.

"I mean, I want you to know I ..." Wayne stops. He swallows. He shrugs. He looks around. The crowd makes a steady, ragged hum. "You see, I thought I was doing Otis a favor. You know? And I was! I mean, he had a chance, really, to really be something, you know?"

"Yeah," Keith says.

"But I feel so goddamed guilty about it! It's eating me up, son."

"It is?"

"Yeah. It is. I didn't know what it was at first, eating at me. But then I started figuring it out. I used the boy, son, and I guess I just want you to know I'm sorry about it."

"Why me?" Keith asks. "Why not tell Otis that?"

Wayne stares at him. "Because, by damn, you're my son, that's why you. Tune in, Keith. And I don't know where the hell Otis is."

"Where is he?"

"Hell, I don't know. Listen to what I say! How the hell should I know?"

"I was just asking," Keith says.

"I figure he's long gone and will send for that old woman eventually. Ain't no telling where he is. But I—"

"Listen," Keith says, "my head. The sun will burn my head. I need to—"

"All right, goddamit," Wayne says. They stand up. Wayne sighs. His son is almost as tall as he is, skinny as a toothpick. His head is like a cue ball. The sunlight glitters on the rings all over his face. "Hell," Cajun Rhodes had said in Leroy's one night, "I heard they put them rings in the heads of their peckers, and girls have em on their nipples and their clits. Beats all. Is that true, Wayne?" "Fuck you, Cajun," Wayne had said, "since when is it your business?" Now, looking at his son, he wonders all that himself. Why? he wants to ask his son yet again, but he does not. If you'd let your hair grow out like a normal person you wouldn't have to worry about the goddam sun on your head. He just stands there. His son starts to walk away.

"You want a barbecue? Some ice cream?" Wayne asks.

"No," Keith says, "the sun, man."

"All right," Wayne says.

⮑

A couple of days later Wayne borrows Tom Stabler's bass boat and trailer. There is a series of ponds on government land up along the Warrior River, some of them sloughs of the river itself, and Wayne thinks he remembers where the biggest and best of the bream beds are. Keith actually brightens once they're on the water, even though it is just day-break and Keith had complained and resisted getting up.

"You're just doing this to punish me," he had said.

"For what?"

"For Karla. All that. For everything."

"No. All that's your business, son. Your business."

The boat has a small trolling motor, and they move quietly and steadily toward a large stand of willows on the other side of the pond from the boat landing. The early morning sun is vague and pale behind heavy clouds, and the new day is muggy and still. Wayne anchors the boat off the willows and they begin to cast, both of them using small yellow popping bugs. Almost immediately they begin to catch thick heavy bluegills that strike with a ferocity and fight with a tenacity that belie their size and weight. Almost every cast results in a strike. Keith loses many of them, laughing at himself, and Wayne laughs with him, pokes fun at him. They boat three stringers of the bluegills, each one as big as a man's hand, their scarlet throats glistening in the sunlight that filters through the clouds. Wayne is already thinking of cleaning them and frying them in deep fat for their supper; he will make hushpuppies with lots of onion and cole slaw with pickles and tomatoes, and they can eat until they can't move and then watch the Braves and the Reds on television. He hopes that Keith doesn't have something planned for this evening.

He watches his son, watches his profile as he casts a smooth, even cast that Wayne remembers patiently teaching him. Keith is a better fisherman than Wayne is. His back cast is strong and controlled; the line rolls out behind him with precision and welds neatly with his forward cast, which is direct and accurate and gentle, the lure floating down to the surface of the water underneath the overhanging willows and landing with just a delicate ripple, like a real insect.

Keith will spend the summer with his mother and there's not a damn thing Wayne can do about it, and then his son will be thousands of miles away in New York. Paid for by Mister Meadows. Keith doesn't know that Wayne is observing him. He looks small and vulnerable in the boat. The rings in his lip. The studs in his eyebrows.

Keith's touch with the fly rod and heavy line is restrained and controlled, and as he watches him Wayne can almost hear the strains of the Mendelssohn concerto that Keith has been practicing, that he will play with the Birmingham Symphony as his recital for old man Smiley. The rhythm and the sounds of the music are bound up with Keith's movements with the fly rod. Wayne sees the connection; he knows the connection, but he cannot put it into words. He wants to express it to Keith; it would be something substantial for them to talk about. But he knows that anything he says will be cheesy and inadequate. He sits looking where Keith has cast. The leader is invisible on the water. The bug lies still, then moves with a barely discernable ripple, followed by a sudden strike, the water spraying outward, the leader suddenly taut and disappearing underwater as the bream turns its flat body sideways and begins to fight against the pressure of the line.

By midmorning they have both grown tired. The sun peeps out from behind the clouds now and the air is heavy and damp. They are sweating freely. It has been in the high eighties for a couple of days, the beginning of the fierce Alabama summer that will set in and not relent until October. October. Another football season. The first one in a while in which Wayne will not be coaching. Coaching is all he knows, but he will not be doing it. The sun's emerging from behind the clouds turns the air over the lake into an oven.

They reel in their lines and break their rods down. Wayne looses the anchor and lets the boat drift. Wayne can see the sunlight glinting off Keith's rings, his studs. He would give anything to have back those years when the boy was a child, those blurred, innocent years. Wayne pushes the electric starter button and the little motor putters into life. They cross the lake.

They secure the boat on the trailer and then cover it. They stand in the bright sunshine by Wayne's dusty car. Wayne opens the trunk for the water cooler. He sees Keith look carefully; he knows the boy is looking for Wayne's beer.

"Nothing there. I quit, I told you," Wayne says, and Keith just looks at him. "I mean it."

"I know you do," Keith says. He looks Wayne in the eye, and then he looks off across the pond. Dark green cedars stand in a row along the bank, like Christmas trees waiting for their tinsel. Wayne stares at his son's profile.

"You and Karla," Wayne says, "I mean, you love her, or what?"

"Sure," Keith says. His gaze seems fixed on the trees. "But things change, Dad. They never stay the same."

That's right, Wayne thinks, that's sure right. And as he stands looking at the boy, his son, that same immense sadness he had felt in the boy's room that other afternoon—listening to the Mozart—wells up inside him again, coming out of nowhere like a sudden summer thunderstorm on a sunny day, and he thinks he can hear the Mozart and then the Mendelssohn. He hears the music in his head. He feels clumsy, self-conscious. Wayne does not ever want to let his boy go away again. But he will have to.

Wayne hears the distant cawing of a crow. He looks around him, at the cleared fields littered with broken rust-colored rocks and clumps of Cherokee roses. Thin woods line the old logging road that leads up to the pond. Wayne is thirsty, and he grabs the water jug from the trunk of the car and runs a cup of water. It is icy, jarring. It makes his teeth ache. He wipes his mouth with the back of his hand and looks at the boy.

Wayne hears the music clearly now in his mind. He has played the CD over and over again in Keith's absences—the Mendelssohn that Keith will play—and he has listened to Keith practicing. It is sweet and clean and as pure as the child that still lies somewhere within his son, that is still his child and will always be his child. He looks away, at the way the sunlight glitters on the water. All around them is quiet, stillness. He can feel the power of the sun on the top of his head, on his shoulders.

Wayne has never loved his son more than he does at this moment. He feels tears beginning to gather in his eyes. He keeps looking at the lake. He does not want Keith to see him cry. He swallows heavily. He does not know what to say, and he does not know how to tell Keith what he's feeling. He wants a gesture, something, some way to express it. Then he is aware that Keith is observing him closely. He shakes his head. He spits on the ground. He grins.

"How about a swim?" he asks.

"A swim?" Keith is looking around, at the muddy gravel of the landing, the dark water. "Here?"

"Hell, yeah," Wayne says. He is already pulling off his damp shirt. He unzips his shorts, lets them drop and steps out of them. He stands there in his briefs. "It ain't a swimming pool, but it's cool and wet," he says.

"It's April," Keith says.

"It's hot, ain't it?" Wayne leans back against the car and pulls his sneakers off. He rolls his briefs down, feeling the air suddenly cool on his exposed private skin, and he wades into the water. The gravel bites into the bottoms of his feet. He feels the mud squishy around the pebbles, soft between his toes. The almost liquid mud—and the water—is startlingly cold. It takes Wayne's breath away. He feels the cold water rising on his legs. He squats in the water, feeling his privates float freely. It is liberating, cooling, secret. "Come on in," he says, raising his feet, floating into the pond.

He watches Keith begin to undress. The boy shyly turns his back. His sweat-splotched shirt comes off, then his battered sneakers. He takes off his jeans. He wears white jockey shorts and he seems to hesitate just a moment before pulling them down. Wayne can see his thin back, very white, his narrow buttocks with the mushroom tattoo, his skinny legs. Wayne remembers changing his diaper, cleaning him down there with tissues treated in that sweet smelling baby oil. He remembers Keith's little pecker the way it had been then, on a pee hard, stiff as a little rubber nub, the unimpeded stream suddenly spewing all across the room and he remembers Bobbye's laughter, how they had laughed together. Tears mist his eyes again and blind him in the sunlight.

He can barely see the boy coming on into the water. He hears him splash. He sees his shape moving toward him.

"Wait, Dad," Keith says, "wait for me."

And Wayne floats. He lets his face go under the cool water. He splashes back to the surface, shaking his hair, watching the droplets spraying around him and glistening in the sun-filled air. His son is smiling as he paddles up to him, reaching out to clasp his hand and hold it.

⌐

Darlene Vick stands on the stage of the Piper Twin Theater. It is no longer really a "twin" theater, because Duane Justice ripped out the partition dividing the auditorium into two smaller ones that allowed him to show two movies at the same time. The curtain now goes all the way across behind Darlene, hiding the two smaller screens. Darlene wears a black eye patch over her right eye. She is thinner. Even though her skin still shows the marks of the beating she had taken from her father, she is beautiful. Her radiance is visible from even the backmost rows of the theater. Hundreds of sets of eyes are glued to her, expectant and eager. Television cameras are trained on her. Over her head is a wooden cross Duane Justice had nailed to the proscenium.

Darlene wears a long flowing purple robe. The theater is packed with people, standing room only. Uniformed and armed soldiers stand along the walls and at the back. Tickets for the event had gone for $45 each and had been snapped up within hours of going on sale. Darlene wears the eye patch because the injury to her right eye was so severe she had lost all vision in it. The eyeball was crushed and had to be removed. The eye patch had been a gift, bought for Darlene at the thrift store by Cody Klinger, who had brought it to her Aunt Brenda's house, where Darlene is now staying. He had presented it to her with a flourish.

"You'll look like a lady pirate," he said. "Wear it with panache, girl!" He bowed from the waist. He hung out at her Aunt Brenda's house. Darlene had been shocked to learn that he sometimes slept in her Aunt Brenda's bed.

When Brenda had driven Darlene home from the hospital in her rattly old blue Toyota she went straight to her own house. "You can't go back there," her Aunt Brenda had said, "I won't let you. The son-of-a-bitch!"

Her Aunt Brenda is angry and sad. She stomps around the house. Darlene can hear her crying during the night. Ever since Jimmy disappeared from the hospital, Brenda has been so distraught she can not even do her work.

"We have no idea," the hospital people had told her, "but there has to be some explanation for it. There is no way he could have walked out. The police are working on it."

"I've hired the best private detective agency in Atlanta," Coles tells her. "They'll get to the bottom of it."

"No," Brenda says, "I don't think so." Her eyes are red-rimmed from lack of sleep. Her long dark hair, usually so shiny and full, is dirty and matted. "I don't think anybody will ever explain it to me, ever!"

"Pull yourself together," Coles says. "I'm here for you."

She just looks at him. He can see what looks like sheer hatred in her eyes. He knows it is fear and panic over her son. Finally, she says,

"Why don't you go to hell?!?"

"You're upset," he says.

"You're goddamed right I'm upset!"

"Marry me, Brenda! Let me take care of you," he says. It is an order, not a question.

"No. Never."

"It's that boy, isn't it?"

"What boy?" she asks.

"The boy. From Hollywood. Cody whatever his name is."

She laughs bitterly, without mirth. "I wouldn't marry you, Roger, if you were the last man on this earth," she says. "Cody has nothing to do with it."

"Then you don't deny it? That you've been...that you've been intimate with him? He's young enough to be your son."

"I'm young enough to be your daughter, Roger," she says. "In fact I'm the exact same age as your fucking stupid daughter!"

"You're upset," he says.

She is losing her mind. Anybody could see that. She is having a nervous breakdown. "Take all the time off from work that you need," he says, "and you need to see a doctor."

"A doctor? That is the very last thing I need! The very last thing I need in all the world is a fucking doctor!"

When Roger leaves her he feels more determined than ever to marry her. He knows that this is just a momentary lapse, a brief breakdown. He wants to make her well, to nurse her back to health. He will. He drives through town, going too fast. He had been astonished the day he returned home and found Helen Grace crying in the kitchen. "Daddy," she had blubbered, "she's dead! She's dead!"

"Who? Who's dead?"

"Damuddy!" Tears were streaming down Helen Grace's face. She sat perched in the chair like a bird. She gripped a white handkerchief, which she twisted around and around her fingers.

"No," he said. "You must be mistaken. Your grandmother is alive and well. She is as alive as the flowers, as full of life as a fresh young girl! Whatever are you talking about?"

His daughter stared at him, a peculiar horrified look in her eyes. "Don't you ... can't you ... smell it?"

"Smell it?" He sniffed the air. "Smell what?" he said, smiling broadly. "I only smell the springtime!"

His daughter had seemed afraid of him. Everyone these days seems afraid of him. Except Brenda. She defies him because she is spunky and full of spirit. A spirit to be broken and bent to his will. Like a wild filly. All the people gathered on Main Street watch him go by. They know who he is. They point him out to their children and to newcomers. He is famous. He sees his soldiers in front of the theater. He sees them up and down the street, at their posts. A contingent of them is stationed out at the construction site of the Twenty-First Century Mall, to guard against possible sabotage. He has had Leeds Scroggins and Calvin Bluett set up inspection posts at the county line where each highway comes in, except for I-65, and they have a plan for that one as well, a plan that can be implemented at a moment's notice.

Byron Bailey stands before the full-length mirror on the closet door in his bedroom. He poses, first one way and then another. He cannot detect the bulk of the dynamite beneath his fatigues. No one would ever notice. His uniform fits him loosely anyway, leaving plenty of room for the explosives. He has practiced this so often that his skin is raw from the tape. He fingers the switch in his pocket. He marches in place, his eyes following his every move in the mirror. He drops to his knees, holding an imaginary rifle. He does not move, posing as still as a statue. After a minute he jumps to his feet and stands at attention and salutes his image in the glass. Then he stands very straight and draws imaginary pistols, two of them, and shoots himself. "Pow, pow," he says. His cheeks are flushed pink with excitement. He smiles.

COLLEEN IS NAKED, WITH SPRING FLOWERS IN HER THICK black hair. The delicate white blossoms—called thrift—are woven into the hair itself. She prances on the altar, displaying to them the aborted human fetus they have gotten from the Women's Health Center. Keith has brought his portable CD player, the one he got from Mr. Meadows for Christmas, and it plays *Le Sacre du Printemps*. A bonfire crackles and roars. The thickening trees blot out the stars. Willie Clyde is here, and Otis, and Jimmy in a wheelchair stolen from the hospital.

They have all snorted several bumps of Special K. In addition, Colleen, when she was still robed, had—in an elaborate ceremony—presented Jimmy with a peyote button that he chewed and washed down with Old Milwaukee. Jimmy's head feels swollen and full of soft red and green lights. The flames from the fire seem like giant crimson snakes. The flames reflect on Colleen's pale body, on her pudgy breasts. Her thighs are thick and sturdy. She holds the fetus and screams at them:

"I am the tempter of life that lurks in every breast and belly! A vibrant, torpid cavern, nectar laden, with sweetest pleasures beckoning!"

"Sustain us, dark lord!" the others chant in unison. Keith and Jayne Ann Dewberry are there, and Karla, and Lolly Phillips. Everything swirls around Jimmy in a palette of bleeding smears that run together to form new colors and shapes. The K makes his whole body tingle and his eyes burn, and the peyote causes the leaves on the trees to turn into birds that flutter around him and brush against the skin of his face, and the music punches the back of his head in a series of thumps like from a baby's fist. He wants to rise from the wheelchair because he knows he can walk. But at the same time he knows he cannot. He knows he can fly. He is certain he can fly. He sees that Colleen's head is gone, that she has been decapitated. She dances with only a bloody stump for a neck.

"I am a thrusting rod with a head of iron," she shouts, "drawing to me myriad nymphs, tumescent in their cravings!"

"Yes, yes, dark lord!"

"Through jagged ice my father leers with cavernous eyes, below the sphere of earth that is my mother, moist and fertile whore of barbarous delights!"

Lolly Phillips has joined Colleen now, throwing off her robe. Jimmy's eyes fix on Lolly's body. Her skin glows like neon, plump soft flesh that grows larger and then shrinks, that sways with the music, which Jimmy can now see in front of his eyes, the notes in physical form leaping about like the myriad strings of spiders' webs. He has never seen anything more beautiful or desirable than Lolly's flame-streaked body. Her breasts are bathed in the firelight and her legs are molded from the smoothest stone. Her entire body is covered in curly black pubic hair, and it smells like a million roses jammed into his nostrils.

He feels his erection growing. He feels it inside his head, as though his entire body is his penis, burning like fire and about to erupt and explode. He looks down and his entire lower body has become a mass of green liquid, bubbling like mercury, giving off spurts of steam, the heat from it moving up through his chest and out along his arms and into his hands and fingers, and he kneads the flesh of Lolly's breasts, the tight hard nipples, Lolly and Colleen together now pressing against him and smothering him so that he drowns in the soft hot meat, four breasts caressing his mouth and his feverish face. He is rising from the chair, his body floating, every inch of his skin as sensitive as his glans penis, and he feels himself merging with them, absorbed by them, sucked deeply into them and disappearing up and away like rising mist into the greater blacker sky.

The voices drift. The voices suffuse like twilight. They drift over the valley, over the trees and rooftops. Whether or not a radio picks them up and gives them life, they are there in the air like spirits. They are like matter: they can be neither created nor destroyed. The voices are constant and immortal; they exist beyond the larynxes that give them sound. They have existed since before the sunrise of time.

A man: "Yahweh our father is at work setting the stage for the final act against the Christ-murdering Jews and their father, Satan!" And Alex shrieks,

"You are insane! Insane!" Beads of sweat cling to his forehead. Mrs. Norton watches him with alarm. He is even thinner now. He is at the station all day, insisting on working both shifts. He does not break for lunch, and Mrs. Norton is convinced he's not eating well at all. She had brought him a green bean casserole and had found it, Pyrex dish and all, in the dumpster behind the station.

"The People Speak," he growls, switching to another line, "go ahead. Go ahead!"

She had not known he was religious at all until he showed up the day after Ash Wednesday with a smudged black cross on his high forehead. "Why, I didn't know you were Catholic," she said and he looked at her with his eyes feverish and unfocused, looking straight through her, and he said,

"I'm not. But I'm going to die! Just like you and everybody else!" and cold shivers ran all up and down her spine. He has become almost like a son to her. She doesn't want to meddle in his business, but she hopes he isn't about to kill himself or something. She had seen him one Sunday afternoon talking to that young man from Hollywood who was in town scouting locations for a movie. They were in the park, and the young man from Hollywood had his video camera trained on Alex, and Alex was talking and gesturing, unshaven, his clothes as dirty and wrinkled as a bum's. He looked insane. He had worn the black cross on his forehead for days, until it finally faded away. She supposes he isn't washing himself. He smells like he isn't, anyway.

"GO AHEAD!" he shouts into the microphone.

"Alex, the birds is back." It is a black woman who called before and told them she is blind. She sounds very old. Her voice trembles. "The birds is back. I hears em singin and carryin on, and I know, Lord, that the springtime is here! Hallelujah!"

"It doesn't take much to please you, does it?" Alex snarls.

"No, sir, it don't. It sure don't."

"Birds are filthy," Alex says, "they nest in the eaves and they carry diseases! They are worse than rats!"

"No sir, you got the wrong idea there!"

"Birds will attack you. Didn't you see that old Hitchcock movie?"

"I can't see nothin, sir."

"Oh, that's right. You claim to be blind. Well, how do I know you're really blind? Can you prove to me, over the phone, that you are actually, really, blind? Let's see, what can you tell me that will convince me that you are actually, really blind? Huh?"

"A man that ain't got no feets can't walk," the old woman says, and Alex screams,

"What the hell has that got to do with anything?!?" and Mrs. Norton bleeps out the "hell." She is terribly concerned about Alex. He is totally agitated now. He is bouncing in his chair. He is furiously licking his lips. "Huh? Tell me? Tell me?" There is only silence on the line and Alex jabs another flashing button. "The People Speak!"

"Alex, this is Newton Grable, Pastor of the Church of the New Light with Signs Following—"

"Oh, my God!"

"Alex, I am founding a new group called the Missionaries to the Preborn. These precious children need someone to preach to them and save their souls before they are murdered! These—"

CLICK. "The People Speak."

"I just want to put in my two cents' worth! We need to teach our young people to be responsible Freemen! The most loving thing you can do for a child is to buy him or her an SKS rifle and five hundred rounds of ammunition! We need to quit playing these silly little games like blindfolding em and telling em to pin the tail on the donkey! We need to blindfold em and sit em down on the living room floor and tell em, 'Now put some weapons together.'"

"Yeah. Teach them all that in Sunday School, right?"

"Why not? I tell you—" CLICK.

"Alex! Listen here! You remember that Oklahoma City bombing?"

"No," Alex says, "what bombing was that?"

"Oh, come on! Anyhow, listen here. Clinton ordered that bombing! That's the God's truth. With the help of his co-conspirator, Attorney General Janet Reno, that cigar-smoking butch lesbian who owns forty-seven pet peacocks, all named Horace. He—"

"Wait now. How do you know all this? Did you read it in the *Star?*"

"No sir. I read it in a flyer circulated by Mr. Roger Coles! Our Probate Judge. And, son, he don't lie! And he's got a shrine right down there in town to prove it! Something that Jesus put there—"

"How do you know it was Jesus who put it there?"

"Who else was it if it wasn't Jesus? Huh? You can't argue with that logic, son!"

Alex laughs. He cackles. His whole body shudders with it. Mrs. Norton watches him with her eyes narrowed. He sounds like one of those mad scientists in the picture shows. He keeps laughing long after anything would cease to be funny. He laughs and laughs. His laughter crackles and sparkles on the airwaves. Mrs. Norton sits still and quiet, her finger poised over her bleeper button, watching him shake and gasp for breath, hearing the forced bursts of hilarity, his body convulsing with the effort. His laughter goes on and on and on.

Ethel Belle Lilly, one of the two women who had been on the church bus that Sunday morning some nine months ago when Byron Bailey had hitched the ride into town, is walking on Pettus Street when she sees the girl again. Ethel Belle Lilly wears the same flowered dress she had on that Sunday morning, and she has told the story of seeing the little girl in the church many times since then. When she sees her this time the girl is older, a teenager, but Ethel Belle knows it is the same girl. She is certain of it. The girl wears the same white dress, too, and has the same hair. The girl is with two boys. She is with Otis Hunnicutt and a white boy in a wheelchair.

Ethel Belle watches them go on down the street toward the woods beyond the Women's Health Center. The girl and Otis take turns pushing the white boy in the wheelchair. They are laughing and making a game of it. Then they vanish into the woods. They don't walk into the woods. They just fade out and sink into the new green, like three yearling catfish disappearing suddenly into the depths. One second she is watching them, and then she simply can't see them any more.

†WELVE

The large high-ceilinged auditorium is charged with electric energy, like lightninged air before a storm. Darlene stands on the stage in her purple robe. Music plays through the speakers: *I come to the garden alone ... while the dew is still on the roses ...* Some in the capacity audience stir impatiently and whisper among themselves and others shush them, urging them to maintain a reverent silence. The Militiamen in their uniforms, holding their rifles, stand along the walls and across the back. The air over the heads of the gathered throng is thick with anticipation. Darlene squints with her one good eye; she loves her black eye patch. It gives her confidence. Cody is in one aisle with a camera set up on a tripod, taping everything. Darlene lets her eye take him in. He is fine, all right. He's a hotty. She is already more than half in love with him.

Darlene focuses inwardly on what she is here for. She has no idea why she knows that this will be the time, but she does. She is sure of it. Duane Justice paces nervously in the back. When she looks at him she feels a chilly emptiness inside. The memory of the naked girl on the floor waving to her from the pool of blood is indelibly etched in the forefront of her brain. It is as though she has given birth to her own self. "It is piss, too, Darlene," the girl whispers to her in her waking and sleeping dreams, "piss and blood!" Darlene knows the girl, has known her all her life, knows her as well as she knows herself, and yet she cannot recall ever seeing her before.

⇌

Her Aunt Brenda helps her get dressed before she goes to the theater. "Maybe this is the end of everything, the apolcalypse," Brenda laughs. Her laughter is harsh and hopeless. She talks on the phone constantly with the Birmingham police and the FBI and the private detective that Mr. Coles has hired. "Find him," Darlene hears her plead, "I just want my son back!" She looks at Darlene with hollow hurting eyes. "I think he died and they're just not telling me," she says.

"Yeah," she says now, "the apocalypse, and I can go out and meet God face to face and pull Her hair and claw Her eyes!"

"Reverend Grable and his people are preaching that it is the Rapture," Darlene says. "It's the beginning of the New Millennium. Jesus is coming. He's coming to Wembly County. That's what he says."

"Reverend Grable is full of shit," her Aunt Brenda says.

Brenda laughs again. Darlene watches her face in the mirror. Brenda laughs that way all the time. She is trying to keep up her spirits. It has been over three weeks now since Jimmy disappeared. She pulls Darlene's hair back with both her hands and they look at it in the mirror. Brenda's face is drawn; it looks thinner. "Like that?" Brenda asks.

"Yeah," Darlene says. Then she wants flowers worked into her hair. White thrift, which she has already gathered and lays on the dressing table before the two women.

↩

Darlene's arms rise. They move of their own accord. A silence falls over the crowd. People crane forward. Hundreds of eyes are fastened on her. Then she speaks, speaks in a clear loud voice that is not her own, and she says,

"It is in beauty that we come." She senses someone behind her, behind the thick red velvet curtain. The curtain smells of dust and disuse. She knows who is back there. She feels her whole body relaxing and easing. A film of cooling sweat breaks out all over her body. She has known this is the way it will be without having to be told. "We come into a great darkness so that you can see a great light," she hears herself saying, or she hears Mary's voice coming from her and saying, as clearly as a tinkling silver bell.

"AMEN!" she hears someone shout, and there is a restless stirring.

"And how great is that darkness," she says. "Oh, how great is that darkness!"

"Tell it, sister," someone else shouts.

"Our name is Legion, and we are many!" she says.

"Yes! Yes!"

She feels Mary behind the curtain. Mary gives off heat like an oven. The spotlights are bright in Darlene's eyes. She feels herself lifting from the floor. She is levitating, and she feels it, and a stunned hush settles over the audience. She hovers two feet above the wide boards of the stage. Darlene thinks she is going to swoon, to faint dead away. She sees Duane Justice in the back. She sees Mr. Roger Coles and his daughter and her husband in a roped off section on the aisle, and she sees her Aunt Brenda, who looks at her with wide, astonished eyes. Someone, a blond young man in an Army uniform, is standing up down front, glaring at Darlene. Darlene searches the audience, looking for her mother and father, but she doesn't see them. She doesn't remember how long it has been since she has seen them.

She looks back at the young man down front. He is standing in his seat now, staring at her with open and intense hostility, and he waves his arms over his head. People behind him begin to yell at him to sit back down. He looks familiar to Darlene; she has seen him around town, in McDonald's or somewhere, but she does not know him. He looks upset.

"FAKE!" he yells. "It's a TRICK!"

"Shut up, Byron!" someone yells to him.

"Sit down down there!"

He turns around to face the audience. "It's a trick on you poor ignorant sons-of-bitches!" he screams. The soldiers now surround him. They try to grab his arms but he jerks them away. "Wake up, you people! Don't you know what's going on?!?"

"Come on, now, Byron," one of the soldiers says, in a voice meant to calm.

"Don't you know when you're being taken for a ride? Huh? This ain't nothing but a trick on white people, and you can't even see it! I'm the one with the real message!"

"Now Byron, just calm down," the soldier says. They grapple with him, grab him, and he steps down to the floor in their grasps. They begin to hustle him up the aisle. Everyone begins to boo and hiss at him. "Git that little piss-ant outta here," Boligee Phil shouts, and there is much laughter and hooting. Cody Klinger is getting it all on tape, swinging his camera around to follow the action.

When they disappear with him out the door in the back, Darlene is standing flat-footed on the stage. She does not remember being lowered and she realizes she is back down at the same time the audience does. There is a loud collective gasp and a ripple of whispering that drifts across the crowd like a breeze on an alfalfa field. And then Darlene realizes that the people are not looking at her any longer but at the stage to her left and she turns fully expecting Her to be standing there but She is not. It is Jimmy Boykin, in his wheelchair. Darlene feels giddy and lightheaded.

There is not a sound. Darlene doesn't know if he were rolled out or just appeared there. She does not know where he came from. She stands gazing at her cousin. She feels the heat from Mary even stronger now, behind her and through the old musty curtain. The spotlights sparkle on the chromium of the wheelchair. Jimmy is even thinner now and his legs are like sticks beneath his jeans. Darlene remembers how he looked in his football uniform, his green jersey with the white number 80. She had been proud to be his cousin but too shy to ever tell him so. Back then she had been too shy; football season seems like a hundred years ago. She doesn't think she is the same person now that she was back then.

Her arm stiffens and extends out toward him. She points to him. Her hand feels hot. It feels as though it's going to melt. Jimmy looks startled. He stands up. There is another gasp from the audience, a sudden unified and violent intake of breath. Darlene hears several voices crying out in wonder and surprise. Darlene is not surprised; it's as though she has long known this was going to happen without really knowing it. Jimmy begins a slow jog around the stage. There's a big smile on his face. Some people laugh, some begin to applaud. Brenda runs down the aisle toward the stage.

Brenda's heart is jumping around so violently that she thinks it's going to bounce out of her chest. She almost loses her balance on the downward sloping aisle, as though she is running down and Jimmy and Darlene are up. She becomes disoriented. She can feel the heat from the white lights. They blind her because her eyes are full of tears. She sees Jimmy standing, moving around. He is whole. She has seen him walk again so often in her dreams, just as vividly as now. She is not sure this is real and not some vision. She hears her mother's voice saying to her that it is really happening, but her mother is not real herself; she is dead.

There are stairs at the side of the stage and Brenda runs up them, hearing her footsteps amidst the laughter and cheering and applause that rise from the crowd. She is in the spotlights now, aware of their shafts coming down like darts from the vast gloom above. Jimmy stands there looking at her. He is flesh and blood. She approaches him cautiously and puts her arms around him. He is her son, the familiar thin body and the scent like old milk and tennis shoes. He embraces her, clings to her. The same arms and hands that had pulled at her breasts and tangled her clothes, the same legs that had been short and chubby and stumbled to first walking. She wants to pull him back inside her to the warmth and safety of her womb. She tries to. She squeezes him so hard that he whimpers.

She feels him sag against her. She feels him begin to grow heavy. She pulls away from him, looking into his face. His skin is pale and beads of perspiration stand on his forehead. He staggers. He begins to move back toward the wheelchair, walking like an old man. She helps him, holds him, and Darlene grabs his other arm. They guide him into the chair and he sits heavily, like dead weight, and all the strength seems to leave his arms at once.

He stares at her, his eyes as wasted and full of dread knowledge as an ancient statue of a long dead boy. The auditorium falls as silent as outer space. She feels her heart shrivel and burn. She smiles. She is grateful to have him here, back, alive.

Thousands of people outside the theater who could not get in crowd the streets of Piper. All the roads and highways leading into Wembly County are clogged with cars. The word spreads by mouth and radio and television that the one-eyed girl has spoken with the voice of the Virgin Mary and has made the crippled walk.

⌒

Easter Sunday dawns bright and chill. Thousands of people gather in a pasture outside of town for a sunrise service conducted by the Reverend Newton Grable. There is an adult choir and a children's choir. As the sun comes up over the green wooded hills—a flaming orange disk that rises straight up into the blue morning air like a runaway helium balloon slipped from the fist of a distracted child—the combined choirs and the multitudes sing "Jesus Christ is Risen today! Allelujah!" Miss Minnie Vice plays a portable electric organ that has been towed out on a flat-bed trailer from the church. It is powered by a generator the Men of the Church rigged up.

All over town children search for brightly-dyed eggs under shrubbery and tufts of fresh new crabgrass springing up on the lawns, while sleepy parents still in their nightclothes watch from the front stoop. They squeeze their upper arms against the chill, but the children don't seem to notice it. Already lawns are littered with shattered eggs and candy wrappers. Already the Sunday School room in the educational building at the Hidden Valley Church of the New Light With Signs Following is streaked with egg yellow and fast-drying sticky yolks because Miss Alexandra Harvey and Miss Katharine Harrison, two maiden ladies, soft-boiled the eggs for the nursery before dying them. When the toddlers discover that, there is chaos.

Byron Bailey has been up since dawn. He sits in his bedroom in his parents' little house on the edge of his single bed, the bed he has slept in every night of his life, his back very straight and the soles of his boots flat on the floor. The bed is made up in crisp, neat military fashion, with a blanket on top and the corners sharply creased. It is as though Byron is poised for something, about to spring into action. Any second now he will move. But he remains still. Tense. He wears his fatigues and his cap. The dynamite is strapped around his chest again, the fuse switch in his pocket. He caresses the button softly with the fleshy under-tip of his thumb. He is not breathing. He has held his breath for a long time, longer than he can remember, and he suddenly exhales and then takes another deep breath. He sits as still as an image in an old photograph. He hears his mother talking to herself in the kitchen. She has gotten old and tired, just in the last years. His father has not come home. He is off drunk somewhere again. His mother is preparing pancakes, which she fixes every Easter Sunday morning without fail, whether his father is there or not, or preaching or not. They will have pancakes and sausage and maple syrup, and then they will go off to church. Except that this time Byron is not going to church with his mother. This time Byron is going to a church of his own making.

⸻

Cody Klinger wakes up in his motel room with Rasheedah Mangruen, a television correspondent with Fox News. Rasheedah is tall and soft butter brown with black curly hair and eyes as green as winter grass. They had snorted coke and eaten fresh strawberries and made love into the night. Rasheedah doesn't have a hair on her body, except for her head.

"What'd you shave it for?" Cody had asked her and she had looked at him and shrugged her shoulders.

"I ain't shaved it, man," she said. "Lasers, baby. The latest. Ain't it cute?"

"Jesus, didn't that hurt?"

"You goddam right it hurt, man," she said. "But it's where it's at, don't you know?" They were both naked on the bed. She lay propped on one elbow, looking at his body. She looked him up and down and licked her lips. "Hey, buddy, you got it goin on, man! You the shit!" She sounded to Cody as if she was right off the street; on the air she was proper and had a British accent.

"Let's go get some coffee," he says when they are dressed.

"What's happenin today, man? Remind me. We in the zoo, man!"

"A rally. Speech. This guy Roger Coles, he's making a big speech down in the middle of town. Down at the shrine. Lots of politicians and big shots gonna be there."

"Where'd all these white folks come from?" she asks with a laugh. "I ain't seen so many honkies in one place since the Republican convention!"

"This is some big shit goin on."

"Yeah," she says.

"Militia shit."

"These people are wild," she says. "They crazy. I'm gonna watch my black ass."

"You'd better," Cody says.

→

Otis and Willie Clyde sit in the lower branches of a tree down along Shell Creek and watch a rabbit skitter out of the bushes and out onto the running track. "The Easter Bunny," Otis says. "Peter Cottontail," Willie Clyde says. The jackrabbit stops and sits up on its haunches and sniffs the air; its nose is wrinkled and its ears are flat down its back. The rabbit's gray-brown fur is rippled by an early morning breeze. The trees in the woods are already almost fully leaved and thick. It has happened overnight. The world is fresh and new. There are only high, puffy white clouds in the sky and the mostly unobstructed sun warms the day. The rabbit hops on across the cinder track and disappears into the undergrowth.

Behind the clouds are the cherubs, the angels, the hundreds of souls of the tiny fetuses and clusters of cells that have left the physical world in the Women's Health Center. They make themselves invisible, hiding behind the cottony clouds. They hover over the town, over the tall trees and the downtown buildings. They dance behind the clouds like plump pink bumblebees. Their laughter drifts on the wind.

→

Jimmy is asleep in his room. Darlene sleeps on the couch in the living room. Brenda moves through the still darkened house scratching and stretching. She smells the coffee from the large automatic Krupps coffee maker Coles had given her. Jimmy has not walked since that day on the stage. But he had definitely walked then. Brenda had seen him walk with her own eyes, and hundreds of others had seen him, too, in the flesh, and millions more on television. "Make it happen again," she says to Darlene, and Darlene shrugs. She looks away with tears in her eyes. "I want to," she says. "I want to!"

"Well then," Brenda says, "do it! Please!"

Darlene breaks down and sobs. "I want to," she says, over and over again. "I will, I promise I will!"

"You will? How do you know?"

Darlene is smiling now. Her face shines with the drying tears. "I just know. It'll happen. I know it will. It'll happen. He'll walk just like new."

"All right," Brenda says after a pause. She smiles, too. Darlene's black eye patch is slightly askew on her face. Brenda reaches out and gently straightens it.

Wayne and Keith sit on one of the outdoor church pews on Main Street, enjoying the morning sunshine, watching the crowd gather. They eat sausage biscuits from McDonald's. Wayne wears a blue T-shirt and white shorts, and he sits sprawled back with narrow black sunglasses on. He nods to people who pass and greet him as "Coach." Wayne smells the sausage and popcorn and cooking grease in the air, and something sugary and sweet. Wayne thinks the air smells like Easter when he was a boy. Little girls wear frilly pastel dresses and women wear hats. Keith wears cut-off jeans and his legs are pale white and thin. He chews his biscuit and grins at Wayne.

Since the day they went swimming they have taken to listening to music together. They've moved Keith's stereo into the living room and they sit and listen, the volume turned up, the music rolling over them like thunder. They listen to Mozart's Jupiter Symphony. Now that his son is about to leave home, Wayne feels together with him for the first time in years. He hears the music swelling against his inner ears. He sees his future stretching out before him. He is sober but he is day-to-day. One day at a time.

He envisions Keith in New York growing into a man. Putting away his body jewelry and letting his hair grow out. The streets of New York teem with people, and the air smells like garbage and car exhaust, and there's always the sound of the rattling of a jackhammer over the honking of the taxis. Keith is in a hurry to wherever he is going. Wayne is younger in his vision, as energetic as he has ever been. He may be in New York, too, but more likely he's in Atlanta, slimmed down, coaching at some dream college, some ideal university that treats him like a king. He has found a new woman who holds him when he shakes in the night.

He thinks of Brenda and the music batters against his eardrums, a physical thing he can feel all over his body. He looks over at Keith and his son has his eyes closed, a look of ecstasy on his face. He looks like a tiny baby with his bald head and his pale pure skin. He is the baby that he and Brenda had together. It is as though Bobbye never existed, and there is only Brenda, the two of them like some primal Adam and Eve creating their own lives, their own two threads unraveling into the future, spooling away and up into some vast and mysterious space that glows bright and full of promise and hope.

"They got the wrong Jesus," A.C. Grist says to Karla. He spoons scrambled eggs and grits onto her plate. "Jesus was a black man."

"And he wore earrings and a ponytail and he had his nipples pierced," Karla says. She wears a pale blue nightgown that matches her eyes and her hair is sleep mussed. The late morning sun slants through the kitchen windows. Everything is bright in the yellow kitchen.

"Ain't it the truth?" A.C. says. He sits down across from her and picks up his fork. He begins to eat, chewing, his eyes watching her. He has no idea what time she got in last night. Nor who she might have been with. She senses him watching her and looks up. Her eyes are still full of sleep. Her skin is as flawless as porcelain. He thinks her face must have been put together personally by God. She is more beautiful than her mother was. "That's how come that picture of Mary downtown ain't got a face on it," he says. "These crackers couldn't take what she was. A black Madonna."

She puts her fork down and looks at him. He has already put on his tie, even though he will not go to his office today, and they will not go to church. She is already taller than he is. He is wiry and quick, full of energy. She does not doubt that he will run for Probate Judge. She feels sure that eventually he will be Probate Judge of Wembly County, if that is what he wants. She can't imagine why he would want that. All people of his generation are a great puzzle to her.

He senses her staring at him and he looks up and says, "What?"

"I'm not going to that school," she says, "and that's that. I've got all the integration I want, thank you very much."

"All right," he says, surprising her. He is calm. She can tell by the way he looks at her that he knows all about her and Keith. He couldn't know everything, though. There's no way he could know that she's leaving with Keith, going to New York City, because Keith doesn't even know it yet. Her father will have a conniption fit. But he married her mother, a white woman, so how could he really object? And Karla has no intention of marrying anybody. Not Keith, not anybody.

Roger looks at his face in the mirror. There is lots of gray back in his hair now, and the dark color looks spotty and artificial. He doesn't care. He knows that the way he looks has nothing to do with Brenda's hesitancy, her reticence about marrying him. He knows that when Wembly County secedes from the state of Alabama—and effectively, at the same time, from the United States of America—Brenda will be so impressed and awed that she will be swept off her feet. All her resistance will vanish. He finishes shaving and goes into his dressing room. He begins to dress, pulling on fresh khaki pants and a crisp, ironed khaki shirt and a pair of brightly polished ankle boots. He is ready.

He has allowed Calvin Bluett to be in charge of defense plans. Units of the Militia are now stationed near each highway or back road into Wembly, including checkpoints on I-65. The county line, all the way around, is well fortified. They all fully expect the U.S. Government to bring down its military might against them, just as they did at Ruby Ridge and Waco, and they are ready. The government will think that Roger's forces will ultimately be no match for the New World Order allies of the United Nations, which control the U.S. Government like a puppet. But they will find out. It is God's plan. Wembly County will defend their rights to the end. And Roger knows that God is watching.

That is the message on the huge banner draped between the office building downtown and the Piper Twin Theater: GOD IS WATCHING! The violet and blue image of Mary with its mysterious indeterminate face shimmers in the bright spring sunlight and the giant banner sways gently back and forth in the tender breezes. The Piper Academy Band plays "The Bonnie Blue Flag," "Oh What a Beautiful Morning," "Up From the Grave He Arose," "Morning Has Broken," and "Come Ye Faithful Raise the Strain." The crowds gather and jam Main Street and all the side streets so that cars are parked everywhere, even bumper to bumper on the curbless streets of MineTown, blocking the driveways of the cursing residents. Enterprising youngsters all over town sell parking spaces in front yards and driveways. Vendors sell T-shirts with the image in the glass reproduced on the fronts. There are pennants and icons of every description, miniature plastic statues of the Virgin, reproductions of the Pieta and Jesus on the cross. A pink-costumed Easter Bunny goes up and down the street handing out jelly beans and coupons for a free family portrait from Owen Elder Photography: School and Glamour Shots Our Specialty.

Byron Bailey gets so tired of looking for a parking space that he leaves his Honda Civic right in the middle of Sycamore Street, near Ticen's Paint and Body Shop. He just gets out and slams the door and begins to walk. Even before he rounds the corner headed for downtown he hears the frustrated and angry honking of horns. He has left his key in the ignition. They can move it if they want to. He feels the weight of the dynamite, the irritation of the tight tape. He touches the toggle switch in his pocket as though for reassurance. He is sweating in the sun beneath his heavy fatigues. His legs feel shaky and weak.

He scurries along the sidewalk on Main Street, on the edge of the crowd. He feels so bulky and awkward that he's sure anyone looking at him can tell, but no one pays him any notice. There's laughter and chatter everywhere. Music comes from several different sources. In the distance he hears the Academy band playing above all the other noises, hears the rattling of the snare drums and the high shriek of the trumpets. The sun is so bright and hot and piercing that he fears for a moment it will set off the dynamite. He knows, of course, how irrational that is. He has studied the hardest, been the most diligent, in their courses on explosives out at the Militia compound.

The crowd parts for Roger Coles as he walks through, followed closely by Boligee Phil and his son-in-law Putt, who act as his bodyguards. They both carry AK-47 assault rifles and .45 pistols strapped to their hips. They wear camouflage fatigues and heavy polished boots and they are sweating in the spring sunshine. Roger has had a platform built in front of the shrine, a wide wooden structure five feet high that can serve as a pulpit and a podium for speeches, important speeches such as the one he is about to make. Dignitaries line the back of the stage in folding chairs. Even the governor is there, a short stocky balding man in a boxy navy blue suit, sitting simian-like next to Randy Capshaw, the mayor. The state senator from Wembly County, Steve Shields, who specializes in sponsoring bills designed to repress sex in any form, is there, too.

Everyone knows Roger Coles, and they cheer him. The line of men sweating in dark suits rises as one, applauding him as he mounts the steps to the stage, and the crowd goes wild. Outsiders know him by reputation and they follow the leads of the natives, clapping and cheering as Roger and Phil and Putt make their way up onto the freshly painted boards of the stage. As they emerge into full view even more cheering goes up and the band plays louder. The crowd packs Main Street from one end to the other and they push and shove to get closer to the stage.

The image of Mary in the glass towers over them all, three stories high. It seems to radiate its own light, taking the sunlight and heating it to even whiter boiling and hurling it back to the Easter sky and its hovering puffs of clouds. The tall glass wall vibrates with the thousands of shuffling feet and with its own lifeblood and soul. It dwarfs all the men on the platform and seems to loom out and over them as though it is about to embrace them.

The crowd begins to chant "We want Darlene! We want Darlene!" and Roger is annoyed that the girl is not here. She was supposed to be here, to be displayed to the crowds on Easter Sunday. Roger suspects it is some of

Brenda's doing. He dispatches Boligee Phil to run over to the house on Pineview Road and find out what's going on. "I want her here!" he says to Phil. "Now!"

They continue to chant, and Roger raises both arms over his head. Immediately they begin to fall silent. The band ceases abruptly with a ragged stinger note—and a great hush gradually falls over the entire down-town, broken only by scattered voices and children's crying and giggling. Byron has made his way to the very front row, by the church pews, and he watches Newton Grable go up and adjust the microphone and begin to pray, his voice booming out and echoing among the brick buildings and the trees and hills in the distance, the sunlight blinding on his bright cobalt-blue suit. Byron cannot understand what Newton Grable is saying. It is a foreign language, nothing but cryptic sounds and syllables that make no sense.

Byron is in another realm, a parallel world in which only the feel of the slick button in his pocket is intelligible. He fingers the fuse switch lovingly, a long slow caress. His mouth and throat are parched dry and he cannot swallow. He looks around, trying to spot Cody and his camera. He does not see him, but he knows he is here. Cody will get it all on tape. Every last second of it. For all the world to see. Byron's arms and legs feel so fragmented from the rest of his body that he thinks they must belong to someone else. They seem to move of their own accord. He feels his boots moving up onto the steps of the platform. Nobody stops him. He is in uniform. Putt sees him and assumes he is taking Boligee Phil's place. He is their patrol leader, after all.

Newton Grable prays forever, for a mini-eternity. And then his ampli-fied Amens ring out to the farthest hills and valleys. He is shaking Roger Coles's hand. Roger Coles's hair is patchy black and mostly gray, like the coat of a Dalmatian. His ankle boots are spit-shined and reflect the sun's glare, and Byron has to squint at everything. He squints up at the huge image in the glass. He has never before been this close to it. He looks into Mary's face. He is stunned to see his own mother's face staring calmly down at him, her eyes fixed on his, the shawl covering what he knows to be her gray hair, and she smiles at him, her lips turned up in a gentle sweet acknowledgement of him, and then she nods, she nods yes, and Byron says "Yes" out loud.

At the sound of his voice Coles turns. He looks at Byron. He looks impatient, irritated. He waves Byron away. He is moving toward the microphones. Byron feels himself moving toward him. He does not think he is even walking but gliding along without effort, sailing along as though the boards beneath his feet are ice and his mother—disguised as Mary —blows a tender wind at his back. He puts his arm around Coles, and Coles pushes him away. He smells Coles's cologne. It smells like the ocean. Coles looks at him, annoyance on his face. The back of Coles's shirt is damp with sweat. Byron gets his free arm around Coles again and holds him, and he sees confusion and curiosity in Coles's eyes, and then suddenly something else, a dawning recognition of danger followed by a quick anxious terror, and Byron presses the button.

⤙

The crowd is watching the strange dumb show going on behind the bank of microphones, the soldier and Mr. Coles—Judge Coles ... King Coles—struggling as though jockeying for position, and in the next split second both men disappear in a great rushing of flames and black smoke followed by a thunderous boom that can be heard as far as downtown Birmingham thirty miles away. The force of the explosion pushes those sitting in the front three rows of church pews—including Wayne and Keith—over backwards. The crowd nearest the platform is lifted off its feet and thrown backwards through the air, splattered with shrapnel from the dynamite and bits of metal from the microphones and splinters of wood from the podium, bits and pieces of Byron Bailey and Roger Coles themselves, fragments of bone and flesh, specks of blood and hair and shreds of clothing.

The VIPs sitting in the folding chairs are slammed forcefully back against the glass wall of the building, and those sitting directly behind Coles and Bailey—including the monkey-like governor and Senator Shields and Randy Capshaw and the Reverend Newton Grable—are hurled through the glass as it breaks with loud protesting shrieks and shatters into millions of sparkling fragments that come crashing down onto the stage and street in a deafening clamor. Metal folding chairs and shards of glass fly through the air and those suited men and nearby onlookers not directly killed by the explosion itself are bloodied and maimed by flying wood and razor sharp glass. The force of the blast deposits Putnam Greer's lifeless body on the sidewalk in front of LEROY'S GRILL AND BILLIARDS, where it lies death-still, its eyes open, a knife-like icicle of blue glass penetrating the forehead.

The crowd surges backward, away from the explosion, away from the loud torrent of dust and debris. Everyone on both sides of Wayne and Keith are killed instantly, but the two of them are protected somehow, as though by some kind of invisible blanket. Neither of them has a scratch. They both scramble to safety on the other side of the street, among the stampede of feet and legs as people begin to run wildly about, little children in pastel Easter clothes pushed haphazardly here and there and some—along with Easter baskets and chocolate bunnies—trampled beneath the shoes of frightened adults and teenagers. Dogs bark. People scream and cry out. They push and shove. Angry shouts and curses. The entire front plateglass wall of the building has come down, exposing desks and computers and twisted pipes and dangling electrical cords.

The marquee in front of the Piper Twin Theater is heavily damaged, the letters dangling and missing, spelling: E S ISEN and EAR MA EAK ERE. The huge banner is ripped to shreds and the two ends flap blankly in the hot gusts. The shop windows all along Main Street are broken and chunks of glass litter the sidewalks and crunch beneath the fleeing feet. And stores' signs hang precariously over the sidewalks and swing back and forth, and some of them fall down on the dodging people below. Crowds run in circles, bunching in the middle of the street and surging back and forth. No one knows what has happened.

At all the outlying encampments of militiamen the explosion is heard. They assume immediately that the U.S. Government has somehow subverted them and attacked the downtown area of Piper: so their tanks and personnel carriers begin to roll toward the village. Cody, from his perch atop the Spalding Furniture Company building across Main Street, has gotten every last second of it on tape, and his pulse is racing. He sees a news helicopter circling, with a television logo on the side, and as he watches it he hears the rattling of gunfire and sees a sudden spurt of smoke from the fuselage of the helicopter. It begins to sputter and shake and spin out of control and Cody swings his camera around and follows its progress as it goes quickly and sharply down behind a row of trees. There is another explosion and streaky flames and sooty smoke shoot high into the air.

"Jesus," Cody mutters, thinking of Rasheedah Mangruen and her sea-green eyes and her hairless body. He swings back around and keeps on taping. As the dust rises into the breezes he can see the mangled stage and the crater where the bank of microphones had been. He sees ripped bodies flayed into the street, and the bloodied and wounded limping and crawling away. He can look directly across the street into an office, where a calendar hangs on the wall with a picture of a woman sticking her bare ass at the photographer and smiling over her shoulder. Cody gets another panoramic shot of the street then zooms in on the calendar.

Those few people in town who have shunned the local excitement for the Braves on television or after-dinner naps are startled by the explosion, some even dumped from their beds by the violence of the blast. The television screens shimmy green for a moment and then all the televisions in Piper go blank as the cable is severed. Lights flicker and in some parts of town the hum of refrigerators and air conditioners goes silent.

The lights go off in Brenda's house and they all three sit at the table, Brenda and Darlene holding their and Jimmy's bacon, lettuce and tomato sandwiches. They look around questioningly. The blast has rattled the dishes in the cabinets and the windows in their frames. The three of them sit in the soft light that filters in from the outside day. Jimmy sits in his wheelchair pulled up to the table. He has a smear of mayonnaise on his upper lip. Darlene squints her good eye at the window. She shakes her head.

"It's gone," she says.

"What?" Brenda asks.

"It's gone," Darlene repeats.

"What the hell was that?" Brenda says, to no one in particular. "A bomb?"

Neither Darlene nor Jimmy answers her. They go on eating, slowly and hesitantly. Darlene feeds Jimmy. They shiver. They all know that something terrible has happened. They don't know what to say. There is a knock at the front door. Brenda puts her half-eaten sandwich on her plate. She looks at the other two, who stare back at her. Brenda goes up the dim hallway. She can see the silhouette of someone, a man, on the front porch.

She opens the door and the day is blindingly white and warm. She has to blink and focus against the glare. Phillip Moon is standing there in his uniform. His face is pasty white, his eyes wide with a kind of mute astonishment. He just looks at Brenda. In the distance begins the high wailing of sirens. And there is the sound of what appears to be gunfire, the rattling of machine guns.

"What?" Brenda says. "What is it, Philip!?" The boy says nothing. "What was that explosion? What's going on?!"

"Mr. Coles," Boligee Phil says, "he's dead!"

⟳

The sun hangs low in the western sky like a shimmering orange, and it will be their target, their guide. They have Cody's van packed to capacity, with Cody's equipment and much of the tape he has shot (he has overnighted some of the most exciting footage to Coates, and Coates is ecstatic) and all Brenda's and Jimmy's and Darlene's stuff, too, their clothes and other belongings. Brenda leaves other stuff behind, like the boombox Roger Coles gave her and the stack of CDs. And the dishes. They have packed what was left of the Jack Daniels and the good coffee and the Krupps coffeepot. And they take the recliner, which Cody has secured in the back of the van for Jimmy to sit in. The van has only one narrow back seat, and Darlene will sit there. Darlene wears a new eye patch that Cody found at a thrift store over in Alabaster. It is done in a leopard-skin pattern with a wide open blue eye painted on it. They will strap Jimmy's folded wheelchair to the top of the van. Brenda has decided to simply junk the old Toyota, to leave it sitting in the driveway of the little house.

But first she has one last trip to make in it. The floorboards are practically rusted out completely now, and she can smell the exhaust and hear the metallic rattling of the muffler. She never got around to having the car fixed. Sometimes, when she stops at a red light, the car shudders and jerks and goes dead, and she can't start it again. When she finally gets it started it goes dead again as soon as she puts it in gear. "It's the transmission," Cody has told her, "it's about worn out." She knows the car would never make it to California. It has four hundred and thirty-five thousand miles on it. It is like me, she thinks, chuckling to herself.

She stands at her mother's grave, looking down at the new-looking stone.

"I always wanted to go to California, Brenda," her mother says. "It's the land of money and men."

"You're so sixties, Mom," Brenda says. "That's what Cody would say." She stands there in the sunshine. "So," Brenda says, "now you're going."

"I don't know."

"I'm going. So you're going."

Spring has thickened, begging summer to take over. There is music high in the sky, behind the clouds. Many sets of eyes watch Brenda from the green thickness all around.

"Look over there," her mother says, and Brenda turns her head. And there against the kudzu and the honeysuckle, standing on a flat gray lichen-covered gravestone, is a young woman. She wears a white linen suit. She wears white high-heeled sandals. Her hair is blond, silver-gold in the sun-light, parted in the middle and hangs shoulder-length and straight. She looks to be in her early twenties.

"Hello, Mother," she says.

"Yes," Brenda says, "yes, yes, oh yes." Tears spring to Brenda's eyes and her breath catches in her throat.

"Why don't we all go to California?" the girl says, and she smiles. Even as Brenda takes a step toward her she begins to fade and grow transparent against the green, and Brenda can see her smile and her eyes and then nothing, and Brenda stands very still, alone now in the dense quiet, in the now empty air.

"Yes," Brenda says again, "oh yes."

⌒

They have the wheelchair strapped to the top of the van. They will drive all night, straight through to Austin, where Cody has an old girl-friend he wants to see. Then they will continue west. Jimmy is smiling, sit-ting in Coles's rich leather recliner, strapped in with a makeshift seatbelt made out of elastic straps. Darlene looks around. She is excited. She is get-ting out of Alabama for the first time in her life. She loves the new eye patch. She poses with it on for Cody and Brenda.

"This is definitely California," she says. She holds her hands out to her side and curtsies.

"Yeah," Cody says, "that is definitely California! That is the bomb, man!" And they all laugh. They laugh at anything anybody says. Everything strikes them as funny.

Cody has a cold beer in his hand and he drives with the other. Brenda sits on the high seat, watching Piper pass by the windows and then begin to fade behind them.

They have beer and soft drinks and sandwiches packed away. They have everything they want or need.

They drive into the sun.